BABYLON STEEL

BABYLON STEEL

GAIE SEBOLD

SOLARIS

First published 2011 by Solaris
an imprint of Rebellion Publishing Ltd,
Riverside House, Osney Mead,
Oxford, OX2 0ES, UK

www.solarisbooks.com

ISBN: 978 1 907992 37 7
Copyright © Gaie Sebold 2011

10 9 8 7 6 5 4 3 2 1

A CIP catalogue record for this book is available
from the British Library.

Designed & typeset by Rebellion Publishing

Printed in the UK

To my parents,
who wouldn't have approved.

CHAPTER
ONE
Day 1
6 days to Twomoon

WHEN I HEARD the shriek, I bolted up the stairs. That's one thing about being my height, I can take stairs three at a time.

The sound had come from Laney's room. I slammed the door open, and there was Laney, curled like a kitten at one end of the bed, and her client, flat on his back with his eyes shut. "What happened?" I said.

Laney just giggled.

I looked at the client lying in the crumpled pile of rose-pink sheets. He was one of those padded, flushed men who always remind me that people are basically made of meat. He had a glazed look, and although he had a sheet over him I was fairly certain that I could see either steam or smoke rising from the general area of his groin.

"Are you all right?"

He squeaked, swallowed, and said, "Oh, *yes*."

"Laney..."

"Sorry, Babylon. We were just having a little fun."

"Yes, well, I'd leave that sort of fun to the Twins, if I were you. I thought someone was being murdered up here."

"Oh, really, Babylon, as if I *would*." She patted the client on his balding head, bounced up, flung on a wisp of pink silk that served her as a dressing gown and danced past me. She grabbed my hand and dived into my office, pulling me behind her. She snatched up a red, leather-bound book I recognised all too well. "Babyloooon..." she waved it at me. A few scraps of paper fell out.

"Not now, Laney," I said.

"If someone doesn't do these soon, we're in trouble."

Laney's tiny: all big green eyes and masses of blonde curls, but she can glare like a hawk. Plus, she's a Fey. You don't mess with Fey. Not if you've more brains than the average plant. Like every being of power, she can't use most of it here on Scalentine – but she's not helpless, not by a long way.

"I know," I said.

"We need to order new bed linens, and curtains, and replace that lamp, and we haven't paid the glazier yet. We might even have enough money, but no-one actually *knows*. Because no-one's done the *accounts*."

"You do them, then."

"You know I don't do *numbers*. That's a completely different sort of magic from mine. But somebody has to do them."

"What brought this on?"

She jerked her head towards her room. "Him. He's an accountant."

"Can't we get him to do them?"

"Well, not right *now*," she said, her mouth twitching. "And once he's recovered he won't be back for at least two weeks, he's broke."

Frankly, a broke accountant didn't sound like someone I wanted doing my paperwork. I had enough problems. "All right, all right, I'll do them tonight."

Laney made a face in which hope, exasperation and disbelief were nicely mingled. "Well you need to sign this, anyway," she said, waving more paper at me. "Clothier's bill."

I looked at it. "*How* much for that silk?"

She pouted. "One must *dress*, Babylon."

"Amazes me that so little material can cost so much," I said. I dipped a pen in the inkstand, signed the bill, and sealed it with my ring. Laney blew me a kiss and sashayed out. I hoped there *was* enough in the kitty, but I doubted it. There are usually six or seven of us working, but what with Laney's taste in clothes,

Flower's taste in ingredients, and the Twins asking for new equipment every five minutes, considerably more had been going out than coming in. For a while, in fact.

I went back down. A few of the crew had gathered in the hall in case there was trouble; even the Twins had emerged from the basement.

"Everything smooth?" asked Cruel. She's got cropped hair the colour of frost, and skin like midnight.

"As silk."

Her brother, Unusual, glanced up the stairs. He's the other way around, great mane of pitchy hair and silver-white skin. Well, they *claim* to be twins. Don't ask me, I only work here. "Is that the culprit?" he asked.

Laney's client was peeking over the banisters.

"Culprits should be punished," said Cruel, smiling at him. Her smiles are... interesting. I saw him blanch and back towards the comparative safety of Laney's room. It probably wasn't just the smile; it might have been the leather, the spikes and the whip.

"Behave, you two, or you can help Flower in the kitchen."

"Yes, Babylon." They rolled their eyes, and withdrew to the Basement.

I looked around. The floor of the hall is honey-coloured wood, and the long windows let in the western light and have red velvet curtains, unfortunately now fading rather drastically to a sort of stripy maroon. I sighed. Laney was right, we really did need some new things. I started, reluctantly, to head back upstairs, but I'd barely got halfway before I heard the front door and Flower's rock-crushing tones booming, "Babylon?"

I went back down to the hall to see Flower, and, in the doorway, the Chief of the City Militia. Flower made a worried face at me behind his back. Well, over his head, really. The Chief is tall, but Flower *looms*.

"Right, come on, you know the drill," the Chief said.

"Yes, Chief." I led the way into the small parlour, sighing. He was going to make my life a misery, I knew it.

He stood in the middle of the small, blue-and-white room, with its big wing-chairs with their blue-velvet upholstery, its crackling fireplace, and its brass lamps with their pearly glass shades. He looked tough and tired and about to snarl. "Money," he said.

"Money?"

"Money. Babylon... come on. How many times? I don't want to have to arrest you, you know that."

"You wouldn't."

"If you don't pay your damn taxes, Babylon, I don't have a choice! You're six months behind, woman! You've got ten days."

"Ah. Ten days?"

"They've extended it twice already. This is the absolute last time they'll do it. And this is the last time I'm warning you. Just pay them *something* to quiet them down, even if you can't pay the whole lot." He frowned down at his sword hilt. "I'd lend you some money, but if it got out..."

"I wouldn't let you."

"I know. So do me a favour and just damn well pay it, will you?"

Ten days. I really *was* going to have to do the accounts. And see if I could increase the client roster, too. Though I doubted even that would get us out of the hole.

"All right, all right," I said. "I'll throw them a bone."

"Good. My move, I think," he said. He sat himself down in one of the big wing-chairs and picked up a pawn from the chess board.

Chief Hargur Bitternut. He's one of those lean, wolf-haired, long-faced types who looks like he should be carving out new territory in some untouched land, but as head of the militia, he spends most of his time just trying to hold back chaos right here.

I sat down opposite him, looking at the board, turning the ring on my forefinger around. The sword and lotus caught the light. "You moved something. Before I got here."

"You think I snuck past Flower? How? Babylon, one of these days you're just going to have to learn to trust me."

"You, I trust. Your chess game I don't trust."

"That's because I always beat you," he said.

"True. Let's arm-wrestle instead."

"Now, or in a week?"

"That time again? Ah. It's a Twomoon, isn't it?" I said.

He nodded, looking more lugubrious than ever.

That's Scalentine. It's on a planar conjunction, for one thing; and it has two moons. And once a year, they're both full at the same time.

In a city endowed with a thousand different sorts of madness, not to mention a fairly wide variety of weres (the Chief's one of them), you can imagine what a double full moon does. We put on extra security, don't let in anyone we don't recognise and stock up on cures.

I moved a pawn, and the Chief sighed. "Babylon. Come on. You're not trying."

I made a face. We played for a while in silence. Well, he played. I moved things around and swore under my breath when he destroyed another pawn.

"So," he said. "Heard anything that's going to make my life more complicated?"

"I've not heard a thing. It's been unusually quiet, to be honest."

We all hear things. We're not in the habit of betraying bedroom confidences; *not* good business. But I know a lot of the local whores, plus their attendant hangers-on. They tell me the gossip. If it's a bit of petty skimming I don't bother the Chief with it, but anything that sounds likely to cause serious trouble I drop him a hint. In return, he warns me about anyone who might cause *me* difficulties, and tries to teach me chess.

Somehow I don't think I'm ever going to get it, though. I don't have the patience.

"Well, I should warn you... the Vessels are on the warpath," Bitternut said. "Diplomatic Section had another delegation trying to get all the pleasure-houses closed down."

The Diplomatic Section is three times as big as the militia and pretty much runs the joint. In a place like this, you need a lot of people who can exercise multilingual tact at short notice.

"Not *again*," I said.

"I doubt you need worry – even the Diplomatic Section realise what a bad move that would be. But you may get some Vessels giving you noise." He moved a knight.

"Can't you arrest them for something?"

"I can't arrest a whole community, Babylon. And annoying as they are, they haven't actually shown any sign of breaking the law."

"Painting nasty slogans on our walls? Hassling my crew?"

"*Apart* from that. And they've been warned. They haven't done anything serious – at least, I don't think so..."

"You don't *think* so?"

He scowled, and moved the knight back where it had come from. "Girl got attacked down in Ropemakers' Row, the other night."

"Oh, shit. One of the freelancers? Who?"

"New girl. Straight off the boat. No instinct for a bad client, probably."

"How bad is it?"

"She's going to be all right, though she'll need a good healer to reshape her face."

"Bastard. She got money for a healer?"

"Not a lot. Few of us helped her out a bit."

That's the Chief. No wonder his clothes always look like they're older than he is. I'd give him a discount, only he's never been a client. Just a friend.

Then I realised what he'd said. "Hang on... don't tell me she was attacked by a *Vessel*? They've started to take the law into their own hands? You could have told me before we started playing, Chief."

"You wouldn't have concentrated."

"I can't concentrate *now*."

"There's no real evidence the Vessels had anything to do with it. I've already talked to them."

"So why *did* you talk to them?"

"The girl said the attacker was wearing a Purity mask, but that doesn't mean a lot. It's not impossible to get those masks copied. Could have been a previous client or someone she'd turned down, who didn't want to be recognised. We set dogs on the trail, but by the time she got up the courage to report to us, more than a day's worth of trade had gone down the street, including half the pigs in Scalentine." He shook his head. "You know what it's like. We're lucky she talked to us at all."

"I know. They'll come around, Chief, just give 'em time."

"I hope you're right, Babylon. Anyway. I just wanted to let you know. Don't go thinking it means more than that there's some idiot out there with a taste for using his fists. Not like they're unknown."

That was true, sadly enough, but personally I wouldn't have much trouble believing that the Vessels had stopped talking and started hitting.

As religious orders go they're a pain in the arse. Heavy on the general 'Shalt Nots,' and with the weird but not uncommon idea that all sin starts below the neck.

"You know if they come anywhere near me or mine I won't be responsible, Chief."

"Yes, you will, Babylon."

I slammed a pawn down at random. "Yeah, I will. *I* don't say, 'the gods made me do it.'"

"I know you don't. Trust me, if they break the law, *provably*, they'll be in as much trouble as anyone else. Just tell your people to be careful."

"Right." Just then something skittered past my foot, and I stamped out, making Bitternut jump.

"What?"

"Beetle." I ground the thing underfoot.

"Hah. There's me thinking you were scared of nothing."

"I hate beetles."

Bitternut stood up. "I have to go, gorgeous." He looked at the chessboard and shook his head. "Work on your strategy. Read some military campaigns."

I made a face. I've seen war; books don't carry the stink.

"You take care of yourself, Chief."

"Always."

"Laney's been asking after you," I said, quirking an eyebrow at him.

"The lovely Laney, eh?" He gave me that melancholy grin. "Maybe I'll drop by again before Twomoon. See you, Babylon."

He nodded to Flower, who was filling the doorway, and left.

Flower's one of the few creatures I know who makes *me* feel fragile. He's huge. And green. A nice green, like polished jade. I don't know what his life was before he turned up on my doorstep; but he was wearing a slave-cuff on one ankle, and he had a lot of scars.

Flower handed me the glass of wine he was holding; it looked breakable in his big green hand. "You may need this."

"Flower, you're a treasure."

He grinned. That's quite a sight in itself; he's a tusky sort. He's one of my favourite people, is Flower. We call him that partly because no-one can pronounce his name, which is all glottal stops and consonants, but mainly because he's such a sweetie. Just the sight of him will usually calm down the most rambunctious of punters, but he's the gentlest creature in the planes, and one hell of a cook to boot.

I took a sip of the wine. "How did you know? Did the Chief tell you?"

"About that girl? Yes. But that wasn't why."

"Oh?"

"Visitor."

If Flower brought me a glass of wine for every visitor we got I'd never be sober. "Tell me," I said.

"Darask Fain."

I almost choked on my drink.

TIRESANA

I WAS A BAG-*child. An unwanted baby, hung on a door in a linen bag, in the hope that the family inside the prosperous-looking house would be generous. It was hard times on Tiresana, and a lot of babies ended up in the river, or left in the desert for the wild dogs to find.*

Philla, the master's daughter, was on her way downstairs when the head servant found the wriggling, bawling bag; nothing in it but me, wrapped in undyed linen, and a few chips of white marble. Philla was fifteen, sentimental, taken with babies. She begged for me as if I were a puppy. Her parents saw no reason why the servants shouldn't look after a baby, so long as it didn't interfere with their duties; they'd get a trained house-servant out of it, eventually.

Philla named me Ebi, after the little desert cats.

It was a stable household and servants were rarely dismissed; the master and mistress liked familiar people about, who knew their ways. For the rest of the servants, I was mainly extra work on the whim of a silly girl, who came to the kitchens to play with me when I was tiny, but lost interest quickly as I grew.

I remember the stone-flagged floor; a bone spoon for a toy. I remember Philla, a little – mainly as long clean hair and a scent of jasmine. When she left the house on her marriage, she left the bag I'd been found in to be given to me when I was old enough not to lose it. I was ten or so when someone remembered, and it was the only thing I'd ever owned apart from the clothes I stood in. It was nothing much, a stained linen bag and a few chips of white stone, but I kept it by me. As though there were another life somewhere, and that bag was the key.

CHAPTER
TWO

DARASK FAIN. HE'S never been a client, but I've heard of him; everyone has, somehow. He moves between the different levels of society smooth as a dancer, but he always seems to skate the surface; runs a gambling den called the Singing Bird, and has a reputation for being a very dangerous man with his fingers in a lot of pies. That sort of client can be an asset, or a major liability.

He's also the most devastating thing on two legs in Scalentine.

Flower had shown him into the red room (the one we call 'Punters' Parlour' among ourselves). It has red divans with masses of cushions in all the shades of a rose garden, (including pink and yellow – Laney's choice – you wouldn't think it would work, but it does), and some pictures. Sexy pictures, but subtle; I don't like paintings that look like an instruction manual, and they can have the opposite effect to what's intended.

The red room's the biggest room we have, but it was verging on packed. There were two other punters: one was a new face, young and nervous-looking, the other was an elderly and delightful clockmaker who turned up mainly to reminisce about his wild younger days with whoever was prepared to sit around with very few clothes on and listen, though he could still be pretty sprightly when the mood took him.

The rest of the crowd was made up of the crew. Laney, in three wisps of green silk that matched her eyes, was perching on the arm of the clockmaker's chair, gesturing extravagantly as she pretended to believe some outrageous story, and everyone else was either offering Fain a drink, plying him with food, or just gawping. Essie, a curvy, pretty creature with dark curls and cinnamon freckles, was holding out a plate of pastries, Jivrais was pouring a large glass of the really *good* wine, and Ireq was leaning against the wall, watching. Flower was in the kitchen, but the Twins were hovering, and they didn't usually pay much attention to what they called the 'prose punters.' No-one was paying any mind to the new lad. *Not* good. I was going to have to do some dressing down.

Hard to blame them, though, when you saw Fain.

He was seated on one of the sofas, with a glass in his hand and a plate of pastries at his elbow. I have rosy-shaded lamps in there; they give a rich, flattering light. Fain didn't need it: with those dark eyes, high cheekbones and glossy black hair, he would look good under a noonday sun. Unlike some new clients, he looked utterly at ease.

This all went through my head in less than a moment. Fain had spotted me as soon as I walked in, and stood up. Everyone else did too, even the clockmaker.

It made me nervous. It's been a long time since people did that when I entered a room.

"Madam Steel."

"Mr Fain. I hope you're being looked after?"

"Quite charmingly. But I wonder if I might beg the privilege of a private word with you?" He had a voice like velvet-clad fingers running down one's naked back.

"Certainly. I'll be with you in just a moment." I held out my hand to the young lad, who bent over it and stammered something about it being an honour. "I just came to... I mean I thought... I'm terribly sorry..."

I managed to get out of him what it was he was after, and sent him off with Ireq, an ex-soldier. Ireq had sleek grey fur and rich brown eyes, and the fact that he had one arm missing below the elbow didn't seem to hamper his popularity and might actually have enhanced his inventiveness. He was taciturn to the point of near muteness, but lots of people seemed to like that. He'd know how to deal with the boy's nerves. I ordered everyone else back to their duties, sharply enough to let them know I was peeved, and took Fain into the blue parlour, aware of more than a few envious looks directed at me as I went.

"This is an unexpected pleasure," I said.

He settled himself into a chair like a cat into a sunbeam. "You run a very pleasant house, Babylon. I'm already regretting that I haven't been here before."

"Now you are, what can I do for you, Mr Fain?" I had several ideas in mind, and they were getting more extravagant by the moment.

"I am prepared to offer you a large sum of money in return for a certain service I believe you may be able to perform for me."

That put me on edge. I didn't know enough about Fain to guess what his personal tastes might be, but if he was prepared to offer much over the going rate, it had to be something a bit out of the ordinary. And though the motto of the House is 'All tastes, all species, all forms of currency,' there are tastes we don't cater for. Anyone who prefers an unwilling partner, or one too young, had better not step through my door. Anything resulting in permanent injury and such, we don't do; and we insist on taking measures to protect ourselves. Disease is not a problem on Scalentine the way it is elsewhere, because of the peculiar nature of the place; but pregnancy is. At least, for some of us. Fain was not a man I wanted to antagonise, but I have principles. That may be why I'm often broke.

I sat down, arranged myself in an encouraging posture, and waited. Not for long.

"Someone has gone missing. I'd like you to look for her."

I managed to shut my mouth, eventually. "I'm sorry, what?"

"A young woman – a stranger to the city – has disappeared. I am extremely concerned for her welfare."

I was thoroughly bemused, not to mention pretty disappointed.

"Why me?" I said. "This isn't the kind of request I usually get." I wasn't entirely able to keep the regret out of my voice.

"Because I think you have the qualities I am looking for. I'd know better if you came to the club, of course..."

"Gambling's not really my game."

"But I suspect you'd be rather good, if you decided to take it up."

"I'm not sure about that. I think it requires a level of concentration that's beyond me. Besides, I'm not good at numbers."

"But judging by what I've heard, you're good at people. Often, that's all that is required."

"You must be pretty good at people yourself." Somehow that had come out sounding a lot more inviting than I intended. Ye gods and little fishes, I was practically *purring*.

It had to be the voice. No-one should be allowed to look that good *and* have a voice like that. It eased past the brain and curled itself right around the privates.

I dragged my concentration back into my head. "Anyway, this girl. What qualities have *I* got? Why not go to the militia?"

"I believe you can talk to people who won't talk to the militia. The last Chief left a long shadow."

The Chief before Bitternut had been a nasty little pusbag; corrupt as a dead dog in high summer. It made the new Chief's job harder than it needed to be. I still heard stories from some of the other whores. A lot of them come to me when they fancy a bit of advice or a gossip. Them and ex-soldiery.

"But still," I said, "why me?"

"You need the money."

That acted on me like a dash of cold water. "What do you mean?"

He shrugged. "I *do* run a gambling house, Madam Steel. I know when someone's overstretched."

The fact that he was right didn't make me any happier about him knowing, and I wasn't sure I believed his explanation, either.

We kept the place in good order. Maybe someone had been gossiping with a client, and word had got out. Discretion, or lack of it, works both ways.

Still, he *was* right. "So who is this girl and why are *you* looking for her?"

Fain leaned forward, and I could smell his scent; a mix of clean male, and something dark and woodsy. I was increasingly aware that I really didn't trust him and that I was having a damn hard time keeping my hands off him anyway. I tried to concentrate on listening to his words, rather than watching his mouth.

"She's the daughter of people I want to keep happy. If I can find her for them they will be extremely, not to say lucratively, grateful. I'm prepared to invest against the possible returns."

"How much?"

He told me. I swallowed hard.

It was a lot of money. It would certainly keep the tax office quiet; it might even pay Laney's clothier's bill as well. We had a good reputation and generous clients, but we were picky and planned to remain so. Unfortunately that can thin the coffers no end.

"What sort of business are her people in?" I said.

"Does it matter?"

"It might."

He sighed. "They're not precisely in business. They're more... government. They are, however, highly influential and helping them out could be extremely advantageous for us both."

"Government where?"

"Incandress."

"Oh." It sounded vaguely familiar; it might have been one of the places I passed through on my way to Scalentine, but then, there had been a lot of those.

"It's a satrapy of the Perindi Empire. The Ikinchli come from there."

"They do?" There are quite a few Ikinchli in Scalentine, and I knew at least one of them pretty well. "This girl's not Ikinchli, though?"

"No." Fain rummaged in a pocket and held something out to me. "They call themselves Gudain."

It was a gold locket. Not exactly the most delicate thing; it weighed so heavy in my hand I could probably have brained someone with it, and it was thick with scrollwork, curlicues and turquoise cabochons. I flipped the catch with my nail.

Inside was a portrait. It looked to me like the sort of thing that gets done by a court painter, so only the All knows how accurate it was. But she was a pretty creature, humanlike, with thick, straight, greeny-gold hair, skin with a seawater sheen, and astonishing eyes, huge and brilliant yellow. I'd never seen eyes like that on a human, but they touched some memory in me. Not the colour, but the look.

"She was visiting Scalentine with her family," Fain said, "and the family of her betrothed. I believe they were here to buy... something or other. Some frivolity, jewellery perhaps, to do with the forthcoming wedding."

That actually made a certain amount of sense. Scalentine being the way it is, we do have things here from all over the place.

"They were staying at the Riverside Palace."

I whistled. "Fairly well to do then."

"Fairly, yes."

"What's her name?"

"Enthemmerlee Defarlane Lathrit en Scona Entaire."

"There's a handle and a half," I said. "So what happened?"

"They were at the Hall of Mirrors when there was some kind of disturbance, and the next thing they knew she was gone."

"What sort of disturbance?"

"Oh, a scuffle in the crowd, and some visiting grandee or other in a jewelled litter, creating fuss. Nothing to do with the Incandrese."

"Just gone?" I said.

"So they said. Vanished."

"No ransom demand?"

"No. Nothing."

I looked at the picture again. The girl had a calm, serious stare, and looked terrifyingly innocent. Though it's hard to tell with different races, I'd say she was no more than sixteen.

"They're government, you say. Ruling families?"

"Yes. Noble class."

Nobility has a habit of pimping out their children, though they don't call it that and it's done with a deal of ceremony. Maybe the girl didn't want to be married, and had seen the chance to do a runner. I sympathised, but it meant she was on her own, in a city which, much as I love it, is not the safest place for a pretty innocent. And she was noble class, which almost certainly meant she had no more idea how to look after herself than a kitten.

Not that poor girls are necessarily safe, either. I looked at the portrait. Something about that solemn stare sent a quiver down my back. Memory, or guilt.

"All right," I said. "I'll ask around. But I need to borrow this. I'll get some copies done, get it back to you."

"Keep it as long as you need. There is one thing, though..."

"What?"

"Timing. The wedding *must* take place before Twomoon. The family are somewhat insistent on that point."

"Doesn't give me long to find her."

"I know."

He took a bag of coin out of his pouch and laid it on the table, then he took my hand and bowed over it, and though he just brushed it with his lips I felt the touch all the way down. "Thank you, Babylon."

"I'm not promising anything other than that I'll look."

He smiled. "I know."

I saw him out, and watched him walk away, with a smooth elegant stride. The money weighed heavy against my hip.

I WENT BACK into Punters' Parlour. Laney had taken the clockmaker upstairs, the Twins had presumably retreated to the Basement;

only Jivrais and Flower were still there. Flower was bending to refill the plates of snacks we always kept on the sideboard, the strings of his apron straining across his broad green back. Under the apron he wears plain linen trousers but nothing else – he gets hot in the kitchen.

"I'm going out," I said. "We haven't anyone due for a couple of hours."

"You should eat," Flower waved at the plates.

"I'll eat when I get back."

"Never mind that!" Jivrais was positively wriggling with curiosity. He's a young lad, part faun and all mischief, otherwise known as Trouble. "What happened? Mr Fain just *left*? You didn't even take him upstairs!"

"No," I said.

"Aw, Babylon... didn't we have *anything* he wanted?" Jivrais pouted.

"Yes, we did, but it wasn't someone to bed. He's asked me to look for a girl who's gone missing." I showed them the portrait.

"Ooh, she's lovely," Jivrais said. "Those *eyes*."

"Yeah, I know. And she's walking prey. She's called Enthemmerlee – hang on – Enthemmerlee Defarlane Lathrit en Scona Entaire. Honestly, even Laney's real name isn't that long."

Flower looked at the portrait and sighed. "You can't save them all, Babylon."

I knew what he was getting at. I have a certain soft spot, or maybe it's a raw spot, for young girls in trouble. "Yeah, well, let's hope this one's just playing 'let's worry the parents' and doesn't *need* saving. And let the crew know what Chief Bitternut said, okay?"

"The Vessels. Right." He shook his head. "That is one weird bunch. Those masks give me the *bihadash*."

Vessels above a certain rank wear Purity masks: white, ugly things like a bird's skull. If the higher priests have to leave their temples, they wear masks without eyeholes, and are led by sighted servants: the 'truly pure' (truly something, all right) blind themselves, to avoid accidentally spotting anything sinful.

"Bihadash?" I said.

"You know how you feel about beetles? Like that. The sight of them makes me want to squish something."

"Well, I sympathise, but I'm afraid you're not allowed to squish Vessels, more's the pity."

While I took my stroll I'd keep an eye out for some of the freelancers, ask them if they'd heard anything that might lead to Enthemmerlee. I'd mention the Vessels, too, but most of them would already know about the girl who'd been attacked. News like that spreads faster than fever in a siege.

Previous was on the door. She's a stocky, freckled redhead who barely comes up to my chin, and a damn sight faster than she looks. You have to be careful picking bouncers; I don't usually put Flower or anyone that big out front – a mountain of muscle between them and their fun can put some customers off, plus it can make them feel inadequate. Previous, in her dented armour, hits the right balance. We hooked up some years before I came to Scalentine; both of us acting as caravan guards to a manically nervous merchant whose cargo of spices, we discovered rather too late, hadn't actually belonged to him. When I left she decided to come with me; I was glad to have her.

"Hey," I said.

"Hey."

"What was that with the gorgeous Mr Fain, then?" she said, grinning. "Talk about take your fun and run."

"No fun. Just talk."

"Shame."

I told her about the girl. She frowned at the portrait. "Looks pretty snappable, don't she? All right, I'll listen out."

"Getting chilly."

"It is."

I handed her my flask, and she took a swig and handed it back. We stood for a moment looking out towards the square, with its cool greenish-glowing lights and the great clock. It showed the cycles of the sun, the moons, and the planes – those that had cycles anyone could follow, at least – in a series of interlocking wheels; brass and silver, copper and gold, lapis and jade and chrysoprase.

"Not as cold as the time we were on guard duty up in the Clarissen mountains," she said.

"Don't remind me. If I had nadgers they'd have frozen off, I swear. Remember those poor boys trying to get a fire going, and the snow came down blue?"

"Hah, blue snow. Made it even colder, somehow." Previous shook her head.

"What *was* that warlord's name?"

"You should know. Got to know him lots better'n I did," she said, grinning.

"Hey, I had to keep warm *somehow*. He was all right. What the hells *was* his name?"

"Don't think I ever learned it," Previous said. "Too busy trying to keep that cousin of his from sneaking through the pass and cutting *his* nadgers off. Families, eh? Can't remember the cousin's name, neither."

"How'd you get yours again?" I said, casually. "Previous?"

She gave a snort. "Oh, you'll have to get me a lot drunker before I tell you *that*."

Damn. I'd been trying to get it out of her for years. I shook the flask invitingly but she just laughed and waved it away. I made a face at her, then headed down to the river.

The city had that silvery-blue, glamorous feel it gets on an autumn evening like this; a little mist rising off the river, lights dancing in the water, the eye-twisting greeny-pink glow in the sky over one of the portals. There's always music from a dozen different taverns and street-musicians, the rumble of wheels, barrels rolling, laughter and yells and the crackle of magic. Little plaster faces watched me from the walls. They're something of a feature in Scalentine; it's as though every race that's ever passed through, someone has decided to commemorate a few of them. They're on almost every building, sometimes one or two, sometimes a frontage so covered it's like a crowd caught in time. I like them. They feel friendly.

I leant on the bridge parapet for a moment and watched the river.

TIRESANA

THE GODS, OR *the shadows of them, were everywhere. The mistress taking Philla to the temple of Meisheté before her marriage, to offer up gold for fertility and easy births.*

One of the servants burning a black feather to Aka-Tete, asking vengeance and swift passage to the Far Lands for his brother, murdered in some brawl.

Even in the tarot pack there were the Sun, the Moon, and Death.

The gods were in everyone's lives, referred to every day. Of course, they hadn't manifested on our plane for generations, but we still prayed to them. Gods don't just cease to be because they're somewhere else. Besides, their temples and their priests were very much here. The temples were everywhere, and so were the priests: they were government and law and militia. The master paid his temple taxes and didn't dare grumble, in case the gods overheard and decided to let his caravans get raided or his ships wrecked. And of course, for fear of the Avatars.

We all knew about the Avatars, even if we never saw them; beings of wondrous and terrible power, created by the Gods to take their place on this plane, to rule their priesthoods and govern their people in their name.

Shoved off on whoever had work that needed doing and time to teach me, I learned a bit of everything; picked up the habits of worship along with everything else. I never was much good in the kitchen, but by the time I was twelve, I knew how to scrub and stitch; by fourteen I could dig a garden or empty a privy or mend a stable door, and make a garland of moonflower to lay on Shakanti's altar, in the hopes she'd help me preserve my virginity.

Because the master had started looking at me with a certain eye. I knew enough by then to know what he was thinking about, and to know I didn't want it. Firstly, he was three times my age, greasily fat, and had a liking for drenching his hair with heavy-scented oil. Secondly, it would have caused trouble and I'd have been blamed.

Shakanti having shown no interest in helping me out, I was still chewing over what to do when the trade caravan came back, to load up for the next trip. The family traded in spices, and it was always a bit of a celebration when the caravan came in; gifts all around, and a feast – or as much of one as could be had.

The head cook prodded the haunch of goat provided for us with a dissatisfied look. "Used to be when the caravans came in, back in my father's day, a whole ox for the servants. And the best beer, not this thin stuff."

"Beer's not what it was anywhere," the mulemaster said. "Well, can't expect it, with the harvests so poor."

One of the kitchen girls leant over and whispered to me, "And the ears of grain used to be big as your hand, the harvest carts came in piled so high the beasts could barely pull them..."

"...twice as much good growing land, forests full of deer so fat and lazy they'd walk onto your spear..." I whispered back. We heard these stories all the time.

Others, too. About how there had been fewer of what they called 'shadowed births.' Babies born... not right, one way or the other. But we were young, the world around us was all we knew.

After the feast, the master handed the gifts out and gave me a length of crimson cloth for a gown – a pretty colour, but hardly subtle, especially with his hand on my leg and his wife glaring like a hen disturbed on the nest.

Poor woman. She was welcome to him. I decided then and there that I'd always choose who I bedded. Given the chance, that was.

I put the cloth aside (when I was supposed to have time to make it into a gown, I don't know) and went to listen to the caravan guards tell their stories. They usually saved the best ones for when the master was out of earshot. One of them, Kyrl, had started teaching me dice last time they were home; I saw her grinning at me across the fire, flushed with wine, and shaking the dice-box invitingly. I went over, accepted a sip from her bottle and told her what was going on.

She wasn't too drunk to listen. She looked at the master, who was congratulating himself on his profits, his big red face greasy as his hair in the heat of the torches, and swore. "The older they get, the more some of 'em want young flesh," she said. "You want to come out with us? I reckon I can swing it, if you're up for it. You'll have to pull your weight, loading and looking to the beasts, but you're used to work. You just have to stay out of his way for ten days or so 'til we're out again – and he should be busy getting the new loads arranged for most of that."

"Yes, please," I said.

Ten days later, the pack boy who'd been hired got called home at the last minute. How Kyrl had managed it, she wouldn't say. I asked permission from the Mistress to go instead, which she was more than happy to give, and set out in the mood for the highest adventure.

Most of the time it was nothing but sitting and swaying and a sore backside; poor food, bad inns and learning to deal with the damned sandmules, one of the ugliest, orneriest beasts that'll ever try to kick your guts through your backbone.

Still, I loved it. I realised the world was a good deal bigger than I'd had any idea of. How big a universe lay beyond it was another thing again. I heard of a portal, in a town called Mantek; apparently some of our spices went through it to places of strangeness and magic, but we never travelled so far. Even the caravan guards, adventurous as they seemed to me, never speculated about going beyond the portal. Our goods got taken on by others – strange, mad people, travellers.

It wasn't until later I realised just how provincial, how closed off Tiresana was. It's a small plane, the habitable part barely larger than some countries. It was bigger, once, or so the rumour goes.

But we didn't think, or look, beyond it. We were Tiresans. Tiresans didn't look outwards. And Tiresans didn't leave.

As well as Kyrl, there were two other guards. Radan was fiftyish, stocky and quiet. Had a wife he didn't get on so well with, but still cared for; him travelling suited them both. Then there was Sesh. He was in his twenties, rangy and restless. A real storyteller; he could have made a living in the marketplace if he fancied. I fell for him, of course, but he wasn't having any of it. He treated me like a younger sister – teased me half to death and threatened to bloody the nose of any man who looked at me in a way he didn't like.

Kyrl was a little over fond of those dice. Ten days after she got her wages they were gone, though sometimes she won, then she'd buy everyone treats. It wasn't the money she wanted, it was the game. Had a tongue sharper than her blade when the mood took her, but she always watched your back. Funny, too, in an acid sort of way. "If you need a six, you'll probably get a three. Life's mostly threes, but you got to play, or what's the point?" She was always going to have her tarot read, but if she didn't like what she heard – and she often didn't – she'd ignore it.

They were my first real family.

Cold early morning, running through a rocky pass, raiders skittering out of the rocks like crabs. The guards up and cursing, a raider trying to crawl onto the wagon. I hit him with the kettle, hard as I could. Smashed his nose; I was startled at the blood, so much. But there was a satisfaction in it. Not in the blood, but because I'd helped. He toppled off the wagon and it gave the others time to deal with him.

Radan slapping me on the back and saying that if I was that good with a kettle maybe I should try a sword.

And, again, I said, "Yes, please."

Radan tried to take it back at first; he was afraid I'd get hurt. But once he saw I wasn't going to give up, he made it his business to teach me properly. I got used to being hauled out of the wagon in the cool of the day, given rags to wrap around my hands and worked until I could hardly stand. He was patient, Radan, but he wasn't beyond slapping me with the flat of his blade if I did something stupid. The first time he did it I was shocked, because I thought he was my friend; I stared at him with tears starting in my eyes.

"You know why I did that, Ebi?" he said.

I shook my head.

"I did it because you make that mistake in a real fight and you're likely to die. I'd rather have you bruised and alive. Yes?"

I got it.

I wondered, later, if I meant something to him – not as a lover, but as a child. He didn't talk about his family much, but the little I heard, he'd only the one son, who he saw even less than he saw his wife. But at the time, I just took whatever training he was willing to give me, feeling ready to leap mountains whenever he said I'd done well.

Being on the road, we were seldom at a temple in time for the major ceremonies. But Kyrl always muttered a prayer to Hap-Canae before she shook the dice; the sun-god had jurisdiction over gold, and profit. Sesh had a fondness for Babaska, inevitably, since he spent a lot of time visiting whores, and Radan would stop now and then at one of Meisheté's shrines, to leave a gift, and ask that she watch over his family.

I laid some of my few coins on Shakanti's altar. Though it was Kyrl who'd got me away from the master, I thought I had better lay tribute, in case the goddess had had a hand in it too.

As we travelled I became a little, a very little, less ignorant, and discovered I had, for some things, a good memory. I heard a storyteller in one of the towns, telling some gaudy old tale of tricksy genies, of burning gems and green-haired crones and princesses locked in towers. (We had no princesses anymore – the last of the old royal line had died out years ago, perhaps of ruined pride, as the temples took control.)

The next day, Sesh was muttering to himself, trying to remember the story, to impress some girl, I've no doubt – I corrected him, and found I could remember it almost word for word.

It was the rhythm and the weft of the speech that did it. Conversations I could keep in my head only a little better than most; but anything with rhyme or rhythm, given it was short, I could recall pretty well after one hearing. Not that it aided me much with music; I sang like a frog.

One night we met up at an oasis with another caravan, and pooled food and stories. I ended up sitting at a fire with some men who teased and flattered and kept topping up my goblet with drink, and it was only because Kyrl had lost early that she wandered over and spotted them manoeuvring me away from the firelight, and me, drunk as all-get-out, innocently going with them.

She got me away, and next day explained, while I groaned and held my head, why it was a bad idea for a fifteen-year-old girl to get drunk with strangers. I was ready for experience, but no-one needs that sort of introduction.

The next trip out I was able to return the favour, when someone took badly to losing to Kyrl and decided to wait in an alley with a knife. I was the sober one, this time. I didn't kill him, but I put him off.

I learned how to tell a slimy merchant from an honest one, at least some of the time, how to replace a broken wheel and how to doctor a sandmule. They're mostly tough as boiled leather, but those great folding ears that they wrap around their heads during sandstorms are prone to mites and rips, and they'll eat anything. Sometimes to their regret, not to mention that of the poor sod who has to try and get a potion down the bloody animal to cleanse its stomach.

We saw some sights. The whistling desert where the wind sings in the dunes like a lost soul, melancholy but not frightening; at night, lying in the wagon and listening, you could almost swear you heard words in the sound. The Ghata Mai, a huddle of pillars of pinkish sandstone. Kyrl told me they were said to be the ghosts of some desert tribesmen who'd raped one of Shakanti's priestesses and been turned to stone by Shakanti in vengeance.

Once we were waiting for a ferry when we saw a boat attacked by two messehwhy, the great river-dwelling lizards that are one of Tiresana's less appealing features. One of the two men aboard, wearing nothing but short linen trousers, got pitched into the river; we thought he was done, but he came up riding one beast's neck, his arms clamped around its jaw. The other, sweating in his armour, was still trying to turn the boat, and fell, and the other beast bit right through him, armour and all. I wondered, after, what it made of such a thing; like trying to eat a thick-skinned fruit, I suppose.

I spoke with the survivor – he'd been hauled off the beast and onto the ferry, which was too big even for them to bite. He was fairly drunk by then, half celebrating that he'd survived, and half mourning for his friend, but he told me how to jab at a messeh's eyes, and how their jaws, although they could crush stone when closing, were weak the other way – if you could hold them shut, they couldn't have you. "Mind you," he said, grinning, "once you've grabbed its jaw, come there's no help to hand, you have to work out what to do after that, unless you're going to ride the thing until you both die of old age. And they live a long time." Then he remembered his friend, and got melancholy again.

As we travelled, I realised that not all the stories about the old days were people gilding the past. The desert had grown. Sometimes we passed a place with roof peaks showing forlorn above the sand, where a village had been swallowed alive. Sesh told me that there were whole towns buried under the dunes; his parents had lived in one, clinging on until the desert was knocking on their doors. Such places always left me cold, thinking of rooms that had been full of people and voices, choked now with silent sand.

I ended up staying with the caravans for two years.

CHAPTER
THREE

THE EVENING LOST its grey-blue sheen and turned into a carnival of lights. The soft glow of the streetlights, a flare of witchfire, the distinctive lanterns of every kind of shop, chop-house, tavern, theatre... even in the less lively areas, what with two moons on a clear night and the portals lighting up the horizon, the city rarely gets truly dark.

I couldn't get Fain out of my head. If I didn't know better I'd think he had a charisma glamour on him, but he didn't need one.

I'd encountered charisma glamours – actors use them a lot if they can afford it, and so do some of the more expensive whores – and to me they always have that slight artificiality, a sort of tang of metal. I don't like them. I think they distance you from whoever you're with, and that's not what my business is about.

Though, of course, for some in my profession, anything that helps them keep their distance, whether it's glamours, drink, or narcotics like cloud, is the only way to survive. They're in the wrong job, of course, but they don't always have a choice about it. Some have to do it for money, some get dragged in. That was only one of the things that might happen to Enthemmerlee.

I just hoped she was brighter than I'd been at her age.

Near the square, the city is at its most beautiful. Great sweeping boulevards, surrounded by tiny winding streets barely wide enough for two riders to pass each other. The old Church of the Glorification, deep green picked out in gold and bronze; the Sleeping Garden with its statues and pale, night-scented flowers, glowing moths dipping and fluttering among them; expensive little shops like dragons' caves of treasure; jewellery and fine weaponry, gowns and crystal and alchemical instruments gleaming in the lamplight.

But as I moved south into the district called King of Stone, I left all that behind. Fewer lamps, the streets even more narrow, rats and worse than rats shuffling and scratching in the alleys. I kept a hand on my hilt and my eyes open.

From the dank mouth of an alley I caught a glimmer of light. Something in the darkness was breathing heavily. I turned fast, and caught a powerful whiff of perfume mixed with alcohol fumes.

"Babylon-baba! Where you been to?"

"Glinchen?"

Glinchen swayed out of the shadows, clapping one set of hands and reaching out with the other pair, jangling a dozen bangles. Several embroidered silk shawls draped massive shoulders, thick black and scarlet curls tumbled, vast cleavage acted as a display shelf for row upon row of glittering beads.

Glinchen is one of the freelancers, and a Barraklé. Not unlike a human above the waist, not dissimilar to a sort of giant furry caterpillar below, with four arms, four breasts and more than enough of other things as well, apparently. Barraklé are hermaphroditic.

Which in Glinchen's case is the least of hir problems.

I allowed myself to be drawn into a squashy hug.

"Glinchen, what are you doing down here? This isn't a good beat."

Glinchen shrugged, causing a cleavage earthquake. "Girl needs a change of scene, sometimes."

"No-one needs this scene," I said, hopping out of the way of a trickle of sewage that chose that moment to appear from a side street and aim for my boots.

"So what you down here for, honeysweet? Not your beat, neither."

"I need to talk to some people. There's a girl who's disappeared." I got the picture out and moved under a guttering lantern some shopkeeper had hung out. "She was at the Hall of Mirrors, with her family. Ask around, will you?"

Glinchen peered at the picture. "Sounds like she in trouble, poor little honeychick. Hokay, I ask."

"You heard about the girl in Ropemaker's Row?"

"Yes, I hear. Bastards."

"You be careful, all right?"

Glinchen sniffed. "Hah. Don't worry about Glinchen, sweetie." Ze waved a hand at the rolls of flesh under the gowns and shawls. "Anyone try that with Glinchen, I just squaaaash him." Ze laughed again and undulated off down the alley, waving. "You be good, Babylon."

I shook my head and made for the Break of Dawn.

It crouched in its alley like a sick toad, dingy yellow light just about managing to crawl through the windows. I didn't go in through the front; there's a dartboard on the back of the door. I ducked in through the back.

Carefully.

The place was fairly quiet: a few figures murmuring in corners, a card game or two. I looked around, and spotted a comatose figure in a ragged brown robe. Mokraine. Good, I needed to talk to him. His familiar, unfortunately, was with him; it never left.

Imagine a cold fog mixed with the soil of an unmourned grave, pressed into the shape of a large dog crossed with a three-legged toad. It had three blood-coloured eyes in a triangle above the place where its mouth would be, if it had one. I feel about that familiar almost the way I feel about beetles.

I could sense eyes on me, from under hoods, from people who were apparently concentrating on their cards, from the corners where it didn't look as though anyone was sitting. Bodesh, the landlord, looked up at me, nodded, and had a glass of Devantish golden on the bar by the time I got there.

Golden's my favourite spirit. The cheap stuff strips skin off your throat, but Devantish isn't cheap. Or common. I don't come in here that often, but I reckon if it'd been a century since I last walked into the Break, Bodesh'd remember what I drank.

"Thanks. And another, please."

He nodded. Whatever Bodesh is, he's the only one of it I've ever met. He's thin and bald, with skin like glossy red leather. He has eyes like dark mirrors, and always looks sick, but that may just be his face. He probably wouldn't tell me anything; he doesn't talk about what he hears. If he did, he'd be dead in an hour. He's not one of my customers either; where he gets his jollies, I have no idea. Rumour has it he sleeps with his gold, like a dragon.

"Heard there were some ructions in the Hall of Mirrors today," I said.

Bodesh shrugged. "Too rich for my blood."

"Girl disappeared, too." I showed him the portrait.

"Happens."

"Yeah."

I took the drinks and made for Mokraine's corner table. Actually, they're pretty much all corner tables. It's that kind of place.

I sat there for a while, waiting for him to come to. Someone nearby was having their tarot read. Both reader and supplicant were hooded, but I could see that the reader had long, very pale fingers, with no fingernails.

Tarot's one of those things that seems to crop up everywhere, like chess. Sometimes the minor arcana are different, sometimes even one or two of the major ones, but, somewhere, on every plane I've ever visited, there are cards, and readers, and people asking questions.

A long nailless finger, or possibly tentacle, emerged from a sleeve and tapped one of the cards. "The High King, reversed." The finger withdrew.

The other figure hissed something.

"The failure of mortal endeavour," the reader replied. "Overweening pride. A reach beyond one's grasp. Upright, the High King indicates triumph, a coming into one's own. But reversed..."

The other figure reached out, with a gloved hand, and with a snap of its wrist, turned the card the other way up. The reader gave a low, whispering laugh. "It is not so simple."

The other figure hissed again, threw some coins on the table, and left.

It roused Mokraine, who raised his head, blinked, and focused on me.

"Babylon."

"Mokraine. How are you?"

"I'm..." he laughed. "I'm bathed in splendour, Babylon. Twomoon is coming, and this is a *special* Twomoon, a time of intensity, a syzygy of syzygies. How are *you?*" His eyes were avid, weary, pouched in greyish flesh. He'd been a handsome man, once; still was, if you liked them seriously ravaged, but he'd lost all interest in the pleasures of the flesh long ago.

"In need of information. What's a syzygy?"

"A time when things fall into line. Planets. Planes. Portals."

He reached for his glass. I kept my hand out of the way. Touching Mokraine isn't a good idea.

He's a vampire, of sorts. But what he feeds on isn't blood; it's the stuff of spirit. Memories. Emotions. It doesn't kill, but the effects can be disconcerting to say the least.

He wasn't born that way. It's to do with that creature that walks with him; we call it his familiar, but only because there's no other word for it. Don't mess with arcane magic when you live on a planar conjunction, that's my advice. You never know what's going to leap through the small but perfectly formed portal you just opened and latch onto your soul.

Because Mokraine had been powerful, once. A First Adept Doctor of the Arcane; students had come from all over to hear his lectures. Apparently he'd known the names and properties of every type of talisman, amulet and phylactery in the Perindi Empire. But his real obsession was portals, and at the time, there was a lot of prestige to be had from studying them. After all, we all live with the things, but understand almost nothing about how they work, why they appear, why some seem permanent and others not. And no-one knew how to create one. Mokraine found a way, but afterwards he couldn't remember how he'd done it, had lost all his notes, and didn't care a jot anymore.

"Since when are you interested in such things, Babylon?"

"It's not important. That's not what I wanted to ask you about. A girl disappeared, from the Hall of Mirrors."

I showed him the picture. He glanced at it, then stared into the distance, taking the information in, savouring it. "Ah, this city," he said, like a man describing a favourite meal... or a favourite whore.

"Mokraine?"

"Yes, Babylon, my bright-burning one?"

"I just want to know if anyone's seen or heard anything. I don't want anyone damaged."

"Oh, my darling, you know me."

"Yes, I do. I think. But overstep, and... well, you know *me*, too."

"I'll listen, Babylon. It's what I do."

I left feeling thoroughly low. Mokraine has that effect on me; so does Glinchen, these days, and the two of them in one evening were more than enough.

But you can't save everyone, I know that.

TIRESANA

I WAS SIXTEEN, *and we were home in time for the Choosing.*

Kyrl called on various gods when she was playing, and if she knew there was a fight coming up, she'd kiss her blade and mutter a prayer to Babaska. Radan and Sesh both did likewise, without the kissing. I picked up the habit, but what or who I was praying to, I never thought about; it was just what you did.

We passed whorehouses in the towns, and Sesh sometimes visited; they were dedicated to Babaska, too. There were often little statues of her outside, with bare breasts and a sword.

And though the gods no longer manifested, their Avatars did. I'd never seen one, but everyone knew someone who had or claimed to have; someone who'd been to a festival at one of the major temples, to ask a special favour, or who'd seen one pick out an acolyte at a Choosing.

The Avatars were divine beings. Like genies, they were the stuff of gods, and through them and through the priests the will of the gods was made manifest. And since it just might be the will of the gods that you got picked to be an acolyte, and thus made for life, you went to the Choosing.

Odd, how people can believe two things at once. Everyone knew that it was the children of the rich and influential who got Chosen; more often than not, someone from the family of whichever temple priest was doing the Choosing. And yet the story was that anyone might be Chosen. There were legends hundreds of years old, of simple peasants who went on to become High Priests.

No-one knew anyone it had actually happened to, *of course.*

It's a good way to make people behave. Promise them that if they keep worshipping they, or their son, or their granddaughter, may be one of the gods' Chosen, and kept in luxury.

Promise them if they help some merchant fatten on their sweat, one day everyone'll be rich.

Promise them paradise after a life of toil.

Promise them that if they just keep betting, one day, they'll beat the house.

CHAPTER
FOUR

I HAVE MY own private bathroom; boss's privilege. I always like to bathe before I take clients.

I put my rings on the side of the bath and sank back. Hot scented water, decent alcohol, and food someone else has cooked – the three basics of civilization, if you ask me. I can cook for myself, if I have to, though it's likely to be soldier's cooking (whatever I can find, raw or shoved on a spit and scorched) or courtesan's cooking; which tends to be small expensive items bought ready-made, not too heavy on the stomach, and without need of cutlery.

There were a few people waiting in the Punter's Parlour when I went down. Some people prefer to make such arrangements in private, and we have waiting rooms for them; others are quite happy to sit around and chat while they make their choice or wait for their choice to become available.

There was Maritel Lothley, a warm-blooded, loud, jolly woman who ran half the crockery stalls in the Upper South. She's handsome and generous, but something of a thug between the sheets and besides, generally I prefer men. Next to her was a thin, nervous young man who looked the type to take his pleasure fast and worry about it for a week.

Then there was a genteel commotion at the door and someone said, "Babylon. Princess of the pleasures."

A bald, high-nosed chap strode up to me in a rustle of scarlet silks, and bowed over my hand.

"My lord Antheran, how lovely to see you."

Antheran had gone from impoverished younger son of a fading noble line, to a merchant prince who provided the nobility of the Empire with the finest of jewelled fripperies to hang upon themselves, their favourites and their pets. He always popped in to see us when he was in Scalentine.

"My son, Antheranis," he said, with a flourish, drawing forward a younger, softer version of himself.

My heart sank. The boy was about fifteen, pretty but with a pouty look. I didn't want to offend the prince, but I wasn't in the mood to soothe a sulky lad out of a bad temper.

Antheran gestured the boy back to his seat, and whispered in my ear. "I think, for his first time, you would be a little strong for his blood. Could you recommend someone?"

"Of course," I said, and sent for Essie.

Antheran gave me the ghost of a wink. "Perhaps you would do me the honour?"

"I would be delighted," I said.

I would, too. Antheran was courteous, responsive, and always clean; not one of those clients who one has to persuade to wash first. We insist, or they leave. It's simple courtesy.

Antheran liked to be undressed, slowly, and to be stroked and massaged. He was smoothly and completely hairless, with neat, expert fingers and an odd aversion to having his neck touched.

He had a thing for silk, perhaps because it was the first stuff he'd made serious money with. Or maybe he'd made money dealing it because he loved it. I kept some scarves for his visits, but as I was taking them out of the chest, he said, "No, look, I have some new ones." He drew out the first from his bag. It was very handsome – pink embroidered with gold – and I looked at it regretfully, thinking how much better that colour would look on Laney. The second... the second was a rich tawny banded with dark amber. Colours I'd once loved. Fortunately he was looking at it, not at me, and I had my face under control before he turned around.

He liked to draw the silk across my skin, and have it wrapped around his cock and his thighs; sometimes he liked to have his hands or ankles tied with it. Luckily, he never asked to tie *me* up; I don't do that.

It was obvious he had something on his mind, so I took things slowly, but not so slowly he'd have time to start thinking again. I licked and nibbled and generally teased him gently out of his reverie until he lay back, his eyes shut, biting his lip as I stroked his shivering cock through the pink-and-gold silk (I'd got the tawny out of sight as soon as he was beyond noticing, so as not to distract myself.) I flicked the silk away from him, rolled on the snakeskin sheath he prefers and eased myself on top. He slid home. The sensation made me smile, as it always does. I tightened up and grinned when he gasped.

One thing about keeping in fight training, it's good for the thigh muscles. I was able to keep him on the blissful edge for some time; feeling his tight, hard plunge, holding myself back too, then when it felt right, speeding up, pushing him on.

I felt him strain upwards, and he clasped my hips and shuddered, his eyes clenched tight, making a little moan in the back of his throat. I pressed down hard against him, leaning forward, feeling the sweet jab of my own pleasure spiral up through me.

It doesn't always happen, with clients; some are too much work, or too nervous, or too quick. Some just don't have the touch. And sometimes, it just doesn't happen. But it's always nice when it does.

We both sighed, let our breath out together.

After a decent interval, I put on a robe, and poured us both a glass of delicate pale yellow wine from the Lathar mountains; his own gift last visit, and very good.

"Ah. Thank you." He raised the glass. "That was, as always, a delight."

"I'm glad," I said. "I thought, when you arrived, that perhaps something was troubling you, but I'm glad to see I was wrong." I hadn't actually guessed, until we were in bed, but it's never wise to suggest to a client (or anyone else) that their performance is off.

He gave me a quizzical look. "You were right, I was a little distracted. Children, sometimes, are a worry."

"Your son?"

"He is a very moody young man," Antheran said. "He says he is not interested in trade. Over and again, I tell him, without trade there will be no silk robes, no servants, no books. And no clean pretty girls, or boys, in a nice safe house where one will not be robbed. Only an old castle, very draughty, and all the effort of maintaining the appearance of nobility with nothing beneath it; like those painted scenes in the theatre."

"And it's necessary to maintain the appearance?"

"In the Empire, yes. It is a relief, sometimes, to come to Scalentine. Here one may be what one wishes, without people caring whether one was born in a mud hut or a palace."

"Some care."

"Oh, yes; this is true. I dine with them. This is not always a pleasure. But then I must on occasion do business with those who I do not necessarily like. Or trust."

"Perhaps, my lord, you should take a long spoon."

"A long...?" He looked bemused.

"There's an old saying; 'If you dine with the devil, you should take a long spoon,'" I said. "As in, keep your wits about you when doing business with those you don't trust."

"Indeed. But here, I know I can be at ease."

I smiled. "And what does your son think of it all?"

"He wants to be a poet!" Antheran shook his head, making the little crystals hanging from his ears spark in the lamplight.

"A lot of youngsters catch poetry, my lord; like a cold. Most of them get over it."

"I hope so. The world is kinder to accountants than poets." I tried not to pull a face at the mention of accounts. "He says he is weary of appearance, and wishes to speak the Truth."

"Oh, dear. One can only hope he will grow out of that, too."

I sounded rather cynical even to my own ears, but Antheran was nodding. "Among Empire nobility, to speak the truth to the wrong audience can be unhealthy at best."

"Not only there," I said. "Many people find the truth unpleasant."

"True." he gestured at his robes, hanging beside the bed. "Tesserane silk. Before I could afford it, I wore the finest linens I could get, though often it meant a thin diet. Because unless I *looked* prosperous, I could never *become* prosperous. Among the nobles, appearance is everything. Truth is seldom more than an inconvenient detail." He sighed. "If one does not have breeding, one must have wealth. If one has neither, one must strive for the appearance. But beneath it all, it is best to have knowledge. However unpleasant the knowledge, it is the... what is the word... you know how a tent, a pavilion, is constructed?"

"Vaguely."

"There are posts, things which support the cloth. These are like knowledge, yes? And must be strong and firmly planted, otherwise, all the pretty silk will rip and fly away in the wind."

"Your son is not the only poet in the family, my lord."

"Hah." He gazed into his glass. "But knowledge is like these posts in another way, Babylon – it is meant to be covered. If a man cannot afford to be held up by bureaucracy at every border, it is useful to know who is susceptible, say, to a little present. If, perhaps, one has a valued and honest steward, who is detained because of politics, but a bribe in the right place will release him, should one refuse to pay it? If one knows of a swift passage that will improve one's profit, and will not cause harm, but requires that certain... deals be struck, that are less than strictly above board, should one refuse to make them? I like to believe myself an honourable man, yet this is the sort of truth I deal in.

"And this is the sort of truth that my son prefers to ignore. He does not want to see that the fish swims *in* water, not above it; that truth is complex. My son wishes to hit people with simple truths as though they were hammers, and mainly he wishes to hit those who have no desire to hear any truth at all. The rich will hire poets who flatter them, and they, at least, get paid. Poets who care only for simple truths will be less likely to keep a whole skin."

He glanced at me over the rim of his glass, his eyes glittering. "You are a dangerous woman, Babylon. Much too easy to talk to."

"You are a pleasure to listen to, my lord."

"Well, I know I can rely on your discretion."

"Of course."

After washing, we went downstairs.

"Ah, here he is," Antheran said. "Well, my boy?"

The lad was definitely looking happier. The sulky pout had disappeared, and a dreamy, slightly glazed smile had replaced it. "*Dvit*. I mean, yes, thank you, Papa."

"Good, good!"

The boy turned the smile in my direction and said, "Do you have, please, a..." he scribbled on air.

"Quill?"

"Please, yes. And perhaps paper?"

Oh, dear. I glanced at his father.

"Paper?" he said. "You have used it all already? Always more paper! It is expensive, you know."

I didn't want to deprive the poor boy, but I didn't want to annoy his father, either.

"Oh, if you have some," Antheran said, "give it to him, please, and add it to my bill. There is no harm, after all, in a little hobby." He clapped his son on the shoulder.

Personally, I couldn't help feeling that if his first taste of the fleshly delights immediately made the boy want to *write* about it, he might be doomed to poetry whether his father liked it or not.

I glanced up the stairs and saw Essie looking down and grinning. She winked at me and disappeared.

The boy left the poem for her, of course, but he did it very gracefully. He took off one of his own rings – no gaudy trinket, either, but a delicate band of plaited gold – folded it into the paper, and wrote her name on the outside.

There are worse things than a boy having his first taste of puppy love. I would have to remind Essie to be kind, though, and help her think of some tactful things to say about the poem. It was almost certain to be terrible. Especially as he was writing in Lithan, rather than his own tongue. Lithan is the main language of the Perindi Empire, which controls large portions of a couple of our neighbouring planes. It's also the language of the majority of passing traders, and is what we mostly speak at home; though Scalentine has its own pidgin. We have people from so many places, some with languages that bear little resemblance to either Lithan or anything else. Scalentine pidgin is a mishmash of many of them. It's easy enough once you get the hang of it, and surprisingly flexible.

Antheran left a more than generous tip and a promise to drop in before he returned home.

It turned out to be a busy night. We had a slight misunderstanding with a large furry gentleman from Nederan (a country through Throat portal, all ice and sagas) who, due to language difficulties, thought he was getting a girl, got a boy, and believed for a few interesting and quite loud moments that we'd impugned his manhood. We bundled the helplessly giggling young man in question (Jivrais, of course) out of sight, and managed to calm the client down before anything very expensive got broken. Laney, wearing a fragile concoction of sea-foam green and looking far too tiny for such a bulky client, pounced on him like a kitten discovering the best ball of wool *ever*, and whisked him away into her room in a whirlwind of chatter and adept little hands.

I was passing back through the hall when I caught a glimpse of someone and stopped. It was a lad of about ten, strolling through with his eyes wide, looking as if he owned the place. "Oi!" I said. "What are you doing in here?"

"Delivery?" he said, brazen, but he'd already glanced behind him.

"Of what? And from who?"

"Er... buns. Fresh... buns."

"Come here."

But he had already turned and scooted for the front door. Previous, taken by surprise, made a grab, but he evaded her.

"You want me to chase him?" she said, strapping on her dented helmet as we watched the skinny little devil disappear down the street.

"Nah. Didn't seem like a thief, just curious. Hoping to see something naughty. How the hells they get in, though..."

"I'll have a look round later," Previous said. "There's got to be a loose window or something somewhere."

The Twins were very busy, too; I had to go down there and tell them to keep the noise down.

The Basement... the Basement makes me uncomfortable. The Twins specialise in pain, and don't get me wrong, they're an asset to the business. But all those chains and straps give me the grue. I'm always glad to get out of there.

Their current client looked up from where he was tied and got a hopeful look in his eyes when he saw me, but it isn't my style. If I feel like causing someone pain it usually isn't because they *want* me to. "The yells are getting through upstairs," I said.

Cruel put down the thing she was holding (it looked as though it was made of three parts leather to one of steel, but I didn't examine it too closely) and wiped her forehead. "Sorry, Babylon." She gave the client one of her more disturbing smiles. "We're just going to have to make sure someone can't make any more noise..."

He whimpered happily. I left them to it.

Dawn was streaking the sky with chilly orange as the last client left, the ghosts of both moons hanging low and plump over the rooftops. The nights were getting colder. Bad weather for the street whores. Glinchen's probably large enough to stay warm, but not everyone's built to their generous dimensions.

I finally stripped off, bathed and fell into bed, alone, in that state of weariness that feels as though you're wearing armour after you lie down.

But every time I thought I might be drifting off, Enthemmerlee crept into my head, with her wide, solemn yellow eyes. There was something about those eyes; not just the colour. A look. Something fated.

Fain really hadn't told me much. Maybe if I could find out more about the people she came from, I could pick up more of a clue. And I knew where to ask.

TIRESANA

A PROVINCIAL TOWN; *the ceremony of the Choosing. A temple to Hap-Canae, the sun god. The yellow stone, chosen for its colour, bleached to the shade of dead lemons. The great bronze masks with their flame-carved hair glaring from the walls, the sun clashing off their burnished brows. The hiss of cymbals like water on hot stones. The scent of the ghost-lilies down by the great Rohin river, so heavy-sweet they were nearly rotten, mixed with the insistent reek of sewage and the ancient smell of river mud.*

Sweating in our best clothes, hoping the ceremony would be over before the worst of the heat. Watching the priests and priestesses walk among the crowd; distant-gazed and dreamy, waiting for the gods to speak to them – or for the crowd to be impressed enough so that they could pick out the Chosen and get out of the sun. A small child, bored, fussing thinly and being hushed.

Suddenly, as if from nowhere, there was the Avatar of Hap-Canae; magnificent in gold and tawny silks, at least a head taller than anyone around him, and handsome as the dawn.

There were gasps and screams and a tumbling collapse as people fell on their faces.

He always did love to be theatrical.

I'd never seen an Avatar before. He outshone the bronze masks; he was like an alabaster lamp with the sun trapped inside it. His skin glowed, his smile lifted your heart. He was as beautiful as a jaguar.

Once everyone was over the shock, the priests scrambled up, brushing off their robes, and started a praise chant. He gave a little bow, smiling.

He looked around, slowly, but with great focus, like a hunter seeking a target.

His eyes locked on me and I was caught. I couldn't move as he walked towards me. I couldn't move as all around me the crowd drew back to let him through. I just stared at him, with my mouth open.

He stopped in front of me and looked down; I was already tall for my age, but he towered over me. He smiled and put one finger under my chin and closed my mouth. He smelled of cardamom and myrrh.

He said, "You will be an acolyte at the great temple. In time, if you prove worthy, you will become a High Priestess of Babaska."

It was utterly quiet. You could feel the shockwave roll out from us, as though someone had dropped a stone in a pool.

It was just like the stories. An unknown servant-girl had been Chosen.

You could hear the crowd breathing, and a bird down by the river, singing an endless falling trill. Then the priests, who were as flummoxed as anyone, remembered how it was supposed to work, and started the celebration chant and drowned the silence.

He hadn't even asked my name. He took my hand, and led me away from my life. I looked back, and there were the family and all the other servants, agape. The Mistress looked as though someone had doused her with cold water. But it was the guards I looked to: Radan, looking worried; Kyrl, grinning, giving me the thumbs up before she realised someone might think it disrespectful and dropped her hand; and Sesh, frowning, then giving me a tentative smile. I was so dazed, it was all I could do to raise my hand in a half-wave. Then I followed the Avatar.

I don't know, even now, how the Avatar Hap-Canae found me. How he knew I was suitable. Had he planned to turn up for a normal Choosing, just to keep everyone sufficiently impressed with the glory of the Avatars? Had he turned up on the off chance?

Either way, it was typical of him not to have warned the priests what he was planning; it made it all so very dramatic.

And there was probably some girl or boy who was supposed to have been Chosen, standing there in the crowd, surrounded by a family now wondering what the hells had happened. The priests no doubt had to exercise a lot of diplomacy in the next few days – but of course it worked to their advantage, in the end. After all, the legend had been proved, the gods had been shown to be capable of just choices.

Not that the Chosen in question had any say in the matter. And it didn't occur to me then, or until some time later, that it was perhaps a little odd that one Avatar should pick out a priestess for another; that Babaska did not choose her own acolytes. I was an ignorant child, what did I know of the ways of Avatars and Gods?

I WAS IN the blue room when Flower came in with dishes and a scowl on, his apron askew.

"No sausages," he said, dumping bowls of hot rolls and plates fluffily piled with eggs onto a table already loaded with fresh fruit, cream, butter, pastries and all the other things he considers essential to a good start to the day. "I don't call that breakfast," he said, regarding the laden table.

"It looks like breakfast to me." I said, loading a plate. "What's the matter?"

"The butcher hasn't delivered. I had everything planned and now I've got to reorganise three days' worth of menus before I go and shout at her."

I patted his arm. "I'll go have a word." Flower wouldn't shout at the butcher, but I would if I needed to. "I have to go out anyway, see if I can find *anything* on that girl."

He handed me a list. "This is what I ordered. Mirril's good, usually; used her for years. And if she hasn't any black-backed hog, tell her I'll take a haunch of red hopper instead."

Previous was on the door again, arms folded, wearing a battered breastplate, ancient leather trousers and helmet, looking stolid and tough.

"Hey. Everything smooth?" I said.

"Yeah. Babylon? Can I take some time tonight? I know we're close to Twomoon, but..."

"Sure, I'll find someone for the door. Doing something nice?"

"Just meeting a friend," she said, staring into the distance.

The blush crept up her neck like sunrise. That's the trouble with being a redhead.

"Previous..." I said, grinning.

"What?"

"So? When are we going to get to meet him?"

"Dunno what you mean," she said, scowling into the distance.

She's a funny lass. She doesn't do the upstairs work, that's never been her style. Her having a hanger-on was new, and we were all wild to get a look at him.

"Ah, come on," I said. "We won't scare him off, promise. Bring him to dinner."

"Maybe."

"Please? Or Jivrais will end up following you, just so he can get a glimpse of your mystery man. You know what he's like."

"Like you aren't as bad."

"Just concerned for you, Previous. You know. Want to make sure he's not taking advantage, you being such an innocent little thing..."

She called me something rude. "All right, all right. I'll bring him over."

I patted her cheek, and she growled at me.

The butcher was in Small Spell Street. Carcasses of every kind of beast – furred, skinned and scaled – hung in the window, different shades of blood dripping onto the scrubbed planks.

Unlike in most butcher's shops, there wasn't a fly to be seen; every board was scrubbed white and the scent of soap was almost as strong as the scent of meat. I could hear a faint, irregular squeak but I'd have bet my sword it wasn't a mouse; I doubted one would dare venture here, for fear of death by scrubbing.

The squeak came from the counter, where a small, vaguely familiar-looking dark-skinned girl, about ten, with the shiny look of a polished apple and wearing an apron so white it almost hurt, was perched on a stool, the corner of her tongue poking out of her mouth as she worked at her letters. She looked up with a smile. "Help you?"

"Missing order, for the Red Lantern?" I recognised her now; she normally delivered our order.

"Just a moment."

She slipped off her stool and disappeared through a curtain into the back. I heard murmuring and the butcher appeared, the girl behind her. She was a big woman, greying hair in a tight bun, with solidly muscled arms and blood on her apron. She was holding a cleaver. "Missus Steel, isn't it?"

"Yes. We put an order in, should have got it this morning?" I held out the list, but she didn't take it.

"I'm sorry," she said. "Order shouldn't have been taken, we can't fill it."

I glanced around the shop; there seemed to be plenty of meat, but I'm not Flower; I couldn't tell what she had and what she didn't. "None of it?"

"Sorry. And we can't take any more orders."

"You can't..."

"Not for the Red Lantern."

"Ah."

It happens sometimes. There are people who don't want to be associated with my business, even when they can make money out of it. She hadn't struck me as the starched-underlinen type, but you can't always tell.

She glanced up at me, briefly. "I'm sorry," she said. Funny thing was, I got the sense she meant it. Maybe she really was sorry, one businesswoman to another.

I just smiled – well, I moved my mouth – and turned to go.

"Missus Steel?"

"What?"

She fidgeted with the cleaver, not looking at me. "You oughta be careful."

It wasn't a conversation I wanted to get into, especially with the girl hanging around looking wide-eyed at me. I glanced at her. Her mother caught the look and jerked her head towards the back of the shop; the girl went.

"Look," I said, "if your husband or whoever's been coming to see us, you need to talk to him, not to me. We don't ask."

"My husband's been dead five years. I'm just saying." She turned away, lifted a skinned animal the size of a small deer onto the slab with one easy swing of her arms and started dismembering it with swift accuracy.

I found another butcher easily enough, though I didn't doubt Flower would soon pick a different one, but the shop looked clean and smelled fresh and the owner, a skinny, furry chap with a wide grin, had no problem filling the order.

From there, I went to The Lodestone. It's all low lighting, staff so discreet they're practically invisible, and the smell of some of Scalentine's most expensive food. I was dressed in my normal street clothes: good boots, leather and... well, leather, mostly. It's comfortable, it's stylish (by my standards, anyway), and it can survive a lot. I'd barely walked in when Clariel saw me.

I love to watch a professional at work. I'm not exactly inconspicuous at my height, even in Scalentine, but she whisked me out of sight without causing so much as a ripple among the clientele. She's something. Always dressed in a dark blue suit so crisply cut you could shave coins with it, glowing white wings folded behind her. She doesn't like the term *angel*, but it gets used a lot.

She raised an eyebrow at me. I've seen strong men quail at the sight of that eyebrow, but I'm not so easy to intimidate.

"I assume you are not looking for a table," she said, giving me the up-and-down.

"Not at your prices, Clariel. I need some information."

"Swift, Babylon." She waved one elegant hand towards the restaurant. "We are busy today."

I told her.

"And why did you come to me?" She looked at the girl's picture and raised the other eyebrow. It indicated that such things as kidnapping were vulgar, and beneath its notice.

"They were staying at the Riverside Palace. People with that kind of money eat here. If you hear anything that might involve this girl, let me know, eh?"

Her eyes are the exact shade of glacial lakes, and about as warm. "If I should happen to hear anything, perhaps you can tell me why I would pass it on to you? Why I should even tell you if they were here? My clients value discretion."

"So do mine," I said, grinning. "Come on, Clariel. It's the high-end clientele like them who bring in the rest. How many of your customers pay for their seats hoping they're still warm from a god's backside, or on the off chance they might spot the Perindan Emperor having a pie and peas with his fifty closest sycophants?"

"There is a difference between people knowing who one's clients are, and passing on private conversation. My clientele will turn up anyway, Babylon. We serve the best food in Scalentine."

"Not all of it," I said.

"Really."

I may not play chess as well as the Chief, but there are games I'm good at, when I have the pieces.

I leaned forward. "You hear anything, and you tell me, and I'll get you Flower's recipe for spiced goulash. If the information's *useful*, I'll get him to come show you how he does it."

She stared at me.

I stared back.

Finally she blew a delicate puff of air through slightly pursed lips. "Very well."

I was smiling as I left, but as I walked towards home, my good mood faded. I still had nothing, and if that girl was in some bastard's hands...

I turned the ring on my finger round and round, crossed the river and headed south.

TIRESANA

SURROUNDED BY THE sort of luxury even my master hadn't enjoyed, I rode by barge to the capital, Akran, and to the Temple of All the Gods.

For five days I lay on a silk-covered couch being fed fruit by beautiful servants and watching land I'd jounced over on a sandmule drift past gently. I felt as though I were in a guilty dream, suspended, waiting for someone to realise it had all been a mistake.

For five days the Avatar Hap-Canae appeared daily and spoke with me, talking about the marvels that awaited me, and asking me questions that no doubt exposed the echoing depths of my ignorance about, well, pretty much everything. Even about Babaska, she I was about to serve. I knew that she took human lovers, though it didn't always end well, and that she sometimes turned up in battle to fight beside a favoured soldier or a company. That was about it. I'd had a lot more education in scrubbing than in religion; what little I knew was mostly from fireside tales.

I was an eager listener, partly because I really was interested, and mad to learn, but mainly because I was half in love from the moment I first saw him. After a few days in his company, drenched in his charisma, the focus of utter and undivided attention from a divine being, I was as hopelessly, helplessly, awe-strickenly in love as any sixteen-year-old girl in the history *of all the planes. Even now the scent of myrrh will bring it back to me; that drugged and burning madness.*

It was the day before we were due to arrive. He lay on a green silk draped couch, the perfect background for his tawny robes; a plate of honey-cakes stood on the little table between us. His robes left one shoulder bare. I watched the smooth play of muscle beneath his glowing skin, and tried not to tremble. I was lying feet away from an Avatar, being treated like a priestess, and I was crazy with desire.

"Have you attended a Sowing?" he said, picking up a cake.

"Twice, so far." I blushed, I swear, all the way to my waist. The Sowing happened at Spring Festival, one of the most important in the year.

Hap-Canae smiled. "Only twice! Well, at least you know what will be expected of you." He bit into his cake.

I hadn't thought of it, but as a High Priestess of Babaska, of course, I would be expected to perform the Sowing. I wondered what it would be like to do it with a man in front of a whole crowd of people. Would everyone guess I'd never done it before? What if I got it wrong?

The thought was probably written all over my face.

He ran a finger down my cheek. My whole body seemed to melt outwards from where he'd touched me. "Well," he said, "you will receive some instruction, before you have to take part. But I think you might benefit from a little practical experience, hmm?"

He took my hand and led me to the covered area where he slept. I hardly felt the deck of the barge beneath my feet.

He had brought a mirror with him, of course; it stood on a gilded stand. I saw my face in it as he undressed me, my eyes wide and solemn.

I knew what went where, and that it was supposed to be an enjoyable experience; but otherwise I was ignorant as a calf. Daft with desire and drenched in Hap-Canae's charisma, utterly stunned with delight at having been Chosen, not just as a priestess but as a lover, I thought it was all wonderful. I was used to feeling too tall, too broad in the shoulder, too big altogether, but compared to him, magnificent in his size and strength, I was fragile, delicate. He could flip me over with one hand.

Just the sight of his hands, the hands of an Avatar, of Hap-Canae, golden and glowing on my ordinary breasts, was enough to send great washes of feeling through me from nipples to groin. I hardly dared glance at his cock, but when he guided my hand to it and I felt it leap under my fingers, I almost fainted with pleasure. I'd done that. I'd made his body respond, to me.

And when he pushed inside me, I welcomed the pain, a willing martyr to desire. Later, I'd understand what pleasure was; that first time, all my joy was simply in having him inside me.

CHAPTER
SIX

THOUGH IT WAS only lunchtime, The Swamp was already busy, the smell of alcohol, fish and riverweed rolling into the street. Kittack looked up from wiping the bar and bared triangular teeth at me; he's Ikinchli, and they're basically lizards. It took me a while to get to the bar, excusing my way through a lot of scales and tails. Kittack serves stuff that I wouldn't drink on a bet, but it's very popular with some of the more reptilian bunch.

"Babylon."

"Hey, Kittack."

"You want a little my special beer? Put scale on your chest, hah?"

I glanced down at myself. "I've got enough on my chest to be going on with, thank you."

Kittack flicked his tongue out at me. It's dark blue, long, pointy, and *very* adept. "I remembers."

"Me too. Put that tongue away before I forget what I came here for. You got a minute?"

He blinked at me, third eyelids pearling his eyes briefly. "Okay, we go back room."

He hissed and clicked at his barmaid, a lamia with deep blue-green scales, hands like an angel and lamplight eyes. If she ever fancies the work, I'm offering her a job. She slid up to the bar and winked at me. "Keep him back there a while, I make twice the tips when he isn't around."

"No respect," Kittack grumbled. We went into his 'back room,' which has heated stone benches and a small pool in the middle. Things swished and whirled in the water.

I settled myself, showed him the picture, and told him what I knew.

His cranial crest flicked up – not a good sign – then he went still. No-one can go more still than an Ikinchli. "Girl gone disappear. Why you ask me, Babylon?"

"Fain told me that these people come from the same place as you, Kittack. I just thought you might have heard something."

"Who you been listening to?"

"I don't get you."

"You been hearing bad old stories?"

"Sorry, Kittack, I don't know what you mean."

"Stories from back home, about my people kidnap pretty girls for sacrifice to Old."

The Old are sort of gods. Kittack's sort of gods.

"I've heard nothing but what Fain told me."

He flicked his tail. "Stories how the Old want pretty girls for make bouncy then cut head off. Waste of pretty girls, you ask me. Is all old foolishness from home."

"Who made up these stories?"

"Gudain." He tapped the portrait. "Master race, hah? Big pain in the tail; think us Ikinchli are made for slave, you know? So we do all hard work, not get nothing for it. Lots like me, we get chance, we leave."

"I don't blame you." I sighed, and shoved the portrait away.

"What's matter?"

"Well, I've promised to look for this girl. Been paid."

"So? Is good. Money is money. I hear anything, I tell you."

"Thanks, Kittack."

He shrugged – he does it with his whole body. "Is no problem. Strange, though."

"What is?"

"That Gudain girl. She got yellow eyes."

"Yeah?"

"I never seen that before. Gudain always grey eyes. Funny. Maybe means she different, not so much pain in arse like other Gudain, hah?"

"Yeah, maybe. You been getting any trouble?"

"From Gudain? No. Mostly don't come to Scalentine. Why would they? Back home, very comfortable, tell everyone what to do. Here, maybe not so much." He waved a foot around in the water. "Me, not so political. Live here now, not there. Some my people, very political. Meeting, meeting, talking, talking. One day we go home, throw down Gudain, all be great, you know? But is all talk."

"I meant, from the locals."

"Bit graffiti, is all. 'Scaly go home,' usual."

Ikinchli are 'Scaleys' only if you're dumb or plain rude, and only to their faces if you're looking to lose a part of your anatomy.

"Idiots," I said.

"True."

"You tell the militia?"

"What's point?" he said. "No head broken, why they care? You tell them about girl?"

"Not yet. I'm sorry, Kittack. I didn't mean anything, you know? I didn't know, about the stories."

"S'okay."

I stood up. "I got a few more people to talk to. You take care, all right?"

"You better tell Bitternut about girl. Otherwise he think you don't love him no more." He grinned, all teeth. "When you going to get smart?"

"Lay off, or I won't let you in next time you come calling."

"Then I waste away, turn into little shrivelled up lizard, you wear me for brooch."

"Like you can't get bouncy anywhere else. I like your new barmaid."

He hissed a laugh. "No bouncy there. She cheek me, not know her place. Also she like girls. Also can break my arm. Too many tough women; what's a poor guy to do?"

"You could visit the Twins, you might get a taste for it."

He gave a theatrical shiver, his tail whipping over the stone. "Pain for fun? Not *this* lizard. You mammals are *weird*."

TIRESANA

As we approached, *with the lesser barges and the trade-boats scuttling out of our way, I caught my first glimpse of the great statues, hundreds of feet high. They were seated rigidly on their thrones, staring out across the desert. Hap-Canae, Meisheté, Aka-Tete, Shakanti, Rohikanta, Lohiria, Mihiria. Babaska. Eight statues, eight gods.*

The statues were older than anyone remembered; they'd been made of some hard red stone that wore well, but even so, their faces were fading and blurring. Behind them, the walls stretched out to either side. "Is that Akran?" I asked. "I didn't know it had walls."

Hap-Canae smiled. "Oh, no, that's not the city. That is just the temple."

I gaped. How huge could it be?

"See how the people love their Avatars?" Hap-Canae said. "Now, it is very dusty. Here." He whisked a scarf of fine white gauze about my head and face. "We will go in the side entrance; the precinct is sure to be crowded."

We anchored at the jetty and I was led, shrouded like the dead, through an ancient side-gate, its thick carved wood silver with age.

I barely glimpsed the precinct before Hap-Canae ushered me inside, and up a set of stairs. All the servants were left behind.

I was slightly breathless by the time he finally paused at a window, looking down on the precinct, and I did likewise, and stood, gaping.

The walls were no deception. The Temple of All the Gods was the size of a town: the very courtyard was so huge the gods all had their own separate temples within it, lined up along the walls. One so white it hurt and all agleam inside with silver, one blood-red, one bright with gold, a gold sunburst mounted above the roof. I had never seen anything so astonishing, and only remembered to close my mouth when I breathed dust and started to cough.

"That," Hap-Canae said, pointing, "is the temple of Babaska."

It was of rich purplish stone, polished to a gleam. Inside I could see a statue, in white, ten feet high. Babaska. Hand on sword, her skirt kilted up and her hair bound back for fighting, smiling. There must have been a ceremony or a festival; the steps and altar were all draped in scarlet flowers, wilting now. I wondered what the festival had been and realised, nervously, how little I still knew about the ceremonies of the goddess I was supposed to serve.

The place was all a-bustle, priests of all sexes, acolytes and lay servants scurrying across its expanse like so many white-clad ants and disappearing into the cool shadows. Guards, very fine with their shields and spears polished bright, stood like statues.

"Come now," Hap-Canae said, and led me on down the corridors, with their silent painted processions of offering-bearers and sacrifices.

We went down more steps into the great mass of buildings behind the main temples, opposite the front gates. In and further in, to what was known as the Inner Temple, the oldest part, from which the rest had grown out over the centuries. It lay within the greater temple like a hidden drawer in a jewellery box, a place to keep secrets.

"Hap-Canae," someone said. "So, finally, you've made your choice?"

A woman with bone-white skin and silver hair that swept around her like a cloak was standing in the doorway ahead of us. She wore black gauze, through which her body showed like the moon through clouds; she was as tall as the Avatar Hap-Canae, and had the same devastating glow; and she frightened the life out of me.

That was the first time I saw the Avatar Shakanti. She looked at me as though wondering if I were ever likely to become worth her notice, then shrugged, and turned away into the room.

It was a cool white room with a blue tiled floor. There, seated on the benches or lounging on cushions on the floor, I saw the other girls. "These are your rivals," the Avatar Hap-Canae said.

"Rivals?"

"Why, yes." He laughed, that rich gold laugh, his hand resting on my shoulder. The Avatar Shakanti glared at him. "You would like to be a High Priestess of Babaska in a temple like this, would you not, rather than some miserable province, where the temple is of dried mud?"

I could hear the laughter still bubbling under his voice, but I didn't understand it, not then.

CHAPTER
SEVEN

SCALENTINE HAS ALWAYS been a city of mixtures. It's a *planar conjunction*, for the All's sake. We link to seven planes permanently, and new portals pop open every now and then, more of them during Twomoon. Some of them only spit out a handful of wanderers before they close again. In some unfortunate cases, all we get is, well, bits; some portals close fast.

Scalentine is a city surrounded by a few miles of farmland and forest, but after that, there's... nothing. A wall of air. Sometimes you see things in it, patterns, swirling, sometimes... other things. Watching it for too long can be addictive, and doesn't tend to be healthy.

We're a small plane; a sort of bubble caught between portals. Some say the whole plane is no natural thing, but something built. But who built it, or for what purpose, well, there are as many theories as there are students of the Arcane, not to mention people who've had a few too many drinks.

And there are those who think Scalentine was made for *them*, and no-one else should be allowed in.

But we get people from everywhere. Planes, and worlds within planes, and races within worlds, and tribes within races. We have Fey and humans, fauns and Ikinchli. We have people with tusks, people with fur, we have Barraklé and Edleskasin and even Monishish or Dra-ay from the Perindi Empire. Hells, there are at least thirty known races within the Perindi Empire alone, and half of them seem to end up here.

No-one knows who the original builders of the city were, or what they looked like. If there *were* builders. The city feels so alive, sometimes I think it just set itself here, and waited for people to start arriving, to fill its lungs with breath and its veins with blood.

I headed to the Hall of Mirrors. It looked spectacular, as always. Its dome is a fine framework of black-painted iron, lacing together panes of multicoloured glass; by day it's pretty enough, but at night, with all the light spilling out, it looks like a giant coloured lantern. (If you're of a cynical turn, of course, it's more reminiscent of one of those deep-ocean fish I've heard of, that uses pretty lights to lure its prey).

The smell of expensive perfumes, the subdued notes of a small orchestra, and the discreet murmur of a great deal of money changing hands greeted me as I went in, and looked up, like I always do. I had a drunken conversation with a friend once who suggested the panes of glass are in a mystic pattern which hypnotises people into spending money. We had just been on a bit of a spree, admittedly, but I think he was wrong. Although the first thing I saw when I dropped my gaze was Bannerman's, and his window display got me, like it always does, dammit.

I told myself I wasn't here to shop, but I did go over for one quick look. Okay, there wasn't anything there I actually needed, but it was all so shiny. And I was pretty sure the centrepiece was a Gillalune. Elegant, gorgeous, just the thing for day or evening wear... but I really, really didn't need another sword, and I couldn't afford a Gillalune anyway. I was still there, trying not to drool too obviously, when I heard my name being called.

"Hey, Chief," I said. "How's it going?"

He strolled over, saw what I was looking at, and whistled. "Splashing out?"

"That wouldn't be a splash, that would be a flood."

We both looked at the window for a bit longer, and Bitternut sighed. "Beautiful."

"You think it's a Gillalune?"

"Looks like it, doesn't it?" he said. "Look at that wave-pattern on the blade. Bet it sings like a bird."

"Yep. You got time for spice tea? I need to talk to you about something."

He gave a quick glance around. "Looks quiet enough, so long as we stay on the square, but I can't stop long."

We settled ourselves at the only café where we could both fit our legs under the table.

"So how are you?" I said.

"Crazed. Carnival opened last night."

"Ah."

Carnival's a portal. There are seven permanent or near-permanent portals. Four are fixed ones that always open onto the same planes. Portal Bealach is the biggest, our main trade route. It links to a spot on the border between the Perindi Empire and the Flame Republic (lot of work for the Diplomatic section). Portal Eventide links to the Fey lands; Throat Portal links to a plane that seems to be mostly ice, darkness, and brutally ferocious beasts, but also contains several powerful if not very appealing countries (more diplomacy); and Portal Spirita, which is an anomaly – it's a permanent portal, but the plane on the other side changes. Very little comes through Spirita, and what does is strange. Stranger, that is, than what comes through the others. Lunatic travellers, self-proclaimed saviours, victims of obscure curses and scholars of lost tongues.

The other portals seem to open up almost at random, but they all have a feel, or a mood, if you like. There's Crowns, through which we get generals without their armies, weapons-makers, runaway heirs to distant thrones, royal retinues, escaped slaves (that's where Flower came through), wandering bureaucrats, occasional legions that walked into a mist somewhere and turned up here. There's Nightwind, not far from where we were sitting. Through Nightwind come refugees from horrors: lost souls, sick gods whose powers have gone, lone wanderers from dying planes. The haunting and the haunted.

And through Carnival we can get *anything*. Any time. With the other unfixed portals there's apparently some sort of pattern about when they open and what plane they link to (not to me, but then I don't study the Arcane; I just live with it). But not Carnival. No wizard, alchemist, or Doctor of Obscure Magicks has ever worked out why it decides to open, or when, or for how long, or what plane it might be connected to when it does, but whatever comes through is pretty certain to be, well, colourful.

Sometimes literally. We had streams of tiny, rainbow-coloured birds no bigger than my thumb come through once; thousands of them, for about two hours. They flew all over the city. Oddest thing, they were completely silent. Not a twitter or cheep. Most of them died within hours, littering the streets with sad limp little heaps of bright feathers. I've heard rumours that a few survive in the houses of the very rich. I wonder about them, sometimes, and what it was like where they came from, and why they never sang.

"What'd we get this time?" I asked.

"A bunch of six-foot, four-armed... *things*. Look like insects, unless it's some kind of fancy armour, and carrying something we thought was weaponry but could be cutlery for all I know. Anyway it got confiscated, which they didn't like. Eighteen ornery green pack-animals with blue teeth, which they don't mind using" – he rolled up his sleeve to show me the bruise – "and a gold teapot. That came through on its own, half an hour after everything else." He grinned. "'Course, we had a rookie, went straight for it. Should have seen him jump when the whole room yelled '*Don't rub that!*'"

I laughed, although it wasn't funny last time someone released a genie here. They're not exactly gods, but some of them have a fair amount of oomph, more than most beings of power do when they get here. Scalentine has some kind of damping effect on magic; it's why Laney can only do minor spells. I've always wondered, with genies, if it's something to do with coming through in a container; being sealed up keeps it preserved, like jam.

Jam doesn't usually come leaping out of the jar threatening to rend all and sundry to splinters, though. Still, if I'd been stuck in a pot for a couple of centuries I reckon I'd be a bit peeved, too. They ended up calling me in to help calm him down, which was... interesting. Fun, too, but he took a *lot* of calming. I had to take the next two days off.

"So," the Chief said, "we've got a couple wizards checking it over."

"Busy night."

"That wasn't even all of it."

"Seriously? What else?"

"Got a call to a Barraklé pie-shop. Newcomers, you know? Only just bought the place. Some idiot painted slogans, broke their windows and tried to set a fire spell. Don't know who he bought it off, but we caught him because he was sitting on the pavement staring at the place where his fingers used to be."

"How terribly sad."

"Isn't it? I mean, there he was, innocently trying to set fire to a shop that still had people in it, and he loses his fingers. Felt for him no end."

"Human?"

"Yep."

"Sometimes I'm ashamed to be the same race."

The Chief shrugged. "Why should you be? Idiots come in all species. I think someone from every race in Scalentine's been hauled into the Barracks since I joined."

"You must be wiped. Shouldn't you be off duty?"

"Probably."

"I hear there was a bit of a ruckus here too, a day or so back," I said.

"Ah, there was a bit of a barney in the crowd, plus we had some high panjandrums, demanding attention. This lot claim to be demigods. Whoops! Watch the tea, there."

"Demigods?" I said. My hand had jolted a bit while I was pouring, but most of the tea had made it into the cup.

"Yeah."

"Where from?" I said, trying to sound casual.

"No idea. That's Diplomatic Section's area, not mine." He eyed me. "You want me to ask?"

"Would you?" It was probably fine. Almost certainly fine. There was no real reason why anyone from Tiresana would be looking for me, not after all this time.

"You going to tell me why?"

"There's some people I'd rather not meet, that's all."

"Hmm. All right."

I knew I was only off the hook temporarily. He's a digger, the Chief. He'd keep digging until I told him or he found out some other way.

I hadn't told anyone all of it. Not even the crew; not even Previous.

"Anyway," he said, "we were just doing crowd control. You know what it's like, everyone wants an eyeful of the powerful."

"Why, do you suppose?"

"Maybe they think it'll rub off, or something. But we had a lot of people on."

"Not completely popular, then, these bigwigs?"

"You never know. Remember The Most Exalted Father of His People the All-Beloved One, about two years back?"

"Oh, yeah. Did you ever find his head?"

"Nope. That was one narked-off bunch of peasantry," he said, with something that sounded a lot like admiration, and probably was. "This was nothing like that. These were just making a fuss because there were ordinary people about, it seems. You know how paranoid they can get, when their full powers don't work. I wasn't there, just got a report afterwards;

not to mention several hours of chat with the Diplomatic Section." He rolled his eyes.

"So?" he said. "Why'd you ask?"

"Ah. Well, there's a girl who went missing, during the ruckus."

His eyes sharpened. "How the *hells* did you hear about that?"

"Um..." Fain hadn't actually *said* not to mention his involvement, but I didn't think he'd appreciate it being shouted. And although I didn't know for sure (I didn't know anything about Fain for sure), I was fairly certain that not all of his dealings were legal. If the Chief found out I was pillow-partnering Fain, if only in the business sense... well, let's say I wasn't keen on the thought.

"Never mind," the Chief said, when the silence had gone on a little too long. "I know, I know, discretion. We're already looking for her."

"Yeah, me too."

"Oh?" He said.

"I've been asked to. Anyway, I thought I should let you know."

"How much do you know about the girl?"

"I know her people are important on Incandress, and that she was here buying something for her wedding. That's pretty much it." Now I came to say it, I realised it really wasn't a lot.

"Important's definitely the word. Important enough to run the country. Watch where you tread, Babylon. If you find her, you bring her straight to me."

"I'll try," I said.

I was fudging. Not because Fain had a prior claim (after all, the important thing was that Enthemmerlee was found) but because she herself did. If she'd been raped or abused in any way, she was going to get time with me in comfort and safety before people started throwing questions at her. Not to mention a chance to tell me whether she actually *wanted* to go back to her family.

The Chief drank the rest of his tea and rubbed a hand over his face.

"You look like you need time off," I said.

"Going to get it anyway, soon." He pushed himself back from the table. "Thanks for the tea. I'll see you later."

I sat over my cooling tea for a while, wondering what to do next. A few people came over and said hello, a few more gave me that nervy side-glance that meant they hoped I wasn't going to come over and claim acquaintance with them in front of their wives, or husbands, or three significant others. As if I would. If people can't admit to having a little fun, I reckon it's their problem, but I know my business and it isn't to play tattletale.

I showed the picture to one or two of those who stopped, on the off chance, and hoped the spice tea would get my brain working. When there was nothing in the pot but dregs, I went home.

TIRESANA

EACH OF US girls had been hand-picked by an Avatar. There was the Avatar Meisheté; her jurisdiction was fertility, midwifery and childbirth. She had a broad-hipped, big-breasted figure that should have suggested hugs and comfort, but didn't, and about her eyes and upper cheeks lay the darkened skin they call the 'butterfly mask' that some pregnant women get – though hers was not patchy as such a thing usually is, but symmetrical, perfect as though painted on, giving her a look of wisdom and mystery. She could touch a man or a woman and render them fertile – whatever age or physical condition they were in. I don't know how long it was before it struck me as odd, as a sign of something out of kilter, that she herself was childless. Eventually I realised that all the Avatars were.

Meisheté could make crops grow in barren earth, if she chose, but she had a preference for babies, even if those babies were going to starve. She was pretty powerful, but blinkered. So long as nothing interfered with what she saw as her sphere, she didn't care.

She changed quite a lot. I had to get used to that; not just being around Avatars, which I'd never expected, but the fact that their aspects changed. The Avatar Meisheté was sometimes a heavily pregnant young woman, sometimes she was an ancient crone. It wasn't just appearance, like an illusion or a glamour. She actually changed; but she never gave birth. What, *if anything, was growing in her when she walked swollen-bellied and swaying, and what happened to it, I never dared ask and hardly dared think about. She'd Chosen Velance, a pretty round thing with wide hips and milky skin.*

Then there was the Avatar Aka-Tete. The death-god. Always smelled slightly of rotting meat, but somehow you got used to that. He wore a belt of human skulls and gloves made of dead men's foreskins. Some of us giggled about that, imagining what would happen if he rubbed his hands together, though we never saw him do it. Sometimes he was a warrior, all muscle and scars, his hands dripping red; sometimes he was a vulture the size of a man. He'd Chosen Jonat, a slender, dark honey-skinned girl with a sharp mind and too much intensity burning in a slight frame. She wrote a lot of bad poetry and was, like me, desperately in love with the Avatar who'd picked her.

The Avatar Shakanti. Shakanti the silver-eyed. Avatar of the Moon Goddess. She could draw up the waters of the sea, increase the power of spells and drive people mad. She was mad herself, Shakanti. Mad as moonlight on a knife blade. She represented virtue, so she never lied, but she could open a wound with the truth and twist it to make you scream. Sometimes her face was a skull, and even then, somehow, she was still beautiful. She'd Chosen poor little Renavir, frail and fierce.

The Avatar Rohikanta, Avatar of the river god. Older, and quieter than the rest. I always saw him in the same aspect: a huge, muscular man, with a beard and hair of running water. Two great reptiles walked with him; the Messehwhy, the sacred crocodiles. The ones that lived in the Rohin were bad enough, but these were another kind. Something that, like the gods themselves, no longer walked our plane. They were huge, big enough to bite a horse in half. They could barely fit through the temple doors. I like lizards, as a rule, but those things gave me the raging horrors. Rohikanta had Chosen Brisein, who was quiet too – so shy she hardly spoke.

We were all different, we girls, but we all shared a certain look, at times. I saw it in my mirror. A wide-eyed, solemn look; knowing we had been chosen, none of us certain of our fitness for the fate we'd been chosen for.

There were the Avatars who represented the gods of the winds, Lohiria and Mihiria. Twins; high-boned and lush-lipped with great twining sheafs of hair that were never quite still. It took me weeks to even tell them apart and I never was entirely sure which twin was which. Of all the Avatars I began to lose my awe of those first; fussy as hens, both of them, and about as much brain.

But though I may have lost some respect for them, I didn't let it show. I'd not been there ten days before I saw the wind twins, their hair whipping around their heads like wild flames, in an argument that culminated in the wind ripping the roof off a shrine, sending it flying over the wall like a great sail. I heard screams from outside. Whether anyone was hurt, I don't know.

Lohiria had Chosen Seili, a girl with a sheaf of glorious dark red hair and the plane's most irritating laugh; Mihiria of the East Wind had Chosen Calife, a sultry-looking creature with a taste for sweets and a habit of falling asleep whenever there was a cushion to be had.

They'd all Chosen someone who reflected themselves a little. Even Hap-Canae.

THE SOUND OF *the gongs in the still morning air, the blue light falling across the honey-coloured floor tiles.*

Lessons. So many lessons. Seven of us, to begin with. We sat for hours with slates, learning our letters. Learning to read dusty, cracking scrolls, scratching and trying not to fall asleep as the afternoon heat spread across the floor like treacle. Reading about the Deeds of Babaska: how she tried to lift a sword as soon as she could walk, how she fought the Lord of the Dark World to a standstill in a month-long battle and came at last to an amicable, not to say amorous, agreement.

Dozens of stories. *Babaska and the Bridge of Dawn, Babaska and the Leopard's Child...*

I knew some marketplace legends and a deal of practical things about running a household or a caravan train, but I couldn't read, or write. The amount we were expected to learn was a little frightening, and I was desperate to do well, mainly to please Hap-Canae.

Those marketplace legends came in useful, though. I recalled how the stories told in rhythm stuck in my head, and started making up little chants and mnemonics to help me remember – most of which would have had a professional storyteller howling into his offering-bowl in pain, but they worked.

I knew that Babaska watched over soldiers, as well as whores. It wasn't until later, when I learned of other gods of war, that I realised that Babaska differed from most of them in her military aspect. She wasn't a goddess of leaders, of triumphant campaigns, riding beside the general and whispering the secrets of victory in his ear. She was a goddess of the everyday soldier. A goddess of survival, of getting through a battle with most of your parts attached and some of your mates still alive. A goddess you prayed to for dry boots, a steady hand, a sane commander, and payday.

And she was a goddess who watched over all whores, from the finest silk-hung courtesans to the street-whore who earned in copper coins. In Tiresana, whores had status as artisans, and Babaska was their representative. To her they prayed for generous custom, the ability to charm, for safety from disease and bad clients and unwanted pregnancy.

No wonder Meisheté didn't like us much.

CHAPTER
EIGHT

I WAS LOOKING forward to my lunch by the time I got back to Goldencat Street; I could see two people hanging about outside the Lantern. White robes and beaked white masks. *Vessels.* I sped up.

They did nothing except stand there, hands folded in front of them, those damned masks turning to watch me as I approached, then turning away again, scanning the street, back and forth.

Bliss was outside, his long narrow face looking vaguely worried. He's thin and slope-shouldered and has a sort of bleached, silvery cast, as though you were looking at him by moonlight.

He's a Fade. That is, someone who came through one of the portals but didn't quite make it all the way. It happens, mainly with Nightwind Portal. People lose some part of their essential self. He was some sort of hunter or tracker, back home. He does odd jobs about the place, in return for food, a bed, and company. I don't usually put him out front, but sometimes I ask him to stick around new clients if I'm not sure they're going to behave, because they forget he's there. Of course, sometimes he forgets, too, and just sort of drifts off.

He hadn't drifted anywhere this time, but he obviously had no idea what to do about our visitors.

"What are they doing?" I said.

"Watching. Everyone who comes in. Or goes out."

I heard one of the upstairs windows open and looked up to see Essie leaning out, breasts spilling out of her gown. "Coo-ee, boys! Don't be shy and hang around in the cold! Come in and we'll warm you up!"

I saw one of the masks tilt a fraction, before its owner returned to sweeping his blank-faced gaze up and down the street. It gave me a chill. They looked like some sort of mechanisms, fixed and unnatural.

Then both masks turned. I saw someone who looked vaguely familiar – one of Laney's clients – who got about a quarter of the way to the Lantern before he clocked the Vessels, blanched, and strode off down a side street trying to look as though he'd meant to do that all along.

I wished him luck – the street was a dead end, with nothing on it but a couple of private houses and a shop that was currently empty.

Another window opened. Laney bounced up onto the sill. She was wearing even less than Essie, a whisper of burnt-orange satin, but gave the distinct impression of someone rolling up their sleeves. Her green eyes narrowed. "That was my client you just scared off," she said. "A *nice* man. A *generous* man. Now, let's see..."

"*Laney, no!*" I yelled.

Too late. Something pink and glittering shot from Laney's hand and hit the nearest Vessel, draping him briefly in a festive glow.

I heard him gasp, and he staggered back, his hands coming up defensively. I started towards him, terrified that Laney had lost her temper.

The pink glitter concentrated around the sides of his head. There was a sound like nasty little laughter. The Vessel whimpered.

His mask began to tilt, like a great bird cocking its head to see better. The whole thing kept rising to reveal a bony, large-nosed young man with a loose wet mouth. He reached up to grab the mask, and stopped, frozen, as his hands encountered something furry.

He glared at me. I was laughing, mainly with relief.

"Ass's ears," Laney said, helpfully. "In case you were wondering. *Ever* so traditional."

"And apt," I said. "If you don't want worse, get out of my jalla. *Now.*"

"Replace your mask, Brother," the other Vessel said. "What you sense is merely external, and of what significance is that? The illusions of a whore-witch have no power over the Purified." The hollow beak of the mask gave his voice a strange, buzzing resonance, an oddly insectile sound.

"I said, leave!"

They ignored me.

"It seems," Unusual said, appearing at my elbow, "that they don't talk to women. Or listen to them."

"Then you tell them to bugger off for me, would you?"

"I really would advise you to leave," Unusual told them.

It took the Vessels a moment to decide whether to talk to *him* – Unusual is very obviously male, but he's also very obviously... Unusual. He doesn't wear a lot, and what he does wear has lots of straps and buckles and fits very, very closely.

Eventually the one without the furry ears stepped forward. "We are not in your property. We are standing outside it, in the public roadway, as anyone might do, and here we will remain."

The hells of it was, he was right. I didn't own the road outside the Lantern. They weren't actually doing anything illegal, that I could see.

"Now," Unusual said, leaning against the doorjamb, languid as a snake in the sun, "exactly how long do you plan to stand there? Until everyone in Scalentine gives up sex?"

"We remain until those that have been dragged from the Path see the error of their ways and put their feet upon the Road of Purity."

"Dragged? *Dragged?*" I said. "Excuse me, but we don't *drag*. Not one person has ever been dragged in here."

"Put *in* drag, maybe," Essie said, from above. "Only on request, mind."

"They have been tempted," said the Vessel, still pointing his mask at Unusual. "They have been drawn from the Way. Their souls are endangered. It is our mission to draw all into the light of the Purest."

"Most of our clients aren't even your followers. What business is it of yours if they come to us?" I said. "Oh, never mind, I'm talking *sense*, aren't I? That doesn't work when it comes to religion. Don't worry, just pretend you haven't heard me, you will anyway."

I wanted to hit someone so badly my arm-muscles were twitching. "Bliss, go fetch Flower."

We glared at each other while we waited. Well, my lot glared; the Vessels stared archly at the middle distance, as though listening to some sound none of us could hear. Maybe they were.

Flower ducked through the doorway, saw the Vessels, sighed, and began to undo the strings of his apron.

The Vessel nearest the door shuffled backwards slightly.

"Lovely piece of fresh fish, I had on the go," Flower said. "It'll be all dried out. Ruined."

The Vessel lifted his chin in a 'preparing to be martyred' kind of way. I had no intention of giving him the pleasure – unless he pushed it.

"Flower, stay on the door," I said. "If either of them tries to get in, I believe we're within our rights if you punch them into next week. Sav?"

"Sav."

"Laney?"

"Yes darling?"

"No more spells unless they try to get in, or hurt anyone."

She pouted. "I wouldn't *kill* anyone; I *can't*, here. Not magically, anyway."

"We don't want a repeat of what happened to that client who tried to hit you."

"Oh, him."

"Yes, him. The one who, last I heard, still wakes up screaming most nights. Of course, if you're offered sufficient provocation..."

"Oh, all *right*." She sighed, loosened her gown some more, hitched one hip on the windowsill and started to paint her toenails. I heard a strangled noise from behind one of the masks.

"Did you deal with the butcher?" Flower said.

"I found a new one, and *yes,* Flower, the shop looked clean, and no there were no flies, no vermin at all that I could see. Order will be here tomorrow."

I heard running feet and turned to see Previous, looking pink, sword in one hand, jamming her shabby helmet over damp coppery curls with the other. She skidded to a halt. "What's going on?"

"The Vessels have decided that since the Laws of Scalentine aren't inclined to shut us down they're going to have a go themselves, by hanging around and scaring off our clients."

Someone was coming up the street behind Previous, rather more slowly. He was slight and basically human-shaped, with a pearly-blue tinge to his skin, appealingly mouse-like, rounded, crinkly little ears and silvery eyes currently wide with curiosity, taking everything in.

"Is that..."

"This is Frithlit," she said. "Um..."

"Take him inside, have some food. Sorry, Frithlit." I smiled at him. "Nice to meet you. Got a bit of a situation here. I'm going to go pay the Temple a little visit."

"I'm coming with you," Previous said.

"What about your friend?"

"Don't worry," Frithlit said; he had a soft, lilting accent I didn't recognise. "I don't make trouble for you, okay? Trouble you got."

Taking another woman with me wouldn't gain me any points with the Vessels, which was fine by me. I wasn't going there to make them like me. But I didn't want to haul Previous away from the boyfriend she'd finally decided to let us meet.

"Previous..."

"We going then?"

She had that completely impassive expression that only soldiers seem to perfect; the one that says, *yes, I understand perfectly, I will obey your orders to the letter, but they will somehow turn out to have been ordering me to do what I was going to do anyway.*

If I did leave her behind she'd only follow me. And maybe it wouldn't hurt to take her. Like Laney, I have been known to lose my temper. In a temple full of people with a known capacity to piss me off, that could result in something quite messy. Wouldn't hurt to have Previous along as a brake.

As we got closer to our destination on Littleflower Way, I slowed my pace; just as well for Previous, her being shorter in the leg and a bit flushed trying to keep up. I took a good look around. The temple was a handsome enough building, of that creamy gold stone they bring in from somewhere in the Perindi Empire, if a bit square and blocky for my taste. Its outer precinct was all brute lines and grim statues with so many clothes on even the marble looked hot. Presumably this was in case a bit of exposed stone flesh sparked a naughty thought, though of course it would have no effect on those Vessels who'd blinded themselves. Maybe they were worried they might brush up against a marble thigh by accident, or something.

We went up the wide, shallow steps to the entrance. Heavy bronze doors writhed with carvings of tortured souls, designed to make the supplicant feel desperate for redemption and deeply uncertain about their chances of getting it.

Nothing here was making me feel any more relaxed.

There were two guards in black uniforms, not masked. They gave us that down-the-nose look, or tried, but I was taller than either of them before we'd even got to the top step, so that didn't work.

"The Purest sees all," they intoned. "Abase yourself before the gaze of the Purest."

"I'm not here to see the Purest."

They faltered, glancing at each other, but only for a moment. "Females are not permitted to enter the Temple," one said, lowering his spear across the door.

"I've no desire to enter, thank you. I want one of your priests to come out and talk to me. Specifically, whoever sent people to hang about outside my place of business and disrupt our trade. That'd be the Red Lantern, on Goldencat Street."

"Our priests do not converse with... females," said the one with the lowered spear and the emphatic, shovel-shaped beard. I've no objection to beards as a rule, but I reckon anyone with that much bristling masculinity pasted to their jaw is trying a bit too hard. The other one blinked at the mention of the Red Lantern and dropped his gaze slightly, but didn't budge.

"Fine," I said. "Find someone who does. We'll wait." I leaned on the wall, and undid a few buttons. "Warm afternoon," I said. I heard Previous give a muffled snort.

"You are wasting your time," said Beard. I wriggled a bit to get comfortable against the stone. Beard stared straight ahead. The other one, who was young and doe-eyed – too cute for a Vessel, by far – glanced over and swallowed. I smiled at him. He looked away but I could see the deep red flush creeping up his neck.

"Oh, by the way," I said to Previous, "I went to the Glory Days and checked out that dancer. The one from Losandas?"

I'm always on the lookout for a bit of entertainment, to keep the punters amused if they have to wait, and Losandas dancers are notorious.

"Oh, I've heard about *her*. She does that thing with the oil, the olives and the snake?"

"Yep," I said.

Previous shook her head. "I saw that once. How does someone bend like that?"

"She does this bit where she goes up to a member of the audience and sort of wraps herself..."

Telling stories intended to encourage a certain reaction in the audience was part of my training, you might say. Well, it was that or sing, and anyone who's heard me sing would tell you I'm a fair storyteller. Mind you, anyone who's heard me sing would probably tell you I'm a fair carpenter.

Funnily enough, it wasn't the young guard who broke, it was Beard who started to sweat, his knuckles gradually whitening as he clutched his spear, and tried to ignore what he was hearing. Eventually he retreated with as much dignity as remains to a man apparently trying to conceal a small sailing boat under his uniform.

I wasn't sure if he closed the door with unnecessary force, or if it was just designed to give out that long, rolling boom. Might have been quite impressive under other circumstances. I wondered what it was like on the other side when that thing shut behind you. A lot like gaol, I'd imagine.

"You all right?" Previous muttered. Something must have shown on my face.

"Fine. I just want to get done and get home."

It wasn't long before a man appeared around the side of the temple, looked us over and gestured us to a small door off the courtyard.

It opened on one of those bland little rooms where the daily business of temples is done; a place for things like paying one's bills and dealing quietly with trouble. A window, two chairs, a plain table. Our host wore grey robes instead of the white of the priests, and no mask. He was a type I thought I recognized: the quiet, unassuming, administrative sort. The sort who, behind the bland exterior, is often rabidly ambitious with an agenda all their own. He was narrow-hipped, slight, no more than a boy's height and as thin as a politician's promise.

He gave a bow perfectly judged to be just polite enough, and gestured us to the two hard-backed chairs. Fine by me, he could stand if he thought height gave him an advantage, but he'd be looking down my front, which might give me an edge.

But he didn't seem as susceptible as the guard. Barely a glance.

"I am Administrator Elect Denarven," he said, his voice as quiet and well-modulated as his gestures. The harsh-soap stink of the temple (no dangerously sensuous incense for the Vessels) seemed to concentrate around him. His fingernails were extraordinarily clean; his hands were reddish, water-scoured, like a washerwoman's. Perhaps they scrubbed the temple floors as some kind of penance. I thought about asking him if they'd hire out; trying to scrub the 'sin' out of the Lantern would surely be a perfect penance, and the floors'd come up a treat.

"Why have you entered our precinct?" he said.

"I told the guard. I run The Red Lantern, in Goldencat Street. Two of your priests have turned up. They are disrupting my trade."

He blinked. "Two *Vessels* are..."

"Standing around, in the street, making a damn nuisance of themselves. I want them removed."

"I am merely an administrator," he said. "What action the Vessels decide to take in pursuance of the worship of the Purest is at the discretion of the High Priests."

"If they were *showing* discretion, it wouldn't be a problem. I want them out of there."

"It is part of the beliefs of the order that sin is not permitted to hide, that iniquity be dragged into daylight."

"We are hardly hiding. We're right there, and everyone, including your Order, knows exactly what we do. So who are you dragging us into daylight for?"

He looked at me as though I were stupid. "The Purest," he said.

Theological discussion with fanatics is a lost cause, but I couldn't help wondering how useful their god was, if he couldn't spot us for himself. We're rapidly becoming the best known brothel in Scalentine.

"Selling pleasure's legal in Scalentine," I said, "whether the Vessels like it or not."

"It is not my place to question the Vessels or to tell them how they should act."

"Then why am I talking to you? Why don't you go get me someone who actually has some authority, and I'll talk to them."

"Our priests do not..."

"Converse with females. Yeah, I get it. I tell you what. You tell them what I said, and you send someone to remove those priests before I get back. Because otherwise, I'm going to be doing it myself. And I may be less than polite."

He folded his hands and permitted himself half a smile, as though he'd be taxed on the rest.

"They are standing in the street. Such action is not illegal. Assault, however, is illegal."

"Your lot should know."

"I do not understand what you are implying."

"The whore down in Ropemaker's Row. The whore who got beaten up by someone wearing a Purity mask. That, Mr Denarven, was assault."

"No member of the Order would *ever* behave in such a way," he said, his jaw so rigid with distaste he could hardly get the words out.

"Really."

"You have no comprehension of the Order." His voice had gone very quiet, the way people's voices do when it's that, or shout. "However distasteful a Vessel might find the existence of this creature, they could never attack her in that way. Her attacker had to get close to her, to *touch* her. Impossible. A member of the Order could never again attain purity after touching such a woman."

Well now I *really* wanted to go up to a Vessel and give him a big hug.

He remembered he was talking to 'such a woman,' I saw it on his face, and I wondered if he'd make some kind of half-arsed attempt at an apology, but no. He looked me right in the eye as though daring me to make something of it.

I realised I wasn't going to get anywhere, and my temper was boiling up like a kettle.

"In any case," I said, shoving back my chair, "get them out of there. I can do things legally and make your lives difficult if I choose..."

"I do hope that isn't a threat," said Denarven.

"That? No, that's not a threat. But if I, or any other whore in Scalentine, get any more trouble from your lot, or connected with your lot in any way whatsoever, you will wish, *fervently,* that I'd gone to the militia with this. *That's* a threat. Smooth?"

"I think we understand each other."

"I do hope so."

He bowed. We left.

Previous had even more trouble keeping up with me on the way back; it wasn't until she put a hand on my arm that I realised I was damn near running. Not to mention gritting my teeth and using words, albeit under my breath, that even I don't normally use. Like 'priest,' for example.

"Babylon!"

"Huh? Oh. Sorry."

"So," she said, "you want to tell me what that was about?"

"We do not *need* any more trouble. And I don't care what that administrator said, I'll eat my sword if the Vessels didn't have something to do with that girl who got beaten up. What if they try it on one of the crew?"

"What, like Laney?" Previous said.

"They're not all Fey."

"They all know how to look after themselves, Babylon. Anyway, s'not what I meant."

"Then what are you talking about?"

"You seemed... upset. I mean, you know, the Vessels haven't done anything, really."

"Apart from destroy an evening's business," I said, "and who knows how many more, if we can't get rid of 'em." She was still giving me a quizzical look. I sighed. "Look, I just don't like priests. Or gods. Or temples. I spent a lot of time in them."

"You?"

"Me."

TIRESANA

WE GIRLS, SPRAWLED *on cushions in a silk-hung room. Shakanti seated in the corner, impatient. And our new trainer, a graceful and soft-voiced woman in linen the clean blue of a spring sky. She had assistants with her, two young men, two young women, in loose white robes.*

"My name is Livaia," she told us. "I am here to teach you how to give pleasure, and how to receive it. It is something that almost anyone can learn to do with some degree of craft, and that is well enough. However, it is the subtleties which transform craft into art. Subtlety, the capacity to take that extra care, is the mark of the true artist."

She beckoned forward one of the young men. He was very handsome, with the sculpted body of an athlete and a gentle smile.

"First," Livaia said, "is anyone here still virgin? Come, there's no need to be ashamed."

I happened to glance at Shakanti, who was glaring, and looked away fast.

Renavir's hand went up, spearing the air. She, too, glanced at Shakanti – seeking approval, poor child. Then, after a moment, Velance's hand went up, too. Neither of them surprised me.

"Then we shall start with the basics." She gestured to the young man to take off his robe. There were gasps and giggles – most of us had, of course, at least seen a cock before, but not in such

circumstances. "Now," she said, "I will show you how things work, and then, we shall move on to making them work better. Jalis here is in no need of encouragement, as you can see. I think being in the presence of so many pretty young ladies has had an effect on him. But sometimes encouragement is required."

She took him in hand, so to speak, and so our first lesson in the heart of the seductive arts began.

Growing up as I had, crammed in among the other servants, and later out with the caravans, I'd had neither the time nor the inclination to be especially modest, though with Sesh and Kyrl watching over me like a pair of mother hawks, I'd remained virgin until Hap-Canae. I enjoyed the lessons. When it moved from demonstration by Livaia to the point when we had to take part, I was more than ready. Watching people seduce each other did nothing to damp my own fires, and when it was my turn to sink into the cushions with Jalis, Livaia had to coach me not to take things too quickly.

Jalis. My second lover. Gentle, adept – not, perhaps, overburdened with brains, but exquisitely good at what he did. My own responses surprised me: I had thought things with Hap-Canae were marvellous, and was surprised to discover that they could be much more so.

I began to realise that Hap-Canae's bedroom techniques lacked a certain something. I tried not to think about it. Of course, I wouldn't dream of telling him, or suggesting that he pay a little attention to my own pleasure as well as his. After all I was, still, so grateful.

It wasn't just that he had taken me away from a life of hard work – I didn't mind work. He treated me like something of value. He loved to give me things: robes, jewellery. I'd never before worn anything that someone else hadn't owned before me – the master's gift of scarlet cloth was still, presumably, back in the servants' quarters, or more probably adorning someone else by now. Just to have things of my own was a treat, and such things! Even the mistress had never had robes like this; lusciously dyed, richly embroidered, they were works of art. Necklaces the worth of which could have bought my old master and his entire business.

So yes, I was grateful, and wanted to make him proud of me. But this part of my lessons was hardly a chore.

I loved finding out how to make someone shudder and gasp, and cry out; to feel a cunny or a cock quiver at my touch, the sudden rush of wetness, the flushed skin and quick breath. Sweet tension, and its sweet release. I liked to give pleasure, and it gave me a sense, I suppose, of something I didn't have anywhere else: power.

We were taught what foods to eat to enhance the senses, and which ones would sweeten one's breath and one's... other secretions. Every aspect of the art, from entering a room or pouring a drink, to undressing oneself or someone else with sensual grace.

I had to learn patience, and although grace was never my strongest point, I learned, at least in the bedroom, some subtlety. I became even more convinced that I had been lucky in being Chosen to be one of Babaska's priestesses; I doubted those of the other deities had nearly as much fun.

Others didn't take to it so well.

Brisein, Chosen by the Avatar Rohikanta, was the first to break. I could have told them she wasn't right for it; anyone with half an eye could see she was embarrassed and miserable. She had no reason to be embarrassed, at least; given a choice and the chance to get to know her partner, she'd have been as good as anyone, but whatever her life had been beforehand, it hadn't suited her to this.

One morning she was simply gone. "She's been found a place," the Avatar Rohikanta told us, running a hand through his watery beard; the water vaporised halfway to the floor, surrounding him in a constant chilly mist. He was frowning, but then, he always looked serious. The Messehwhy reared, showing their pale bellies, and hissed.

Jonat scowled. I remember how black her hair was, in that cool-coloured room; she had the high-boned face of the desert tribes and her eyes were as dark as her hair. "Fat lot of good *she's going to be," she muttered, once she was sure Rohikanta was out of earshot, though of course, with the Avatars, it was difficult to be certain. "She couldn't cope with the lessons, what sort of priestess is she going to make?"*

Renavir trembled and bit her thumb. "Hush."

Shakanti appeared silently behind us, as she tended to do. One of her many disconcerting habits. She swept her hand briefly over Renavir's hair, which was fine and light as a baby's. "Concentrate on your own future, if you are to have one," she said.

I could feel Jonat wanting to ask what that meant and held my breath. I'd seen already what Shakanti could do to an acolyte who displeased her; I didn't even know what the boy had done, but he had been giggling and trying to pull his own fingers off when they led him away. I needn't have worried – at least, not about that. The Avatars didn't interfere in each other's affairs, and that meant they didn't interfere with each other's Chosen. Shakanti merely swept Renavir off to her own rooms.

Aka-Tete came for Jonat, Hap-Canae for me. They never left us girls alone together. I didn't care: Jonat made me uncomfortable, and I was anxious to show Hap-Canae what I'd learned. They never let us wander about the temple by ourselves, either; for all the rooms I'd seen, I hadn't explored a fraction of it.

Unless he decided to keep me for the night, he always took me back to my room.

The first time, he said, "Sweet child, forgive me, but I must lock you in."

"Why? I'm not going to run away! I'd never leave you!"

He put his arm around my shoulders. "There are those who might wish to harm you. Jealous of your position, of the power you might – you will *one day wield." He stroked my cheek. "I would be most distressed if anything were to happen to you."*

After that, of course, I took being locked in as a sign of his care for me.

Sixteen-year-old love. Worse for the brain than cloud, and twice as addictive.

CHAPTER
NINE

WHEN WE GOT back to the Lantern the Vessels were still there, and so was little Frithlit – standing on the steps, in fact, looking as though he were about to make a speech. Flower was standing behind him, arms folded, his brow-ridges arched.

"I know law," Frithlit said, his voice soft but quite clear enough to be heard across the street. "And law says," he drew a breath, and with his hands clasped in front of him like a small boy reciting a lesson, continued, "'the loitering, blocking, or acting in such a manner as to deliberately prevent or interfere with the lawful pursuance of trade' is illegal. This trade here, she is legal. You loiter, is not legal, because is deliberate interfering with trade. Is big fine, is big scandal, is maybe prison."

The Vessels looked at each other.

"You know what?" I said, "I think he's right." They take trade damn seriously here, it's Scalentine's lifeblood. That and diplomacy. "Prison, eh?" I said. "Now, that wouldn't look so good. Wouldn't be so pleasant, neither, especially since word about the girl in Ropemakers has got round. I know you say the Vessels had nothing to do with it, but you know, I'm not sure everyone believes that. There's probably people who would be very excited to see you, down in the gaol in King of Stone. Of course, you haven't heard me say that, so it's going to be a nice surprise for you."

"We fear no harm; we are armed in Purity," the young man with asses' ears addressed the air.

"Working so far, then," I said.

The Vessels moved together and began to converse in low voices. I couldn't hear the words, but the tone was clear enough. Whether it was the thought of all the nice new friends they'd make in prison, or the scandal, something was bothering them.

With an abruptness that had me putting hand to hilt, they swung about and strode off, their robes swishing behind them, Asses' Ears holding his mask on with one hand.

I suffered a mean impulse.

"No, Laney, don't!" I shouted.

He grabbed up his robes and ran, not bothering to look back and see that Laney had already left the window. As though he could have outrun a spell, anyway.

"Well, that went better than it could have," I said. "Thank you, Frithlit."

"That won't be the last of it," Flower said. "You wait. And now I have to find something else for supper."

I patted his arm as we went past. "Never mind, it looks like we've no clients to feed anyway."

"Oh yes, that makes me feel a lot better," he said, and grumbled his way back to the kitchen.

He still managed to come up with a substantial supper, which we ate around the big scrubbed kitchen table. "So, how did you meet?" I said to Frithlit. He was very pretty, in a pastel sort of way. To be brutally honest, what with his pearly-blue skin and her copper hair and freckles, he and Previous clashed appallingly, but she was so obviously taken with him that no-one was going to be unkind enough to point it out.

Frithlit flushed lavender and looked down at his plate. "Is embarrassing. She is rescue me. I am maiden in distraint."

"Distress, I *think* you mean," Laney said, gesturing one of her laced sleeves into the pickle. "Drat."

"Yes, thank you. Distress. I am in card game, and is going well, then all of a sudden peoples decide they don't like me to take what I have won, and is go for throw me in river." He shrugged. "Previous is come and kick their heads, and, well, I decide, is sort of woman for me, eh?" He took her hand.

Previous went scarlet (she blushes far too easy for someone who's a doorguard on a whorehouse, bless her heart).

"And what do you do?" Jivrais said.

"I buy things. I sell them. Sometimes I make a little money." He shrugged. "Sometimes not so much. And at cards I am not very lucky. But sometimes I am lucky in other ways, yes?"

He smiled at Previous, who gave him a fleeting half-smile and turned to me. "Here, the Vessels. I've been wondering. Do they actually *have* any women? I mean, they don't allow them in the Temples, but they must get new little Vessels from somewhere."

"So far as I know, the Vessels are an order, not a race," I said, "though all the ones I've met are human, I think. People just join up, somehow. I don't know what happens to the ones who have families before they join, whether they just get abandoned, or what. Maybe they're like those people we met in Lahter, remember? The ones who allow women into a sort of annexe, off the back of the temple, where they can hear the ceremony, but not be seen. You know, just in case any of the men sees them at the wrong moment and gets distracted."

Previous snorted. "Any god you can be distracted from that easily don't seem like much of a god to *me*."

"Oh, speaking of distraction – you been to Bannerman's lately?" I said.

"You joking? I daren't look in the window in case he charges me."

"He's got a Gillalune in."

Ireq's ears pricked up. "Gillalune?"

"He hasn't!" Previous said. "Really? Dammit, Babylon, I'm going to have to go look now."

"You need a new helmet anyway. Yours is so dented I'm surprised you can get it on without a crowbar."

"Not from Bannerman's I don't."

The talk stayed with weapons instead of gods, a much healthier subject.

IT WAS DARK by the time I got out again. Too early to look for Mokraine at the Break of Dawn; I'd try a couple of his other haunts first.

There's plenty of gambling in Scalentine; everything from a handful of brass on a street-bet to entire fortunes exchanged on a gentleman's handshake. For some reason most of it seems to concentrate near Nightwind portal, like a lot of the city's more disturbing aspects.

It's not that I've got anything against people enjoying themselves, not in my line of work. But... I remember Kyrl, and the knifeman in the alleyway. And it's not just the violence. I've seen too many people utterly focused on the turn of a card, their whole body clenched with need. People I knew had children at home eking out the stale loaf for another day and hoping this time Mummy or Daddy wasn't lying when they said they'd be coming home with their pockets spilling over with gold.

But that very need was the thing that drew Mokraine.

I passed The Singing Bird first, not exactly hoping to see Darask Fain, but I admit the thought occurred to me.

The Bird has that discreet, velvety look of serious money, rather like Fain himself. The woodwork is glossy-dark, and the windows are curtained with heavy silk. The bouncers aren't called bouncers, they're called 'courtesy guards.' They look like valets.

It's not the sort of place they'd willingly allow Mokraine in, though he has his means, and most people are, wisely, a little nervous about getting in his way. But the Bird is also the sort of place where most of the punters have plenty of coin to lose.

It doesn't matter so much to them, and that makes them less appealing to Mokraine.

I went on to The Golden Cup instead.

From the outside, it looks pretty good; not as gilded as The Singing Bird, but with richly draped windows and smart doormen.

When you get close, you realise that the silvery sheen on the curtains that makes them look like the best velvet is actually dust, and that the doormen's uniforms are worn over armour, and have patches of neat stitching here and there where at some point someone's put a blade through the cloth.

They checked me over and made me hand in my sword.

Well, I wasn't planning on needing a blade, and I can handle myself without one. It's just an extra edge, so to speak.

Inside, the Cup was brightly lit: hissing alchemical lamps with a harsh white glare. It smelled of drink and pipe smoke and sweat and it was very, very quiet. No laughter, little chat. Just the click of dice, the rattle of cups, the whisper of cards.

This place was *all* about the turn of a card, the fall of the dice. No-one was here for fun, they were here for chance. At least, the punters were. For the owner, chance hardly came into it.

Not that this was a scam joint. So far as I knew, The Golden Cup ran straight games, but you can count on one hand the number of customers who can play them and make a profit. Which is why it needed new doormen every now and then; some people get upset when they see their last coin rolling away.

In the ugly light that cast such hard shadows, the customers were pale, almost transparent, nothing moving but their eyes. They looked like hungry ghosts.

A man got up from one of the tables, swaying, and walked towards me. He had that hit-on-the-head look of someone who has just lost everything they had, and more.

Then I saw Mokraine. He rose from the corner where he had been sitting unnoticed, and put a friendly arm around the man's shoulder. His familiar, grey and lumpen, hopped after him, and leaned its head against the man's leg like a dog.

The man turned his head, slowly, as though in a dream, towards Mokraine. Mokraine bent down, until his hair brushed the man's cheek. I couldn't help but watch, though it made me shudder, as the expression on the man's face went from numb shock to vague surprise to an utter, white blank.

Mokraine straightened up, and closed his eyes with a look of satisfaction which I personally think belongs in the bedroom. His familiar made a snuffling grunt. The man he'd touched stood for a moment, then wandered away in the direction of the door, as though he were sleepwalking.

I moved closer, and waited for Mokraine to come out of his trance. Eventually he shuddered and opened his eyes. "Babylon, my darling," he said. I stepped back, and his hand fell away before it reached me. Some emotion I couldn't quite read crossed his face, quickly replaced by a smile.

"But you look so very anxious, Babylon. Would you not like to be calm, serene...?"

"No thank you." Dammit, it *still* upset me that Mokraine would try and feed off me, we used to be friends. Still are, in so far as that's possible with Mokraine these days. But that's addiction for you. Everything else becomes secondary. You have to feed the beast, and in the end the beast eats you.

"Ah well," he said, moving towards the door. "I think this place has done its duty for this evening."

I retrieved my sword from the doorman and followed him. "So," I said, falling in beside him but making sure I kept out of reach of both him and the familiar, "have you anything for me?"

"Anything? Why, plenty, my darling, if you want it." He smiled, dreamy and distant. "That fellow there, nothing to look at. Dull as a pudding, wouldn't you say? But oh, Babylon, what depths of hunger! And what castles of fantasy built over those gulfs on the most fragile of foundations! And he knows, beneath it all. He knows it is all glass and air, that the gulf awaits his every step. He longs for it, he loves the fall he never has the courage to take."

"Mokraine..."

"What do you think he will do, now, when he remembers? When he feels it all again? Perhaps I should follow him, and wait..."

"Mokraine! Ye gods, man, you get worse. That's vile."

He looked at me, and I could almost swear he looked hurt. "I don't *make* them feel that way, Babylon. I give them a respite from it."

"I've heard about your *respite* from those who've been granted it." Like being an abandoned house, was what I'd heard, all whispering emptiness. Then whatever you were feeling rushes back in, twice as bad for its brief absence.

I hauled on my temper. I didn't need to antagonise Mokraine. I tried to smile. "You know I get my relaxation elsewhere," I said. "I just wanted to find out if you'd heard anything about..." I had stepped backwards and my sword was halfway out of its sheath before I even realised, then I swore. It was that damn familiar, which had been sneaking up on me; I'd been on the verge of trying to cut its vile bloody eyed head off. "Mokraine, can you please keep this thing away from me?"

He clicked at it, looked up at me and shrugged. "It's not a pet, Babylon."

"The girl," I said, keeping an eye on the familiar. "The missing girl. Remember? You heard anything?"

"I have heard many things, Babylon, since last we met. Or, I have tasted them. I have tasted love, dark and sweet as poppy-syrup, and as full of imaginings. I have tasted the suspicions of a cheating merchant, all glitter and edges, like clipped coin..."

I should have caught him before he'd fed. He was quite capable of going on in this vein for some time.

"...and the paranoia of a demigod's slave; living in a sweat for fear of an unwary word. Fascinating."

"We've been plagued with demigods recently," I said.

"Those who rule by fear are always surrounded by the most intense of emotions, bound tight, pressed to a concentration. Most... stimulating."

"And the girl?"

"Girl?"

"The one I'm *looking* for, Mokraine. I showed you her picture, remember?"

He frowned. "There was something..."

Finally. I let him think, picking through the pieces of his own broken memory and those of whomever he'd fed on recently.

If he was interested in money, he'd be able to blackmail half the city – at least for the few days his stolen memories remain with him. The only reason no-one's tried to kill him yet is because they're scared of him. Nobody knows how many of his powers he still retains. Because he was one serious wizard, back in the day. That's how he was able to open the portal, and that's how he ended up like this.

Power. That's another dog that'll bite you in the arse if you don't keep it on a choke-chain.

"Ah, yes," he said. "There was a little child, running about in the crowd, who bumped into me. Oh, really, Babylon, don't give me such a look, I don't feed on children."

I bit my lip, hard, forcing myself not to ask why, since I found it hard to believe he had any morals left on that issue.

"She babbled about something or other, about a pretty lady with sunshine eyes who patted her on the head."

"Sunshine eyes?"

"That was what she said."

Yellow eyes aren't that common, even in Scalentine, except among the Ikinchli, of course. It could have been Enthemmerlee.

"Anything else?"

"That a man had come up and taken the pretty lady away. She thought it rude, that the man had taken her away while she was still talking. Children have such charmingly strict ideas of etiquette, don't you find?"

"That was all?"

"I fear so. Then her father came rushing up, and he was so relieved and angry at once, I had to take a little taste, just a little." His eyes went misty again. "The emotions of a parent. So powerful..."

"Mokraine." I tried to keep my voice level. "Did you get anything that would tell me where to find them? The father, at least?"

Mokraine tilted his head, his eyes on the distance. "A small white temple, the smell of bread. The river, portal light. Masts."

The city has temples like a miser has coin, but the light, and the masts on the river, suggested the docks. Of course, there were at least three dozen bakeries in the area too.

"And do you remember what he looked like? What race were they, do you know?"

Mokraine frowned. He doesn't remember the outsides of people so well. "The race I don't know. Thin. Stretched-looking. His hands were scarred. He was... dusty."

"All right. I'll get down there." I made a face. The day was getting on, I'd have to go tomorrow. Even with Fain's money, I couldn't afford to be away from the Lantern too long.

"Babylon."

"What?"

"I didn't..."

"Didn't what?"

He was looking at me with an expression I hardly recognised. Almost sorrowful. "He was still able to look after the child, Babylon. I didn't take that much."

It hadn't even occurred to me. I had no idea what to say.

DESPITE THE EXHAUSTING day and a hot bath, I couldn't sleep. I suspected Flower was right, and we hadn't seen the last of the damned Vessels. We'd lost a chunk of trade that day; if they came up with many more tricks like that, Fain's money wouldn't last a moon. And I hadn't found out one useful thing about the missing girl yet. Or been to the tax office.

I tried to find a more comfortable position, but my bed's

already extremely comfortable. It's designed to be: firm enough for energetic company, soft enough for sleep.

I finally dozed off to dream uneasily of going to butcher's shops and grocers all over Scalentine, looking for something I had to buy for a special dish Flower was making, only to discover that when I got inside, every shop was a Temple of the Vessels, and I could get what I wanted only if I agreed to be blinded.

TIRESANA

AVATAR HAP-CANAE. *Avatar of the Sun God. Golden Hap-Canae, with his jaguar eyes, his self-confidence, and his desire.*

It's not unusual to have at least one relationship you look back on with a kind of bemused horror. The sort where, once the madness has burned itself out, you wonder who drugged you. You think... by the All that Is, what was I thinking? Where was my brain?

Of course, my brain was where one's brain usually is in this situation, tucked between my legs more firmly than a scared dog's tail. And Hap-Canae was a sun-god. So his Avatar could dazzle like nothing else, fill you with his glitter and glow. He loved it, loved the way people basked in his presence. He could ripen fruit and dry floods – and rivers, if he felt like it. Though he didn't do it. The Avatars didn't impinge on each others' territory if they could help it. His aspect cycled through the day, and he was always weakest at night and strongest at noon (it was a long time before I realised why he always wanted to bed me in daylight), but he pretty much always looked like himself. I saw the most of him, of course; I mainly saw the others when they supervised our lessons.

Of the Avatar of Babaska, who we were to serve, we saw nothing. She was dealing with the business of her own great temple at Don-panat. Or she was out fighting a war. Or she had taken a new lover, and he was occupying all her time. The rumours flew everywhere, but we never saw her. All the other Avatars spent some or all of their time at the Temple of All the Gods, but not, it seemed, the Avatar of Babaska, yet it seemed to me quite reasonable. She had things to do, exciting, important things. Why would she want to come and watch a lot of tedious ceremonies, and a bunch of girls sitting about having lessons? Already, I felt she was slightly superior to the other Avatars. Apart from Hap-Canae, of course.

He fetched me from my lessons one afternoon when the wind was blowing off the desert with a constant itchy whine, making everyone uneasy. He had great skeins of amber beads roped around his neck and a scroll tucked up the sleeve of his gold and tawny robe.

"What is that?" I said, and he glanced over to where Meisheté was standing, and drew me away before he answered.

"Only a treatise on the worship of Babaska. I thought it might help you with your lessons, but it is very dull."

After he had finished with me, feeling restless, and – although I didn't want to admit it – unsatisfied, I slipped out of bed while he was sleeping and looked at the scroll.

It was very dull indeed; a discussion of some minor ceremony I had never heard of, full of ramblings about which incense was most appropriate, with long digressions on how it was obtained; what cloth should be used for the officiant's garments, and whether one dye should be used as opposed to another, whose colour was less good but which was produced in some village Babaska was supposed to favour.

Honestly, *I thought,* What sort of goddess would even *care* about such things? *I kept reading only because I had nothing else to do, and in the vague hope that Hap-Canae would wake and see me studying and be proud of me.*

There was stuff about the proper decoration of the altar, and about how the officiant should stand, and speak.

There was a little phrase at the bottom which I noticed because the writing, while nearly the same, was not quite. The letters wavered a little, and the ink was slightly less faded. "As it is said at the point where the incense is lit: 'And with her sword she cuts the way to power; true godhead comes only with blade and flower.'" The scroll was damaged here. I could see faint scratches near the words.

I came to with a start. Hap-Canae had been right about it being dull; I couldn't even read it without falling asleep.

I folded up the scroll again and looked out of the window at the desert until Hap-Canae woke.

"You tried the scroll, I see. How did you get on?"

Since he had, as I thought, brought it especially for me, I was ashamed to admit I hadn't even finished it. "Well, there was a lot to read," I said.

"Come, you were bored," he said. "Were you not? So was I. Shall we rid the world of a little piece of boredom?"

"How?" I said.

Hap-Canae smiled, and touched the scroll with his finger. There was the toasty smell of burning paper, a brief flare of flame, and the thing was gone – ash.

"Oh!" I said. I felt an odd sense of shock; the scroll might be dull, but it was very old, it had survived so many years, the priest who had written it was long since dust, and yet, now, it was gone in an instant.

"What did you do?" I said.

"The Touch of the Sun. A gift from the God Hap-Canae to his Avatar. Don't look so startled, child. You must get used to these things."

CHAPTER
TEN
Day 3
4 days to Twomoon

I WOKE WITH that ugly hung-over feeling a bad dream smears in its wake, and decided another bath would be a good idea. I was hauled out of it by Essie calling outside the door that the new butcher's boy was here, wanting payment, and no-one knew where I'd hidden the petty cash.

I hadn't hidden it, I'd just shoved it behind a lamp in the parlour.

Frithlit emerged onto the landing as I went downstairs wearing towels. I waved him a casual good morning, wondering whether the normally early-rising Previous was still sleeping the sleep of the happily rogered. He ducked his head shyly and smiled, his pearly-blue skin gleaming in the morning light. I had no idea what plane he came from. In fact, I realised as I went downstairs, for all the chatter he'd done at the table, I hadn't learnt much about him. Still, so long as he made Previous happy.

The butcher's boy was an appealing young thing; same species as the butcher, judging by his coat of thick chestnut fur and round brown eyes. He was looking around with a vast, yellow-toothed grin I didn't think could get any wider, though when a few of the crew wandered in, yawning and half-dressed, in search of breakfast, he somehow managed it.

When I paid him and signed the bill he looked speculatively at the money in his hand and said, "How much is it for, you know, an hour?"

"More than you've got, even of your boss's money."

His grin drooped, then perked again. "Okay, I'll get rich, then I'll come back."

I like a bit of entrepreneurial spirit. "You do that," I said, clapping him on the shoulder. "Now, off with you."

On his way out he gave me an even cheekier grin. "Hey, how much for you?"

"Get rich. Then we'll talk."

He went off laughing.

I went back up to finish my bath, but it was nearly cold and the damn soap seemed to have disappeared somewhere. I gave up, got dressed and put on my rings. My seal-ring, the only thing I had from the past, looked dull. I rubbed the thumb of my left hand over it and it came away soapy. What had the ring done, *eaten* the soap? It was a funny thing, that ring; I often wondered why I kept it. But somehow I always had.

Never mind, it was about to get greased up anyway, because I needed some serious breakfast.

Flower, with a big orange stain down his apron, was still adding food to the table, though there was barely room. "Ah, look at this. I'd better put it in the laundry." He whipped off his apron and tucked it under his arm, his massive green torso gleaming.

"We expecting an army?" I said. "Or are you just planning to keep open house for the Vessels if they come back?"

"Everyone's hungry before Twomoon," he said.

I couldn't really blame him for being extravagant. I'd spent enough time in my life hungry, I wanted my crew well fed, and the punters liked it. It helped add to our reputation as a place where you came away feeling fulfilled and happy rather than soiled and robbed – unless that was how you wanted to feel, of course.

Ireq came in, stretched, and filled his plate. "Morning."

"Morning."

He took a seat and tucked in, having used up about half the words he allowed himself each day.

"So," Laney said, whisking into the room in her pink silk dressing gown, her green eyes slitted as she yawned, and reaching for coffee, "Previous not up, then?"

"No, but her boyfriend is. Saw him on the landing."

"He's sweet," Laney said.

"Came in useful yesterday, I'll say that for him."

"Didn't he? Such a poppet."

So long as he stayed out of the way of the clients I didn't have a problem with him hanging about. If he hurt Previous, though, I'd bounce him down the steps on his head. Or give him to the Twins.

We've a saying – talk of a demon and hear him fart. Frithlit appeared in the doorway.

"Morning," Flower said. "Help yourself."

"Thank you. Is very much food! I eat all this I am go pop, yes?"

"I expect you need your strength," Jivrais said, reaching for another pastry. "Previous up yet?" Laney nudged him hard in the ribs and Jivrais dropped his pastry. "Ow! What?"

Frithlit went an even prettier shade of lavender, and Previous walked in, noticed everyone grinning, and went bright red.

They really did clash.

I tried not to laugh, and distracted myself by digging in my trouser pocket for something that was pressing uncomfortably into my leg.

It was Enthemmerlee's portrait. Any desire to laugh drained away. Two days, already, and who knew what was happening to the poor child? I finished my breakfast quickly, and headed for the docks.

TIRESANA

ALONGSIDE THE LESSONS *in the sensual arts, we had martial training. My friend Radan had been good, but the trainers they brought in for us were the best that could be found, although they never lasted very long.*

"Why do they change them so often?" I said.

Hap-Canae frowned down at me. "Understand that everything we do is necessary," he said. "You are doing very well, I am pleased with you. Your training is working. Do you have some complaint?" He let a little anger show in his voice, then, or at least the potential for it.

"Oh no," I said. "I only wondered... is it so we won't get stale? Miss out on something? After all, if you learn only from one person, you'll only know what they know. If you learn from lots..."

"Clever child," he said, stroking me. "That's it exactly."

He hardly had to make an effort at fooling me, by then I was doing almost all of it for myself.

Livaia showed us how our bodies worked, and how to make the most of them. She showed us how to be graceful in the event of everything from a failed erection to an unexpected fart. How to stimulate the unenthusiastic and hold back the over-eager. How to make someone smile, and how to make them shudder or scream.

One morning, Shakanti was supervising, and Meisheté had come in to check on us too.

Livaia said, "I have been told you are to be priestesses, but one may find oneself, even as a priestess, confronted with someone who desires to hurt you. This is the world we live in."

"Oh, they have no need..." Shakanti said, and I saw Meisheté lean over, eyes gleaming in their shadowed surrounds, and whisper fiercely in her ear. Shakanti shrugged and glared and flounced away. Meisheté leaned back, her hands over her faux-pregnant belly, and waved an impatient hand at Livaia to continue.

After a moment's hesitation, she did so. "If someone is threatening towards you, it is essential to remain calm. Move slowly. Look them in the eye. Speak in a steady voice, say that they seem troubled, and ask them what it is that troubles them. Speak of yourself, tell them of some little personal detail or preference, it makes it more difficult for them to see you as merely a body, or a woman, or whatever it is they want to hurt. And call for wine or food, remaining always calm and courteous. Many are less likely to become violent in the presence of others. If you can, make sure you can get out of the room ahead of them."

"And if none of that works, we can always headbutt them, or get them in a grapple and stab them," I said. We had been doing grapples and throws in fight training, and I was rather overenthusiastic about it all.

Livaia laughed. "Looking at you girls, I'm sure you could. However," she turned serious again. "Sometimes, you may encounter those who are mad. I have seen it, and they are very strong, and seem to feel no pain. In that case, you must just get away."

"How do you know when someone's mad?" Velance asked.

I heard someone whisper, "Just look at Shakanti." Probably Jonat.

"Sadly, it is not always easy to tell. But once you realise, the thing is to get away, whatever you need to do to achieve it."

After the class I saw Meisheté in the corridor, speaking to Rohikanta. I hesitated, because of the Messehwhy. Their great coarse-scaled bodies almost filled the corridor. One turned its head as I came out and yawned, a cave of teeth and carrion stink.

"...endanger us all," Meisheté was saying, the skin around her eyes so velvet-dark she looked like some exotic beast, her belly drum-tight. "They know she never lies."

Rohikanta stroked his watery beard, sending the mist that rose from it into wavering curls. "And what do you suggest?"

"I think..." Two more girls came out behind me, giggling. Meisheté realised we were there and said, "I will discuss this with you later." She beckoned Velance to follow her and walked off in her swaying, gravid way.

She was always in her pregnant aspect when she supervised the classes, as though to remind us what all this rampancy was for, though, of course, Livaia taught us about preventing that, too.

I didn't know, then, that the Avatars paid a price for their power. Meisheté couldn't have become pregnant, even if she had wanted to. I'm not sure she even wanted a real baby: power over other women and their babies seemed to be enough for her. She didn't once, that I saw, make an affectionate or motherly gesture even towards Velance, her Chosen.

But if she'd wanted a baby, there were more than enough that could have done with mothering. They hung in bags on doors all over town.

CHAPTER
ELEVEN

I LIKE THE docks. Loud, interesting, stuff coming in from everywhere in the Empire. Scalentine's main river, the Druthain, runs there, through Portal Bealach.

Portal light bathes the docks, gilded and thunderous. The portal is an arc of flame; a huge shimmering hole in the stuff of the world. Bealach hasn't closed in living memory, but it's still a portal. It could. What would happen then... ask Mokraine, not me. We'd lose a lot of trade, that much I know.

The ships come up the river, clothed in the light, their masts shimmering with fire; the sailors clinging to the rigging glow like seraphim. Light sings gold in the planks and turns the sails to lamps of alabaster. Every ripple and crest of the water is flame lined with lapis lazuli. The low song of the portal, like the purr of a cat or endlessly ripping silk, dampens all other sound, so the ships float silent as ghosts.

Then they steer into the dock, empty casks and broken boxes knocking and bumping against the hull, through cabbage leaves and rotting fruit and drowned rats, and the glowing sailors leap down and swear and yell at friends and wave to the doxies waiting on the shore, and the sweating stevedores start unloading. Great crates of fruit and grain; livestock bawling and shrieking and shitting, wool and spices, silk and copper.

There was a sleek Imperial yacht with scarlet sails, full of chattering... creatures. The current fashion in the Imperial Court was for robes of stiff, heavily embroidered linen with collars that came halfway up the face, and strange starched headdresses that covered most of the rest. Hard to tell what *species* someone was, never mind gender. Their servants were a mix of humans and other species, furred, feathered and scaled, all chosen for their looks, it seemed. No Fey, of course; just try making a servant out of one of them.

There was no-one I knew. Might be a few of the captains I'd recognise, but the dockworkers and the freelancers change fast. Docks are the same everywhere. It's easy to disappear, and easy to make someone else do so. Rats aren't the only things that sometimes turn up dead and floating.

Still, there was plenty to appeal to the eye, what with the Empire folks having good taste in servants, and a lot of husky stevedores around. I had to remind myself I wasn't here to admire the scenery, but if I had to make enquiries... well, there was a muscular dockworker with luscious skin like rich-grained wood and big gold earrings, stripped to the waist, who was yelling a mix of pidgin and pretty inventive obscenity at three men trying to wrestle a swinging crate full of some bright yellow and very lively animals to the dock. I waited until he had time to draw breath. "Heya?"

"Heya."

"You herefrom?"

He nodded. "Not sell hereside. You wantshee, you bid himbig jalla." He jerked his thumb towards the great echoing sheds where they held the livestock auctions. Jalla is Scalentine pidgin – it means pretty much any structure from a temple to a privy. "Sav?"

"Not here for buy." I looked at the crate. The yellow creatures had long noses, eyes like blue cloth buttons and grey, tubular tongues – I found out the last when one spat at me, a thick gluey divot of phlegm I only just avoided. Whatever they were, they didn't look wholesome. "Look-my bread fella, by-by godjalla white is."

"Plenty-plenty godjalla." He shrugged. "Plenty-plenty bread fella." He turned away and started yelling at the men some more.

Oh well. I kept asking, and got a variety of responses, some more polite, and one or two less so. I kept my hand near my sword. One grey-skinned pair whose oddly jerky movements seemed to mirror each other directed me down an alley of fish-stalls, where the shifting light coruscated on the flat, chilly eyes of the merchandise and the glittering scales that coated every surface. It reeked, and the footing was slimy with spilled fish guts. I got a bad feeling halfway down, and turned back, to see that the greyskins had followed me. They got very interested in a tank full of some sort of crabs scrambling and clicking over each other. I walked back towards them, slowly, hand on sword, and they decided to do their fish-shopping another day.

After that I was directed to three churches that had no bakery in sight, three bakeries with no churches in sight, one chandler's next to a very dodgy looking bar (problem in translation, there), all the while fending off threats, promises, and offers. One or two of the offers might have been lucrative, but I had no regrets turning them down. The docks are an even worse area than King of Stone for that kind of business, and just because I can take care of myself doesn't mean I like unpleasantness.

It started to feel like a long time since breakfast, and I was no nearer any answers. I wondered if Mokraine had been playing some odd little game of his own, or whether he was just plain mistaken.

I was thinking of calling it a day when there was a chorus of squeaky yapping sounds. A plump, freckled little critter appeared around the corner. He had a big plumy tail, a little like a squirrel except he (I thought *he*) came about as high as my waist. He was leading six assorted small furry creatures on leashes, though whether they were pets or offspring I couldn't tell.

"Are you lost?" he asked. "Now, now, stop that! *Down!* Lost you? Wantshee help? Oh, dear, I am sorry..."

I disentangled myself from two leashes, at the cost of some enthusiastic licking and paw-marked boots, and asked if he knew of a bakery next to a white temple.

"Oh, yes, just round the corner..." he gestured, and ended up with a lead around his neck, which then had to be unwrapped. "It's not far... *stop that!* Go on down this street, turn left at the inn called the Fighting Gloriana, get *down!* Then right, where they're building the new warehouse. And it should be right in front of you... *waaah!*" He was whisked away as the little beasties spotted something worthy of chasing down the other end of the street, trailing him behind them like a small furry cart in need of brakes.

I followed his directions and passed the place where the new warehouse was going up: noisier than the docks, what with the hammering, the yelling and the grind and slam of stone being dropped into place. I peeked in – lots of pretty muscle, all of it streaked with grey. Then I caught the scent of fresh bread, mixed with some heavy, brain-numbing incense, and there it was. A small dome-shaped building, with round windows and heat baking out of the open door, and next to it a little temple, standing out white as a spring morning against the scramble of houses around it.

Some of them had been dwellings of the rich, once; you could see it. They were still sturdy, though a lot of the gutters were sagging away, and most of the window-panes were cracked or gone.

The little plaster faces were here too – they're everywhere. I saw Fey and Ikinchli, a few who looked a bit like Flower, broad-nosed and tusked. Not many portraits of humans, except one of a little girl who'd been caught just about to make some delightful mischief. She was a treat, even with her ringlets missing their ends and a chipped nose. But the faces were cracked and grey; stains from leaking gutters ran down their cheeks like bloody tears. I saw another little fish; its grin seemed out of place here.

The temple was newish, built in an odd style that made it look like white soap bubbles stuck together.

I walked up and down the street, looking for some clue as to which house might hold the fellow Mokraine had touched. I *could* ask at the temple.

I'd try the bakery first.

I ducked in through the door and the heat wrapped around me like an overenthusiastic lover. The baker was Barraklé; I swear, Glinchen's the only Barraklé I know who isn't involved in feeding people. On the other hand, I guess appetite is, well, appetite.

Ze didn't look in the mood for conversation; there were three ovens on the go and one helper, who was also Barraklé. I don't know much about baking (just ask Flower) but I was pretty sure the tray of flat, dark brown, smoking things over which they were arguing weren't supposed to be either flat or smoking.

I was going to back out and come back when there wasn't a domestic crisis going on, but the bigger of the two whirled around and saw me.

"You come for the order for the *Sweet Marie?* Is regret, is have to wait, my most stupid offspring is ruin order, I am much sorrowful. Please to sit, I bring tea, you wait, yes?"

"I'm not..."

"Please to tell Captain Juggan I am never to be unreliable, is only stupidness of this one" – ze gave the unfortunate offspring a cuff around the nearest ear, unnecessarily hard, I thought – "who is burn all."

"I'm not here..."

"No, no, please, you sit, hey, stupidness, unwanted child of my most unfortunate loin, go, out back, make tea immediate and do not burn it."

"Hey!" I can yell when I have to. If you can make yourself heard on a battlefield you can pretty well flatten walls. They both jolted, curling in on themselves like snails sprayed with salt water.

"I'm not *here* about that. I'm looking for someone." I was getting tired of that phrase. Looking for people isn't my *job*. "I'm not sure of his race. Lives around here. Kind of long and thin, dusty," Mokraine's description made the poor creature sound more like a ghost than anything else.

They looked at each other, then back at me. The baker shrugged. "Lots races round here."

Their offspring, eager to please, poor thing, pointed to the pans waiting to go in the oven. "Dusty! Like flour? Maybe baker?"

"No other baker near here," the baker said. "Me, only."

Dusty... I'd just seen a lot of dusty people. "It's all right, I think I know. Thanks." I smiled at the youngster. "You've been helpful." Ze smiled back.

"Glad this one can be helpful sometimes," hir parent said. "Most unusual."

I saw the smile disappear under a sullen look. *Gah*. Parents and their offspring. That's one problem I don't have.

I headed for the building site, and enjoyed the scenery until the head mason had a chance to talk to me. She was a big, strapping lass, with an eye patch and a cotton hood over her hair, and coated with stone dust head to foot.

"You looking for work?" she said.

"No, looking for one of your workers, I think."

She tilted her head, giving me the once-over with the remaining eye – a deep brown, very pretty. Then she bawled over her shoulder, "Boy! Mint tea quick-quick!"

"Please, there's no need," I said. Everyone wanted to give me tea today. What I needed right now was some answers, followed by a massage and a big, very alcoholic, drink.

A slab of stone slipped from its rope cradle and slammed onto its fellow, provoking another billow of dust, which came straight at me. I coughed, and brushed uselessly at myself. Make that a bath, a massage and a slightly bigger drink.

"So. Who are you and why are you looking for one of my crew?"

"I'd just like to talk to him." I told her who I was, and she nodded.

"I've heard of the Lantern." She looked me up and down. "Heard of you, too. My man cause trouble?"

"Not for me. He may know something about someone I'm looking for, that's all."

"You know his name?"

"Sorry. Thin, I was told, stretched looking. With bushy brows and scarred hands. Might have seemed a tad mazed, day or so back. That's all I know. Oh, and he has a child. Little girl."

She looked down for a moment, frowning, then snapped her fingers. "Badhan."

A young Ikinchli lad showed up with tea. I took mine, grateful for the chance to rinse some of the dust out of my mouth, and she took her time sugaring hers and stirring it before she said, "Why do you want to know?"

"Hoped I might have a word with him."

"About?"

I realised she was protecting him; he'd only worked for her a while, or she wouldn't have taken that long to remember his name, but he was still her crew.

"I don't want to get him in trouble," I said. "He may know something that will lead me to a girl who might be in *serious* trouble. I plan to haul her out of it, if I ever find her."

She looked at me – the gaze of that single eye surprisingly penetrating. "Don't *make* trouble. I got a business to run, and he's skilled. You lose me a good worker, you'll hear about it. Understood?"

"Absolutely."

"All right. He should be heading in for his shift soon, you'll catch him on the way, or maybe still at home. Lodgings're round back of the temple. Brick archway, one flight up, door on the left."

TIRESANA

WE NEVER LEFT *the Inner Temple. We never entered the courtyard, not for the ceremonies of the other gods, not even for Babaska's major ceremonies; they were performed, in miniature, within the rooms, as part of our training.*

"Why can't we go to the main temple?" I asked Hap-Canae. I wanted to get a closer look at it, to try and get a sense of Babaska through her statue, if nothing else. And though the rooms of the Inner Temple were generously proportioned, I was beginning to feel a little itchy at being inside for so long. Fight training in the inner courtyard wasn't enough.

"My dear child, the main temple?" He gestured, suggesting crowds: the scent of myrrh drifted from his sleeves. "Babaska's most important shrine? The Hierarchs of the priesthood, the most powerful in the land, attend the ceremonies there. And you have barely begun your training. Imagine if something went wrong, in front of them all!"

I blushed and mumbled, immediately seeing myself tearing my gown, spilling the wine on some terrifyingly important priestess, falling down the steps.

He stroked my hair. "You will do very well, I'm sure. One day I will see you lead the ceremonies, and the worshippers will all be in awe of you. But not yet."

A few days later another girl was gone. Seili, with her fire-glow hair and her annoying laugh, Chosen by the Avatar Lohiria, she of the West Wind. That night there was a gale at sea, and a trade ship lost with all its hands, its cargo of corn sinking to rot on the sea floor. But none of us made the connection, or if we did, nothing was said.

Stupid? Yes, we were. Stupid and self-involved, wrapped in luxury for the first time in our lives, and so terribly young.

One of our martial trainers was a battered ex-soldier called Farren with one missing eye and two missing fingers, who knew every nasty fighter's trick, throw, tear, grapple and gouge you ever heard of and then some, having learned how to do them all a second time, with no depth-perception and half a hand. He had me in a tight hold, flat on the marble, my left arm halfway to the back of my neck and his knee on my spine. "See what I did there?" he said, and then, bending close, he whispered, "Message for you. Can you keep your mouth shut?"

I nodded, not really understanding.

"Sometimes you find you've thrown a three instead of a six."

"Kyrl! You've seen her?"

He wrenched my arm further up. "Quiet!"

Always someone watching. That morning it was Shakanti, her face glowing like a sick moon in the shadows.

I hated it when she was there. I felt her willing me to fail, hungry for any or all of us to suffer injury, humiliation, despair. Something had twisted Shakanti badly; who knew what, or how long ago? Twisted her enough that she remained determinedly celibate, while she loved to torture others with her beauty; something that becoming an Avatar had only distilled and concentrated to a lethal elixir.

Farren got off me to go shout at one of the others. Then he came back, grabbed me in another grapple, cold marble pressing against my face, and whispered again, "She said she's got a cousin in Babaska's temple at Pryat. If you find you've thrown a three, get a message there, and they'll get you out. That's all."

"Why would I want..."

"Open your eyes, girl." He raised his head and glared around.

"You, girl in the blue. See where my hands are. Now look where yours are. Doesn't matter if your opponent's underneath you if he can still throw you off and break your wrists while he's at it." Velance, the one he was shouting at, rolled her eyes and shifted her grip.

"What do you mean?" I muttered.

"This place reeks of bad luck. You see your blade lying at your feet with two of your own fingers still in the grip, you learn to be watchful, or you die," he said, his mouth so close to my ear his breath stirred my hair.

"Tell her I'm fine, everything is wonderful. And when I'm a priestess, if she needs anything... if any of them do... send to me."

"I hope you're right, girl. Very well, I'll tell her."

He pushed me hard for the rest of the session. The next day he was gone, and we had no fight trainer for three days.

Maybe Shakanti got suspicious and had him disappeared. Or, maybe, he'd scented the wind in time. I hope so, still.

I was in love, I lived in silk, I enjoyed my lessons. And if I felt a growing fear creeping in towards my heart, I pushed it aside. Hap-Canae wouldn't let anything happen to me, I told myself.

CHAPTER
TWELVE

THERE SEEMED TO be no-one about at the lodgings except an orange cat dozing in a patch of sunlight on one of the steps, and a small boy concentrating on some game that involved moving pebbles about and muttering. I stepped around both of them, and went through the archway up to the room. I knocked on the door, and someone called, "Who is?"

"I'm looking for Badhan?"

Mutterings from behind the door. I kept my hands ready, in case. Finally a long, thin, dusty-skinned sort opened the door; he had a slightly dished face, and no nose to speak of, just a sort of a bump, I couldn't see any nostrils. The dust wasn't from building, as he hadn't been to his work yet. It was just the look of him. He was almost my height, but I doubt he weighed half as much; I knew what Mokraine meant about him looking stretched. He stood in the doorway, keeping between me and whoever was in there. "What wantshee?"

I glanced down at the hand clutching the door. It was knuckly and seemed too big for the skinny arm it hung on. Narrow pink scars writhed across the backs of his fingers.

"Can I speak with you? I'm looking for someone."

He looked at my sword. "Trouble no want."

I dropped into pidgin, offered to leave off the sword if it would make him happier. Eventually he edged back into the room, with a jerk of his head.

Someone stood near the window – also long, and thin, one arm protectively across the child peering around her legs. I smiled at the girl. One day she would presumably have the same dusty-looking skin as her parents, but now she just looked pale, as though she'd never had quite enough sun.

It wasn't over-generous, for three people. Floorboards, a window, walls, a roof. A bed. Not much. But at least it smelled clean. Compared to some lodgings I'd seen, it was luxurious.

A small stray feather, perhaps from their bedding, drifted across the floor. The orange cat, which had wandered in from outside, pounced on it. The child squeaked with delight and attempted to lift it off the floor.

I started forward, worried the animal might object to being manhandled. The mother did likewise.

The cat allowed the child to pick up its abdomen while its feet remained on the floor, until it looked like a furry bridge. The child giggled, her mother whisked her into her arms, and I whisked the cat into mine, in case its patience ran out.

With the cat kneading my shoulder and purring loudly in my ear, I tried a smile on the mother and got a tentative grimace in return. The child stretched out her arms towards the cat; the mother sighed and moved closer, took the child's hand and showed her how to stroke the cat's head (she had to reach up a way to do it), saying, *patha, patha,* which I assumed meant *gently*.

There are worse icebreakers than a cat. Especially one that, as in this case, had bright yellow eyes. "Cat," I said.

"Yes, tat."

"Close enough."

"*Cat,*" said the mother, obviously not thinking close enough was good enough.

"You have cats where you come from?"

The child shook her head.

I pointed to the cat's eyes, though they were currently half-closed with the pleasure of being the centre of attention. "Yellow eyes," I said. "Like the sun."

"Like the sun."

"Right. You saw a lady, with eyes like that, didn't you?"

The girl shrugged, more interested in putting her hand on the cat's throat and feeling it purr. "Honey? Listen."

But she was getting bored, and twisted away in her mother's arms. "Down!"

I looked at her mother and said, "Please. Sun-eyes girl in bad-bad is. Needs help my. You sav?"

The parents looked at each other. "Girlchild is?" the woman said.

"Child-woman is." The cat wriggled and I put it down.

The woman knelt and took her daughter by the shoulders, made quick soft-voiced conversation. The child sighed, with every sign of someone kept from massively important business by trivia and said, in rapid pidgin, "Sun eyes lady saw my, sun eyes lady talk my." She patted herself on the head. "Touch my. Nice is. Sun eyes lady smell pretty-pretty. Man come talk, take her away."

"Man look how?"

She shrugged again, watching the cat longingly as it chased the feather into a corner and beat it into submission. Her mother said something to her.

"Man high, but not so high like you."

"Man sun eyes have?"

"Not."

"Man look same-same sun-eyes lady?"

"Not same-same-same. Some same."

Possibly they were the same race, but the child could have meant anything. Hair, even clothing.

Still, maybe I could find out something.

"Sun eyes lady fear have? She see man go..." I made an exaggerated frightened face.

The child shook her head. "Not fear lady have. Have thinking." She scowled ferociously. "Then she go with."

Whatever Enthemmerlee had heard had made her thoughtful; neither angry, nor scared – yet she'd gone with the person who'd said it, apparently willingly.

What had someone said, to persuade her away from her parents and any guards? I imagined her taken by the hand, led away from her life all unknowing, and a shudder went through me so bone deep I had to cough to hide it.

"I play cat now?" the child said.

I reckoned that was probably it, and that I'd been lucky to catch her before the memory faded. "Thank you," I said. She was already picking up a string to tempt the cat with.

Badhan was obviously eager to see me leave, but the woman put a hand on my arm as I was going out. She glanced over her shoulder at the girl, who was lying on the floor, the cat settling against her side, and said, "You find her, yes?"

"I'll do my best," I said.

She nodded, and closed the door.

The small boy who had been playing outside was gone. The street seemed suddenly too empty, and the wind too cold.

I had only passed a couple of houses when light falling across a wall caught my eye, and I crouched down.

A child's drawings, scratched with a sharp stick or a knife when their parents' attention was elsewhere. A sun. A house. A blobbed something or other, coloured in with mud... I hoped it was mud.

A man surrounded by little bent, servile figures; a man with either several horns, or rays, coming out of his head. Like the sun.

Next to him, a stick-thin figure, with long hair and what seemed to be a skull for a face.

I straightened up, slowly.

It didn't mean anything. Plenty of strange creatures pass through Scalentine, and a child's drawing makes them look stranger yet. I had Hap-Canae on my mind, that was all. It didn't mean he was here.

But forget a bath, a massage and a big drink; right now I felt like just filling a tub with wine and a couple of close friends and getting straight in.

HARD AS I tried, I couldn't get the drawing out of my head. Had some child seen Hap-Canae and Shakanti here, on Scalentine? After more than twenty years, were they looking for me? Why?

Worrying makes me hungry, and I wanted the distraction of noise and people. I headed back towards the centre of town and Gallock's. It's not fancy, mainly a place for the performers from local theatres and gambling houses to rest their feet and complain; if any of the Avatars *were* on Scalentine, it wasn't the sort of place they'd go.

I pushed open the door to a roar of conversation in a number of languages and the smell of meat pies and perfume and sweat and coffee. Two dancers of indeterminate sex, with headdresses (or hair, I wasn't sure) of multicoloured feathers and hands with at least twelve long fragile fingers apiece, were at the counter getting coffee and hot sausages. I could tell they were dancers because they wore mainly skin and sequins, their glittering shoes so high in the heel that they stood almost as tall as me. "Come on, Gallock, move yer arse, darlin'. I gotta be back on stage in a lizard's blink."

"Here is, sweetie pie. How is new job, The Lotus? You like?" Gallock is another Barraklé, like Glinchen, though half the weight and with a voice like a troll chewing gravel, all four arms flicking back and forth between plates and pans at eye-blurring speed.

"Yeah, s'all right, but he's a bugger if you're late. Ta, love." The dancers scurried out, clutching their food. How anyone even moves in shoes like that, never mind dances, is beyond me.

"Hey, Babylon," Gallock said, freeing one hand to wave. "Shan't be a... Borlak! *Sh'tin tazik dimankat laiagrai!*" Gallock shoved a loaded tray at a wispy young man, presumably

Borlak, who took it with an exasperated eye-roll and swayed off between the tables. Out of work actor, I'd have bet my best boots on it.

Gallock rested hir lower set of bosoms on the counter and grinned at me. "Babylon, not seen you long-long. How going the world, hey?"

"It keeps on rolling, Gallock. You?"

Gallock patted hir rounded stomach. "Breeding."

Looking at hir beaming face, I gathered this was good news. "Congratulations."

"Is good, no? Soon I get some more help round here."

"Planning to shove the little 'un to the sink as soon as it can... slither?"

"Of course. Start work early my family."

"Hey, listen, I don't suppose you've seen this girl, have you?" I showed hir the picture.

Gallock shook hir head. "Not so's I remember. Sorry."

"Worth a try." I put it away. I wasn't sure whether or not to feel less worried about the girl. It sounded as though she had gone willingly, but who knew what had been said to her, what promises made, what lies?

Gallock looked up as the door opened and hir face changed.

I spun around so fast I knocked a plate off the counter; I was in a twitchy frame of mind.

There were three men in the doorway – all human, all young. "You," Gallock said. Hir voice cut through the chatter like a hatchet, not because it was especially loud, but because of the tone. It was glacial. "You out. Now."

"What?" said one of the men, making a wide-eyed, innocent face. They kept coming towards the counter. There was a lot of silence around them.

"You know what. Get."

"We don't want to order," said another. "We just wanted a chat."

"Don't chat with the likes of you," Gallock said.

"Who are these people?" I said, still raw with relief and annoyed at my own jumpiness.

"*People* is right," said one of them. "The ones who *belong* here."

Great. I can always do with meeting idiots on an empty stomach, puts the edge on the day.

A lot of the customers were staring at their plates, or suddenly very interested in the contents of their pouches. I didn't blame them, really. They weren't professional fighters. Why risk a broken head for the sake of a bacon roll?

I sighed. I didn't put my hand on my sword, not yet; I didn't want to risk anyone getting hurt who didn't deserve it, and this was a bad place for a barney; too many tables too close together and a greasy floor.

"Come on," I said. "No-one wants trouble."

"Trouble?" said one, a lanky type with a cheap tattoo. "Who said anything about trouble? Just want our city back, that's what."

"*Your* city?" Gallock said. I raised a hand to shut hir up.

"Who are you, anyway?" said the other thug, who had badly bitten nails.

"I'm Babylon Steel, and I haven't had my dinner. You want to talk about this outside?"

"All on your own, girlie?" said the third, doughy and raspy-voiced.

"I'm hungry. Let's get this over with."

"We're not fighting *you*," doughy said.

"Then leave."

Instead, he leaned over and swept the dishes off a nearby table. "S'disgusting, s'had their four filthy hands on it!"

The sight of the good food scattered on the floor broke my temper. I grabbed his arm, folded it behind him, ran him out the door and propelled him headfirst into the nearest wall with a boot in his arse for emphasis.

By the time his mates came shoving out I had my sword drawn. So did they.

"Whatcha do that for?" No-Nails yelled, seeing his mate face-down at the foot of the wall. "Bitch!"

"You can walk away now," I said. "No-one's looking."

Tattoo glanced from the unconscious man to his mate, but No-Nails was on his high horse and had no plans to get off until it was ridden. "Walk away?" he snarled, and charged at me, waving his blade like he was trying to attract my attention.

I *hate* fighting amateurs. You never know what the hells they're going to do. I barely managed to get his feet out from under him without running him through – he practically threw himself on my point. Stupid boy. He hit the street hard; his sword flew from his hand, he winded himself, and he got a face full of something nasty. That distracted him long enough for me to lock Tattoo's blade with my quillons, disarm him and get him in a grapple. "Are you going to be sensible," I said into the ear I had his elbow wrapped round, "or do I have to knock you out while I deal with your friend?"

"Sensible," he said, with some difficulty.

"Good." I took his blade. Decent piece, seen some use. "Stand over there."

I picked up No-Nails' sword. He was getting up, his face streaked with filth and plain murder in his eyes. "Back off," I said. "I am all out of patience."

He stepped forward anyway. Honestly, it amazes me how some of them make it to adulthood.

"Come *on,*" his friend said.

No-Nails looked from me to his friend and saw no help anywhere. "That's my sword. You can't steal my sword!"

"This?" I held it up. "I sure as hells wouldn't pay you for it." It was junk, all fancy-work and no damn balance. "I'll leave them both with the militia, shall I? You can pick them up at the barracks."

I saw all the reasons he didn't like that plan pass over No-Nails' face.

"Listen, young man," I said. "I am not having a good day. I have been very, very nice to you, but the strain is telling on me. Keep pushing. Give me an excuse to get unpleasant. *Please.*"

I guess something showed in my face. I saw him swallow, and his friend, who had all the sense in that bunch, grabbed his arm. They started to walk away with undignified haste.

Their other friend, who'd actually been faking for the last few minutes, gave a theatrical groan; they realised they'd forgotten him, edged around me, and dragged him off between them.

I looked up and realised the windows of Gallock's were full of faces. I went back in, to a scatter of applause.

"Yeah, yeah," I said. "Next time, *you* can fight the morons, all right? Gallock, can I have some soap and water, please."

It duly arrived, followed by a plateful of food so vast I wasn't sure whether to eat it or move into it. "On the house," Gallock said. "Next time, too."

"Any luck, I won't have to earn it the same way next time." I shook my head. "Must be the moons."

Gallock slammed pans about. "Moons, no moons, always that kind around."

"Yeah I know. Gallock, you got any security?" That sort might always be around, but customers ready to get involved weren't.

Gallock shook hir head and glanced down at hir swelling belly. "Sometimes, you know, I think about old days. Not want to go back, me, but some things maybe not so bad."

"Well, you wouldn't get hassle from those idiots, I guess."

"Those idiots, no. Other idiots, yes. Other tribes, most. Get you anything else, Babylon?"

"Coffee, please."

Gallock slapped bacon into a pan with one hand, reached for rolls with the other, and for coffee with a third. The fourth rested on hir stomach. "Back home, things get bad with another tribe, is always the *dinan-bathai.*"

I swallowed a grimace along with my coffee. I only knew about the *dinan-bathai* ceremony because of an evening's drinking with Glinchen one time. That was the *last* time I was ever going to try and keep up with *hir* intake – it was amazing I remembered anything at all from that night.

The Barraklé, as well as being hermaphroditic, have another oddity. If a child is kept virgin, and fed particular foods, they don't grow like ordinary Barraklé. They become something else. It's a bit like bees that only turn into queens if they get fed royal jelly. With the Barraklé they have to be virgin as well. There's a lot of rubbish talked about the significance of virginity, but like a lot of things that get twisted into myth, sometimes it has a basis in fact.

It's a great honour to be chosen as a *dinan-bathai*; much adulation and ceremony and the best of everything until it's time for the transformation.

If they survive (they don't always), they turn into a warrior, of sorts. A muscular, damn near indestructible thing, sterile and almost mindless, but extremely effective at killing anything they're told to.

They don't live long. Usually just long enough to wipe out most of whatever village the tribe has a grudge against. Then either they die from the after-effects of their transformation, or their own tribe has to kill them before they turn on their makers.

A great honour, indeed.

TIRESANA

"WHY US?" JONAT said, scowling, her dark brows drawn like bows. As an old woman, she'd be hawk-faced. She was sprawled on the cushions in the window like a cat in the sun, looking down at the courtyard. I could hear the swish-swish of the brushes from below. "They sweep, they wash, they cook, but not us. Fighting and fornication, that's all we do. What's different about us?"

Meisheté, who was watching that day, turned her head, eyes flaring with irritation in their dark surrounds, but before she could speak, her protégé, Velance, stepped in. "We're Chosen," she said, as though it were too obvious to mention. Velance didn't take to the seduction so well, either; she did it, but always with a slight but noticeable air of impatience, as though there were better things to be getting on with. She was much the same with the fighting. Efficient, but no love for it.

"Chosen for what, though?" said Jonat, turning her ring on her finger. Aka-Tete had given it to her; it had her initials carved in the gold. She wore it all the time, never took it off even to sleep.

"To be High Priestesses of Babaska, idiot," Velance said.

"So why isn't Babaska choosing us herself? Why are the other Avatars choosing us for her?"

"You have been told. The Avatar Babaska has important matters to attend to," Meisheté said. "More important than running about after a bunch of foolish girls."

Unlike you, then, *I thought, but didn't dare say. I wished Jonat wouldn't ask such questions; they made me uncomfortable in my skin, made me think of a few questions of my own that I would rather not have been troubled with. Where was Babaska? Didn't she care who got Chosen for her? If I were her, I wouldn't want someone like Shakanti choosing my priestesses for me. She might not lie, but in her hands the truth was a poison blade.*

"All the same, I don't understand why we aren't getting training in temple administration," Jonat said. "I've seen the High Priestess of Babaska here, she's always busy. There are hundreds of people in a big temple precinct like this, they all have to be told what to do, so why..."

"Every temple is different," Meisheté said. "There is no point you being taught how to administer one temple when you will be sent to another."

"Surely the ceremonies and rituals are the same everywhere?" Jonat said.

"If you want to find out," Meisheté said, "you will concentrate on your studies and cease asking foolish questions. If you fail you leave in disgrace. Is that what you wish?" She had a way of speaking that could make everyone cringe and flush and feel six years old.

"Can't we hire someone else to do all that?" I said. "Who wants to do all that boring administration anyway?"

"We all know how you'd rather spend your time, Ebi," Velance said. "A priestess does have duties outside the bedroom, you know."

"Never mind," Jonat said, and turned back to stare out of the window again. She was looking for Aka-Tete; she always was.

Renavir, Shakanti's Chosen one, was so quiet, and small, and thin, you hardly even knew she was there. She often sat half wrapped in the curtains, or with cushions piled over her and clutched in her arms until there was almost nothing visible but her little face with its pointed chin and too-big, pale blue eyes, with their solemn stare. She had a scarf that Shakanti had given *her, a strip of silvery gossamer that reminded me of the Avatar's hair, and she wore it wrapped around her arm. It got torn and bloody during fight training, and she would clean it as gently as if it were a hurt kitten, and mend it with tiny, obsessive stitches. She was doing it now.*

"We have to be broken to be made new," she said, without raising her eyes from her sewing. "But most of you will just get broken."

She often said things like that – sometimes pure nonsense, sometimes not. She'd got worse recently, perhaps from spending too much time with Shakanti. We knew things weren't right with her, but we didn't know what to do, so we didn't do anything. And I stopped listening then, because I'd been summoned to Hap-Canae.

He gave me a ring, too. Perhaps he had noticed Jonat's. He found it in the treasury: he spent a fair bit of time there. He preferred it to the library, though he occasionally browsed there, among the crumbling scrolls with their browning ink. I thought him a scholar, and as I found scholarship hard myself, it only added to his glory in my eyes.

"A ring of Babaska," he said, handing it to me. "Hush! Don't tell the others, they'll be jealous."

It was a heavy, gold seal-ring, its flat, dark red stone carved with a sword and a lotus that still stood out clear and perfect, though the writing that had been engraved along the band was worn away to almost nothing by who knows how many years.

"Aren't you pleased?" he said. "I thought you would like to have something that was connected to her, something none of the others will have."

"Of course! It's beautiful."

It was actually a strange, heavy, solid thing, but once I put it on, I found it pleasing. Having something connected with Babaska was gratifying, though it seemed, somehow, underhand to get it this way. I felt there should have been ceremony attached, to receiving something of hers, rather than have it simply lying around in the treasury and passed on to me so casually.

It suggested to me that Hap-Canae was ashamed of me, or was unsure of my worth. Grateful, uncertain, desperate for approval, I put myself out even more to please him. I was terrified of losing him. And although I hardly realised it myself, I was lonely; I missed Radan and Sesh and Kyrl; I even missed the other kitchen servants. We girls couldn't be friends – apart from the fact that we were never allowed to be alone together, we swam in rivalry like ornamental carp swim in a pond.

Hap-Canae was all I had.

CHAPTER
THIRTEEN

I WATCHED THE café crowd. Now the drama was over, they were providing their own: practicing songs, declaiming speeches, topping each others' stories, having highly melodramatic fallings-out and reconciliations, sometimes both within the space of a cup of coffee. A couple of Ikinchli, a probably human sort with a great shock of black hair and a... something (greenish fur like damp moss and what appeared to be two noses, but one – or both – could have been his dick for all I knew; not everyone keeps them in the same place) were playing some game with counters and little clay figures. The black haired one was moaning about having to go in lockup – yes, he was a were. Not all weres need locking up during Twomoon, but those who do get themselves sorted or face the consequences. If you're caught tearing out someone's throat in Change, the militia are likely to use the silver first and pretty much ignore the asking questions part.

One lad with vast brown eyes and horn-buds caught my eye – I glanced under the table and, yes, furry legs and little hooves. I adore fauns. Always want to pick them up and cuddle them. He was talking about his latest conquest, waving his hands around. "Ooh, and he's taking me to the Lodestone, darling, can you imagine?"

"We are moving up in the world," said one of his companions: a tiny, crop-headed Fey, one of the few I'd actually seen with wings, rainbow-tinted translucent things as fragile as soap-bubbles. "Don't forget your old friends, will you? Bring us some leftovers."

"Oh, sweetie, if I'm going to the Lodestone there aren't going to be any *leftovers*."

"I don't know where you put it all," said the third member of the party, a chunky little redhead who reminded me of Previous, and who was looking down mournfully at his rounded belly. "Honestly, I don't eat as much as you two, how come you never get fat?"

"It's the dancing, honey," the faun said. "You need a part that has you leaping all over the stage. Oh, have you seen the new dancer in the Red Smoke Revue? I didn't even know what she does was *possible* unless you were half lamia and half shameless!"

"You're talking about someone *else* being shameless?" The Fey said, shivering her wings with mock indignation. "Who goes for every *single* part that might mean taking his clothes off in front of an audience? Is it me? No? Why, I believe it's you."

The faun shrugged prettily. "I get them, don't I?"

"I don't," said the redhead, but the other two were too busy sparring to notice. He might have that little belly, but he also had the hollowed look of someone who'd lost too much weight in a hurry, and I'd already clocked him stuffing a stale roll left behind by another customer into his pouch. Acting. Tough business.

But I didn't need another doorman, and he didn't strike me as the type who'd fancy the upstairs work. Unlike the faun, who might, but who'd be far more trouble than he was ever going to be worth. Fauns may be cute, but when it comes to the business, I know who won't suit. I also know a city-sized ego when I see one.

The little redhead paid his bill, bid farewell to his friends and got up to go. I followed, and as we both pushed our way from the warm steam into the chilly street, I leaned down and muttered, "Want some free advice? Take some training in swordplay, mate. It can get you stage work, and anyway, in this city it's always useful."

He looked up, surprised. "Thanks, but I can't afford it."

"Try Bressler's in South Side. He'll often do free lessons for errand runs." I winked at him and went my way. My good deed for the day. And a useful reminder that I needed a little freshener myself; I'd managed in that fight, but they were amateurs. I'd have to set up a session with Previous. Normally we practiced every week, but with one thing and another we'd become slack.

Once out of the noise and warmth, I started thinking about that damn drawing on the wall again. Had I seen a skull, or not? Did it even mean anything?

I should ask the Chief. Or Fain. One of them would know. I was putting it off, like the accounts.

But it was only a suspicion. The faintest of suspicions, really.

Because if they were here, I'd have to run again. I'd spent twenty years doing little else; I'd thought myself settled, finally, and safe.

I'D ALMOST REACHED home when I heard something that sounded like my name, though it was more wheeze than word. I turned around. It was Glinchen, half-collapsed in the middle of the street, one hand to hir considerable chest, panting like a dog.

"Glinchen? What is it? Are you all right?"

Ze flapped a hand at me and eventually got enough breath to say, "You... walk too fast. You come. Is girl."

"What girl? What's happened?"

"Girl is dead."

"What? Which... oh, not Enthemmerlee. The yellow-eyed girl? Glinchen?"

"I don't know. Only know is new girl, and now she dead. You come."

"All right."

As we headed towards King of Stone, me going half-mad with impatience as I slowed to keep at Glinchen's pace, I was hoping, desperately, that the girl wasn't Enthemmerlee. But even while

I hoped, a cold conviction grew in my belly that I had failed to save someone I could have, *should* have saved.

"How did you hear?"

"I was down Slip Street, it all go quiet, you know? Then someone come running out say girl is dead, what we do, and I remember you looking for girl maybe in trouble, and I come for find you."

Every area of the city has its scents and sounds; they change as you move. Round the Hall of Mirrors it's muted chatter, the swish of silk, the clatter of well-shod hooves, the hard click of heels. Perfume and clean linen, cut flowers and high-priced food.

As you pass through the residential area in between, things go quieter. There are more gardens, the shops are smaller, there are fewer eating places; less noise, less smell, less everything. Things are tucked away behind closed doors and curtained windows.

Then you get into King of Stone. Coming in this way, from Buckler Row, you move from murky shadows into smoky light. Cheap lamp-oil and tallow candles. Skinny urchins run everywhere, mostly barefoot, and you don't want to look what they're treading in. They play strange, complicated games that involve chalking patterns on the paving or the walls and shrieking a lot – furred, feathered or skin-clad, children shriek. There are stalls selling food from half the planes, and the smells come at you in waves; delicious or gagging. The smell of cloud, earthy and a little damp, like fungus, the fatty reek of burning oil and tallow. The underlying smell is, always, sewage. You forget to notice after a while.

There are performers singing or reciting – often enough with a friend in the crowd dipping purses while people's attentions are elsewhere – there are people playing cups, people standing in doorways and gossiping. Processions clamour through the streets, ceremonies from worlds away, worlds that sometimes exist only in memory. Dancing and drums and cymbals and instruments I don't even have a name for.

Around Twomoon, things usually get even crazier for a couple of days, and then they lock down.

But tonight it was different. Fewer children running through the street, more parents on watch, eyeing those who were, and the freelancers huddling round the stalls with steaming cups in their hands, or bunching two and three to a doorway.

It's not the safest place for whoring, but there's plenty of business, and the more adventurous respectables often come down here for a taste of something they can't get at home. A stabbing, like as not.

Glinchen pointed to a pair of grimy buildings that leaned together as if they were muttering over some ugly secret. Broken windows, stuffed with cloth to keep the cold out, looked like blind, bandaged eyes.

Someone who seemed to be the same race as the child I'd questioned about Enthemmerlee, with that same dusty skin, was standing by the open door, her arms wrapped around herself, whispering a stream of something. Maybe prayers. I couldn't tell.

"In there. Upstairs," Glinchen said. The stairs led straight up from the tiny, crumbling hallway, into a grey gloom.

I looked at the woman. "You called the militia?"

She didn't respond. I tried again, in pidgin and a couple of other languages, but she only looked at me, whispering and whispering.

"Has *anyone* called them?" I said to Glinchen.

Glinchen shrugged.

"Glinchen..."

"Oh, no, no, no. I not go talking to the millies, me."

"Things are different, now."

"Yeah, maybe, you all cosy-cosy with the Chief. You be careful, baba."

"Glinchen, someone has to tell them."

"You look first. See if your girl. Then you go tell millies if you want, hah?"

I looked up the dank webby stairwell, feeling my stomach contract.

"All right." I had to know.

I found the room easily enough; there were only three. One was empty, presumably because of the gaping hole in the middle of the floor. Broken planks dark with rot surrounded it like a mouthful of decaying teeth. In the doorway of the next room stood a creature of indeterminate species or gender, with skin the colour of mouldy bread, clutching a tattered coat around itself, watching me with big wet eyes like black fruit. It tilted its head towards the end room.

I took a breath and went in.

The room was grey: grey rags at the windows, grey walls, grey cover on the bed. It had the fungal smell of cloud and dingy sex.

She lay on the bed, looking as though she'd flung herself back in laughter, or exasperation, her arms above her head. Her face was swollen and dusky, but the rest of her was very pale, like something grown in the dark.

She was slight, with thin wrists and fragile ankles. I moved closer, taking the little portrait out of my pocket. The locket glimmered dully. Even crusted with gilding as it was, it didn't really shine. It was meant for ballrooms with a thousand candles, charming rainbows from the guests' jewels; for negotiations in fine, high-windowed rooms between the scions of great families. It struggled to glitter in this dank little rathole with its torn curtain and stained bed.

And I could tell, even with the poor girl's face swollen that way, that it wasn't her. This girl's eyes, traced now with red, were brown.

I wished her a good journey, and put the locket away.

I heard the feet on the stairs and knew even before I turned around. "Hey, Chief."

"Babylon. What are you doing here?" In the grey murk, his face looked weary, and older.

"One of the freelancers fetched me."

147

"You should have sent for us."

"I was going to."

"Straight away, Babylon. Not after you'd come up here and had a look."

"I know, I'm sorry. I just... I needed to know whether it was the girl I'm looking for."

"Is it?"

"No."

"Right then. Come out of there."

We went out on the landing. He'd brought two more militia with him; I didn't know either of them. He nodded them into the room and turned to me.

"Aren't you in enough trouble, Steel? What were those Vessels doing around your jalla?"

"Huh? Oh, that. Yeah. Nothing, I mean, they decided to make an example of us, or something, standing around scaring off clients, but someone told them they were breaking the law. They've not been back. Yet, anyway. Why?"

"And I'm supposed to clear it up if you decide to get into a barney with them, am I?"

"I didn't!"

"You went to their temple. You walked right in there. Dammit." He took a breath, and said, "never mind. No-one's dead, this time anyway. Who fetched you here?"

"Chief..."

"Who told you, Babylon? The landlady?"

"The woman outside? No. One of the freelancers came to find me."

"I need to talk to them."

"They didn't see anything."

"You don't know that. This is my job, not yours. Tell me who fetched you and don't... muck... me... about." A suggestion of a growl roughened his voice.

"You sound like that, you're going to scare hir to death."

"Hir? Glinchen?"

I cursed myself for the slip.

"Not the most reliable witness," Bitternut said. "I'm amazed ze didn't fall down the stairs."

"Glinchen didn't come up here. And was sober, last I saw."

"Time I find hir, ze'll be too pissed to talk. Let's walk."

I followed him down the stairs.

"Anything else you haven't told me?" he said, as we reached the street.

There was a small, muttering crowd, but Glinchen, of course, was nowhere in sight – ze'd taken off at the first sight of the millies. Still, I'd bet on hir being around somewhere, too curious to leave.

"Just that Glinchen said she was new. That was why I thought maybe it was the missing girl," I said.

"Well we can both thank our stars it wasn't."

"What, because the missing girl's the daughter of some noble or other? So this one doesn't matter? She's still someone's daughter, Chief. Dead in a shitty back room because of some sick little..."

"*Of course she matters.*" Quietly as he spoke, I'd never heard the Chief sound quite so angry. "Do you think I don't care, just because no-one knew who she was? What I mean, Babylon, if you've *quite* finished making assumptions, is that at least with this girl we won't have some idiot from the Diplomatic Section turning up and demanding we hand over the body *right now* before there's an Incident, and we might actually be able to conduct a proper investigation and find the murdering bastard."

"I..."

"If even *you* think like that, I'm not surprised none of the bloody freelancers will talk to me. I thought you had better sense, Babylon Steel, I really did. Get out of here. Go home." Before I could answer, he turned away.

The sun had dipped below the horizon, and the sky where it had been was streaked with bloody stains.

My whole body felt coated in lead. I went looking for Glinchen but without luck. I could have slapped the stupid creature, even though ze'd thought ze was doing the right thing. Why'd ze have to put me at odds with the Chief? And what else was going on with him, was it the coming Change? He wasn't usually so damn touchy.

My mind swung from the Chief to that poor girl, that miserable little room. That's what too many people think whoring is. Sex as something to use, instead of something to worship – an ugly life and an ugly ending.

Murder happens, of course. Whores get killed. But it's unusual in Scalentine. We look out for each other, and the militia treat us like citizens, too. Well, most of them. The last Chief was an exception, from what I understand – but then, he was bad news for everyone, not just for whores.

Scalentine's different, thanks be to the All, but there's a lot of people on a lot of planes who think sex is evil in and of itself, and so is anyone associated with it.

Which is simply crazed. We all come from it; human or Fey, god or genie – it's how we started. It's how life begins. People like the Vessels hate that, and you ask me, they end up just plain hating life.

Talk of a demon… I was halfway up Buckler Row when I spotted two Vessels. They were moving slowly, and as I got closer I realised why. I could see the front man's eyes glittering in the holes of his Purity mask, as they skittered nervously from side to side, glancing into the shadowed mouths of alleyways.

The man behind him had a hand on his shoulder, and his Purity mask was smoothly white from brow to chin. There were no eye-holes.

Why would a blind man insist on being led into the worst part of the city with night coming on?

"Hey," I said. "Hey, you."

The front man jumped like a rabbit, causing the blind one to lose his grip on his shoulder. Both masks swung towards me. Sighted or blind, I wasn't sure which was creepier; but even with their faces covered I could tell this pair were nervous.

"I want to know what you're doing here. I know you don't talk to females, but you'd damn well better talk to this one."

The blind one recovered his grip on the front man's shoulder and I saw his fingers tighten hard.

The front man stared past me.

"There's been a murder, " I said. "Do you understand? Someone is *dead*."

The blind one turned to his fellow. "Terrible things happen among the unfortunates of this city. There is lust, and hatred; there is fury and despair. Thus we walk among them, to shine the light of the Purest into the dark places."

"Thus do we shine the light," his companion responded, his voice quavering.

"So you've been down here spreading the light of the Purest. Tell me, how does the Purest feel about people getting murdered?"

Still addressing his companion, the blind one said, "We upon whom the Purest has chosen to shed enlightenment know that the Purest does not experience feelings. The Purest is beyond them. Emotions weight the spirit and corrupt the mind. It is time we returned to the Temple, brother."

His grip tightened again. The sighted one glanced at me. Buckler Row is well lit, in comparison with some places; I could see his eyes behind the mask. They didn't look like those of a murderer. They looked frightened. He shook his head, a tiny fraction. A denial? A warning? I couldn't tell.

I put out my hand, and let it drop. I could hardly knock them over and haul them in front of the Chief because they happened to be within a mile or so of the murder; I was in enough trouble already.

But *something* was going on with the Vessels. I watched them make their slow way back towards the temple and respectability, vowing that one way or another, I was going to find out what that something was.

TIRESANA

THEY DECIDED WE *should be tested in a real battle; a little local difficulty, you might say. Not that local, though – we travelled for days to get there. I think it was so there was less risk anyone might recognise one of us, later.*

It still was a risk. One can test aptitude for the bedroom arts fairly discreetly. But war, even a local raiding party, is messy. The unexpected is inclined to happen. People die who shouldn't and people survive who weren't in your plans.

Aka-Tete, the Avatar of Death, accompanied us in his warrior aspect. The skulls at his waist clicked together as he walked, as though they were chattering about us in some secret language; the dark-must smell of death trailed him like smoke.

"Maybe the Avatar Babaska will be there!" I said to Jonat. The Avatar Aka-Tete was getting careless about keeping us apart. We weren't exactly friends, but I was excited, and wanted to share it with someone.

She was too busy looking at Aka-Tete to answer for a moment. When she did turn to me, she looked stormy. Her hawkish nose was even sharper than usual, and I realised she was getting thinner. "Why would she, Ebi? She hasn't bothered with us so far. It's not even a war. It's some little scuffle up in the hills; probably someone lost a goat."

I wondered what had upset her, not that it took much.

"Who are we fighting?" I said, when we caught up to Aka-Tete.

"The enemy," he said.

Even then, I didn't consider that a sufficient explanation, but what could I do? We were lined up and sent in and there wasn't time to ask more questions, even if anyone would have answered them.

It could have gone worse, all things considered, though I had some bad moments. Looking at the soldier I was fighting and seeing, instead of an enemy, a terrified boy even younger than me, holding a rust-pitted sword in a shaking grip. I didn't want to kill him. But he took a swing at me, I blocked it and kicked his legs out from under him, then someone else took a swing too, and I was too busy trying to stay alive to worry about the scared boy. When the fight was over he was there, dead, lying with his cheek cupped in his hand like a sleeping child, and I didn't even know if it was me who'd killed him.

One of the girls had an arm off at the elbow. I had a shallow cut across the back of one hand – I'd been lucky – and once everything was quiet I went to have it dressed.

We had our own priest with us for that, of course. I went into the tent, which smelled of blood and tart medicinal herbs.

The injured girl, Calife, was lying on a mattress. I could hear her muttering and crying. The Avatar Aka-Tete and the priest stood over her; the priest kneeling in his stained white robes, head bowed. Aka-Tete was a great gleaming shadow in the tent's pale gloom, blood smeared across his armour and dappling the skulls. I wondered whose it was, as I hadn't seen him fight.

"The bleeding is stopped, O lord. I've given her poppy; she should quiet soon."

The Avatar Aka-Tete nodded, then bent down, and laid his hand on the girl. Her crying stopped. The priest said, "My lord? What..."

"She is quiet now." The Avatar's aspect changed from Warrior to Vulture. I backed out of the tent, and cleaned my wound myself.

Back at the temple, I stewed on it for two days, before working up the courage to mention it, when I was lying at Hap-Canae's side, cupped in the crook of his arm, smelling his scent of myrrh and cardamom.

"Something happened," I said, "While we were away. I saw something. And it... seemed wrong."

"Oh?" he said.

"There was something the Avatar Aka-Tete did..."

"To you?"

"No. One of the girls was injured. Calife. She was one of the winds' Chosen, I can't remember which one. But I think he... I think she might have got better. Only he did something. And she died."

"Aka-Tete is the God of Death. Do you think his Avatar does not know where the boundary lies? I have told you before. We do not interfere in the actions of another Avatar."

"Wasn't it interfering, though? He didn't Choose her..."

"Trust Aka-Tete to know that she was not going to recover. Now, enough. We have a responsibility, as representatives of the gods, to present a united face to the world." He looked into my eyes. "We have responsibilities to the people, too. How do you think they would feel if they thought we were squabbling among ourselves? Hmm? Come, I know the girl's death upset you, but you must put it aside. These things happen in war, as Babaska's priestess should know better than any."

I apologised, and he pulled me back to him, and the next day he presented me with a gown so heavily embroidered it was like armour, which he'd had made while I was away. He would always rather bask in people's adoration than burn them with his anger, although he was capable of both, as I would learn.

CHAPTER
FOURTEEN

I GATHERED EVERYONE who wasn't with a client as soon as I got in, and told them about the dead girl.

I watched their faces. Sorrow, and anger... but very little fear. I didn't know whether to be pleased or worried. "We all know this happens," I said. "And it may be a one-off. But I want everyone being extra careful, all right? No new clients unless I look them over first. Any of the regulars been acting strange? Off? No? Well, keep an eye out and let me know immediately. And I want everyone to have some training with me or Previous or Ireq, as soon as it can be arranged. You should all know the basics, but if there is a madman out there, you need to brush up. Actually... Previous. Session? After this?"

"'Course. But I thought you had a client."

"Cancelled."

"Because of the Vessels?"

"What? Not that he said, no. Why?"

She squinted out of the window, tightening the strap of her breastplate. "Thought I saw one hanging about, earlier."

"Out front? Like before?

"No. Sneaking. Corner of Lassiter and Brass Fish Street. Just caught a glimpse of the mask."

"Probably hoping Laney'll sit on the windowsill painting her toenails again."

"Hah," Laney said, bouncing up from her chair. She was wrapped in black and crimson silks, and looked like an exotic bird. "*That* was totally wasted on them." She held out her leg and looked at her toes, scowling. "And I don't even like the colour much."

"We can't do anything unless they cause trouble. The Vessels, I mean, not Laney's feet." It was a thin joke, but they made the effort to smile. That's my crew. "All right, everyone. If anyone's worried about a client or just doesn't fancy the work tonight, let me know, and we'll sort something. Smooth?"

They seemed as happy as could be expected. I went upstairs, and changed into my training gear.

Previous may be a sight shorter than me, but she's damned fast on her feet. Made me sweat for every stroke.

I was grateful. There's something about training that focuses you, and training with someone who really knows what they're doing, even more so. You're concentrating so hard on getting it right, on avoiding ending up on the floor with someone sitting on your head, that everything in your mind stops whirling around for a while.

It was night, but the moons were up and fattening fast, and we hung out lanterns.

We called a halt two hours later, both of us panting. Previous grabbed one of the tankards of water we'd brought out, drained it and wiped her mouth. "Your lower right defence is weak."

"I know." I did, since I was now wearing a couple of cracking bruises across my right shin.

"Sorry about that," she said, not quite hiding a grin. "I heard the last one."

"Necessary reminder. I've been getting slack."

She put a hand to her shoulder, wincing. "Me too."

"Better bruises than a missing limb, right?"

"Oh, yeah. Still, I think I'll ask Laney for some of her ointment."

"Drink?"

"Ah. No. Not right now. Actually, Babylon…"

"Yeah?" I said, yanking at a stubborn buckle, longing to get into a hot bath and wash the day off me. I looked up with a strap between my teeth.

Previous leant forward, peering, whatever she'd been about to say forgotten. "Babylon? Did I catch you across the face?"

"What? No." I let go of the strap and my hand went to my jaw, before I could stop it; I could feel the thin raised line. "Old scar." Stupid. Any scar I'd had that long, she'd have noticed. We'd known each other going on seven years.

When had it come back?

"Babylon? Are you all right? What's going on?"

"I can't..." The rush of shame and guilt and deep cold fear came over me like a wave. I leaned against the wall of the garden to steady myself. "There're things I haven't told you, Previous. About me. About what I was running from. I can't, yet." I was still hoping I'd never have to. I took a breath. "What were you going to say?"

Previous was fidgeting with the knot on one of her own bracers, not looking at me. She shook her head. "Later. It'll wait."

I SPENT HALF the night worrying, trying to sort things through in my head. I should find out whether the Avatars were here, for certain. But what I'd do then, I didn't know, other than run again. Leave my life, my crew, my friends. The thought of it felt like something breaking, right down the centre of me.

And there was Enthemmerlee. Every time I shut my eyes, I saw her face on the dead girl's body. I wouldn't, *couldn't* leave without trying to find her. Her, at least, I still had a chance to help. And, let's face it, I could do with the rest of Fain's money, even more so if I was going to have to go on the run; I'd have to leave the crew decently set, with the bills paid. But all I had was a dead girl who wasn't her, and no idea where Enthemmerlee might be.

And I wanted to make things right with the Chief. If I really was going to have to run, somehow I couldn't bear to have him remember me badly. But that, I didn't know how to do.

I decided that the first thing was to talk to Fain. I needed to find out more about Enthemmerlee's background. And the man had contacts. Maybe we could help each other.

CHAPTER
FIFTEEN
Day 4
3 days to Twomoon

AFTER A FEW hours of uneasy sleep, I went out while Flower was still the only other one up; I just caught a flicker of his apron as he whisked past the kitchen doorway. Pale lamps burned against a sky that was still slaty dark but for a brush of cold green above the horizon. Birdsong wove among the rattle of delivery-carts on the cobbles, and the smell of baking bread was everywhere.

The Singing Bird was, to my surprise, already open; or at least the 'courtesy guards' were on the door. "Up late, or up early?" I said. They didn't answer, just gave smiles that looked as though they were worked by counterweights.

"Name, please?"

"Babylon Steel," I said. "Here to see Mr Fain."

After a minute and a muttered consultation with someone inside, they bowed me through.

Inside you wouldn't know it was half past uncivilised, except that the only occupants were two people cleaning tables. The place was a velvet vault, with a little discreet gilding here and there, and booths lining the walls. The lighting was low and lush. It somehow managed to avoid the ugly, stained look places of night-time entertainment often have by day, but then, the curtains were tight shut and not a whisper of daylight was allowed in.

A door in the gilded wall I hadn't even noticed opened and Fain appeared, looking unfairly crisp and laundered. "Madam Steel. Do you have news for me?"

"Some. Not much."

"Coffee, then?"

"Please."

He summoned a waiter with the flick of a finger, and eased us into one of the booths at the side of the room, where we sank into deeply padded seats.

The coffee arrived, in a heavy silver pot of expensive simplicity, accompanied by cups as colourful and delicate as a butterfly's wing. After the waiter closed the elegantly carved door of the booth, I got down to business, trying not to look at the line of Fain's jaw and the way his shoulders moved under the crisp cotton shirt.

"Did you hear there had been a murder in King of Stone?" I said.

His hand tightened hard on his cup.

"Not..."

"No. I thought, in case you'd heard, I'd better let you know first that it wasn't Enthemmerlee."

"I appreciate the courtesy," he said, loosening his grip on the cup. I wondered what hold the Gudain rulers had over Fain that it mattered so much to him.

"I don't have much else, though. It seems Enthemmerlee wasn't snatched," I said. "She went willingly. Doesn't mean it wasn't a con or a pimp, but no violence was involved. Not in getting her off the square, at least. She went with someone who may, possibly, have been the same race, that part I'm not sure of."

"I see. That is, perhaps, comforting."

"I need to know more, Mr Fain. Is there any reason why other Gudain might be here on Scalentine? I've been wondering if there is a rival clan, or some such, who wanted the girl."

"It's a possibility. How much do you know about Incandress?"

"Only that the girl came from there, and so do the Ikinchli."

"It is a rich country, with much to offer, but in some ways very backward."

"So I gathered. I know a few Ikinchli. I'd have left, too."

"Have you spoken to them about the girl?" Fain said.

"One did say her eyes were unusual, if that means anything. He didn't know anything else about her."

"You believed him?"

"Yes." I'd believe him on most things. We've spent more than a little time between the sheets, Kittack and me, and that's one place I'm far less likely to be deceived in someone than anywhere else. Nowadays, at least. It wasn't always the case. But now, though people can, and do, hide their true selves in bed, they have to work quite hard to hide from me.

Of course, if I bedded Fain, I'd have a better idea of whether I could trust him. I wished I hadn't had that thought, because I *really* needed to concentrate, and it was getting more difficult by the minute.

"Hmm."

"What is it?" I watched his throat move as he considered, the skin glowing in the soft light.

"The Ikinchli might see kidnapping one of the ruling nobles as a form of leverage."

"Then why hasn't there been a ransom demand? Besides," I said, "I doubt they'd risk it. You know the stories?"

"Stories?"

"About maidens sacrificed to the Old. If a girl disappears the Ikinchli are in danger of being blamed for it, even though sacrifice is no part of their worship and never has been. They'd be unlikely to do anything so silly; too much trouble for everyone back home."

He leaned forward, eyes gleaming. "Now, that is interesting. No, I didn't know. You do have a way of getting people to tell you things, don't you?"

"It wasn't pillow talk, if that's what you mean. Not that there hasn't been that, too."

"I simply meant you have a capacity for making friends."

"You need them in this life, Mr Fain."

"Indeed."

"My Ikinchli friend said maybe Enthemmerlee was nicer than most Gudain. Admittedly he's prejudiced, but one can hardly blame him."

"There are those among the Gudain," he said, "who are not happy with things as they are, but it is difficult to take a stand, when the culture states that it is not only their right, but positively their duty, to regard themselves as superior."

"Hmm. Maybe."

I got up, partly because his closeness was beginning to make it difficult to think. He looked up as I moved, and *something* crossed his face: satisfaction?

It made me suspicious, although I still wanted to stroke him. There was so much more going on here than I knew about. "Look, Darask. I plan to keep looking for her" – I only just stopped myself from saying, 'whether you pay me or not' – "but I'd be a lot happier if you'd tell me why you're so interested."

He gave me a long, considering look. "I told you, I have business dealings with Incandress."

"What sort of business?"

"You're very protective of someone you haven't even met."

"Someone has to be. She reminds me..." There was something I didn't want to say. But did it matter? My blood was tingling in my veins and I was losing the thread. I didn't realise I'd leaned forward, until I overbalanced and almost landed in Fain's lap.

I could smell something underneath that clean woodsy smell; something heavy and musky.

I gritted my teeth, and with a fairly massive amount of effort, stood upright and moved away. "All right, Fain. I'm leaving. You can have your money back tomorrow."

He stood up. "Babylon, I..."

"Enough. I know that I'm not just reacting to you, attractive as you are, Mr Fain. There is something else going on here, and I don't appreciate people trying to manipulate me." I've had someone try a love potion on me before; when I realised what was going on (thanks to a timely intervention from a local herbwoman who owed me a favour), I broke several bits of the perpetrator. Some of them twice. I don't care how you do it – getting someone into bed without their conscious consent is rape, plain and simple.

Surprisingly, Fain grinned. And even now I knew that he was working something, it was a devastating grin. Partly because it looked so honest.

"You're right," he said. "I'm sorry." He shuddered, and there was suddenly a faint astringent tang on the air.

"The moons," he said.

"What?"

He sighed, and looked, if I could believe it, almost embarrassed. Darask Fain, embarrassed? Now I was *really* confused.

"What, exactly, is going on?"

"I have a... it's what you might consider a personal trait. Around full moon I give off a particular aura. And it has a certain effect on people."

"What sort of – oh, wait a minute. You mean you're in *heat?*"

He looked at me, open mouthed, and gave an utterly undignified snort of laughter.

"Oh, my," he said. "You know, I've never heard it put precisely like that before, but it's actually quite apt. Although I can control it to some extent at a normal full moon, around Twomoon it becomes rather more difficult."

"You *can* control it, but you didn't. You were using it on me."

"Controlling it is difficult; it's tiring, and it doesn't work for long. Not when Twomoon is this close."

"You tried it, nonetheless. I'm sorry, Mr Fain, but I don't think I want to talk to you about this girl anymore. Or anything else. If you wouldn't mind..." I turned towards the door.

"Babylon, Madam Steel, *please*. I'm sorry, it was stupid of me. I would never – I should have been honest with you. One gets into bad habits."

I actually had my hand on the door handle. I stood there, looking down at it. A few little things were beginning to trickle together in my brain, now I could use it again. Darask Fain, moving among all the levels of society, no-one really knowing much about him. Darask Fain, with an interest in one lost, kidnapped, betrayed, but politically important girl. And a habit of dishonesty.

I turned around, folded my arms, and leaned on the door. "Are you by any chance something to do with the Diplomatic Section, Mr Fain?"

His face went completely still. He looked down at his nails. "Well, well," he said. "I think I was right."

"About what?"

"That you are rather sharp."

"If I were that damn sharp I'd never have spoken to you in the first place. Is that a yes, then?"

"If you want proof, I'm afraid I don't carry a badge."

"If you want trust, give me a reason."

"We can help each other."

"Tell me why you want the girl, first."

"We're running out of time, Madam Steel."

"I know. She's supposed to be married before Twomoon. Tell me. Oh, and try that trait of yours on me again and I'll punch you through the wall."

He poured more coffee and leaned back, lifting the delicate cup. "Enthemmerlee Defarlane Lathrit en Scona Entaire is one of those in Incandress who wants to see things get better for the Ikinchli. Once married, at the apex of two powerful families, she could be a major force for change."

"So you – the Diplomatic Section – want her married too?"

"It would suit us if Incandress were a more stable, equitable society. The reasons are complex and I am not free to tell you all of them, but be assured, that is what we hope for."

"I see. So that's why you need to get her back."

"I am not entirely without concern for the girl herself."

"And once she's married? If they keep their women that close before marriage, how much power do they have after it?"

"More than you might think; their obsession seems to be with virginity, not with gender. But from what I know, the girl was kept unusually close, watched with something verging on obsession."

"So how the hells did she get whisked away under the noses of her family and bodyguards and what-have-you?"

"We don't know."

There had been a barney. Fain had mentioned it, and so had the Chief; I'd been distracted by his mention of demigods, but there had been some trouble in the crowd. It had occurred to me that, just possibly, said ruckus had been engineered. A diversion, to turn people's eyes elsewhere. But Fain had said that the girl was guarded to the point of obsession. So that alone would hardly have been enough, not without someone on the inside.

Maybe even the girl herself. Maybe she didn't see marriage as her way to change things. Or maybe she wasn't as idealistic as Fain believed and just wanted the hell out. I could hardly blame her for that.

"So did you have your own people on watch?"

"We had little warning that they were coming here."

"That's a no, then. Surely even a *little* warning should have been enough?"

He shrugged. "Whatever else it is, the Diplomatic Section is also, unfortunately, a bureaucracy. One needs permission, the right orders correctly signed, and official approval in order to do anything. And sometimes they are not forthcoming as quickly as might be wished."

"And did you get your orders signed to try and lust me into agreeing to anything you said?"

"*Lust* you?"

"It's hardly seduction, Mr Fain. Seduction is generally rather more subtle."

"I was hoping to persuade you to continue looking, yes."

"You didn't think that the money would be enough?"

"I wasn't sure it would. That's a compliment, by the way."

"Right." I trusted a compliment from Fain about as much as a lead coin right now. "Do you know anything about why the Gudain are so damned anxious to have the girl married off? Why is the *timing* so important?"

"From what we can discover, it appears to be connected with their history, and with their belief system. Twomoon is not just a time of significance on Scalentine."

Mokraine had said something similar. The various planes I'd passed through had so many different festivals, holy days and so forth, for so many reasons, it had never occurred to me back then that one of them might matter on *all* the planes.

"I don't study planar cosmology," Fain went on, "but those who do tell me that the next few days are highly significant for all sorts of magical and spiritual workings on a number of planes. Marriage, especially among noble families, often signifies more than itself. A return to stability. The rightness of the traditional way of doing things. But I am afraid the niceties of Gudain thinking are still beyond me. In any case, they are frantic to have her back in time; otherwise, the marriage cannot take place. The effects of that could be dreadful. Not only for the Gudain."

"What do you mean?"

"You mentioned the reasons why the Ikinchli would not be foolish enough to kidnap the girl. But if she cannot be found and safely returned in time for the wedding, it is entirely possible that the Gudain will put out the story that they have done so in any case."

"Reprisals," I said, going cold.

"Exactly. They want this marriage, badly. If it doesn't happen, and on time, don't you think they might look for a scapegoat? Or hundreds of them? Ikinchli."

"All right. What do I do if I find her?"

"Come to me. At the Singing Bird, not the Section."

"Why not?" I said.

"Things at the Section can be... complicated. Let's just say it will be in everyone's best interests."

"Including Enthemmerlee's, Mr Fain?"

"Of course," he said, rather shortly. "What will it take to convince you?"

I thought about it. "I don't know."

"I am running out of time." I realised he'd lost some colour. "Personally, I mean. My control's going to wear off shortly, and I'd rather not give you an excuse to punch me through the wall. It's quite solid."

"I will do my best, Mr Fain. That's all I can promise you."

"I'm sure you will, Madam Steel." There was a metal tinge in his voice and his eye. Not a threat, just a promise that he could make things difficult for me, if he chose.

As if I didn't know. I felt a plunging sense of relief that I hadn't asked him to find out whether the Avatars were on Scalentine; he'd almost certainly know, but he'd also want to know why I was interested, and I didn't need him to have anything else he could use against me.

I walked out of there in a state, what with the frustrated desire and the realisation that there was a lot more at stake than I'd realised.

I needed, desperately, to clear my head. And I needed to find out more about the Gudain. There was one place I could think of where I could do both.

TIRESANA

ONE GIRL WAS dead. Another two had disappeared; we were told that they'd achieved a posting, off to be priestesses at one or another of Babaska's temples.

And if I ever thought about what Farren the mercenary had said, I pushed it away. Because I was stupid, because I was in love. And because I was afraid. I was afraid to ask Hap-Canae what was going on.

He'd never hurt me with anything but words. But I already suspected that he might, if I displeased him. That was one lesson it took me too long to learn: if you're frightened of the person whose bed you share, whatever's going on between you, it isn't love.

Now there were four of us: me, Jonat, Renavir and Velance.

We all pretended to be excited about being posted away, becoming High Priestesses and having a whole temple district under our administration – well, apart from Renavir, who was so strange by then it was impossible to have a normal conversation with her.

I think the only one who genuinely liked the idea was Velance. She'd have made a good High Priestess. The rest of us were horrified by the idea of leaving, in case it took us from our Avatar. Not that they couldn't come to us wherever we were, if they chose. Maybe we were all chewing on the suspicion that they could abandon us without a moment's regret.

Jonat may have picked up something. An inkling. She was always the clever one; all that time she spent looking out of the window for Aka-Tete, she was thinking, too.

She flung herself into her studies, badgering the tutors for extra lessons. Like me, she'd quite enjoyed both aspects of our training, though she preferred the fighting to the seductive arts. Now she pushed herself and everyone around her until they were half-mad. Then she would suddenly give up, lose interest, drift away and stare out of the window. Later, when I first saw hawks kept for hunting, I remembered Jonat: all furious focused activity one minute, and hunched silence the next.

Renavir was worse. The fight-trainers came to dread her; she had skill, but no self-preservation. Half the time it was all they could do to stay out of her way without gutting her like a fish. She still wore the scarf Shakanti had given her, though the fragile stuff had been mended so often it looked twisted and humped, like scar tissue. Velance, on the other hand, just ploughed steadily on, doing what was required, hoping, eventually, to stop all this nonsense and be given a temple district and several thousand people to organize. She asked for an interview with the High Priestess, so she could learn from someone who was already doing the role, but she kept getting put off.

Even I could smell something, like coming thunder. I wasn't bothered about being chosen for some grand role, all I wanted was to stay where I was. I certainly didn't want to be sent to administrate a temple thousands of miles away. I had visions of being surrounded by sensible older women like Meisheté, or like the cook back home, who rolled their eyes and tutted at my every incompetent move.

But worst of all, I'd be away from Hap-Canae.

I asked for an interview with the High Priestess too; I thought if I could learn something, anything, about the way this temple worked, I might have a better chance of staying here. But like Velance, I kept getting put off.

Finally I pulled my courage together and asked Hap-Canae. I begged, in fact. "Don't let them send me away; I don't want to be a priestess if I have to leave you. I'd rather stay here and sweep the floors."

He just laughed. "My sweet, you'll never have to sweep a floor again, and I won't let anyone send you away, believe me. I am certain you, of all of them, will be able to stay here with me, where you belong."

CHAPTER
SIXTEEN

THE SWAMP LOOKED much bigger, empty; I'd never noticed that it was floored with cool, silvery tiles. The lamia was sweeping out the bar. She looked up, but obviously didn't recognise me. It was kind of a relief. "Sorry, we're closed."

"I know, I just wanted to see Kittack. He around?"

"Oh, surely. Kittack!"

He came out with a cloth in his hand and grinned at me. "Babylon! Hey, is not even noon, what happen for you be up this early?"

"You don't want to know."

"You here about girl? Sorry." He shrugged. "Not heard nothing."

"Wasn't why I came. Well, not the only reason."

"Oh?"

"You got a minute? And maybe a bed?"

It wasn't just the aftermath of Fain leaving me a little overheated. Sex relaxes me and helps me think. Well, not at the *time,* obviously, if it's any good... but afterwards.

"For that, I got more than a minute." He blinked at me, his version of raising an eyebrow, since he doesn't have those.

"Think of it as a favour. For you or me, either way."

He didn't ask any questions. Nor did he actually have a bed, as it turned out – but he had plenty of cushions.

Scalentine's chilly for his people, especially coming on to winter. He wears loose soft clothes in colours of water and earth. Under them his skin is like fine polished leather, a rich reddish brown; the scales lying close and shining. I can feel their edges if I run my hand upwards, from tail to head; it makes him shiver and grin.

"So soft," he said, running his hands over me in return; he doesn't seem to notice the scars, but then, even they probably feel soft to him. "How come you so soft when you so strong, eh? Strange person."

"I'm strange? You're the one with two cocks."

"Not strange to me," he said.

I stroked them as they began to emerge from the fold of skin that hides them. I've heard the female part referred to as a flower, more than once, but Kittack's two cocks are more like some jungle bloom than any cunny I've ever seen. They looked sleek and new and strangely vulnerable against the rest of him: gleaming pink and delicately curved.

He sent his long blue tongue flickering over my neck and breasts, stroking me with hands and mouth. I did the same to him, finding the soft vulnerable skin at the base of his throat where the scales are small and fine, feeling the smooth flex of muscles in his buttocks and thighs, enjoying, as always, the differences, the structures and surfaces that are so nearly human, so delightfully other.

He has scars himself, Kittack; mostly on his abdomen, where the scales are thinner, faded yellow against the warm brown. Scars of beatings, given when he was a child, and didn't run quick enough to do some Gudain's bidding. He doesn't mention them, so nor do I. We have better things to do.

Tongue to skin, skin to scale, the sleekness of him, curved hollows and long hard muscle and the powerful, always surprising limberness of his tail. Long clever fingers that stroke and probe. Quick, but never hurried.

He knew just the right moment to hook one leg over me and slip in, sideways, the way he does. The curve of him is strange, but pleasant; a tickling pressure that makes me gasp. Once settled, he's fast and vigorous and blissfully uncomplicated. I heard him hiss with pleasure and a moment later pleasure shot through me too, sharp and delicious.

Afterwards, feeling much more relaxed, I looked around, taking a breath before I had to introduce less pleasant subjects. I'd never been in this room before. The walls were grey-green stone, which should have felt cold, but Kittack being the lizard he is, he keeps the place pretty warm; some kind of system of hot water that runs beneath the floors. You get it in Ikinchli houses, something they brought with them from Incandress.

There were little niches in the walls, holding bits and pieces – some decorative, some just things that had been put there, apparently for no other reason than because someone needed to put something down. In one, there was a statue about the size of my hand, a graceful little figure, with chips of yellow stone for eyes. The face wasn't quite Ikinchli – a shorter muzzle, and different proportions.

"Kittack?"

"Hssh?"

"What's that little statue?"

"That? Itnunnacklish. The One who is Both."

"Huh?"

"Old-old story, from home. Legend, yes? Not so many left now, these old statues. The Gudain they not like, when they find, they break, so we got hide. Me, I am not religious, you know? I only keep statue because was old thing of my family, was carve by my many-times grandmother."

"Why'd the Gudain not like these statues, anyway?"

He propped himself up on one elbow, and ran a finger down my hip. His hands were pleasantly cool. "Legend say long ago, there is no Ikinchli and no Gudain. Is only the Kay-ebakat."

"Who?" I relaxed against him, not sorry to put the evil moment off a little longer.

"The children of the Old." Kittack nodded at the little statue. "Like that. Is powerful, almost like gods. But they not good children, is disobey, and make mess of things. They play with the world like toy, and make big trouble. The Old they say, you are wicked children, you be good or we will not be so nice no more. But the Kay-ebakat do not listen, they fight and dance and make the world all broken. In the end the Old say, look at mess. Now you get punish. So the Old, they take the Kay-ebakat and tear them in two" – he made an unpleasantly graphic gesture, and I could have lived without the sound effects – "and so is made Gudain and Ikinchli."

Ouch. "I can see why the Gudain aren't fond of the legend."

"No, they not like at all. To Gudain, Ikinchli is low, is only for do dirty job. And in Gudain legend is no Old. Is only big noble God-Gudain make everything; make high Gudain and middle Gudain and low Gudain and, under that, Ikinchli. Also have legend of Ikinchli take high-born maiden and sacrifice to Old, you know? Any time Ikinchli say, 'scuse us, not like being treat like filth, out come story of sacrifice maiden, and lots Ikinchli get dead."

Religion. If there's a better excuse for beating up the other guy, I've never heard it.

"Your Old, Kittack – they don't manifest, do they?"

"Nah. Is not been Old on our plane for long long time. Some say when we behave proper, Old come back, make us and Gudain one again; everything be good, you know?" He gave that sinuous shrug. "We behave proper, but Gudain don't, so we get sick waiting. Now Empire come, plenty trade, can get away, lots Ikinchli like me go bye-bye, we going elseplace, you do own dirty job now. So maybe when Old come back, find no-one there but Gudain no more." His stroking got more specific and I started to get distracted.

Something was niggling at me, and I held his hand still for a moment. "But who's the statue?"

"Itnunnacklish."

"And the story?"

"That she was best of the Kay-ebakat, and that the Old did not tear her in two, to make Gudain and Ikinchli, because she was behave proper, but put her to sleep, with sacred cup in hand. And if any find cup and drink from it, everything be good, you know? Gudain and Ikinchli be one again, rivers so full the fish can't move, plenty of everything, all thing be wonderful."

"So do people go looking for this cup?"

He hissed laughter. "Sometimes. Maybe very crazy people, who think gods solve everything. But is all very well wait for special cup, wait for planes to move into right place, wait for gods turn up, go, okay, you been good, we make everything nice now. Time of gods, not like our time. Maybe better not to wait, you know? Do things for yourself, even if thing is to leave home."

"Yes," I said. "Sometimes you do have to stop waiting for the gods to intervene. Who knows if they're ever going to turn up? Or what they'll be like if they do?"

He tilted his head.

"You okay, Babylon?"

"I'm fine. Do you ever miss it, though? Home?"

"Is things I miss. Light on the home water; ceremonies in the ancestor caves. The swamp in spring, white flower everywhere, thousand little fish like silver fire in the water. But here is good. Here not got Gudain all time going, do this, do that. Gudain come in my bar, order me about, can smack head and throw out on street. Is okay."

"*Do* they ever come here?"

"Not seen, no. Closest was that girl you show me, the picture. Why they leave home? Got everything they want right there. They come here, they not in charge no more."

I frowned at the statue. "Kittack, I need to tell you. That girl? She was part of one of the ruling families. They're mad to get her back, and married, before Twomoon. Do you have *any* idea why?"

He shrugged. "Is crazy Gudain. Who knows?"

"Because if I can't find her, if they don't get her back, things may get even worse for your people. The Gudain may take it out on them."

He paused, looking down at me. Then he shrugged. "My people, they had a hard time many many years. Used to it. Can be good slave, can do what you told, can hide or run or be angry, what it mean? Only more beatings, more murderings, every way. Better to get out, eh? I got out. Whatever happen, Gudain find some excuse for give Ikinchli bad time. Me, I taken my back away from the whip."

"Yeah," I said, feeling the old guilt coil in me like cold, bitter coffee. "Yeah, I know what you mean. Hey, what are you doing down there?"

I let myself be distracted again.

FEELING SLIGHTLY MORE energised, I went out talking to the freelancers, handing out Enthemmerlee's portrait, and making promises that would eat up Fain's money pretty quick if any of them bore fruit.

There was a bar off the docks, the Dog's Head, that was so grimy it looked as though it had been smoked like a side of bacon; I was getting hungry, but I'd sooner eat off the floor in Gallock's than risk the food in the Dog. I knew a few of the freelancers worked out of there, but the place was near empty except for the sort of drinkers who like to start early. There was a commotion in one of the corners and I heard, "Babylon-Baba!"

Glinchen was sitting with a middle-aged faun and a thin, long-nosed type with the pouched eyes and collapsed face of a man whose closest relationship for a long time had been with the stuff in his glass.

Not that Glinchen was in a much better state. Hir eyes were crossing with the effort of trying to focus on me, and one of hir necklaces had broken. As I watched, a glass bead slid from the thread and bounced away like a frozen tear.

"Come on, honeysweet, come have drink."

"Another time, all right?"

"Ah, come on, baba."

"Glinchen, I'm still trying to find that girl."

"What girl?"

"The yellow-eyed one, remember? You thought it might be her, the one in Rolldown Street."

"Oh, I remember," Glinchen's already swimming eyes spilled tears. "Poor little, who do such a thing? They know who was done it yet?"

"No, they don't. It would be a real help if you'd go talk to Chief Bitternut, Glinchen."

"Oh, nonono. Not talk to no millies, me. Here's to poor lost girls," Glinchen said, and downed half hir drink.

"Who?" said the faun.

"Girl got murder by some crazy person."

"Ah, that's bad. Friend of yours?" he said to me, and slid off his seat. I don't think he meant to, but he very gallantly offered it to me anyway.

"No, no, I didn't know her," I said. "But thanks."

The faun, with some effort, climbed up next to Glinchen, and started whispering things in hir ear. Glinchen began to look more cheerful. I wasn't going to get anything useful here.

"I got to go," I said. "Another time, all right?"

"Nono!" ze said. "Wait, I remember now, girl, yellow eyes girl," ze elbowed the comatose man. "Heyyou! Be wakesome! You know 'bout new girls."

He opened a smeared eye. "New girls? Where? I like 'em fresh."

I thought of Enthemmerlee and the dead, nameless girl, and lifted him by the hair. Woke him up all the way, at least.

"What do you know? Talk, or I'll..."

He was gasping and clawing at his head, his toes just scraping the carpet. "Gah! All's sake, let go! Let go!"

I lowered him until his feet could take the weight, but kept hold of his hair. Glinchen was, helpfully, laughing like a drunk jelly. The faun was watching what laughter did to Glinchen's cleavage. He grinned, poured the remains of his drink down there, and went after it.

I said, "I have got problems and no time to be nice, so talk."

He looked hunted. "What about?"

"Girls. New girls, who don't know a bad client. You been wearing a mask lately? Or supplying 'em?"

"I don't know what you're talking about!"

"No?"

"No!"

"There's a girl, dead. I take that very seriously, little man. There's another girl, with yellow eyes, who might have been pulled into the business against her will, and if she ends up the same way, *someone* is going to regret it, especially if they knew something that could have stopped it and *didn't tell me*. Now, you heard anything?"

"No!"

"You hear *anything,* you come to the Red Lantern. And stay away from young girls. That kind of thing can be entirely unhealthy, you get me?"

"I get, I get!" His scalp was starting to bleed. I let go, and wiped my hands on a filthy, beer-wet rag, which was still better than having that wretch's hair-grease on my hands.

"Glinchen? Glinchen!"

The faun had disappeared down Glinchen's cleavage most of the way to the waist. Brave man. I don't know how long I'd have had to wait for Glinchen's attention if ze hadn't suddenly shrieked, and used all four arms to pull the faun out, holding him in midair looking ruffled and slightly short of breath. "Sharp horns!" Glinchen said, shaking him. He flopped back and forth. "Sharp-sharp! Naughty boy. Next time you file them down or no play with Glinchen no more."

He got his breath back, gave a lopsided grin, and shrugged. "Sorry, beautiful, it's kinda hard to avoid poking *something* in there."

"No poke!" Glinchen put him down and jabbed him with a finger. "You go buy more drinks, make up for stabbing me in the chestings. Babylon-baba, you stay, have a drink?"

"No thanks, Glinchen. And hey, you really care about poor lost girls, sober up long enough to bloody well talk to Bitternut, all right?"

Ze looked at me, with reddened eyes, and I'm not sure which of us felt more ashamed.

But I couldn't think of anything to say, so I left.

TIRESANA

I CAUGHT VELANCE being sick in the corridor on the way to our lessons. "It's just the smell of fish from the kitchens," she said. "I shan't be eating it, it reeks."

But it wasn't the fish. We'd been taught what to do to avoid pregnancy, how to make a preventive out of a plug of vinegar-soaked wool or a sheath of waxed linen. Which herbs to use to make the foul-tasting tea no amount of honey could sweeten, which nonetheless was more reliable than wool or linen for pregnancy, though less good for disease. Not that we ever had to make these things for ourselves; servants did it all. But it was in the scrolls that Babaska's priestesses knew these things, so we were taught them.

And, of course, we'd been taught to spot the signs if the avoidance didn't work.

"Are you going to tell her?" Jonat said, tart as ever.

"Meisheté?" Velance said. "Of course. As soon as I'm sure."

"You don't think she'll be angry?" I said. I knew, somehow, that Hap-Canae would be if I should slip up that way.

"Why should she be?" Velance said. "She's the Avatar of the Mother Goddess."

Jonat looked at me, and I at her, and it was as though something walked by us, like the shadow of a predator.

It wasn't even a month later, when one night there was a terrible howling from somewhere in the Inner Temple; it woke *me and I looked out of my window, wondering if some beast from the deep desert had wandered in.*

I saw Jonat at the lesson next morning, but not Velance.

"She's gone," Jonat said. Her face was sallow, with shadows like smears of mud beneath her eyes.

"Velance?" said the Avatar Meisheté. "Yes. She's to be a priestess at the great temple at Nard." But her face was rigid when she said it, her shadow-surrounded eyes glittering with fury. I could feel the anger coming off her like heat. She looked at the three of us who were left like someone working out how to make one skinny chicken feed ten people.

"Did you hear the howling? There was blood in the corridor," Jonat said, in a whisper, as soon as Meisheté's back was turned.

"What do you mean?" I said.

"Meisheté likes the idea of babies. I don't think she likes actual babies. And all of them, the Avatars... there's something wrong. When have you seen..."

She shut up as Meisheté turned around.

Meisheté had a temper, even though she controlled it better than Shakanti. I imagine there were a lot of miscarriages that month. A lot of wailing women at the temples, whose hopes had been washed away in blood. A lot of love built up only to have nowhere to go.

But maybe some of them were grateful. It was hard times in Tiresana; hard to feed another hungry mouth, however small.

High summer, and the air so hot it scraped like sand. The stench of the river Rohin and the middens reached us even in the heart of the temple. I was surprised to find myself missing Velance. That stolid practicality of hers had been a kind of cushion of sanity.

Now there was only me, and Jonat, and Renavir.

Lying awake, I could hear the splash of a river-horse, though it must have been a half-day's walk to the Rohin, and the yipping of a dog, half-crazed by the heat and the moon.

I heard the sound of the lock and sat up. Had Hap-Canae come to me? He never did that.

No-one came in. The door creaked open an inch, and stopped. I got up and looked out.

There was no-one. The moonlight fell like sliced metal in the empty corridor. The habit of obedience was so ingrained that I hesitated. We were always locked in, always.

But tonight was different. I wrapped a robe around me and went out, feeling as though I were in a dream.

I heard a clink, in the room where we'd had our lessons in serving wine. I looked in, and there was Jonat, standing with a silver cup in her hands. I didn't think I'd made a noise, but she turned, ruffled up, glaring at me like a hawk disturbed from its kill.

"Was your door open, too?" I said.

"What do you think?" She lost that hunched look. Whatever she was afraid of, it wasn't me.

"Who do you suppose did it?"

"I don't know. I was asleep. There's some wine left, do you want some?"

"All right."

She thrust a cup at me and picked up the wine-jug. "Come on."

"Where?"

"Shut up and follow me."

I did.

We crept through the temple like mice in the walls. Jonat took me along corridors I didn't know, through the back of Aka-Tete's temple, to the outer wall of the precinct. On the other side of the wall, outside the precinct, the back of Aka-Tete's statue reared above us, hunched against the stars. Moonlight poured down over his shoulders like a silver cloak.

The guards never saw us; they looked outwards, not in. "Look," she said.

"What? Oh, there's a crack..." The wall was split by a crevice, about two hand spans wide.

Jonat said, "Hold this. And be quiet." She gave me the jug and wriggled through the crack.

Her hand came back through, gesturing, and I, bemused, put the jug in it.

"Well, come on!" she whispered harshly.

I writhed after her in the gritty sand, scraping my back against the broken edge.

I emerged from the wall, the first time I had left the precinct without supervision since the moment I arrived, to find myself in a narrow space between it and the statue's base. The moonlight couldn't reach back here, but to either side I could see the bare sand outside the precinct and the gleaming weapons of the guards.

Something pale fluttered in the dark – Jonat's arm, beckoning. There was a crack in the statue, too, bigger than the one in the wall, and she was inside it.

I hesitated, scared, wondering what she had done, what she wanted. The dogs were, briefly, quiet. The night wind whispered across the sand, and one of the guards shifted his stance. I scurried for the hole in the statue, in case he should turn and see me, and tell Hap-Canae that I was outside the walls.

Jonat lit a lamp. There was a tinder-box; how long had she been coming here? She stared at me in the flickering light, her eyes huge wells of darkness. "It's hollow," she said, as the light danced on the inside of the statue. "I think all of them are."

"How did you find it?"

She just shrugged. "I wanted somewhere..."

"Doesn't Aka-Tete lock you in at night?"

She snorted. "I was living on the street when I was Chosen. I learned to get round a lock like that before I was ten years old."

I brushed the inside of the statue with my fingers. "This is strange. We're outside, but we're still... inside."

"Yes." *She poured the wine.* "Well," *she said,* "what do you think's going on?"

"What do you mean?"

"You're not stupid. Not that stupid."

"Oh, thanks a lot."

"When we went out fighting... how many priestesses did you see on the battlefield?"

"I wasn't really looking, I was too busy. Anyway, how would you tell? They'd hardly fight in their official robes."

"Have you ever seen a priestess of Babaska fight? Or seen one whore?"

"Well, hardly. I mean I've hardly even seen one."

"And why's that?"

"How do I know?"

"You're going to be one, aren't you? Why haven't you asked?"

"We're the Chosen," *I said.*

"Chosen by who, though?"

I glanced at the wine-jug, wondering how much she'd had.

"I'm not drunk," *she said.* "We weren't chosen by her, were we? Why didn't the Avatar of Babaska choose us herself? None of us have ever even seen her."

"I think she waits," *I said.* "I've been thinking about it." *I sipped the wine, which tasted of spice and iron.* "See, I think Babaska's the strongest of them all. I mean," *I looked up, at the hollow inside of Aka-Tete's statue, and lowered my voice even more as though he could hear me.* "She's the best, isn't she?"

"What do you mean, the best?"

"Babaska's goddess of all the good stuff. The fighting and the sensual arts. She gets to have more fun than anyone, and so does her Avatar. What, you think there's better?"

"Death's stronger. Death's stronger than anyone." *I might have expected her to leap to Aka-Tete's defence, but she said it in a flat, chilly little voice.* "But you're right," *she said, to my surprise.* "Babaska's different. Different from all the others." She shrugged. "She's... I don't know. I don't think the others like people much."

"Hap-Canae likes people!"

"He likes people to like him."

Something about that stabbed me. I yanked the subject back to Babaska. "I saw an old scroll, about Babaska." It had stuck, the way anything with rhythm or rhyme tended to do. "'And with her sword shall cut the way to power; true godhead comes only with blade and flower.'"

Shadows chased each other across Jonat's face. "True godhead?"

"Yes."

"So what's false godhead?"

"I don't know. It's just an old rhyme. But the other Avatars are still doing Babaska's bidding, aren't they? They're choosing priestesses to serve her. I think they try and pick people who'll please her. And Babaska waits until we've had our training and then she picks the best ones herself to be priestesses."

"So when did she come and pick the others? In the night? Why? Babaska's not a night goddess. Wouldn't it make more sense to Choose us herself from the start? You'd think she'd have come to see us, if only to make sure we were getting proper training. What if we're picked and it's all been done wrong?"

"Oh, you worry too much." She was saying things I'd only thought, and I was frightened.

"Have you family?"

"Bag-child."

"I never knew mine. Velance was a bag-child too, did you know? And Renavir and Shanket. No family, anyone."

"All of them? So it's true the gods can Choose anyone, then. I always thought you had to be rich."

"Are you trying to be stupid? None of us with people back home expecting an influential priestess to help them out, get *their goods bought by the temples, get them favours. No-one to worry if we never come home. Why do you think that is?"*

"I don't know." I thought about telling her what I'd seen, in the tent after the battle. But I was scared, scared all the way to my bones. "Well, once we're priestesses, we're certain to meet Babaska's Avatar. We can ask her all these things, surely?"

"Yes," she said, with a thin, bitter smile in the darkness, "once we're priestesses."

The words dropped into me like stones in a well, echoing cold. And I ran from the meaning that followed them down. "I'm going to practice," I said.

"In the middle of the night?" Jonat shrugged. "Go on, then." She swallowed the rest of the wine down at a gulp. I remember her fingers were so tight on the cup that her knuckles stood out like little skulls.

I dived back through the hole in the wall, back into the precinct, and ran to the empty practice room, where I drilled until I was exhausted, until my limbs burned. Staggering, I walked back to my room.

Something landed on my bare arm as I passed the window; I thought it was a spider-thread at first.

It wasn't. It was a long, silver hair that glowed with its own lunar shimmer.

Shakanti.

Had she opened my door? Had she opened Jonat's, too? Why?

Did she want us to get into trouble, without anyone knowing she'd 'interfered'?

I stood shuddering in the silent temple, and hauled on the door myself, until it locked again.

Despite my exhaustion, I lay awake the rest of the night, listening to the maddened dogs barking at the indifferent moon.

Two nights later, death prowled the corridors. I saw several bodies being carried across the courtyard. And next morning

Aka-Tete hunched on the roof of his temple in his vulture aspect, the dark reek of death spilling from his feathers, and Jonat was nowhere to be found. They said she had gone to the temple of Broseid, far to the North; a cold place to send a desert girl.

CHAPTER
SEVENTEEN

PREVIOUS MET ME at the door of the Lantern with a grin. "You'll never guess," she said.

"What?"

"We had a delivery. From the Vessels, no less."

"What? What was it?"

"Money."

"You're joking."

"Nope; it's in your office. There's a note, too."

"Did Laney check it?"

"Babylon, come on. Of *course* she checked it. And she says it's fine; it's money. And paper and ink. And a bag. No curse, no dodgy spells, nothing she can find."

"What in all the hells are they giving us *money* for? Do they think they can *buy* souls, or what?"

"You could just read the note and find out."

I took the stairs fast, and there it was, sitting on the table in my office. A bleached linen bag. Well, of course, they'd hardly go in for velvet and embroidery. And a note, neatly folded, and sealed with blue wax; or at least, formerly sealed. Laney, or someone, had opened it – to check whether the seal would do something nasty when broken, for one thing, and for another because they're my crew, and nosy as pigs after truffles.

'The High Council of the Vessels of Purity of Scalentine have been given to understand that their actions may have been seen as intended to cause the disruption of business and might have been considered to be an infringement of Scalentine's laws. While the Vessels of Purity in no way condone the encouragement of sin, the Order has always chosen to site its temples where the laws of the land do not directly conflict with the Rules of the Order, and therefore we neither condone nor encourage the breaking of any law. In regard of which we send this coin, believed to be an adequate recompense for any loss that may have resulted from any misunderstandings.'

A masterpiece of maybes, that was. It could have been written by a lawyer. Perhaps it was.

I tipped the coin out onto the table. It was pretty close to what we'd have made in the hours we'd lost while the Vessels hung about outside, on a normal day. How had they found *that* out? Who'd done the research?

And never mind how, *why?* Had the Chief gone and talked to them after all? They weren't admitting anything; they *very carefully* weren't admitting a single thing. But something had put the wind up their tails all right.

I scooped the coins back into the bag, put it in the cupboard in my office, and went to my room to have a think.

THE NEXT THING I knew, there was whispering outside the door. I sat up and groaned. I hadn't meant to doze off. "Who's there?"

Laney poked her head around the door. "There's someone to see you."

I sat up, holding my head. The pain felt like a hangover, which was hardly fair since I hadn't had a serious drink in days. "Who?"

"Not a client, I don't think. Sit still." Laney put her narrow, cool hands either side of my head, the silk of her sleeves brushing against my hair, and I felt a tingling through her fingers. I got a brief vision of a stream running through a forest, tumbling down between mossy, water-glittering rocks, the brilliant blue flash of some bird flicking down to the water. Then it was gone, and my headache with it.

"That's better. Thanks, Laney. So who's our visitor?"

"I don't know. They're wearing a deglamour."

A deglamour is the opposite of a charisma glamour. Makes anyone's glance sort of slide over you, without pausing. Not cheap, and something the militia are constantly trying to get outlawed. They weren't unknown among rich clients who preferred discretion, but since it was getting close to Twomoon I strapped the sword on before I went down, and signalled Laney to hang about, just in case.

The visitor was standing just outside the main door, wearing a great hooded cape – deep blue, the lining crimson. Previous, hand on hilt, was between them and the entrance, not in an aggressive stance, just a ready one. She glanced at me.

"Take the deglamour off, if you please," I said.

The visitor turned so their face was hidden from Previous and tipped back their hood. The glamour dissipated.

It was Clariel, from the Lodestone.

I recovered my balance. She must have her own reasons for not wanting to be seen coming here. Clariel had reasons for everything. "S'all right, Previous. Stay on the door, I know this one. Come in, then." Clariel put her hood back up, and I led her through to the Little Parlour. "Drink?"

She waved a hand, as though a fly were buzzing round her – not that I think one would dare. "No. I can't stay."

I was briefly distracted by wondering whether the cape had slits cut for her wings, or what; I'd never seen her in outdoor gear. I don't think I'd ever seen her outside the Lodestone, come to that. Her face was the same calm, pure-cut cameo as ever. But under the cape I could see her wings shifting constantly. The sound of feathers against satin lining made an odd, jagged whispering.

"So. You have some information for me?" I said.

"What?"

"I assume that's why you're here."

"Yes," she said, fixing her gaze on a painting of a basket of cherries. It wasn't a great painting, but I liked it. Clariel, however, was staring at it as though it contained the secret of the ages.

"Clariel, is everything all right?" This was *not* a question I expected to be asking. If anyone ever gave the impression of being utterly in control of their personal universe, it was Clariel.

She kept looking at the painting. "Babylon, you understand, I have a business to run. I depend on the goodwill of my clients and those they speak to."

"I thought you depended on providing the best food in Scalentine."

She shook her head. "Never mind. The point is that I may have some information for you, but it is essential, you understand, that no-one, *no-one*, knows it came from me."

"I'm not a total blabbermouth, Clariel. For the All's sake, if you wanted to pass something on that secretly, why come here yourself? Don't you trust your staff?" But I knew the answer to that. Clariel's staff were just that, staff. Not crew, like my lot, not friends. She paid them, they did their jobs. If someone made a better offer, or they couldn't take the pace, they left.

Why she hadn't got a message to me, though, asking me to come to her...

"If it *should* come out that I was here," she said, "I came to get a recipe. Flower's skills are well known."

I tried to hide a smile. So she didn't want anyone to think she'd come here for the skills the house was really well-known for.

"All right, I'll bite. Give. What is this so-dangerous information?"

"Not dangerous, that I know of. Merely *awkward*. I have heard something about a girl who has gone missing. A very important girl."

I wasn't going to let Clariel think I was that easy to get round. "A thousand girls go missing all the time, across the Planes. What makes you think it's the one I'm looking for?"

"The fact that a number of people are seeking her with great eagerness, including her family. The fact that they seem to believe she disappeared *here,* at the same time that the Avatars from Tiresana arrived..."

The room fizzed, darkened. Everything started to spin away. I could hear Clariel still speaking, but I had no idea what she was saying. I rested one hand on the back of the nearest chair, gripped it until my fingers hurt. *I'd known. I'd known as soon as I'd seen the child's drawing on the wall.*

I could *not* pass out. If Clariel picked up on my reaction, if *that* information made its way back to the wrong ears, I'd be dead, or worse.

I curled my free hand so my nails dug into my palm. *They're here; they're here, in Scalentine. Keep your wits about you, Babylon. You need them. Lose it now and you're a long way worse than dead.*

"...so you see, her family have a great deal of influence. If they find out that I was talking to you – indeed, to anyone..."

"I understand." My voice sounded odd to me, but Clariel didn't seem to notice. Just as well for me she was so distracted at the thought of losing business.

I had to hear this. I dragged up every rag of concentration I possessed. "Run it by me again, Clariel. Then we're done."

"Oh for the All's sake, Babylon. Very well. Members of two of the high families of Incandress dined at the Lodestone. I overheard a fragment of their conversation. The girl is the daughter of one of them, and affianced to the other. She has eloped. They are anxious, *extremely anxious*, to get her back."

"So I should hope."

"Specifically, they are anxious to retrieve her before Twomoon."

"Yes, so I'd heard. But why before Twomoon? Don't tell me she's a were."

"Not that I could gather. But Twomoon on Scalentine reflects a time of change on Incandress, and elsewhere. It is a syzygy. You know how these things work."

Well, no, I don't. I'm not convinced anyone does, however many warlocks with a mouthful of measurements try and tell you otherwise.

My mind was running away with irrelevancies, trying to think about anything except the words 'Avatars' and 'Tiresana.' I *had* to concentrate. "So why Twomoon? They're not just worried about her for her own sake?"

"I did not get that impression. Nor does it seem to be a matter of mere... preservation of virtue." She ruffled her wings with distaste.

"If the poor kid's been taken by a pimp, it's somewhat late to worry about that, unless they're keeping her as a special treat for some bastard." I saw Clariel's face go slightly more rigid, but I was too thrown to worry much about her sensibilities at the moment. "So, what *are* they worried about?"

"It wasn't clear. They were talking among themselves, greatly agitated. They seemed to be in accord that the daughter must be retrieved, and *married,* before the 'becoming time.' Which, as I say, appears to coincide with Twomoon. Possibly. My knowledge of Incandrese is imperfect."

Typical. Clariel had a working knowledge of a ridiculous number of languages. Well, I guess it goes with the territory. Ordering in a restaurant's more complicated than in a brothel; you can't rely on sign language so much.

I tried to wrench my thoughts into enough order to run through what she'd said. So far it pretty much matched what I'd heard from Fain. "None of this helps me find her," I said.

Her eyebrows snapped down like two spears at the throw. "Babylon, I came here at some personal inconvenience to tell you this and you appear not to have been listening at all."

"I'm listening. Tell me, Clariel."

She sighed with impatience. "They talked... I'm not certain. I heard a word like 'revival,' or 'resurgence.' Something from the past. A dead past that should stay dead."

That's the problem with the past. Too often, it doesn't.

"Nothing else?"

"No. Except that the families were united in their desire to get the girl back. There were no recriminations, no arguments. Both families seemed... frightened."

"That's weird."

"Indeed." Clariel seemed to have regained all her equilibrium. She cocked her head as the great clock in the square began its run-up to the fifth hour; a rising shimmer of notes. "I must go. You will send Flower to me?"

I still had enough of my wits about me not to be outplayed. "I'll send the recipe. You get Flower to show you how to do it *if* your information helps me find the girl."

Something crossed her face that might almost, if you were feeling generous, be a smile. "Very well." She touched the ornament at her throat and the deglamour spread over her again, rendering her dull, normal, unrecognisable. She reached out a hand to me, and I shook it.

As soon as she had gone I dropped into the nearest chair. I felt sick. My hands were freezing. I wondered if Clariel had noticed. Hers were smooth, cool. Marble hands.

I SAT IN the wingback chair by the window of my room. I could see down the street to the town square, and the clock. *They're here.* I watched the interlocking wheels tell their jewelled minutes; the circles that showed the planes moving almost imperceptibly into alignment as the syzygy grew closer. *The Avatars are here, on Scalentine.* It was still afternoon, but dropping to dark; the lamplighter was doing his rounds, the town square lights coming on in pools of warm yellow. The two moons were up, their light falling where the last of the day and the first of the lanterns didn't reach, casting mauve and green shadows.

In the shadows at the corner just before Goldencat Street opens onto the square, I thought I caught a flicker of movement, smoke-grey, skull-white. Something tall and faintly birdlike; it gave me a grue. I peered, trying to focus. There was a yell to my left, some drunk being thrown out of the Sailor's Last Hope, the tavern just down the street, and when I looked back to the square, the pale figure had gone. Maybe it had never been there; just a fear, or a memory.

Tiresans don't leave. Even, especially, Avatars. Whatever they want, they want it a lot.

I settled back in my chair and looked out at the moons.

A room, familiar, crowded with people. Walls of warm creamy stone painted with hundreds of small, brilliant figures of people, trees, birds, beasts, doubling one crowd with another. The floor of polished red granite glimmering in the light of torches. The slow solemn chant, the slap of sandaled feet and the hush of robes.

I was moving with the others, towards the inner doorway. I wanted to back away, to run, to scream, but I couldn't. My feet kept moving forward. I looked down to see I was holding a cup carved of some deep green stone veined with glimmers of gold. I knew that if I got through the inner doorway and they noticed the cup, it would be smashed, but I couldn't make my feet stop moving forward.

I realised Glinchen was next to me in the procession, holding an infant Barraklé, wrapped up in white gauze, in hir arms.

"What are you doing here?" I said.

"They've promised to help me," Glinchen said. Ze held out the infant. "This one's going to be the next *dinan-bathai*."

A fold of cloth fell from the infant's face, revealing a twisted, furious gargoyle. It began to cry in great whooping wails, and soon they would hear us, and take the cup.

"Make it be quiet!" I pleaded.

"I can't," Glinchen said. "It's too late for that."

People were turning towards the noise. Any minute now they would see me.

I woke with my heart crashing against my ribcage and sat straight up in the chair, panting, looking frantically all around me. I was in my familiar, beloved room in the Red Lantern, with its wide bed and deep rose curtains. It was dark, the moonlight flooding in on my face.

They say you shouldn't sleep in the moonlight, especially not on Twomoon. They say the dreams can drive you mad.

The wailing I'd heard was a fading drunken song from somewhere down the road. My neck hurt from sleeping in the chair. I got up and stumbled back towards the bed, my mind spinning like a child's painted top, a blur of colours.

Then like a top, as it began to slow, something, a pattern, started to emerge. Kittack. The Barraklé and their *dinan-bathai,* the warrior beasts created in times of need. The little statue in the wall-niche in Kittack's room, with the yellow chips for eyes. The One who is Both, the one who was the best of the Kay-ebakat; the original, single race, before Ikinchli and Gudain. Enthemmerlee, and her golden eyes.

I looked down at my hands, which had held the green and gold cup in my dream. In Kittack's legend, the last of the Kay-ebakat had been buried with a cup.

Cups turn up often in legends across the planes. Sometimes they represent the female part, or the womb. A cup that must be filled, or stay empty.

Among the Barraklé, the *dinan-bathai* could only be created from a virgin.

Enthemmerlee's people were damn determined to have her wedded, bedded, and safe. She was that unique thing, a yellow-eyed Gudain. Were the Kay-ebakat more than a legend? Was *that* what Enthemmerlee's people feared; that, left virgin, she would change with the moons, that she would become living, physical proof that the Gudain and the Ikinchli were once one people?

I was flailing in the dark, I knew absolutely nothing for certain, but it certainly sounded like the Gudain believed it. Kittack, practical creature that he was, might not, but maybe his political friends among the Ikinchli believed it too.

Was Fain right, had she been kidnapped by Ikinchli? To keep her virgin until the change happened, so she could be paraded as proof? Used as a symbol?

I knew about that. It seldom ended well.

Why the Gudain hadn't just had the poor child bedded themselves, with or without her consent, I didn't know; the upper classes weren't usually too fussy about what their daughters thought. Possibly I had got the whole thing arse-uppards and was making a great big fancy from nothing but a runaway girl who didn't fancy the man her parents had chosen. Which still meant she needed help.

But how the hells was I going to find her? Fain had asked me because I could talk to the people who wouldn't talk to the militia. But if she hadn't disappeared among the street-girls, who did that leave me to ask, except the Ikinchli? The only one I knew was Kittack, and he knew nothing and had no desire to get involved. And who was I to blame him for that?

I had to go back to Fain. But if I was going to talk to the man again, I needed a little protection.

I went to find Laney.

"I DON'T LIKE these kind of things," Laney said, frowning, while she chopped herbs with eye-watering speed and shook drops from bottles with a snap of her wrist.

"Nor do I. I'm not planning on using it unless it's an emergency."

"You're expecting one?"

"Maybe."

She gave me one of those looks, like being jabbed with emerald spears. "You know, Babylon, if you don't tell me what's going on soon, I'm going to get *annoyed*."

"Laney, you know what's going on. Fain's asked me to look for this girl. I need to be able to talk to him without losing my head."

"And that's *all* you're worried about?"

I sighed. "No. I'm worried about the girl who was killed. I'm worried about the Vessels. I'm worried that I'm no closer to finding Enthemmerlee, and if I *don't,* it could mean bad trouble for a lot of people, not just her."

Laney sniffed, and thrust a small glass stopper with unnecessary force into the neck of a bottle no bigger than the top joint of my thumb. "There," she said. "A preventative against lust. And by the way, I know how to make a truth potion, too. Or I could make you swear a Fey oath to tell me what's going on. I know you know one. I taught it to you."

"Laney..."

Fey oaths are a damn sight scarier than truth potions. Once you've sworn one, it will get itself fulfilled, one way or another, unless the swearer's dead, and sometimes even then. They work here on Scalentine, too.

Laney had indeed taught me one, in case I ever needed it, but she'd never threatened to make me swear it myself, in all the time we'd known each other – she must be seriously worried. I would have to tell the crew *something,* and soon.

Part of me still hoped that whatever had brought the thrice-damned Avatars here would take them away again, without effort on my part. But that sort of attitude hadn't got my taxes paid.

"Babylon!" Essie called. "Visitor!"

I really wasn't sure I wanted another one. The only person I really wanted to see right now was the Chief, and I didn't think that was going to happen.

TIRESANA

I DIDN'T SLEEP much, the next few nights. I told myself it was the heat. Looking out of my window, I saw Renavir standing with Shakanti in the empty precinct; Shakanti was stroking Renavir's hair, and Renavir leaned against her like a dog. There was something wrong, something horribly wrong, and I didn't know what.

I saw Renavir in the corridor the next day; she looked straight through me, at some terrible ecstatic vision. Her arms were scored with cuts, although we hadn't had fight-training for days. I tried to say her name, but my throat closed.

Two nights later the tide rose, out of season, drowning people and crops, and the moon seemed to shudder in the burning air, and every dog for miles around howled and wailed the night through. I heard dreadful sounds, a voice I was sure was Shakanti, shrieking with fury.

The next morning Meisheté came to my door; she brought food, and told me, looking me up and down in a measuring way, that Renavir was gone. The shadows around her eyes were sharply defined, as though brushed in with paint. "Eat up," she said, brisk and forceful. I had a million questions, but I was locked in silence, afraid to ask them, afraid of the answers.

I picked at the food and thought about Renavir, with her little pale face and endlessly restless bony hands; I tried to imagine her running a temple, dealing with supplicants and

*corn-merchants and acolytes, and the image wouldn't coalesce
in my head.*

*I waited in my room, looking out at the inner precinct where a
few cranes bobbed and pecked. Faintly, I could hear the sounds
of life in the Outer Precinct, voices carried on the hot still air.
Why was the inner precinct empty?*

*For hours, no-one came to fetch me. There were no lessons
anymore.*

*I would have killed to see a friendly face. Radan, Sesh, Kyrl.
Suddenly I longed to be going out with the caravans, where the
biggest mystery was how a sandmule managed to get its own
harness in such a tangle you had to cut the leather to get it out,
and the biggest problem was how to avoid being bitten while
you were at it.*

*I fell asleep, having nothing else to do, and woke with a gasp
from ugly, heat-thick dreams of wandering through tunnels of
sand, to see Hap-Canae standing in the doorway of my room.*

"Wake up, child," he said. "This is your day."

*Behind him was the Avatar Meisheté in her aspect as a crone,
her little black eyes like chips of obsidian in their wrinkled beds,
the butterfly mask still clearly marked but riven with deep lines;
the marker of pregnancy somehow obscene on such an aged face.*

*"Go with Meisheté," Hap-Canae said. "You need to be
prepared."*

"What? What's happening?"

"All will be explained soon. Go, go."

*Meisheté started to walk away down the corridor, without
waiting for me to get to my feet. I dragged a robe around me
and ran after her.*

*"Prepared for what? Am I to be a priestess? Is that where
we're going?"*

*She turned then and looked at me, with a sort of weary
patience. "If you are going to fulfil the role for which you have
been Chosen, you must learn to comport yourself with dignity,
and with strength, and not chatter like a silly girl."*

We reached a room I'd never been in before, full of heavy wooden chests and robe-stands and pots of kohl and eye paint. Meisheté yanked a comb through my hair and dressed me, briskly, in a white gauze undergown and a robe of crimson silk so heavily embroidered with gold and jewels that it weighed like chain mail. She pinned up my hair with jewelled combs, and strapped gilded sandals on my feet.

I kept quiet, and let her pull me about like a small child being dressed for a festival day.

I was thinking as fast as I could. Was this how it had been for all the other girls? Perhaps the Avatar of Babaska herself would be here at last, to take me to my new posting. Could I beg her to let me stay here, to work in this temple? I could say that having been here for so many months I had learned about the temple and its district and would be a perfect High Priestess for it; it was rubbish, of course, what did I know, outside my own little world? I had never spoken with the current High Priestess, and knew almost nothing of the duties she performed.

Not that it mattered, in the end.

I entered the room where all the Avatars were waiting, and it was like seeing Hap-Canae for the first time all over again, only more so. Meeting one Avatar, you can feel the power in them; it's a little like standing in front of an open oven. A room full of them was like standing in the desert sun.

I searched for Hap-Canae, and he smiled at me. He seemed happy, and my heart calmed a little.

I glimpsed Shakanti's face and looked away in a hurry, because it was a glaring, screaming skull.

Hap-Canae came forward and took me by the hand, just like that first time. "Child," he said, "a great destiny is to be yours. You are to become the next Avatar of the Goddess Babaska."

I simply didn't understand. I couldn't speak, I was so confused.

So Hap-Canae spelled it out, or as much of it as they decided I should know.

Avatars weren't divine beings, god-like, created from the stuff of gods, as we had been told and taught, and had believed without question all our lives.

They were created from the stuff of men. Every single one of them had once been entirely human.

And the Avatar of Babaska was missing. Gone. That was why we had been Chosen, that was why we had had to learn and to be tested in the arenas of fighting and seduction, to see which of us was best suited to take her place. "The others were suited only to be her priestesses. You are the one who has been chosen to be her Avatar."

"But what happened to the last one?" I said. "Where did she go?"

"She proved unworthy of the role," Shakanti said. "Let us hope you are more suitable."

"It was a great sorrow to us," Hap-Canae said.

I looked around me. Meisheté, the crone. Rohikanta with his running-water hair and beard and his webbed feet and the ugly great Messehwhy always at his side. Aka-Tete, who even in his human form had the claws of a vulture, and the smell of death he wore like a cloak.

"Will I change?" I said. "Will I be..."

"You've seen the paintings of her," Hap-Canae said. "In her aspect of desire, or her aspect of war, Babaska is always a woman. She has a scar, of course. She flung herself in front of a spear to protect one of her lovers." He stroked my cheek. "You will become even more beautiful. And as to the scar – if you were flawless, how could mere men look on you and not go mad?"

I told myself I believed him. I wanted to, after all.

CHAPTER
EIGHTEEN

As I HEADED for the hall I stopped, wondering, for a horrible, paralysing moment if my visitor was Hap-Canae. Or Shakanti, which might be worse. *Stupid*, I told myself fiercely. If they were looking for me, they wouldn't just *knock*.

But it was Kittack. He was pacing the hall, his tail twitching

"Kittack? What's happened? Are you all right?"

"Yes, yes, fine, not to worry," he said, waving a hand at me. "We go talk, okay?"

"Yes, right, come up." He didn't bound up the stairs like he normally did, eager to get to business, but plodded after me, his tail flicking at the banisters. "What is it?" I said, pulling the door of my room shut. "You don't look like you're here for bouncy."

"After much excellent bouncy already today? Ask younger lizard, hey?" But the grin fell off his face almost as soon as it appeared. "Is damfool politics. Is big stupidness and I probably get head kicked in."

"What do you mean, Kittack?"

"I mean is maybe know someone might know where is Gudain girl, or maybe help you find."

"Kittack, that's wonderful!"

He shrugged. "No. Is political. Big trouble for everybody. But maybe sometimes got to deal with trouble, even when you think have left it behind, goodbye. Been long time since the ancestor caves, long time since I leave Incandress, but me, I am still Ikinchli. Don't want everyone back home get head broken because of political stupids. You come?"

"Come where?"

"Meet with talky-talky politicals, maybe know where girl is."

"Of course I'll come."

"You bring some friends, hey? Is political. Is get maybe excitable."

"Right you are."

Cruel was on the landing. "Need some help?" she said, smiling at Kittack, who just nodded instead of, as usual, pretend to hide behind me when he saw her. She frowned. "What's up?"

"I need to go have a word with some people. Should be back soon."

"We need to know where you're going?"

I looked at Kittack. He shrugged. "Witchspring Street, first, after that, I don't know."

"Well, be careful," Cruel said. "Oh, Babylon, can I borrow your cloak? That little sod Jivrais has gone off with mine again. Laney offered me hers but it's *pink*. I don't *do* pink."

"It's on the banister," I said. It's a little short on me, so it would be about right on Cruel, especially with the heels she was wearing. "Cruel, how *do* you walk in those things?"

She gave that cool smile. "Practice. Whatever you're up to, good luck."

I took Previous and Bliss. I'd have taken Ireq, but he'd eaten something that disagreed with him and was in his room, groaning over a bowl. His fault, as Flower said smugly, for eating outside the Lantern.

Bliss still had his moonlit pallor, but looked slightly more solid than usual, and was going through one of his more alert phases. I didn't know if we were actually going where the girl was, but if we met someone who'd got close to her, there was a chance Bliss could pick up her trail. Besides, I clung to the hope that giving him tracking work when he was capable of it, reminding him of his old life, might counteract the effect of Fading, pull him back to himself, at least a little.

As we walked up the street I noticed Previous was wearing new bracers. They gleamed on her forearms, the first bit of new armour I'd seen her with in years. They looked expensive, too; delicately engraved with leafy branches and twining beasts. They were a tiny bit long for her: she'd have to have the ends shortened, or they'd chafe the backs of her hands.

"Nice," I said.

She tugged at a buckle, trying not to grin. "Present," she said.

"Frithlit?"

"Mmm."

If she was wearing them even though they didn't quite fit, it must be love. I knew a good armourer where she could have them shortened, but it might be tactless to mention it.

Kittack took us to the north of the city, into a district where the Ikinchli had bunched together. The sound of running water and wafts of steam trickled from several windows; the scent of fresh fish, mingled with a clean green-water smell. We passed a statue that I recognised, although this one was considerably bigger than the one in Kittack's room, a good head taller than me. It was of deep red polished stone, carved with a kind of rough grace; it had an Ikinchli's long jaw and flattened nose, but the high forehead of the Gudain. Its yellow eyes, with their long pupils, stared across the street at a window hung with iron pans.

The door of the house Kittack took me to was half off its hinges, sagging into the street; the windows were broken, stuffed with rags. I remembered the dead girl and had a moment of chilly doubt.

I caught a flicker of movement in the darkness behind the door. Kittack held up a hand and I stopped where I was while he went forward. There was a brief, chittering exchange of which I understood not a syllable. I could feel I was being watched; I hoped the locals were in a receptive mood. I've heard about Ikinchli slingshots; the best of them can take out a fly's eye with a pebble. One small rock aimed with enough accuracy and it's Goodnight Brain.

Eventually, when I'd had time to get very antsy indeed, I was beckoned forward. I turned to the others.

"Previous, Bliss, you stay out here. If you hear trouble, you know what to do."

A little light struggled past the cobwebs in the unbroken windows; a big stone tank, steaming gently, stood in the centre of the room. Two Ikinchli stood either side of it, one male, one female, statue-still. The male's cranial crest was up. Only their eyes moved. After they'd had a good look at me, the woman stepped forward. She had a slingshot, plus a couple of efficient-looking little knives at her hips. "What you know?" she said.

"Not much, and the rest is guessing. But I know that if this girl isn't found, it could mean a lot of trouble for Ikinchli back on Incandress."

"Why you care?"

I shrugged. "I don't like people getting punished for something that isn't their fault. But frankly? Mainly I'm worried about the girl. I want to find her and talk to her, to make sure she's safe and has some sort of choice about what she does next."

The Ikinchli woman exchanged a few words with Kittack, then turned back to me. "Why you so worried about girl?"

"I see a lot of young girls, on the run, scared stupid and prey to every lowlife on the street. You understand? I used to *be* one, but at least I had some training in looking after myself. I..." My breath caught in my throat, suddenly, surprising me. "I want..." The sound of desert dogs, yipping and whining. Jonat, lampflames dancing in her dark, terrified eyes.

I shook my head, hard. "I want to help her, if I can. Oh, also, I got paid to find her." I'd almost forgotten that part.

"Yes." She nodded at Kittack. "He say. How we know you find, you not take her straight to paymaster, hey?"

"Because she comes first. If I have to give the... paymaster his money back, then so be it." Right now, that was among my smaller worries.

The Ikinchli woman came right up to me, stared into my

eyes, and then sniffed at me, slowly, all over. I stood as still as I could. The other Ikinchli never moved except to blink.

She stood back. "We find her," she said, "you talk to her, you understand. Then, is decide."

For the first time the other Ikinchli moved, bursting out in a furious chatter. She spoke to him, pretty sharply by the sound of it, without taking her eyes off me.

"He says, you will not understand. He says, you will not believe. He says, you will betray us."

You will not believe. Believe what? That she really was the Itnunnacklish, the One who is Both? Had I been right?

"I say, we see. I say, I think we trust you, and maybe you be help to us. If we think you betray, we kill you. Yes?"

"Seems fair," I said. "What about my friends?"

"You bring them, maybe they get killed. You tell them this."

"I think they know, but yes, I'll tell them."

"I am Rikkinet," she said. "You come with us."

TIRESANA

THEY GAVE ME *spiced wine and took me, bathed and scented and dressed with silk and flowers like a sacrificial goat, into the altar room.*

I'd never been there; I hadn't even known it existed. It was right at the centre of the temple, in a place no-one ever went. The floors were so thick with dust it puffed up around my feet as I walked, rising up in smoky curls and drifts. There were no guards, no acolytes. Just me and the Avatars.

Double doors, with carvings worn almost to invisibility. There was neither lock nor handle; no apparent means of opening the doors at all. But Hap-Canae read out words from a scroll. I don't know what the language was, but the words rang in my head as though cut from bronze.

Insiteth

Abea

Iatenteth

Hai ena

The floor hummed under my feet, and the doors swung open.

I'd expected a room lined with gold, at the very least, but this was just a plain box of a place, walled in great blocks of rough-cut sandstone.

There were no windows; the only light came from the window in the corridor.

In the centre was the altar. No carved and painted glory, this, just a chunk of iron-red rock, hacked into a rough cube. It looked so ancient it was as though it had been there before temples, before gods; as though it had been there first, and everything else had grown up around it.

There was nothing else in the room.

Silence, except for the shift of cloth, and the chink of jewellery, and the click of Aka-Tete tapping his nails against the skulls he wore around his waist.

They told me to put my hands on the altar. There were hollows there, too big for my hands. Above them, in the centre, a round indentation, the size of a copper coin. I looked at it, and my mind made some curious sort of weaving, and I thought of the times I'd been casually tipped just such a coin, when I was with the caravans. Of how enough of them to clink in my pouch had been riches.

That had been Ebi. If I put my hands on that altar, I should never be Ebi again.

I looked at Hap-Canae, and he smiled at me.

So I put my hands on the rock.

I shut my eyes. It was like looking down a long, dark tunnel, with a tiny light at the end. In the tunnel were voices, whispering; some near, some so far away that my mind shrieked at the distance.

I heard one voice getting clearer, closer; a woman's voice. But there were only fragments. She spoke my name, Ebi, then I felt her watching me, so clearly that I turned my head to look for her, and then the light wasn't at the end of the tunnel anymore, it was rushing towards me, bigger and bigger, huge.

It hit.

It was like having a firebolt the size of a city go through me. It roared, smashed everything apart, brain, body, pulled it backwards through itself and rammed it together again. By the All, it was incredible. I felt huge. As big as the world and flaring with light. I felt... magnificent. I felt I could stride across worlds like stepping-stones.

My hands jerked free of the altar.

I was all flesh and fire. I wanted to fight and I wanted to fuck and I didn't know which to do first. I was laughing with the sheer force of it.

Hap-Canae took my hands. "Now you're one of us," he said.

I grabbed at him, trying to pull him down to the floor with me, not caring in the least that the others were there. He stood back out of reach, laughing, and Meisheté made me take some drink that doused me a little.

Once I was calmer, Hap-Canae took my hand and led me away.

My new rooms were ridiculously luxurious: silk and marble and gold. I hardly noticed, because there were weapons laid out, and the first thing I did was pick out a sword and a dagger. They were good, but not wonderful. I knew that in a way I hadn't before, and I decided I wanted weapons made to my hand. I told Hap-Canae and he laughed.

I caught a glimpse of the mirror, and went to it, and stared.

It was as though my old face had been an apprentice-piece, and the new one was the work of the master. I'd never been beautiful; striking, maybe, though at sixteen I'd not yet grown into a definite nose and a strong jaw. Now, even I could see I was beautiful. The scar was there, and I ran my fingers over it. It felt warmer than the rest of my skin; a little trail of heat.

I was taller, and broader, and had muscles I wouldn't earn for another ten years.

The next thing I did was pull Hap-Canae down onto the bed.

I'd never taken the initiative before, but he barely seemed surprised.

CHAPTER
NINETEEN

"YOU DON'T HAVE to come," I said to Kittack, who'd fallen in with us.

He shrugged. "Want to get a look at this girl everyone so crazy for."

I glanced at Rikkinet. She was moving ahead with that sleek Ikinchli glide. "Rikkinet, I think this girl... well, I think she may be the Itnunnacklish. Or at least, they believe she is."

"I know."

"You don't think so?"

"No. Me, I do not believe; is story to make happy little Ikinchli. But maybe she is Gudain who want to treat Ikinchli like people. Is novelty, yes?"

"It doesn't bother you, that someone would pretend?"

"Maybe she believe it too. Or not. If can change things by pretend to be old legend from past, why not? If works, is good."

Yeah, maybe – or maybe it would just get her torn apart by fanatics on one side or the other. Or both.

We went down into the docks, into a blind alley that ran behind a scruffy chandlery. There was a carving of a little fish on the wall; its grin looked too knowing for my liking.

Rikkinet had her weapons ready.

Previous and I did likewise. Whatever was on the other side of that wall, it might react badly to unexpected company.

Bliss doesn't carry a weapon, or at least, not for long. He always loses them somewhere. It gets expensive.

Rikkinet stood on tiptoe, and traced the outline of the carving with one long finger.

The fish seemed to grin more widely, and tilted silently upwards.

With only the faintest gritting noise, no more than might be made by a mouse crossing gravel, a section of the wall slid backwards.

I could hear running water, and smell dank stone and more than a hint of sewage. A little light fell through the opening, just enough to show ancient-looking paving, and a shimmer of water to the right.

Rikkinet lit a small lantern of pierced brass, and we followed its dancing glow into the darkness.

Once the door was shut behind us, my eyes began to adjust. The lamplight didn't reach far, but it showed us solid brick to our left, about ten feet of path ahead and, to the right, the satiny glimmer of running water; we were walking alongside a river, of sorts.

Sometimes we passed a crumbling archway. Some were open, tunnels beyond them running silent into the dark; others were blocked with ancient doors or a criss-cross of iron bars. Bliss moved ahead, humming, running his long pale fingers along the wall, sniffing the air, occasionally stopping and staring about.

There was no need for him to track, as it seemed Rikkinet knew where to take us, but it was good to see him looking so awake. Twomoon. A time of transformation, Darask Fain had said, and he was right. It's not just weres who feel it. I stroked the scar on my face, and wondered. If Enthemmerlee really was what they said she was, would she have begun to change? What would it feel like?

Rikkinet stopped and raised her hand, then disappeared.

I blinked.

She reappeared, and gestured. "This way."

When we got closer I could see what had happened. There

was another of those side tunnels, but it angled back into the wall, its entrance concealed by an outjut of brick that had been carefully designed to look like just another part of the wall until you were practically on top of it.

Perfect place for an ambush, in fact.

Previous gave me a questioning look, and I shrugged.

We followed Rikkinet down the tunnel.

The lamp burned steadily, but it seemed as though the darkness got thicker until you could feel it pressing around you, sucking at the light, wanting to make it gone. There was a deep chill striking up from the paving that the damp encouraged, and I began to wish I'd worn a warmer jerkin. All the Ikinchli, including Kittack, were wearing thick padded jackets and trousers.

If the girl really did have lizard in her makeup, I hoped she was sensibly dressed.

Rikkinet was moving faster – too fast. "Hey!" I hissed. "Hold up!"

She paused, and I caught up with her. She glanced over my shoulder and said, "That one. What is?"

She was looking at Bliss. I realised that he was shuddering like a man with a fever. Always pale, he was now so white he glowed, and his grey eyes had a peculiarly luminous cast.

"Bliss?" I said. "You all right? Man, you're freezing."

"Oh, yes," he said, "but it doesn't matter."

"I don't want you catching your death down here."

"I didn't think that was who we were hunting," he said, and grinned. "Don't worry about me, Babylon. It's good to be on a trail again. I feel..." – he held a pearl-pale hand out before him, and looked at it – "much more myself."

There was no sound except footfalls, breathing, and the lap and ripple of the river. The Ikinchli all moved whisper-quiet, but the rest of us couldn't match their stealth. What with the noise and the lamplight, if anyone was on watch they'd have plenty of warning we were coming.

Previous stumbled and said, "Oh. Ugh." Then she turned aside and threw up.

"Previous?"

She pointed. Lying on the paving was a fish, or something like one. It was a pallid pinkish-yellow and had no eyes; they weren't gone, it didn't even have a place for them. Its head was just a smooth glistening lump, gashed by a needle-toothed mouth.

"Previous? You all right?" I whispered. She wasn't normally the squeamish sort.

"Fine," she said, wiping her mouth.

I looked at her, wondering, but she was glaring at the dead fish, her mouth pulled down.

"Let's not go swimming," I muttered.

"Yeah, and I really fancied a dip," she said.

Kittack came over to see what we were looking at. "Cave fish," he said. "Been breeding in the dark for so many years, they don't got eyes. No use for them. No flavour to them, neither."

I could really have done without the thought of eating the thing, and so could Previous, from her expression.

Rikkinet was getting ahead again. I was glad to hurry after her and leave that poor blighted fish behind.

She held up her hand a moment later, and everyone stopped dead. She extinguished the lamp, and after being plunged in a darkness so absolute it felt like death, I could eventually make out the faintest glimmer of light ahead. It was too faint for me to see anything but a smudge.

Bliss came back towards me and I realised his eyes really *were* luminous; his pupils glowed yellow-green.

He gestured for me to bend down. "Up ahead," he whispered. "A fire. Several others, I think an Ikinchli, couple of humans, the rest I'm not sure of. Maybe five or six. There are more around, I can hear them, and smell them, keeping out of sight."

"Right," I said. "This is Rikkinet's show. We're not here to fight. We're here to talk to the girl. She's priority, and I don't want anyone hurt or even scared unless it's necessary. So let's try not to look like a bunch of throat-slitting mercenaries." I looked around. Previous, all scowl and battered armour, except for her fancy new bracers; Bliss, glow-eyed and shivering with some suppressed excitement. And me, of course. "Let's try quite *hard, all right?*"

As we got closer, we could hear voices. Sounded like an argument.

The fire threw bloody shadows on the crumbling brickwork. We were approaching the end of the path. A crude, or just very ancient, jetty poked a rotting finger out over the river. Behind it was a wall, with three arches. The centre one was occupied; crowded, in fact. The two either side appeared to be empty.

And there was Enthemmerlee, alive, looking utterly out of place in this dank, forgotten hole, her long fair hair gilded by firelight. She was standing between a male Ikinchli and another man who looked, to me, like a Gudain. Had he been the one she had met at the Hall of Mirrors?

There were a couple of people with their backs to us, silhouetted against the flames; one slight, one heavy, that was about all I could see.

"...paid enough," the Gudain was saying.

"People *looking* for you. This'n our jalla. Millies come, big-big trouble everybody."

"You say so many days, so much money," the Ikinchli said, his accent thickening with anger. "Now you say, not enough money, more, always more."

Bliss tilted his head towards one of the side rooms as we moved up, then skimmed away out of sight, quiet as smoke. From the side room came a skitter of feet on stone, and a scruffy individual with bad teeth and a tarnished gold scarf wrapped around his head appeared in front of us. "Who the hells are you?" A couple more appeared out of the shadows. They looked hard, nasty and well armed; but they also looked a bit glazed, and reeked of cloud. No wonder we'd managed to get within bowshot before they'd clocked us.

"Cap! We got comp'ny."

There was some incomprehensible language I'm pretty certain was obscene, and the figures by the fire turned around.

The dumpy human had pale, elaborately plaited blonde hair piled onto his head and gleaming with oil, a broken nose and a silk shirt that had probably been white, once, bulging open over a stomach like a pallid mushroom. The slight one was all in faded black; grey-furred and long-nosed with an unfortunate resemblance to a rat.

This was a ruffians' jalla if I'd ever seen one. What in all the hells were the Incandress lot doing here?

The Ikinchli and the Gudain had already moved protectively in front of the girl, and I saw the Ikinchli's hand come up, holding a sling. He was moving slow, but whether from caution or cold I wasn't sure.

Rikkinet stepped forward, made a strange, ducking, twisting movement with her head, and said something in the Ikinchli tongue. There was a brief but furious-sounding three-way argument between her, the other Ikinchli, and the young Gudain man, while the girl just watched.

"You shouldn't be here," said the pudgy type in the silk shirt. "Bad idea, come down here. Trespassing, is." He scowled at Rikkinet. "You ask for private, safe place, now you bring half the city down here. Is not so private."

"We don't want trouble," I said. "I want a conversation with Enthemmerlee, and then we'll be out of here. We're not millies, we're not looking to make any difficulties, and if this greasy little arsehole doesn't stop trying to creep up on me I'm going to slice him into chops and kidneys."

The greasy little arsehole in question drew back, muttering.

Pudgy gestured us to come forward. "Come to light. This all you?"

"As you see," I said. That being Previous, Kittack, and

Rikkinet. Bliss was out of sight, the All knew where. I hoped he could keep out of trouble.

Pudgy grinned, showing a mix of glitter and stumps where his teeth should be. "Tell you what. You pay good lucre, you have nice quiet talky-talky, then you be gone. We escort you out, all polite."

"No lucre," I said. "We didn't come for talky with you."

"Who are you, and why do you want to talk to me?" Enthemmerlee said. She had a low, clear voice, with a faint huskiness to it.

At least she spoke Lithan. That would make things easier. "That's a longish story," I said. "And requires privacy."

"Who are you working for?" said the Gudain.

"Well... That's a question. See, I *was* paid to find Enthemmerlee," I said. "But now I want to hear her side."

"Why should we believe you?" He was a young man, his Lithan well-educated but his voice quivering with nerves and anger. The girl, on the other hand, remained sublimely calm. I began to wonder if they'd drugged her. If that was the case I was getting her away from the bloody lot of them until she had a chance to make some decisions for herself.

Pudgy grinned at me, looking me up and down. "What say you me have our own private talky-talky, hey?"

"Maybe some other time," I said. "I need to talk to the girl. If you want I'll ask my friends to back off, and you... gentlemen... can do the same."

"Fine by me, we not want hear nothing," he said. "No politicals, us. More trouble than we's want. You give money. You talky-talky. We wait, you finish your business, you get gone. *All* you get gone."

The Gudain said, "We've already paid to stay here for another day!"

"Yeah well, you not say, so many people after you, all these come looky-looky. Maybe next time type we don't want see here, maybe is millies, maybe is business competitors, maybe all sorts unsavoury peoples come tramp around our private place, right? So original contract made on basis of undeclared factors, not so valid now, right?"

"We didn't know people were going to come looking for us!" the Gudain said.

"Could have taken good guess, no?"

"You have no..." He obviously couldn't come up with the word, in Lithan, and waved his arms furiously. "And I have to say I don't think much of your guards; they let these people walk right in here!"

Rikkinet muttered something under her breath. I hoped the remark wasn't going to get the young Gudain into more trouble than he could cope with, but Pudgy merely put his hand on his chest with a wounded air. "Good faith businessman, me. And you don't like my guards, we take them away." He gestured and the three guards began to back off. "You talk. We go over there, not listen."

I wouldn't have made any bets on that. Information is currency, and I suspected Pudgy wouldn't pass up the chance to know more about his paying guests. Though his so-called guards smelled of cloud, he didn't.

They swaggered past me. Pudgy blew me a kiss, which gave me an unrivalled opportunity to smell his breath. Man needed a better diet.

The Gudain glanced at the girl, looking worried. "This isn't..."

"It's all right, Malleay," she said. "I'm willing to listen."

"I'm not leaving you alone!"

"And why not?" I said. "Afraid of what she'll say?"

"How dare you!" Malleay might be a revolutionary type, but he had all the arrogance of someone who'd grown up a member of the ruling class. But he was young, and the way he stood – badly, off balance – and the way he kept fingering the dagger in his belt, told me he wasn't an experienced fighter. "Tell these people to go away!"

"Previous?" I said, "back off, if you would. Don't get lost and don't kill anyone if you can help it." She nodded, and walked away.

Kittack didn't move. He was looking at the girl, his head on one side.

"Kittack?"

He blinked. "Oh. Okay." He followed Previous, glancing over his shoulder every now and then.

"Tell me who you are," Enthemmerlee said. "And why you are looking for me."

"Will you talk to me alone?"

"Yes."

"Enthemmerlee..." the Gudain boy said.

She put a hand on his arm. It was a fragile hand, fine as bone china, and I noticed small, delicate webs at the base of her fingers. "Malleay."

There was another brief exchange, and then, reluctantly, looking frequently back at us, the three Ikinchli and the Gudain lad moved away, around the corner.

"Well," I said. "I thought you might be here against your will. Are you? Because if you are, I'll get you out. Somewhere safe."

Enthemmerlee smiled. "There is no need. They are my friends and fellow soldiers."

"You're sure."

"Yes. Who is the person who paid you to look for me?

I told her – leaving Fain's name out of it. Someone in power on Scalentine, I said, someone who was concerned about the way things could go on Incandress, and didn't want them to get worse. "I don't understand the details. I'm no politician. But for some reason there's worry here about what will happen if Incandress gets more unstable, and they think that if you aren't found, it will get bad. Reprisals against the Ikinchli, for one thing."

"I see. But this is not why you are here?"

"First," I said, "I thought you were just a girl who didn't want to marry the man they'd chosen for her, then I realised that some of them believe you're the... Itnunnacklish. The One who is Both. I don't know about that. But either way, I thought you might need help."

"And why would you do this? If you were to hide me, and get me away, you would not be paid, surely?"

"More to life than money," I said, despite a little crawling sensation in my abdomen when I thought of the debts hanging over my head. "And let's say I've a certain fellow-feeling for young girls in trouble."

"My family wished to use me to keep things as they are, yes. But these here with me want the same things I do."

"They're still treating you like a symbol. You're a person."

"But sometimes a person must be a symbol," she said. "You see, it is true. I am what they believe. I am the Itnunnacklish."

TIRESANA

Before I was allowed out they dinned into me how I was to behave now I was an Avatar, how I owed it to those who'd given me this opportunity, to do what they told me, how we were the foundations of all that held the land and the people together and that a single misstep could have terrible consequences.

"And no-one, no-one, is to know who you were," Hap-Canae told me. "The past is dead to us. It has to be."

"Why?" I had very unworthy reasons for asking, like wanting to show off to the other girls who had become priestesses, who had all got posts before me and no doubt thought I was a failure. Priestesses! I was an Avatar! *The thought that I might go back and terrify the life out of the bossy old cook at home, and make the master tremble that he had ever considered laying a hand on me, had crossed my mind, too.*

"Listen to me." Hap-Canae put both hands on my shoulders. He was as serious as I had ever seen him, wrapped in all the dignity of his office, looking the way he did when presiding at a major festival. "Tiresana is a plane whose gods have withdrawn from her. You understand?"

"But... but we still worship them. All the ceremonies are for the gods."

"Of course we worship them. But the ceremonies? They are for the people, who have no gods. We, the Avatars, are all that is left. Why do you think we took on this mantle? Do you

think it is easy, to be what we are? Our powers are greater than those of ordinary people, but they are limited. Tiresana is poor, and its people struggle. We are their hope. Without us, what would they look to? Who would they see, watching over them? Only a void. And that is a terrible thing." He sighed. "Believe me, one day you will understand. For now, be guided. Use your powers with care, do not exhaust them. You are young in them yet, and they will take time to grow. You cannot afford to make mistakes in public; to the people, you must be, always, an Avatar, and nothing else."

I was an Avatar. I could fight like a demon, without having to practice much, although I did pay for it eventually, in exhaustion; later and less heavily than a normal person, but pay I did.

Weapons could wound me, and they still hurt – I found that out after a particularly careless moment in practice, overexcited by my own newfound abilities – but I healed, within hours. I asked Hap-Canae about it.

"Oh, yes," he said. "We are very hard to kill, child. Not impossible, but even then, only by another Avatar."

It never occurred to me, then, to ask how he knew that.

When I was finally allowed to show my face, which they wouldn't let me do often, people went silent or cheered, paled, flung themselves down in front of me, wept at the sight of me or begged for my blessing.

I realized, after doing it purely by accident, that I could make someone fall madly in lust with a glance. I could make a woman who'd never known pleasure laugh aloud with delight in the arms of a callow boy – or a callow girl, for that matter – which gave me immense satisfaction, but wiped me out for days.

Hap-Canae scolded me for overdoing it. "Remember, we have limitations. It is a great sorrow to all of us. Think what we could do, if we had not such limits!"

"I could make everyone as happy as we are!" I said, stroking his hair. We were, of course, in bed.

"My sweet girl, how generous you are," he said, laughing. "We are seeking out knowledge, we have been seeking it for a long time. And one day we hope to have the capacity to do everything we wish to. Think what we could make of this land. Cities of gold and brass, cities of marble and jewels... oh, we could create such glories! One day, my child. One day, and you and I will ride in a barge made all of sunset clouds and drawn by dragons. Would that not be a marvel?"

"Oh, yes!"

I dreamed, one night, as I lay beside him. We flew in a chariot of sunset clouds, surrounded by glowing pink and gold. Yet the stuff of the clouds was sticky and damp, and clung to me like spiderweb. I realized Hap-Canae was spinning it out of his own body. We were flying high above the land; below us were the cities of gold and brass, the cities of marble and jewels. "Are they not magnificent?" Hap-Canae said.

In the way of dreams, I could see the cities in detail even though we were so high. The streets were full of tiny figures. They too were made of gold and brass, of marble and jewels; automata, mannequins. As we flew lower they all fell to their knees, in perfectly synchronized, perfectly meaningless worship.

"But they're not real," I said.

"They're as real as they need to be," Hap-Canae said, and then he was on top of me, inside me, the glowing stuff of the chariot still extruding from his skin, and I realized that he was drawing out my life, to make his cloudy chariot and his pretty mindless dolls.

I woke up in a gasping sweat, and told myself it was just a stupid dream.

But he'd miscalculated. They all had, and perhaps not for the first time.

Babaska of the double aspect; Babaska of war and love. I did more fighting once I became her Avatar. Once you've had someone knock aside the spear that was heading for your guts or stood back to back with them while you held off some maniac whose only perception of you was as something to be got through, you're connected, you have a bond. Yes, I was an Avatar; yes, human blades couldn't have killed me. They could have hurt me, of course – even Babaska herself bore a scar. But I'd fought before I became invulnerable, and the soldiers still fought alongside me the same way. It makes it harder to remember that you're supposed to be separate, superior, different.

As for sex... it's a sacrament, don't get me wrong. Always was, always will be. It's one of the most powerful forces there is. And misused, it's devastating.

But sex is also intimate, essentially fairly ridiculous and very, very human.

They couldn't keep me apart from people, as much as they'd have preferred to, because that wasn't how Babaska worked. The others might take human lovers, but they didn't talk to them; Babaska did. The others might appear at battles, but they didn't fight alongside the common soldiers; Babaska did. It was in the scrolls and the carvings, in everything about her legend.

And sometimes, when I stopped an enemy blade from gutting the soldier next to me, when I made someone cry out in pleasure, I thought I felt something. A sense of being watched, as I had been at the altar when I became an Avatar. It was neither friendly nor hostile; it was... assessing. And it felt as though it came from a very long way away.

I came to look for it, and was aware of a faint disappointment when it wasn't there.

I studied hard to be as much like Babaska as I could, to be a true Avatar; yet in doing so, I remained more human than an Avatar was ever supposed to be.

CHAPTER
TWENTY

I LOOKED AT Enthemmerlee, down there in the reeking dark. "Ah," I said.

"You do not believe me?"

"Does it matter?"

She looked thoughtful, then smiled again. It was an extraordinary smile, so sweet and open it should have looked childlike, but didn't. "No, it does not matter, but it is true, nonetheless."

"So why are you here?"

"It was necessary for me to stay out of the way, until the time of transformation."

"So you made a bargain with the sewer-crawlers who run this place, so you'd be out of sight? Am I right that you need to remain – how can I put this – 'untouched,' for the transformation to take place?"

"Untouched?" She blinked. "Oh, unmated, you mean?" She shook her head. "No, it is not a matter of virginity. If I remain virgin, according to what we have been able to discover, I will only die."

"Only?"

"It would be a waste," she said. "It has happened before, in the family bloodline; yellow-eyed girl children, not mated in time, through fear, or ignorance. If I mate only with a Gudain, then" – she gestured at herself – "this is what I remain. To become what

I can be, for the transformation to be complete, I must be mated, at the time of transformation, to two men; one Ikinchli, and one Gudain. You understand? Then it will happen."

I managed to close my mouth, after a moment. And opened it again. "That's why they were so eager to get you married."

"Yes."

"Why wait until Twomoon? Why didn't they just mate you off as soon as possible?"

"Because until then I will not be..." – for the first time, she blushed, a soft greenish glow in the firelight – "physically capable."

Well, she looked similar to a human, but Ikinchli had two cocks, after all. Who knew what was the case with Gudain, or indeed with her, who was neither one nor the other? I had no idea what was going on under her robe and didn't think it was the time to ask.

"You really want to do this?" I said. "To become something else?"

"I have thought very hard. As Itnunnacklish, I can do so much more for both my people than I ever could if I remain Gudain. The transformation will be hard, I know, and painful. I may die, even if everything is done correctly. But I have to take the chance."

I said, "You know, being turned into an image... well, it doesn't always work out the way you expect. Trust me, I know this."

"Symbols have great power."

"Broken symbols do, too. If you survive the change, the Gudain may try and kill you."

"Yes," she said, "but even martyrdom can have its uses. Although I would prefer to avoid it. One can do so much more alive than dead."

It was a moment before I could talk. "You're a very brave young woman," I said. "And if that's really your choice, I'll do what I can to help."

"The mating must take place at the right time, and somewhere I will be safe for several days. During the transformation I am vulnerable."

"Down here may be out of sight, but it's a long bowshot from safe. We'll think of something."

She called, softly, and the others reappeared. I whistled, and Previous and Kittack returned to the firelight. "Sorry, Previous – would you go back out, keep an eye?" I said quietly. "I don't trust our hosts one bit."

"Me neither. I'll watch." She disappeared again.

"You have told her," said Rikkinet.

"Yes," Enthemmerlee said.

Kittack was still staring. He spoke, a question.

Enthemmerlee answered.

There was a long silence. The water dripped. Kittack drew a long, shaky breath, and then sat down, abruptly, on the stone flags, and made a choking noise. I put a hand on his shoulder. He touched it briefly and got to his feet. "Forgive," he said, looking at Enthemmerlee. "Is not often a legend is walk out of the story and say, 'hello.'"

He made a strange, ducking, twisting movement with his head, as Rikkinet had done when we entered the firelight. He said something to Enthemmerlee, first in Ikinchli, then in Gudain.

She answered him, first in one, and then in the other.

He made that odd movement again, and backed away, towards me, almost as though he were afraid.

"Now you're a believer?" I muttered.

"I believe what I see. She is Itnunnacklish." He shook his head. "I remember some saying, about living in interesting times. Suddenly everything getting very interesting, yes?"

"Too right. We need somewhere for Enthemmerlee, somewhere safe."

Kittack said, "She come to my place, I keep safe."

"Is Ikinchli bar," Rikkinet said. "You think Gudain don't come look?"

"Haven't yet," Kittack said.

"No," I said. "Rikkinet, I'm assuming there was a reason you didn't keep her where I met you? With the other Ikinchli?"

"There is Ikinchli who do not want to believe in Itnunnacklish. Who think that to say Ikinchli and Gudain are one is evil; that we should kill all Gudain. If they hear of Enthemmerlee, they will kill her. That was why come here, where no-one know."

"Look. I can get you out of here, and take you to my jalla, but..." I rubbed my face, and my fingers found the scar.

My home, my safe haven, might not be safe any longer. What if the Avatars turned up while Enthemmerlee was there?

I began to pace the few feet between the walls, not really seeing those around me, trying to think.

"The man who paid me," I said. "Maybe..."

Malleay snapped, "You will not betray us! I will kill you!"

"I'd love to see you try, boy. Now shut up and listen. This man wants stability on Incandress. *If* we can persuade him that Enthemmerlee can help provide that, then maybe we can also persuade him to keep her safe, with her two mates, until the transformation's complete. That way, he has a fait accompli to present to the Gudain high court, *in* the safety of Scalentine."

"Safety?" Malleay said.

"Scalentine's diplomatically neutral territory. It's where people come to negotiate without killing each other. If we can get you under the protection of the Diplomatic Section, perhaps we can..."

Then we heard a yell and a splash from further up the tunnel.

I heard a clash of steel, and a grunt. There was a brief, blinding flare of alchemical fire, lighting up the crumbling walls and the black flow of the river, then everything went dark again. Someone shrieked. Blinking furiously and totally failing to rid my vision of white-edged purple smudges, I drew my sword and dagger. "Enthemmerlee? Stay behind me."

"What's happening?" Malleay said. I could make him out, shaking, but with his dagger in hand.

"Wish I knew." I still couldn't see a damn thing beyond the firelight, that flare had mangled my night-vision. On the other side of me Rikkinet was swearing softly and steadily; the sling wouldn't be much use to her if her vision was as messed as mine.

A voice from the darkness said, "Hey now, no need for this, just hand over girl and everything be fine, we all friendly as can be."

That pudgy sod in the greasy shirt. I should have known. Guess they'd tried to sneak up on us and the others had spotted them.

"Changed your minds, have you?" I was stalling, waiting for my sight to come back. I couldn't just run off with the girl, I had no idea where in these bloody tunnels I might end up. And where were Previous and Bliss?

"Give us girl."

Malleay yelled, his voice shrill, "Don't you touch her!"

"I not touch nobody, am businessman, me. I do public service, return her to grateful family for reward as offered."

I should have known the bastard had listened in. He must not have realised who Enthemmerlee was before, or she'd already have been handed back to her family – in a sack if necessary – and her companions and fellow-soldiers slaughtered and slung in the river.

I brought my sword up just in time as someone ran at me out of the darkness, sliced; there was a soft thump. I caught a glimpse of a pallid face, mouth open in shock; blood spattered my skin, and there was a hand lying on the ground, a dagger still in its fingers. The face backed into the darkness. My night vision was beginning to come back, I could make out the shape as he went tottering along the jetty. Then the rotting wood gave way and he tipped into the water; there was a sudden violent churning, and a bubbling scream.

I thought of those blind fish with their vicious little teeth.

Swimming for it was out, then.

More running feet, a shriek. I saw Previous, holding off the ratty thing; her sword catching the firelight as she flicked and parried, but the rat was fast, an ugly-looking short sword in each hand. I couldn't see the brute Pudgy anywhere.

Beside me, Kittack hissed, clutching his arm, blood streaming between his fingers.

"Get back," I said. "You've no weapon."

"Yes, have, but is behind bar. *Politics,*" he spat.

"Come here, and I'll bandage that," Enthemmerlee said. "I have a scarf."

There was a thud, a shriek. The ratty thing ducked as Previous swung, stabbed at her and missed. Previous kicked out and sent it flying into the wall. It slid down and lay in a heap.

Previous backed towards us. She was breathing hard; it echoed off the tunnel walls and roof. We had a solid wall behind us and the sides of the archway on either side, but there was no knowing how many reinforcements that greasy bastard could summon.

"You seen Bliss?" I said.

Previous shook her head. "I was a ways down, keeping an eye on you, when a couple of them tried to sneak up."

"You all right?"

"Yeah."

"Don't you be foolish now," Pudgy said from the darkness. "We not want to hurt nobody, you give us girl, all be fine."

"Not believing that," I muttered. "Where the hells is Bliss?"

I could make out more shapes, down along the tunnel. Moving towards us. Crap.

And yet there was part of me that relished it; a sword in my hand, enemies before me, mates beside me. Even in this mess, I could feel myself grinning.

I glanced to the side; Rikkinet was by me. I never even saw her draw, but one of the moving shapes pitched backwards.

Two down.

The Ikinchli man – I didn't even know his name – must have followed suit; someone else squawked and doubled over.

"Okay," Pudgy's voice came out of the shadows. "You want be stupid, fine. Go, boys."

They ran towards us, a tatterdemalion line of rags and glitter. One of them had a dagger in his teeth. Idiot. Elbowed him in the mouth; he dropped, choking on his own blood, his jawbone gleaming in the firelight.

I swung, parried. Managed to defend my lower right when a blade swept low. He left himself wide open; took him in the side. He didn't notice at first. Sometimes they don't. Then he fell.

Thrust forward. Remember the girl, don't get too far out, got to stay between her and these fools, what do they think they're doing? Going to kill their bargaining chip if they're not careful.

Almost backed into the fire. Dammit. Not enough room. The stones slippery with blood.

Splashes of light in the darkness. Rikkinet's run out of stones for her sling, using a dagger. She's fast, but it's risky. Lots of longer weapons. Spray of blood in my eyes, blink it out.

Rikkinet's down, taken through the shoulder. Alive, I can hear her swearing.

I keep swinging. Can feel the grin on me, there's one in front, got a grin too, I grab his arm on the downswing, punch my hilt through his grin. He falls back, goes down in the press. They keep coming.

Then someone yells, "Hold up! Hold!"

Not very disciplined, this lot; they back off in pieces, and we get a couple more before they're out of range. I fight down the impulse to belt after them; get as many as I can.

Silence, except for hard breathing, a whimper, the drip of blood. And the river.

"EVERYBODY BACK," PUDGY'S voice, a little tight and sounding slightly less full of itself. "Okay. You too much trouble. You go now."

"Stay where you are," I said, when Malleay started forward. "I don't trust him any further than I can spit, and at least here we've a wall at our backs."

"We can't stay here!"

"No, but I'm not risking it when he could send more after us from a side-tunnel as soon as we're on the path." I raised my voice. "Come out where I can see you!"

I could hear a muffled argument from somewhere above and to the right. Then the sound of footsteps scrabbling down towards us. Finally I could see a bobbing, rounded shape making its way cautiously downwards; there must be steps or something cut into the wall. Pudgy. And behind him, a lanky pale figure I knew.

"Bliss? How the..."

I elbowed Previous in the ribs to shut her up. I didn't know how the hells he'd managed it, either. He didn't carry weapons, but somehow he'd not only cornered our plump friend but persuaded him he was in mortal danger.

As they got closer, and I saw Bliss's glowing eyes and the predatory tilt of his head, it was a little easier to understand. He didn't look a lot like the gentle, faintly grieving creature I knew. He looked like a cat on the hunt.

I just hoped that no-one would notice that the cat didn't have any claws.

Bliss kept Pudgy close to the wall, where his cronies couldn't get between them, and edged him towards us. Pudgy looked around at the bodies of his gang that littered the walkway.

"No need for this," he said.

"No, there wasn't," I said. "And we're leaving."

I could see the men all watching their boss. "Yes, yes," he said, his voice sounding strangely prissy, "please all to go away now."

"Bliss? Let's take him with us, shall we? Just as far as the way out."

Pudgy started to protest and then made a little breathless squeak. "Fine! Fine! I show you way out!"

Malleay didn't look happy about the idea, but Bliss edged the man ahead of us and, moving in a close bunch, weapons at the ready, we followed; me and Rikkinet bringing up the rear.

We made it to the exit without attack, and emerged blinking into the daylight. It felt as though it should have been evening already, but it was only just past midday; this is what happens when you get up so damned early.

I stood in front of Pudgy. "Now," I said. "You stay out of my way, I'll stay out of yours, all right? Are we done?"

Pudgy, squinting in the light, had a kind of stretched, tiptoe look. He nodded, but carefully, as though afraid to lower his chin too far. "Just get crazy fadefreak away from me!"

I tossed his weapons through the open doorway, back down the tunnel. "Go," I said. With an expression of intense relief, he dived after his gear. Rikkinet and Malleay dragged the door closed after him, and I turned to Bliss. "How in the hells..."

Bliss just smiled and held out one of his pale hands. A single long, very sharp fingernail glimmered like metal. "I had his... full attention," he said.

No wonder the pirate's voice had gone squeaky. The cat had claws after all.

Malleay was looking at Bliss's hands with something between horror and delight. Previous simply guffawed, and slapped Bliss on the back. "Unexpected, you," she said. "Right, what now?"

"First, we need to get away from here, before our nearly-castrated chum decides to come back with all his friends," I said. "Let's move."

"We're not going anywhere with you!" Malleay said. Fervent, that boy, but a little behind the times.

Rikkinet said, "We go with her. You want to be sliced up by sewer rats? You no good to Enthemmerlee, then."

I couldn't help wondering how much good Malleay was going to be to her anyway, but presumably he had the necessary equipment.

The male Ikinchli caught my glance and let one of his eyelids droop fractionally, as though he'd caught my thought.

"Kittack's," I said. "Safest place I can think of until I can talk to the... paymaster."

WE MADE A pretty conspicuous group, even for Scalentine near Twomoon; I tried to hail a couple of cabs, but the drivers took one look at us and snapped their horses to a fast trot. Admittedly even Enthemmerlee had streaks of gore on her gown from Kittack's injury, and Previous and myself were bloody from head to knees.

Somehow, we reached The Swamp without attracting either a mob or the militia. Kittack ushered us in through the back, in case someone got curious. We stood in a store-room surrounded by smells of alcohol and soap and fish. I fingered the bottle of Laney's lust-preventive potion I was still carrying.

"One of us must come with you," Malleay said, "to hear what you say."

"All right, all right. Fine. Rikkinet?" I said. "You want to join me? If it goes bad, I'll try and keep the guards occupied, you get yourself out and get them out of here, wherever you can."

She nodded. We tidied ourselves up a little, and I swallowed the potion.

The 'courtesy guards' at the Singing Bird were well trained. "Madam Steel, how nice to see you. Are you planning to play the tables this afternoon?" said one.

"In a manner of speaking," I said.

They bowed us through. Rikkinet made a low whistling sound which indicated either that she was impressed by the surroundings or that she, like me, was made distinctly nervous by the ease with which we'd got in.

Fain appeared almost instantly through one of the hidden side doors, and flicked his glance over us both without so much as raising an eyebrow. "Madame Steel. And friend. You have news?"

"We have something to discuss," I said.

"Please." He gestured towards one of the booths.

Laney's potion had worked, and fast. I could still see Fain was attractive, but in a distant way, as though he were a well-made statue of some subject I didn't much care for. He could have stripped his shirt off and I wouldn't have been interested. It was a weird feeling; like water in the ears, a sense of deafness, and silence. I caught myself shaking my head as though I could dislodge it. Fain himself looked tired; I wondered if it was trying to control his trait that did it. I wasn't going to tell him about the potion, though – let him think I was still susceptible. Any advantage I could get over him, I wanted.

"Can I offer you anything?" he said.

I glanced at Rikkinet, but she shook her head.

"No," I said. "Let's get to business. I know where Enthemmerlee is. But before I can pass her to you, her associates require assurances that she and her companions will be kept safe and together until after Twomoon, and that you will then provide facilities here on Scalentine for negotiations between herself, the leaders of the Gudain, and the leaders of the Ikinchli. That she will be protected from any attempts to harm her, and that you will provide her with asylum here on Scalentine if the negotiations are unsuccessful." I looked at Rikkinet. She nodded, her eyes fixed on Fain. I wondered if Ikinchli were susceptible to his trait; well, at least one of us would have a clear head.

"And you are?" said Fain, looking at Rikkinet.

"I am servant of Itnunnacklish," Rikkinet said. "Also am negotiator for my people in this."

"Itnunnacklish?" Fain said. "I'm afraid I don't understand."

So she told him.

Fain's face went utterly expressionless.

"Is this true?" He said to me.

"I believe it is. So do both the Gudain and the Ikinchli."

"And this mating must take place during Twomoon?"

"Yes."

He leaned back, lacing his fingers together on his chest, staring at the wall of the booth above my head. "Madam Steel."

"Yes."

"How did you discover this? All the time we have been on Incandress, we have not heard of the Itnunnacklish."

His ability to pronounce the name perfectly after one hearing irritated me. "Well the *Gudain* were hardly going to tell you about it, were they?" I said. "Did you actually talk to the Ikinchli at all?"

"Attempts have been made," he said, glancing at Rikkinet.

She made a hissing sound. "You go first to Gudain, then you come to us? We think you cosy-cosy with Gudain, why we talk to you?"

Fain sighed. "Mistakes have also been made, it seems."

That seemed pretty damned obvious to me. "Look, Fain. We need an answer. Can you give us one, or not?"

"And what do you get out of this?" he said, leaning forward again and looking me in the eye.

"Relief from the sensation that I have been bought," I said. "I sell sex, not my soul."

I thought I caught the faintest crinkling of a smile at the corners of his eyes, but I could have been wrong. "I see."

"So," I said. "What's your answer?"

"Really, Madam Steel, these sort of negotiations take time."

"'The right orders, correctly signed?' We haven't *got* time, Mr Fain. Twomoon is upon us."

"Actually, yes..." he gazed at the wall again, drumming his fingers against his crisp shirt-front. "If I were to make such a decision, in unseemly haste, well, the fact that I didn't even know what the truth was until the last minute would be an excuse no reasonable being could ignore... of course, that assumes one is dealing with reasonable beings. However." He sat upright, and said, "Yes. My answer is yes. If you bring them here, I will arrange for somewhere safe. For you, too, if you wish?" he said to Rikkinet.

Rikkinet looked at me. "You trust?" she said.

"Mr Fain," I said.

"Yes, Madam Steel?"

"I'm not satisfied, Mr Fain."

"No?"

"No. I want something more from you."

"And what would that be? You'll receive the other half of the payment. I'll even include a bonus, since the result has been... more interesting than expected." Despite the bantering tone, he sounded slightly disappointed.

"That isn't what I meant. I want an oath."

"You have my word," he said.

"I didn't say I wanted your word, Mr Fain. I want your oath. A Fey oath."

"Ah. You know, that could make my life extremely difficult."

"Only if you attempt to break it."

"No. Because in my position such a thing is *highly* discouraged. I ask again. Why?"

"Why what?"

"I might, *might,* swear one. If I thought it sufficiently worthwhile. But a Fey oath is a large counter to play at my table, Madam Steel. Why would *you* spend it on someone you never met before today?"

"That, Mr Fain, is my business. Will you swear to provide Enthemmerlee with what she's asked for, and do your best to protect her, or not?"

He grinned, suddenly, and if I hadn't been under the influence of Laney's potion, it would have floored me. As it was, I still wanted to smile back, but I held off.

"On one condition," he said.

"That being?"

"Dinner. After Twomoon."

"Dinner?"

"I have a... proposal to put to you."

"Another one?"

"Yes. Well?"

I looked him over. Pretty, dangerous Mr Fain.

"Can I bring a long spoon?" I said.

"I've DONE MY best," I said to Enthemmerlee, on the doorstep. I'd spoken the oath to Fain; he'd made the required response, and there had been a sort of pink shudder in the air, and a deep click like the sound of a turning lock. According to Laney, that was it. I just hoped it would work. "I'm still not convinced you can trust him," I said, "but he should be on your side now, whether he likes it or not."

"If I am to change anything," Enthemmerlee said, "I must begin with trust. I must believe that people can choose to do what is right. After all, you did."

"I hope so," I said. "I wish you good luck."

She held out her hand, and I clasped it, gently. Those delicate little fingers. She seemed so damn fragile, to change a world.

TIRESANA

I STROKED HAP-CANAE'S *bare shoulder, the skin golden and glowing. My own flesh had that same light, though not as strongly as his.*

"It would be appropriate," Hap-Canae said, "for you to take your place as Avatar of Babaska at the Sowing at the great temple of Nard."

"Take my place? But I thought... I thought I was to stay here." New to my post and eager, I attended every ceremony they would allow at Babaska's temple in the precinct. Hap-Canae usually accompanied me; if it was one of his own major ceremonies, such as the dawn worship at the sunburst temple, he would send another Avatar with me.

I was conscious, always, of being watched by the Avatars, but I was almost accustomed to it by then. I assumed that once they knew I would fulfil my duties properly, things would change.

Babaska's priestesses always dealt with me with immense respect, even the High Priestess, who was gravely and unfailingly courteous. I found it odd from a woman the same age as the head cook at home, who had treated me more like an untrained pup likely to widdle on the floor. Of course, I couldn't have killed the cook – or at least, wasn't likely to. The priestesses, I came to realise, had no such surety.

I took my place out front for some ceremonies, in the shadow of Babaska's statue; for others, I stood behind the screen while people laid gold, weapons, lengths of cloth on the altar, and begged for Babaska's help in love and war. I tried to use the powers I was still learning as judiciously as I could, to pick deserving cases; I had attempted to behave as I thought an Avatar should, and now...

"Don't look so devastated, silly child, I'm not sending you away. But it is one of Babaska's major temples, and the Sowing is her festival. Therefore, it would be a good time for you to appear to the wider world."

"Will you come with me?"

"Of course. Remember, now. We are Avatars. People need us to be different, Babaska. They need us to be more than they are. Take yourself some lovers – nothing else would be expected of you. But remember what you are now, treat them appropriately, and let the past lie unspoken."

"Hap-Canae?"

None of the Avatars addressed each other as 'The Avatar so-and-so,' just by the name of the god they represented.

"What?"

"How long have you been an Avatar?"

"A long time. The gods chose me many years ago."

"And was the ceremony the same for you?"

"Now, you know that our powers were gifted to us directly by the Gods. But otherwise, yes, it was the same."

"There was a woman at Meisheté's temple today," I said. "She was praying for her family's fields to be fertile..."

"And?"

"Meisheté could do that, couldn't she?"

"Of course. If she wished."

"So why won't she?"

He sighed, and sat up. "I have told you. We do not interfere in the affairs of other Avatars."

"I know. But..."

He put his finger over my mouth. "Listen to me. You know that we have limits. Knowing that, we must use our power *appropriately. There is a village, along the Rohin, flooded. Yes, I could dry up the floodwaters. Yet that might offend Rohikanta, and it would leave me weak. What if I was called upon again, the next day, for some truly dreadful need? 'Hap-Canae, save us,' they cry, and I cannot, because I dragged one fishing village from the mud. What then could they believe in, pray to, hope for? We are what they look to, the light in dark lives."*

"The last Avatar of Babaska, what did she do? Did she help them? Or..."

"Enough questions; we are what we are. Remember, you were Chosen."

The unspoken half of that little speech being, of course, that I had been Chosen not by a God, but by an Avatar, and that having been Chosen, I could be... unChosen.

And so we went to Nard. I had heard of the temple, but couldn't remember why. There were long, solemn processions, people coming forward to lay offerings upon the heaping piles, elaborate dances and chants and choking clouds of expensive incense.

We performed the Sowing. It was all done with great solemnity. I thought of Livaia, the woman who had taught us; I was grateful, and wondered what had happened to her. I thought I should like to send her a gift.

Yet something felt wrong. I was the Avatar of Babaska, it was part of my function to increase the life-force that flowed into the land, the crops, the people. But as we performed the ceremony, to the quickening beat of the chant and the little drums, I felt detached – from Hap-Canae, from the land, from myself. The power was in me, I could feel it, but it spiralled in on itself, going nowhere. Intoxicating, but hollow.

I assumed something was wrong with me. Hap-Canae had no trouble completing his part, and I cried out at the appropriate moment, though for me nothing had happened.

Except that I had had that sense, again, of being watched; of that silent, assessing gaze that existed nowhere but in my own head. Afterwards, there were more days of ceremony. The flattery and adulation which had already begun to wear on me even before the Sowing were now troubling; I felt I'd done nothing to earn it. And I was, frankly, bored. I'd worked every day of my life since I was old enough to turn a spit. All the sitting about being chanted at left me too much time to think.

Brooding behind my smile, I remembered that this was where Velance was supposed to have come, as High Priestess of Babaska. But the High Priestess was a middle-aged woman who bore no resemblance to her.

"Oh," Hap-Canae said. "Meisheté must have been mistaken about the place. You know how she is. Anything outside her sphere is of little interest to her; if it isn't to do with babies, she hardly troubles herself." He pulled me to him, then made a face. "The incense they use here! Where do they get it, the street market? Your hair reeks of it. Tell them to use something more appropriate to your status."

I was hurt. After all, this was supposed to be my temple, and my festival.

Then, sitting on the great chair in the temple, smelling the incense (which I rather liked – a rich, dark, cedary smell) as yet another ceremony rang and chanted around me, I realised, no, it isn't my temple, my ceremony. It's Babaska's, not mine.

And my mind would not be quiet. Things I saw, things I remembered, clustered around my chair and whispered below the chanting of the worshippers.

Meisheté was supposed to have jurisdiction over pregnancy and childbirth, things of life. The bee-hive and the cattle heavy with milk. And yet... There were the babies born wrong, and fewer cattle, and little honey to sweeten the coarse bread.

They prayed to Shakanti for success at the hunt, but where were the deer?

They prayed to Hap-Canae for success at trade, but what gold flowed into Tiresana?

At least, I thought, with a first jab of rebellion, I do my job as best I can. I make people happy, as best I can. When I'm allowed.

And then, frightened of my own thoughts, I shoved them back down and straightened my back and tried to be dignified.

I had plenty of help. Everywhere I went, respect and awe followed me like hungry dogs. People prostrated themselves before me. And yet Hap-Canae stood behind me, in the shadows, in case I said the wrong thing, or overreached myself. To them, I was an Avatar. To him, I was a child. And to me, I was a confusion, with too many thoughts and questions and no-one able or willing to answer them.

When we were back at the Temple of All the Gods, I went to the seer, in search of something solid. Something understandable in the midst of it all. Something that was truly mine.

I had kept with me, all this time, the bag I had been found in. I'd decided to try and track down my parents. I had some idea that I would find, at least, my mother, and present myself in all my glory as an Avatar, and she'd fall on her knees, I would reveal who I really was, and all around there would be tears, reconciliation and so forth.

I'd listened to too many storytellers.

I had no plans to tell the seer why I was seeking what I was; I knew the Avatars would never permit it. But I thought I could manage it somehow. I was pig-headed and romantic and, well, sixteen.

The seer had no temple – only the gods, or their Avatars, had those, but he had a set of rooms in the outer precinct. They were full of wind-chimes, which tinkled and clinked in the slightest breeze; one couldn't move without brushing against them.

The other supplicants moved aside to let me pass; though I'd have waited, I went on, knowing how Hap-Canae would react if I let mere humans go before me. Bad enough that I'd slipped away without telling him where I was going. I wasn't letting myself think about that, about the fact that I had to deceive him, that I didn't really trust him.

That he frightened me.

I saw the Seer raise his head as I entered the inner room. He was young and clean-shaven, with a certain tilt and lift to his chin as though the world were beneath his notice.

"An Avatar," he said. "I am honoured." He prostrated himself. Everyone did, in the presence of Avatars, but there are ways and ways of doing it; his was that of a man interrupted in some important business, performing a necessary but irritating courtesy.

He made me uneasy; the smooth dents where his eyes should have been troubled me more than the wounds I'd seen in battle; and though he couldn't see me, I felt watched. Marked. Judged.

"They tell me you can find things," I said.

"I hope they did not tell you I was infallible," he said. "I would risk the Avatar's anger if I did not warn her of possible failure." But his words said one thing and the cool lift of his mouth another. He seemed not at all frightened of me, and I realised how accustomed I had become to others' fear.

"Oh, no. I won't be angry. I suppose it's like betting, you can't always get it right."

"Indeed." That cool, not-quite-smile again. "What is it you seek?"

"I'd like to know where this came from, and if you can tell me anything about who it used to belong to," I said. I handed him the bag I'd been found in, with the marble chips shifting and rattling in the bottom.

He took it in clean, pale hands. "I will try," he said. "But my gift is more towards lost things, than lost people. I have found lost coins, lost earrings, lost crowns, even. I have a bent for metal. People have not enough metal in them."

I wasn't sure if everything he said really had more than one meaning, or if it was just that he made me nervous.

He reached into the bag and took out one of the chips, turned it over in his fingers, and put it back; another, a third. He ran the stuff of the bag through his fingers, then shrugged. "I am sorry," he said. "I have nothing. If you will permit a suggestion, though, a stonemason might be able to tell you where these chips are likely to have come from. Perhaps."

"Thank you," I said. I was disappointed, but hardly surprised. I dropped gold into the offering-pot and left, thinking, as I did so, that he was strangely self-possessed, almost arrogant. As though he knew things that no-one else did, and they made him see the rest of us as ignorant, and foolish. In my case, of course, he'd have been right.

CHAPTER
TWENTY-ONE

FAIN HAVING PAID me, I dumped another fat purse in my room. I really had to take the blasted money to the Exchange.

I checked on Ireq, who was recovering but wouldn't be working for at least another day. "Sorry," he said.

"Don't be daft, Ireq. Just get better."

There were shrieks next door and I found Jivrais and Essie engaged in a tussle for lip-paint in Essie's room, breathless and giggling, and with water all over the floor from a jug they'd knocked over. "Oi, you two! Look at this place! And the pair of you, talk about dragged through a hedge backwards. Jivrais, get a cloth, get that water up. Essie, come here, let me do your hair. Honestly."

"Yes, Babylon."

I combed and oiled Essie' dark curls into some sort of order. I spend more time on the crew's hair than I do on my own – mine's curlier than Essie's, practically ringlets, long, and black. Most of the time I just wash it, run my fingers through it with a bit of scented oil and leave it. Too much else to do. But Essie' hair pays for having a fuss made.

"Ooh, not that oil, Babylon, I think it's gone over."

I sniffed at the bottle. "Gah, you're right. Which one?"

"The Ghost of Jasmine, please."

"Niiice." I rubbed a few drops of the richly scented stuff through her hair. "A present?"

"My little princeling. Antheranis. He's *such* a sweetie."

"He's been back already? You have made a conquest. What do you think of him?"

"Oh, well, he's such a boy, you know. But I'm teaching him a few things." She smiled at me through her reflection.

"His next one will thank you." I kept an eye on her in the mirror, but there was none of that wistful look when she talked about him that meant trouble in store.

We can all fall for clients, but most of the time, you'll break your heart for nothing. I suspected Antheran's ambitions for his son didn't include him taking on a girl from a whorehouse.

"So," I said, wrapping her curls around my fingers. "What do you make of Frithlit?"

She shrugged. "He seems all right. He was wandering around the top floor, looking lost, so I chatted to him a bit."

"Oh? Where was Previous?"

"Not sure. Anyway I told him about what happened with Mirril the butcher – I'm not going *there* again; I mean, who does she think she is, the sour-faced old bat? Jealousy, that's what it is, bet she's never had a good..."

"Essie? We were talking about Frithlit?"

"Oh, yes. He's not been in Scalentine long, you know. He said that was why he'd got into a bad card game. I told him I was local, and he asked me what places he should stay away from."

"In so many words?"

"Well, he said, 'Where is places of bad peoples, villains, card sharpeners?' Something like that. I thought it was rather sweet."

"And you told him?"

"Of course, I didn't want him getting into trouble. I told him to stay away from King of Stone, and the Break of Dawn of course. He's awfully young," said Essie, all twenty or so years of her.

I smoothed a last curl into place. "There. Now you're gorgeous again. Try not to spill anything expensive on anyone who's going to mind."

"You don't think Previous would be bothered, do you? That he was talking to me? I mean she knows I wouldn't..."

"Of *course*. Don't be daft, Essie."

Something about Previous's little friend bothered me. Not that he hung around – we always kept open house for friends – but he did seem to be forever *hovering,* somehow. It wasn't that Previous had a lover; after all, it was about damn time, I could barely remember the last one. But something about the way he was with her felt slightly tinny, off, like a charisma glamour.

But maybe I was overanxious. Though Previous was tough as a soldier's boot in most respects, I wasn't entirely sure her heart was as hard as the rest of her. And maybe I was a tiny bit jealous. Casual companionship and a pleasant time in bed I could get. But someone to be close and tight with, someone who knew my heart? That had been a *very* long time.

I was just capping the oil when I heard a yell from downstairs. "Laney! Babylon! Get down here!" That was Previous. *Now* what?

I took the stairs fast, and saw Ireq standing in the doorway, holding someone up.

It was Cruel, the hood of my cloak sliding off to show her short white hair matted red, her eyes rolling up. Blood rolled down her neck and into her cleavage.

I caught her as she slid off Ireq's shoulder. She hung from my hands like an empty gown.

"What the hells?" I said.

Ireq said, "There was a bang, and then I saw her stagger out of Twodice Row, dripping everywhere, grabbed her, brought her here."

"You see anyone?"

"No."

"Cruel? Talk to me."

She groaned. Laney was beside me in a blink, running her hands over Cruel's head. "Somebody fetch some water," she said, "and the blue bottle from my dressing table. And the green wooden box. Bring her into the Little Parlour."

I scooped her into my arms as gently as possible and took her through. Her blood soaked through my sleeves. "Someone tell Unusual, get him up here," Laney snapped.

I laid Cruel on the sofa. Her eyes were closed. She always seemed so self-contained, even dangerous; now she looked vulnerable and strangely young. Her nose was obviously broken; some of the blood was from there, but most of it was from her head.

Jivrais appeared with an armful of bottles and boxes, it looked as though he'd just swept everything off Laney's dressing table. She sighed with exasperation, plucked out what she needed, and told him to put the rest on the table.

"You need me?" Ireq said.

"Yes, on the door, " I said. "Go."

The All bless ex-soldiers, he did, without a word. Frithlit stood in the doorway, silver eyes wide, his mouse-like ears shivering. Unusual, normally so graceful, shot past him into the room, banging his hip on a table, and dropped to his knees by the sofa. His arms were full of bandages and bottles; he looked around wildly as though he didn't know what to do with them, then shoved them onto the overcrowded table, sending one of Laney's potions off the edge. There was a crash and a green smell of herbs. Unusual rested a shaking hand on Cruel's cheek. Against her midnight skin, his pale fingers seemed to glow. He whispered to her, stroking her face.

"Laney?" I said.

Laney parted Cruel's hair carefully with her fingers. "Scalp wounds always bleed a lot. She's going to have a nasty bump and a worse headache, but nothing's moving that shouldn't be." She cleaned Cruel's face and scalp with a wet cloth, took one of the bottles from Jivrais, rubbed a few drops of ointment into her scalp, then more around her nose. "Hold her shoulders, Babylon." She pinched the bridge of Cruel's nose between finger and thumb. There was a cracking sound and Cruel yelped awake.

"There, there," Laney said. "That's the worst of it."

Cruel said something in her own tongue, and Unusual answered her; he had tears in his eyes. Cruel looked at him, rolled her eyes and said something else, and Unusual gave a gasping laugh. "She called me a soft idiot," he said. "I think she'll be all right." He wiped his eyes, and started wrapping one of the bandages around her head.

"Cruel? You remember what happened?" I said.

She frowned, and winced as it pulled at the wound. "I was in Twodice Row, coming back from the saddler's. We had some harnesses needed mending. I had both hands full. Someone put their hands on my shoulders. Then I hit the wall and everything went white."

"Ouch. Good thing you've a hard head." I tried to keep my voice light. "Thought I told you lot to keep in training?"

"I thought I *was*. But it was just..." She shrugged. "So sudden. Whoever it was, they were strong. Really strong. And fast."

"You didn't hear anything?"

"I think they said something, maybe. I thought I heard a sort of whisper. After that, nothing." She shut her eyes again.

"You see anyone else in the alley?"

"No."

"Anyone else see anything? Frithlit?"

"I am sorry, I was upstairs, not see. Heard loud bang, yes?"

"All right. Laney, any more you can do for her?"

She shook her head. "I've given you a little bit to help the pain," she said to Cruel, "and your nose will be fine if you *don't touch it*. In fact, I'm going to make you a plaster."

"I am not wearing a plaster on my nose," Cruel said. "Really, Laney. What would I look like?"

"Then don't blame me if it mends crooked," Laney said, glaring.

"You've done what you can, sweetie," I said. She's a Fey, not a healer, and a Fey on Scalentine at that; she can only do so much. "Cruel, have you any clients booked?"

"Only one."

"Unusual, you send a message, put them off. We'll give 'em a discount next visit. Previous, Bliss, come with me."

Twodice Row was empty. It's only a short street, nothing but a cut-through between Goldencat Street and The Panney, the road that runs down to the river. It smelled of soap and steam from the laundry on the corner.

Bliss stared thoughtfully at the smear of blood on the wall; a little of it had spattered one of my favourite stonework faces: a laughing faun no bigger than my hand. There was more on the ground, splashed over cobbles and mud, looking dark as ink.

If I was ever squeamish I lost it in battle the first time someone's guts spilled over my boots. The smell's pretty bad, and the sound is... memorable, but I was more worried about slipping in the mess and giving someone the chance to rip open my own frontage than I was about going 'yuck.' One reason I'm still alive, I guess.

But this was different. On a battlefield, when people know why they're there, it's one thing. A random attack on a lone woman, and a friend, is another matter. That was *Cruel's* blood. Looking at it made my eyes feel hot.

"Don't get too close," I said. "Whoever it was, they might have left something..."

Bits of leatherwork were still scattered over the paving. We started to pick them up.

"Not a robbery, then," Previous said.

"Doesn't look like it, does it?" I said. "Unless they meant to take the stuff and realised it wasn't what they thought." They'd have been fools, though. The gear Cruel and Unusual use costs a lot more than horse-harness.

"Looks to me," Previous said, "like maybe whoever did it was drunk, or just plain clumsy. Saw her from behind, just meant to grab her, maybe, or grab what she was carrying, but tripped. Slammed her into the wall by accident, and bolted when they realised they'd knocked her out. Or when they heard the bang."

"What was the bang?" I said.

"No idea."

"Not drunk," Bliss said. He was trying, but he was getting that drifty, bemused look again.

"No?"

"I don't think so."

"How can you tell?"

Bliss just shrugged. "Smells like a laundry, not an inn."

"There is a laundry, Bliss. It's just over there." I pointed. Steam was rolling out of the open door. "You took the sheets there, last week."

"Yes, I did. Was that right?" He gave me that worried look he gets when he's trying to remember which bits of life are important.

"Yes, don't worry about it." I patted his shoulder and went into the laundry, leaned on the wooden counter, and yelled into the warm soapy fog.

A red face finally appeared, surmounted by a white kerchief that had probably been crisp this morning. Now it drooped damply over grey locks. The laundress pushed her hair out of her eyes with a forearm. "If it's an order, we can't take it. We just lost a boiler."

"What?"

"Panel just blew off one of the boilers. We're behind as it is."

That must have been the bang everyone heard. I explained what had happened, and she half-listened to me, head cocked for sounds of more trouble from the cavernous room behind her. I could hear knockings and sloshings and shouts.

"I wondered if anyone might have seen anything?" I said.

"No-one's been out front for at least three hours. I'm nearest the door, that's how I heard you yelling. If anyone'd come out I'd know. No-one has. We've a big order on, gotta be done before Twomoon. And now the boiler..."

Her shoulders sagged. "Right, well, thanks anyway..." Her body was already angled towards the inner door, and she'd disappeared around it before I'd finished.

We went back to the house.

"Previous, a word. Unusual, stay with Cruel. The rest of you, back to what you were doing. *Now*, people."

They scattered. I motioned Previous into the hall. She wasn't saying anything, but she was giving me a look.

"What?"

She shrugged. "You sounded a lot like my old Sarge, for a minute there."

"Sorry. Look, Previous... Someone may have it in for us."

"You think?"

Her tone was neutral. I decided to take it at face value. "Maybe. Stay sharp. Keep an eye out."

"For what?"

"Anything that looks like trouble."

"Yes, of course. You all right, Babylon?"

"No," I said. "This is getting to me. First the Vessels, and then the dead girl down in Ropemakers Row; I hate that I don't know her name, Previous. No-one knew her name. And now this. If they'd had a knife instead of just their hands, Cruel could be dead."

"You going to the millies?"

"Yes. Yes, I'd better." I started for the door.

"You might want to change first," Previous said.

"Oh, right." I'd been about to stroll down the street spattered to the elbows with blood; well, it's just not stylish, is it? Plus I had enough trouble without being suspected of Unspecified Slaughter.

"And Babylon?"

"Hmm?"

"What sort of trouble should I be looking out for?"

"Weird people."

"*Weird* people? Babylon, it's Twomoon."

"You've got a nose for trouble, Previous. Use it. You get worried, shut the place up, keep everyone inside, and send someone for me."

"And when are you going to..."

I headed upstairs without answering. I got the worst of the blood off, pulled on the first clean shirt that came to hand, grabbed some weaponry and headed out before anyone else could start asking questions.

Trouble among the powerful gets dealt with by the Diplomatic Section, poor folk mostly get the militia. So they keep the barracks between the docks and King of Stone.

TIRESANA

PRELLA WAS A *village on the coast. Not much of a place. The people there scraped a living with fishing and stone-quarrying. There was a vein of white marble in the rocks, in demand for temples to Shakanti, because of its pallor and glow. Shakanti decided to take an interest in the place – perhaps to discourage the use of the marble for anyone's temples but her own – and was going there to conduct a ceremony.*

It was rare; the Avatars seldom left the Temple of All the Gods. It hadn't yet occurred to me that this was strange, especially when most of them could hardly stand the sight of each other. But except for brief excursions to their most important temples for the major ceremonies, they stayed clustered about it. Later, much later, I realised that they were afraid; that they feared losing their powers if they got too far from the altar, or stayed away too long. Feared most, perhaps, that one of the others would somehow find a way to steal their power from them.

I was learning a little cunning by then. Enough, at least, that I made up a story about wanting to see how Shakanti dealt with her worshippers, so I could learn from her example.

The real reason was because of those chips of white marble that had been in the bag with me when I was hung on the master's door. I had had one sent to a stonemason, and he had said that it looked to him like the stuff they quarried at Prella.

I took a barge to Prella, with the full complement of silk, delicacies, servants and priests. It was spring, the rushes a tender brilliant green, the little scarlet warblers that nested in them darting about like living jewels.

One of the priests was only a few years older than myself, with huge, dark, thickly-lashed eyes and beautiful black hair. When he rose, with grace, to his feet after the formal prostration, he looked at me with an adoration as sweet and tempting as ripe grapes.

The Avatar Lohiria, of the West Wind, was also on the barge, ostensibly to help speed its journey but more probably to keep an eye on me. She watched me constantly, having little else to do, when she wasn't combing her writhing hair. She could not, however, make any objection to my taking a lover. It was what Babaska's Avatar was supposed to do.

Hap-Canae could hardly have objected either; he'd encouraged me himself. Nonetheless, I felt both guilty and defiant when I took Ranay's hand and led him to the pavilion they had made on the deck for me.

Why Ranay? Yes, he was handsome enough. Yes, I was beginning to find Hap-Canae's techniques a little wanting now that I knew more, and to hanker for some variety. But it wasn't just that. It was the way he looked at me: not as Hap-Canae did, as though I were a doll to be decorated or a child to be chastised, but as a woman.

He smelled fresh, like green growing things. And he played the flute. I remember the music, sweet and melancholy, counterpointed with the lapping of the water and the creak and clop of the oars. At night the stars blazed so brightly it seemed they should crackle.

We lay, Ranay and I, with the canopy drawn back, and watched the constellations. The Wheel, the Leopard. "I love the stars," he said. "I would like to study them, know their stories and their meanings. They can tell so much; everything is written there, one only needs to learn the language."

"Why don't you?" I said.

He gave a sad little smile. "I am to be a temple administrator. It is a post of great prestige, and my family will never want for anything. But I wonder... once the family's farms would have kept us, but the desert has encroached, and sand covers what were fields in my grandfather's time.

"I am sorry, this is of no interest to you..."

"Yes, it is. Go on."

"The livestock breed poorly, there are so many shadowed births; calves born eyeless or without... no, forgive me, this is too ugly a subject."

I thought of the Seer, with those smooth dents where his eyes should be, and wondered.

Ranay went on, "Only that I have wondered if perhaps the answer lies in the stars. There are many scrolls that I would like to study, too; about the nature of the world, and..." – he gave me a sideways glance, smiling – "and of the Avatars. But they are all locked away. Even the highest priests must seek special dispensation to study them."

I was guiltily glad. After all, would Ranay love me if he knew I had been merely human? I tried to smile.

"Ah, what is it?" he said. "I am sorry, I have distressed you with my foolishness."

"No, not at all. How could you be foolish when you are so wise, and study so hard?"

He laughed a little. "Well, I think one must have something to study in order to be wise... perhaps I can become wise in the ways of administering a temple."

It seemed unfair, that he should be doomed to drudgery. He was one of my priests. Surely I could do something? I must have frowned, thinking.

"There, I have bored you," he said. "I shall talk of pleasanter things. Look, There's your sword," he pointed up.

The Sword of Babaska, drawn in fire on the black sky.

"I'm only her Avatar," I said. "I'm not her."

"You are my goddess, I ask no more."

For some reason that made me want to cry, but that doesn't come easy to Avatars. I just pulled him close, and breathed in the scent of his hair.

CHAPTER
TWENTY-TWO

"BARRACKS" IS A bit of a misnomer, though they do have sleeping rooms there. It's a combination of holding cells, armoury, courthouse and training ground, and this close to Twomoon it was in even more than the usual chaos. I made my way through the loud, odorous crowd to the front desk, passing by a rather delicious young officer – tall, blond, human, with unfairly long eyelashes and looking quite edible in his uniform – who was talking to a small, neat man in a highly embroidered waistcoat.

The officer at the front desk nodded at me and went on taking notes, so I waited. I could hear the neat man saying, "I am embarrassed, that I was tricked so easily."

"Classic bait and switch," the cute officer said. "Well, we'll do what we can, Mr Bannerman."

"Help you?" The desk officer said.

"Got an attack to report."

"Right, sit down, with you when we can."

Eventually she called over the blond officer, which was definitely the best thing to happen to me all day. "That was *Bannerman?*" I said.

"You heard that, eh?" He smiled. "What I wouldn't give for one of his swords... Someone managed to trick him out of some gear. He's *not* pleased. Now, how can I help?"

Just then a door slammed and the Chief came barrelling out through the crowd, hair flying behind him like a battle-banner, looking ready to rip out throats. He skidded to a halt when he saw me. "Babylon!"

"Hey, Chief. You look like you've got something big on, don't let me stop you."

"No, no... I just heard... you all right?"

"Me? Yes, yes I'm fine, but Crucl's hurt."

"I'm sorry to hear that," he said, straightening up. "Will *she* be all right?"

"Yes. We think so. Laney's looking after her."

He jerked his thumb at the young officer. "Roflet, get on to the next one, I'll take over here."

Roflet got up, gave me a little bow, and looked at the next person in line. It was an elderly, not very fragrant gent with a small, even less fragrant dog under one arm and an umbrella hanging from the other like a dead vulture. Roflet sighed. "This job's not as much fun as it used to be," he said, going off to deal with the old boy.

"Come into my office. And stop corrupting my officers," the Chief growled.

"Never laid a finger on him," I said, trying to smile.

He didn't answer, just stalked off ahead of me to the tiny, bare room he called his office. "So." He sat down on one of the ancient wooden chairs, gestured me into the other, and eased his shoulders. The Change was getting more obvious: his musculature was thickening, and his stubble was now a silvery beard. It didn't make him any less attractive. "Tell me," he said.

I told him. I realised my hands were clenching, by themselves, into fists; I hid them under the table, staring at the stained wood. It looked as ancient as a tomb.

"It wasn't even a robbery. She was... whoever it was just walked up and slammed her into the wall."

"Anyone see anything?"

"I asked at the laundry on the Row, but they hadn't had anyone out front. They'd just had a boiler blow up or something."

"That may have been what disturbed the attacker. Any of your clients tried to get nasty recently?" he said.

"After what Laney did to the last one?" I shook my head. "Word gets around. I thought we'd be all right, after you put the wind up the Vessels..."

"What?" He blinked.

"The Vessels," I said. "Didn't you go and see them?"

"I already told you I had, Babylon, and there's no evidence..."

"I didn't mean the *first* time you talked to them. I thought someone had warned them off, recently."

"Who? And why?"

"I thought it was you. Because they were breaking the law standing around scaring off clients. I told you about that."

"You did?" He tilted his head. "Oh, yes, you did. I'd just seen a murdered girl. I had other things on my mind than the Vessels, right then."

"Well that's the thing. Because they sent some money, and an apology, afterwards. I don't like them, Chief, I never will, but if they were planning on causing us trouble, why'd they do that? I mean, we've caught glimpses of people who *might* be Vessels, about the place, but I haven't seen any face to face since I ran across them in Buckler Row, coming away from... you know. The girl. I thought they'd decided we were beyond redemption and were trying their luck converting down in King of Stone. You haven't heard anything?"

"About the dead girl? No, Babylon. I haven't. I haven't been able to get anyone who *might* have seen anything to talk, have I?"

I felt a jab of irritation. *I* wasn't the one who'd scared Glinchen off.

He sighed. "Cruel didn't see anyone?"

"They came at her from behind. She thought she heard some whispering, that was all."

"That doesn't sound like the Vessels, does it? They're more inclined to the obvious, get it all out in the open where their god can see. We'll need to talk to her."

"You'd have to come to the house; I don't think she should be moved today."

"Won't be me. Probably won't be anyone until after Twomoon. I've got about a day to lock this place down before I go off duty."

"Of course."

"See any boot prints?"

"Nope. It's been dry. Bliss said he smelled soap, but, well, you know Bliss. And with the laundry so close... There was some of Cruel's blood on the ground." I had to stop and look away for a minute. When I looked back he was glaring at me as though I'd done something wrong. "What?"

His eyes were changing, too. The pupils had elongated, and the irises had taken on a purplish bloom.

"Go on," he said.

"Well, there might be something there. The only one who got close was Bliss, and he didn't tread in it. But that's not much good, is it?"

"Why not?"

"There was plenty of time for more people to walk through the alley before we went to look. And even if it was the culprit, what are you going to do, go through every set of shoes in the city looking for a bloody one?"

"You're right, it may be useless, but it might not." He motioned over one of the officers and said, "Send a scraper team to Twodice Row."

"I'll try, Chief, but we're short."

"Who's on?"

There was some brisk chatter about duty rosters and trainees, and the Chief scowled. "Whoever you can get – that new trainee seems pretty sharp, just make sure she has someone check her work. Tell her to get there now, before it rains." He turned back to me. "I suppose I should be pleased you came straight to us, instead of running off after the first person you saw, waving your sword."

"Now that's not fair."

"Isn't it? You charged into the Vessels' main temple, you walked into a room where a girl had just been murdered..."

"What is this, Chief?"

"You can't just go blundering into things, Babylon!"

"Blundering into things? Where would Enthemmerlee be if I hadn't gone *blundering in?*"

His mouth dropped open. His teeth were getting longer. "You *found* her? When? Where is she?"

"Safe. She's at the Diplomatic Section."

"And when were you planning on telling me about this?"

"As soon as I got a chance. It only happened today, for the All's sake."

"You found out where she was, and it never occurred to you to come to me?"

"There wasn't time!"

"Really."

"Yes, *really.*" We glared at each other. I wanted to hit him. I was pretty sure, from the way his arm-muscles were rippling, that the notion wasn't far from his mind, either.

He leaned forward, his changing eyes hard on mine. "What else aren't you telling me?"

"What do you mean?" I felt my hand go to the scar on my jaw before I could stop it. He watched the move like a cat.

"Well?"

"I..." I shut my mouth, hard.

"Right." He stood up. "I have things to do."

I stood up, and made for the door. As I opened it, he said, "I can *smell* a dangerous secret. They get people killed."

"Trust me, I'm not planning on getting killed."

"No-one ever is, Babylon. No-one ever is."

TIRESANA

I SPENT THE *next few days in a strange state: guilty, delighted, bemused. I had thought I was in love with Hap-Canae, but this was... sweet. Sweet and gentle and fun.*

His eyes were as rich a brown as good earth, and he smelled like spring. We talked, solemnly, for hours, about stars and beasts and rivers and worlds, but also we laughed. A lot.

And as for the sex... I hadn't realised just how ignorant I was. Oh, in terms of technique, I knew more, certainly, than Ranay, but technique is only, in the end, mechanics. With Ranay, within days of our first meeting, just the touch of his hand on my arm sent me closer to swooning ecstasy than Hap-Canae had ever managed. Being close to him was like swimming in warm clean water; touching him was painfully sweet, always, even if all we did was lie in each other's arms, just breathing. When he slipped into me, lithe and easy as an otter into water, I felt a kind of ecstatic terror, because I wanted him so much.

I began making plans. Plans to free Ranay from his drudgery, to bring him to my temple and get him access to the knowledge he craved. I built whole futures in my head, as beautiful and false as the city of mannequins I had dreamed of in Hap-Canae's bed.

And yet always, between us, was the awareness that I was an Avatar, and he was not. We didn't speak of that, or of the other Avatars. Though we seemed to talk about everything, the silences where we didn't venture were, by the end of the voyage, beginning to swallow our words.

The last night on the barge I looked into his great dark eyes, and saw all the questions that were hiding there. I was afraid of what would happen if he asked. I was afraid that I might answer. I pulled him down with me, and kissed and licked every part of his sweet silky body as though I was trying to take the taste of him into me forever, as though I was trying to consume him. I suppose I was. But I was also trying to distract him and exhaust him so that the questions would never be asked.

I was very good at what I did. But he knew. The next morning I saw him watching me, with a brooding look, as the barge drew close to Prella.

Lohiria saw it, and laughed, running her fingers through her hair. "I see you've got yourself a dog," she said. "Pretty, too. Does he do tricks?"

I thought how like a nest of snakes her hair looked, writhing and twisting on itself.

"Oh, don't look at me like that," she said. "Don't let him get above himself, dear. You know what happens to Babaska's lovers."

"I'm not her," I said. "Any more than you're Lohiria. And anyway, they didn't all die."

"Not by her hand, no," Lohiria said. "But they still die, little Avatar. They all die... one way or the other."

She waved to Ranay, and he bowed deeply.

When we pulled up at Prella, there was a somewhat thin display of priests and priestesses, and no Shakanti; I was told she had been called away, to her regret, and would meet me later.

It was a manoeuvre, intended to put me in my place. Most of the Avatars cordially disliked each other, but Shakanti loathed me, in particular. I think it was the sex thing: she despised it, and everything to do with it. Perhaps I should have felt sorry for her; for whatever it was, that had made her like that. But other times I just wished the crazy bitch would disappear, instead of breathing icy disapproval over everything about me and the goddess I was supposed to represent.

So when she wasn't there, I was less insulted than relieved. I would only have to avoid my escort and a dozen or so priestesses, rather than Shakanti herself. Lohiria was easily distracted by rumours of a ship driven aground, down the coast; she went charging off to see if someone else was impinging on her territory.

Ranay I enlisted to make a demanding fuss about my accommodation, to keep everyone occupied.

Once their attention was elsewhere, I swathed myself in scarves to conceal my shape and wrapped cloth around my face. Many of the quarry workers were similarly draped, to keep the dust out of their lungs. I headed into the town, with no clear idea of what I was going to do.

Of course, I hadn't thought it through. I wandered the streets, looking at the stalls in the market where people bargained for worm-eaten vegetables, undersized fruit and scrawny chickens. It was so long since I had walked among ordinary people, without an escort, that I felt lost; I couldn't ask any questions without revealing myself, and, I realised, I had no idea what questions to ask. All I knew, all I had ever known, was that I had been left hanging on a door, in a bag, with chips of what might have been Prella marble wrapped in a bit of cloth. I clutched one of the chips in my hand as I walked. What was I going to do? Walk up to some respectable matron and ask if she had abandoned a baby girl in my hometown sixteen years ago?

I looked for anyone who looked like me – or looked like me as I had been. But on Tiresana, high-nosed faces and black curly hair are hardly unusual. I searched every passing face, scrutinised stall-holders and weary women, bent and coughing quarriers and skinny children scurrying among the dusty legs.

I saw a woman, who could have been any age from thirty to fifty, stooped and grey. Was there something familiar about her face? Or not? Another, another. Any of them could have been my mother. Any of the men could have been my father. I stopped, in the middle of the street, suddenly overwhelmed with fear and shame. Why was I going to try and walk back into my mother's life? After sixteen years, she might be dead. She might be respectably settled, she might have no desire at all to have a reminder of her past turn up on her doorstep.

I had been thrown away with only the marginal kindness to hang me on a door rather than leave me to wail in the desert until the wild dogs found me. How did I even know that it was one of my parents who had left me there, and not some stranger, with just enough compassion to give me that chance?

People were beginning to glance at me curiously, to smile in my direction. The Avatar charisma was seeping out despite my attempts to conceal it. I turned and ran, scooting down side streets and out to the outskirts of the town, where I went on running up into the wooded hills.

Finally, in the cool shade, I stopped. Birdsong embroidered the silence. I was crying. I had let the piece of marble fall at some point. I stood there calling myself a coward and an idiot. I wanted to talk to Ranay, but what could I say?

And then, not before time, I started to think.

All those people looking, smiling. Because I was an Avatar. Instead of running off like an idiot, with no plans, perhaps I could use that, use my power and my influence to find my parents, if either of them were alive; I might have sisters, or brothers. I could act as their benefactor, from afar, and then when I was sure, when it could be done safely, I could reveal myself to them.

CHAPTER
TWENTY-THREE
Day 5
2 days to Twomoon

I DIDN'T WANT to get out of bed. Unfortunately we had no clients; so there was no good reason for me to stay there. Eventually, I got up, dressed, and checked on Cruel. She had swapped her white bandage for a scarlet one, which looked very dramatic against her black skin, and was already up and dressed, seeing no need to stay in bed as she felt, she proclaimed, perfectly well.

I went to glare at the accounts. The thing about life's tribulations is that sometimes you can avoid one by dealing with another. If I put the papers into some sort of order, I'd know which bills I needed to pay first. Then I'd take the rest of Fain's damn money, if there was any left after I'd paid the bills and the tax office, and put it in the Exchange before it all got spent.

I stared at the bits of paper. All I could see was the Chief's face. A dangerous secret. If only he knew.

Now things were quiet, I couldn't avoid thinking about the Avatars anymore. They were here, right here on Scalentine.

All right, I'd been... a little distracted the last few days. But knowing they were here, I'd done nothing. I'd been keeping my head down, afraid that if I got within a mile of them, if I even asked questions, somehow the past would burst through the skin of the present, and destroy my life. But what was I going to do, just hide and hope they went away?

Because I knew, as well as I knew *them,* that whatever they were here for, it wouldn't be anything good.

More than twenty years had gone by, but I didn't think they'd have changed that much.

Half an hour later, I was down in the welcome warmth of the kitchen, watching Flower, in a crisp clean apron, marshal his pans like a battle leader.

"You got a minute?"

"Jivrais, watch that pan, stir that pan. Do not allow that pan one minute's peace. If you let it burn, you go in it," he said, ushering me out.

"You're busy," I said, backing off. "This can wait."

But he'd already spotted the bunch of receipts in my hand. "Not if it's the accounts, it can't. How broke are we?"

"Not completely. Fain paid me, but I need to know what's urgent, and I can't even *read* half of these." We went into the blue room. "Most are stuff from the butcher; how's the new one, by the way?"

"All right, I suppose. We had a bit of mutton that was older than I'd have liked. That was that stew, yesterday."

"That? If it's the one I'm thinking of, it was gorgeous. How's Jivrais doing?" Jivrais had decided he wanted to learn to cook. Flower had offered to teach him. I viewed this with some trepidation, given Jivrais' capacity for chaos.

"He can cook, *if* he keeps his mind on it. Trouble is every time someone he likes the look of walks past the window, he gets distracted. Or anyone wearing clothes he can make fun of, or clothes he wants to buy. Or just clothes."

"Obviously not enough naked people walking around."

"I'm not sure that would help," Flower said.

"Maybe not. Can you teach someone to cook blindfolded?"

"Jivrais'd still find a way of being distracted. Like you." He tapped the papers.

"All right, all right. Just go over these with me, will you?"

He flipped through them, muttering. His hands are huge, but he has long, clever fingers. He keeps his claws fairly short. Otherwise they get in the way when he's cooking.

"That's odd," he said. "All the stuff for the kitchen's here, so far as I can tell, except the copy of the last order for Mirril."

"Our old butcher."

"Mmm." Flower frowned. "Did you ever find out what was going on there? She was so reliable. I mean, the new one's all right, though that lad of his has a neck and a half, but the quality just isn't as good."

"She just said she couldn't serve us anymore. You know how it is, Flower."

He kept flicking through the papers, sorting them into order. "That's what's strange about it. I mean, *she* knew how it was, too. She's always known what sort of place this is, never bothered her before."

"Maybe she got *religion*," I said.

Flower looked down at me. "Ouch." He took a glance around, but there was no one else near us. "Babylon?"

"Hmm."

"We've never talked about where either of us came from. You took me in and I was grateful..."

"Flower, I couldn't run this place without you."

"Pff. Anyway, I just wondered if you ever felt like talking, you know, I've got some pretty good golden hidden away. Thought we could break it out, maybe tonight. No customers, after all."

"What brought this on?" I said, sharper than I meant to. "Did you... has someone been asking about me?"

He shrugged, looking down at the bills. "No. And I wouldn't tell them anything if I knew it. You should know that."

"I'm sorry, Flower. It's been a little crazy."

"I had noticed."

"As for that golden – yes. Soon." I patted his arm. Actually I wanted to throw my arms around him and hold on; I wanted to put my arms around the whole building and hold on.

We went back to the office and looked for the copy of the order for Mirril, but it wasn't around. It was just a bit of paper with my signature scrawled on it; I told Flower not to fret. Rather wished someone would tell me the same thing, not that it would have helped.

I packed the bag of Fain's money inside my coat and headed for the Exchange.

We were close enough to Twomoon now that the streets were getting lively; I could hear the clash and shriek of a band from Hayanna howling through the streets. The music was supposed to drive away the evils that lurked under the double moon. I don't know about evils, but it would work on me.

Pity it wouldn't work on the Avatars. *Could* they be here looking for me? They didn't know me by my current name, but eventually it would occur to one of them to start checking brothels. Or sending someone to do it, more likely. What could I do? Shut the place down? Some of my crew had places to go, like Laney, and Flower could get a job anywhere he chose, but what about Jivrais? Essie? Ireq? And the thought of them all scattered to the winds... dammit, they were my *family*.

I barely managed to duck a bit of random magic that fizzed past my ear, and roundly cursed the bloody wizard who was too busy experimenting to look where he was throwing his spells. But you get a lot of that around Twomoon; I should have been keeping my eyes open.

I tried to concentrate on my surroundings, but I couldn't. Instead I thought about maybe taking myself off somewhere; hiding out, at least until the Avatars had left Scalentine, but I'd have to come up with some kind of explanation for the crew.

And was I really going to run? Again, after all this time?

Unwillingly, I thought of Kittack, who hadn't wanted to get involved, but had. Of Enthemmerlee herself. She could have turned away, she could have lived the easy life of someone at the top of the Gudain hierarchy. Instead...

My life, my people are here now.

But in the dark behind my eyes I saw Jonat's face, shadowed, looking at me.

TIRESANA

FEELING A LITTLE *calmer, not exactly making plans but at least thinking of doing so, I went back to the temple, where Shakanti had just arrived, draped in gauze of midnight blue and silver. "Oh. You," she said, when she saw me. "Why are you here?"*

Possibly, she had actually forgotten I was coming. I reminded her.

"I have many worshippers," she said. "So close to the sea, they know my tides. They think of me as the shine of the fish in the net. They think of me as they dig, as they cut the stone, as their blood stains its purity..." she was staring ecstatically past me at something I was quite glad I couldn't see. "Remember who you are," she said, coming back from wherever she was to glare at me. "I may choose to answer a prayer, but it will be of my choosing. Remember, always. We are not at their beck and call, to do whatever they ask."

We couldn't have done everything they asked anyway, of course. But the worshippers weren't supposed to know that. Avatars could be capricious; they just couldn't be less than godlike.

There was whispering at the temple door; the acoustics were disturbingly good, perhaps designed that way. Shakanti sighed. "It is still afternoon. That is hardly the proper time for worshipping me." Her face became a veiled skull for a moment. "Let us see who is so desperate that they come to my temple in daylight."

It was a young girl, perhaps sixteen, with the peachy bloom of youth and health. She was kneeling at the altar. Shakanti and I stood behind a screen of white marble carved as fine as lace; the carving was angled so that we could see the girl, but she couldn't see us.

She knelt, her long black hair tumbling over her breasts and thighs, looking up. "Shakanti, goddess of virgins, help me. Oh!" She picked up her rush basket. "I bring offerings. It's not much..."

A handful of herbs, a few pretty stones she'd found on the beach – some of them the very marble of which the temple was made, polished smooth by the sea. A shell, a feather. She got up to lay them on the altar, and knelt again, bowing her head.

"We don't have much, you see. That's why I'm promised in marriage. Only, he's old. And he grabs. And..." – she looked up, her eyes very wide – "I'm scared of him. He had another wife, and I don't think he was nice to her. She died, they said of childbed fever, but there were people said other things, too. Can you help me, Shakanti? I'd rather marry someone else. Someone younger, and, you know..." She blushed.

After all the formal chants, the solemn processions, the offerings, it was strange, almost heartbreaking. The handful of pitiful treasures, and the heartfelt plea. This was what people wanted gods for.

A few watchers had gathered at the temple door, perhaps knowing of Shakanti's presence. They had enough sensitivity to stay where they were, not wanting to disturb the supplicant at her prayers.

Shakanti looked up and saw them. Witnesses.

Maybe she was still feeling bruised by the fact that Hap-Canae's choice had become an Avatar, instead of her own. Maybe she really believed it was the right thing to do. Just maybe, there was no understanding her.

"Stand up, child," she said; she did something to make her voice drift through the temple like chilly smoke, so that even

those by the door heard it. They gasped and fell to their knees. The Goddess was among them, or at least her Avatar was, and who, now, remembered the difference?

The girl, her eyes huge, scrambled clumsily to her feet, clutching at the altar.

"What is your name?"

"Adissi."

"Adissi. Sweet child, I will save you from this unseemly marriage," Shakanti said, her voice clear and strong, even caressing. "Stand straight. Look up."

Adissi did, trying not to tremble, her hands clasped in front of her.

I saw her eyes searching for what was behind the screen, seeking a miracle.

I heard Shakanti draw in breath.

There was a shiver in the air, and where a living girl had been, there was now a statue of the whitest, gleaming marble.

One of the watchers screamed, and Shakanti clutched the screen, weakened, but smiling.

I was too shocked to move.

I stood there while the people crept towards the altar, pallid and shuddering. I stood there while the girl's mother, bustled to the temple by neighbours, dropped the bundle she was carrying and howled with grief and horror.

I stood there.

And Shakanti stood watching, still smiling.

"TURN HER BACK?" Shakanti said, looking at me as though she'd found me on her shoe. "What, into a mere girl, when now she is an object of wonder? She will remain beautiful, virgin, perfect. Proof of the power and compassion of the gods."

"You turned her into a statue!" I was shaking so much I could hardly get the words out. "That's not compassion, it's murder!"

"We do not *interfere in the actions of another Avatar*," Hap-Canae said.

He had decided to follow me; suspicious, or uncertain how well-trained I was. What would have happened if he hadn't... well, if I'd gone up against Shakanti alone, who knows? There might not have been much left of Prella.

I could feel my power beginning to surge up in me like water coming to the boil. It was part of what was making me shake. My sword was in my hand; Shakanti looked at it. "Hap-Canae..." she said.

He took me by the shoulders and made me look at him; our eyes were almost on a level, now. "Babaska. She has been saved from a marriage she feared, from a poor, short, miserable life. Instead she will remind them all that we see and know their lives, that we are always there. She will matter, now."

She will matter, now. Because before, at least to the Avatars, she hadn't.

I looked into those leopard eyes, and began to realise what I'd loved. I looked at my sword. I could attack Shakanti, but even if I could, eventually, kill her, the other Avatars would stop me. And I would never persuade her to reverse what she had done.

I let Hap-Canae take me back to the temple. I saw Ranay looking after me as I left, but I took no leave of him; I turned away even though it felt like someone tearing my chest open. I was terrified for him. They said they didn't interfere in the affairs of another Avatar, and yet I didn't trust that to apply to me or mine. What if one of them noticed him, as Lohiria already had? How could they not? He was so wonderful, so much better than any of them. How could anyone not notice him?

But it wasn't safe to be noticed by an Avatar. And now I knew what an Avatar really was; it was nothing that anyone should love.

As for seeking out my family... better for them to remember an innocent, if they remembered me at all.

CHAPTER
TWENTY-FOUR

THE TAX OFFICE is near the Exchange hall, but a lot less bumptious. The Exchange is all pillars and cherubs and women carrying sheaves. The tax office is small, grey and unfriendly. I handed over an unpleasantly large chunk of Fain's cash to the equally small, grey and unfriendly person behind the table, who didn't seem at all impressed with my efficiency and good citizenship. I was briefly tempted to take it back until their attitude improved, but I suppressed the notion and went to the Hall of Mirrors instead, to reward myself with some spice tea and a look in Bannerman's window.

It occurred to me, just as I took the first sip, that the Avatars might come to the Hall of Mirrors. It's where everyone comes, especially if they have money to spend.

I clutched the cup in front of my face, and looked over the rim, feeling suddenly raw and cold. I told myself I was being stupid – more than twenty years had passed, they would hardly recognise me now. I was just another Tiresan.

Only I'd never met another Tiresan since I left. Tiresans don't leave. Idiot, I told myself, there are other people on Scalentine who look like you, dark-haired and copper-skinned, so don't be a fool.

All the same, I lost my taste for the tea; I left it unfinished and dived into Bannerman's.

At least if the Avatars did turn up I'd have plenty of weapons to hand. I wondered if they'd work on them, here on Scalentine. It was a tempting thought.

I wasn't really looking at the merchandise at all; I was staring out of the window when someone said, "Can I help you?"

I turned around. The assistant was a long, pale creature who reminded me of Bliss, but whose eyes were much more sharply focused. "I'm just looking," I said.

Then I actually *saw* what was in the window. A pair of greaves, finely chased with leafy branches and twining beasts. Where had I seen something like those before?

Previous. Her nice new bracers, the ones that had been a present from Frithlit. I couldn't possibly afford them, but...

"I like those," I said. "Is there more in that style?"

"There should be bracers," the assistant said, "but regretfully they are not available at the moment. They would have to be re-ordered. That could take some time."

"Oh? Pity," I said, my mind whirring. "Why is that?"

"I regret to say that the original set was stolen."

Oh, mulecrap and dragonshit. They were the ones Bannerman had been tricked out of.

And now I knew who'd nicked 'em. What was I going to tell Previous?

TIRESANA

Hoping for something, *I attended the ceremonies at Babaska's temple in the precinct; listening from behind the screen, in the shadow of Babaska's statue. At the Ceremony of Petals, a celebration of the sensual arts and their practitioners, the place was crowded for days: there were great courtesans who came with their own households, and street-whores who charged in coppers or in food. I tried to answer too many pleas, and exhausted myself. What I could actually do for them was mainly show; I could increase someone's power to attract, but I couldn't protect them from bad clients or disease or poverty. My powers were hollow as a painted gourd, benefiting myself far more than anyone else.*

I even, in desperation, tried praying to Babaska, but my prayers sounded like nonsense – so many dead leaves, drifting into a void. There was only, sometimes, that gaze in my head, distant, unanswering. I was no longer sure it was Babaska at all.

At every ceremony, they came with their offerings, and I saw Adissi in every face – warm with life, laughing – or the young soldier who'd been killed in my first battle, who'd lain like a child with his head cupped in his hand. Every day my own guilt, my own complicity, ran in my blood like sickness.

Once I had experimented with my Avatar power, enjoying it, trying to find its limits; now, even when I used it for something halfway worthwhile, I felt it in me like a loathsome parasite and longed, more than anything, to be rid of it.

If any of the other girls had been left, they might have noticed; Jonat almost certainly would have. I was going out of my mind. Burning up with guilt, barely able to drag myself through my days. Missing Ranay as though I'd lost a limb, longing to try and contact him, not daring to.

I couldn't bring myself to bed anyone else, but went on with Hap-Canae because I couldn't think of an excuse not to; he didn't seem to notice my lack of eagerness. Though maybe he was aware of something, since he took another lover, a fiery little priestess with tiny feet and beautiful eyes, and started to spend half his time with her. I felt a sort of numb relief.

One day I hid in Aka-Tete's statue, where Jonat and I had had our last conversation. I was there for hours; staring up into the hollow god, trying to work out how to kill myself. But it's hard to kill an Avatar.

Eventually, the thought came to me. I had been made an Avatar.

Surely, somehow, I could stop being one?

It wasn't hope, exactly; it was more a lessening of darkness. A smudge of cold grey light that might, or might not, promise dawn.

I crawled back into the precinct, moving a little less heavily.

I couched my questions very carefully, and asked most of them in bed. I seduced priests, priestesses, even Avatars. Being what I was, I was good at it, though my Avatar abilities worked least well on other Avatars. For that I had to rely mostly on the lessons I'd been given, and on my own human self.

At least the sex itself gave me some pleasure. It is the nature of the goddess, and my own, and going against it would in the end have left me as twisted as Shakanti.

There was another advantage to putting myself about; it helped convince Hap-Canae that I had accepted my role and was happily fulfilling it.

I found out that the Avatars had already lived the span of a dozen normal lives since the gods had left this plane. I found out that Ranay – ah, even thinking of his name hurt my heart – had been telling the truth; the writings that dealt with the creation of the Avatars were all locked away, and only an Avatar could give permission to study them.

Of course, they never gave such permission. Someone might discover their true nature. But I discovered that the Avatars themselves sometimes poked about among the scrolls. I'd known Hap-Canae did, but not that the others did too.

I was long past thinking Hap-Canae was any kind of scholar, and no more were the rest of them. What were they looking for? I watched, and I listened, and I asked questions, and I stayed silent.

I heard the dreams of Avatars. Dreams of statues, solid gold and ruby-decked, so tall their shadow would span the desert. Dreams of Emperors of other worlds laying tribute at their feet. Dreams of armies millions strong, spreading fear of their names across the planes.

That was it, that was what they wanted. Their powers were terrifying, but limited; they wanted to be gods in truth.

But they were caught in a dilemma of their own making: they didn't have the scholarship or the dedication, and at least in the case of the wind Avatars, they didn't have the brains, to find out the information they desired for themselves. They dared not set human scholars to study for them, for fear their secret would get out.

I managed to get a glimpse at a few of the scrolls, but I was afraid, too. Frightened of drawing attention, frightened they would guess. And I had only recently learned to read; trying to decipher words written two hundred years before I was born was often beyond me. I found nothing.

I was walking across the outer precinct after leaving the bed of yet another priest who'd been able to tell me nothing, frustrated, frowning at the ground, when something made me look up.

Ranay. Walking towards me, smiling. I felt a wave of love and terror so strong my vision blurred.

"Avatar Babaska." He prostrated himself on the dusty stones.

"Ranay. What are you doing here?" My voice seemed to come from very far away.

"I have offended you," he said, scrambling to his feet. "Avatar Babaska, I will remove myself from your presence." Oh, his eyes, so dark, so hurt.

"No," I said, "Follow me. Keep your head lowered."

In the room behind Babaska's statue I closed the door and leaned on it. "Ranay."

I longed to touch him with my whole body, with my whole self. I shook with need. But I stayed where I was. He lifted his hands, as though to embrace me, but I was an Avatar. He could not, without my permission.

"My lady."

"How did you get here?"

"I asked to be transferred to the Temple..." his voice tailed off.

It was obvious he had asked to be transferred to be close to me. I breathed in his fresh, green scent; it was like sweet air after being closed in a sickroom.

"Oh, Ranay. You shouldn't have come."

My eyes were dry, though inside I was wailing like a child. How I hated not being able to cry.

He knew, though. He reached out a hand to me, but I waved him back.

"What is it? My goddess, what is it?" He looked both miserable and frightened, and I hated myself even more. But I couldn't tell him the truth. I didn't dare.

I looked at him. My sweet, my lovely man; so gentle and so dear.

"Ranay, if I asked you, could you help me do something?"

"Anything," he said.

"It's dangerous. They mustn't know."

"Danger? Who can threaten you?" he said.

"The others. The other Avatars. I've seen... I've seen them do terrible things, Ranay." The thought of his sweet warm body

*turned to stone finally wrenched a tear from me; I could feel it,
burning against my cheek.*

"It's you they'll hurt," I said. "I couldn't bear it."

*"Let me help you," he said. "Please. Seeing you cry, it's like
darkness on my heart. Please."*

He was crying, too.

*I thought, if I can stop being an Avatar, we can escape. We can
run away together.*

*"I have to tell you something," I said. "But if anyone finds out
you know this, they will kill you. You understand? You mustn't
ever speak of it. Ever."*

"I will take an oath, if you want me to."

*"No. There's no need." Even now, it was hard to say; fear and
the habit of obedience closed my throat, until I could only whisper.
"Ranay, I'm human. Or I was. All the Avatars were, once."*

*I held out my hand, and looked at it; it cast a faint golden
light, not enough to read by.*

"You're..."

*"My name was Ebi, and I was a servant. There was another
Avatar of Babaska before me, but she's gone. Disappeared. They
chose me to take her place."*

*He believed me, immediately. Perhaps some part of him had
already suspected. Or perhaps it was just because he trusted me.*

"How?" he said.

I told him about the altar-stone.

*There was a silence. His eyes were on me, but I didn't dare
look at them; fearing I'd see contempt, or hatred, or just the end
of love.*

"Ebi," he said.

It was so strange, to hear that name again. "Yes."

"Why did you tell me?"

*"Because I want to be human again. I want to find out how to
stop. Will you help me?"*

"You want to stop being an Avatar."

"Yes. Ranay..."

For the first time, without asking permission, he reached out, and touched my face. "Ebi," he said. "Tell me what you want me to do."

So I took him in my arms and kissed him, and it felt like coming home. But there was a darkness on my heart, too.

CHAPTER
TWENTY-FIVE

I HEADED BACK towards King of Stone. I needed somewhere big and crowded, where no Avatar would be likely to lower themselves to venture, where I could have a drink and get my thoughts together.

I had to stoop a little to get through the door of The Sideways Road, but once I was inside there was room enough and more. It's a big old barn of a place, goes back further than it looks like it should from the street. It smells of burned meat and old beer and smoke, and could do with a cat or six to keep down the healthy population of vermin who thrive on its leavings. Of which there are plenty; the food's terrible. But they keep surprisingly decent wine, and right now, I needed some.

It was fairly crowded; must be due for another scouring out by the militia. They don't bother until enough passing trade complains loudly enough about being scammed. Most of the locals know better than to get into any kind of game in the Sideways and most of Scalentine's *important* visitors don't venture down to King of Stone. I pushed my way through the press of bodies, after making sure my pouch was well hidden. There were a few card games, there always were, but there were more than a few other scams going on, old and new. "This ring was my mother's, it's worth more than I'm asking, but I have to get through Portal Bealach tonight and the captain won't take it as surety, he wants forty silver..."

"The coin's under this cup... or is it this one?"

"I'll give you one silver, that makes it proper, see? Makes you a real poet, that does. We'll print up your book of poems pretty as you like, then you just have to sell it, you see, to all the fine folks...."

"One silver?"

Whoa, I knew that voice. Right enough, it was young Antheranis – last seen in the afterglow of his first bedding – looking with wide eyes at a grease-nailed slime crawler I knew of old. Pettifer Crewe; well-known talent vulture.

"Pettifer, get your claws out of this boy. Lord Antheranis, this is no place for a young man like yourself, and this is no-one you should be talking to."

Antheranis looked from me to Pettifer, and clutched his sheaf of poems to his chest.

Pettifer swelled like a boil. "I was about to give this fine poet the chance he deserved! I'm a respectable businessman, and you're..."

"I'm an *honest* whore. Whereas you're a vile, envy-ridden dream-thief who wouldn't recognise fine verse if you stepped in it."

He looked towards Antheranis and spread his palms. "Don't listen, my lord. She's trying to crush your hopes! I can...."

But Antheranis was already tucking his poems away in his coat, and if there were tears trembling on the ends of his lashes, I for one was prepared to pretend I hadn't seen them.

Pettifer looked as though he were about to burst with fury and frustrated greed. Sadly, he didn't. "You... you... I shall..."

"Sharp with language as ever, ain't you?" I said.

He actually shook his fist at me. "You'll regret this, Babylon Steel!"

The man even talked in clichés. "Oh, get in line," I said. "But right now, get your arse out the door, Crewe, before I slice myself some pork." Finally, he went, leaving the air a little fresher, in my opinion.

I turned back to Antheranis, who was looking bemused. "My lord, what in the All's name are you doing here? And alone? You don't have an escort?"

He poked his lower lip out. "I am not *prevennis* – a child."

"No, but you don't know Scalentine. There are places *I* don't go without an escort." Okay, it wasn't true, but I was trying to save what face the poor lad had left. And I had to get him back to his father before anything worse than his dignity got damaged.

"I am wishing to see the real life," he said. "Not just the pretty."

I didn't want to knock him out and carry him – that would do nothing for his dignity. And even in here, someone *might* think it suspicious.

All save us, a young boy on a runner from his father's care and innocent as an egg was *not* what I needed. Sometimes this town was just too damn small, but now I'd seen him, I had to do something. I looked regretfully at the bottles behind the bar. So much for my drink.

A skinny rat of a creature tried to sell Antheranis some cloud. I'd have intervened, but the boy knew enough to give a very firm *no*. The rat-like dealer disappeared sharpish before I could make my displeasure known. He looked pretty similar to the creature I'd seen below ground, but then, a rat's a rat.

"Good lad," I said to Antheranis.

"My father, he take me to the street where many beggars, all beg for cloud, even when they have only skin over bones." He made a face. "I do not want to be like that."

"Your father is a sharp man."

"Yes, but he does not understand. I wrote about the beggars. They were..." he waved his hands. "I do not have the Lithan. But in my tongue, I write about them. People should know, yes?"

"Well, yes, but lots of people only want to hear about... what did you call it? The pretty."

"That is what my father says."

"He's not wrong, you know."

"Sometimes the ugly is more important." I didn't have an answer for that, since I couldn't help but agree with him.

"Tell me about this man Pettifer," he said.

"Oh, he's the ugly, all right. If you want to hear, I'll tell you, but we'll have to do it while we walk, my lord. I need to go to the Exchange hall." Fortunately it was near the good hotels – money tends to pool together, I've noticed – and I knew which one his father was staying in.

Antheranis sighed, and looked around. "I have seen this place now. And I do not think they appreciate poetry here. Will you show me another place?"

"Maybe," I said. "Your father ever taken you to Nederan? Beyond Throat portal. Icy place. Inhabitants tend to the hairy."

"No, but I would like to go very much. They have a great respect for poets."

"Good poets, yes. If you please them you can fatten for a year on what they'll pay you. Pettifer Crewe tried to make it as a court poet. Did one recital and barely got out with his life. They threatened to nail his tongue to the wall if he ever crossed their border again. They take the phrase 'murdering the language' fairly literally, the Nederans."

"Indeed?" He looked thoughtful. "Perhaps I will practice some more."

"Anyway after that, Crewe decided to leech off other people's talents instead of attempting to improve his own. He'll take someone's work with all manner of fine promises, but all they get is lots of excuses and empty pockets."

We turned towards the square. As soon as he saw the cluster of fine hotels, dominated by the Riverside Palace with its soaring white marble frontage, the boy's face grew sulky again. I only just managed to grab his collar before he made off down a side-street. "Oh, no, you don't," I said. "What do you think your father would do to me if he knew I'd let you go wandering off by yourself?"

"You make me a *fath*, a trick!"

Then I saw who was coming out of the Blue Sun. It's only two doors from the Riverside Palace, and the most expensive place in Scalentine. Cold sick fear dropped through me all the way to my boots. I put my hand over the kid's mouth and hauled him into an alleyway. He was struggling madly, reaching for the little dagger in his belt. I whispered in his ear: "My lord, if you value your life, be still and *shut up*. No trick. I've just spotted someone who wants my hide and they won't have any compunction about taking yours to go with it." He stilled. "Are you going to stay quiet and do as I say? *Please,* my lord. I don't want either of us dead."

He must have felt me trembling. I felt him nod against my palm, and let him go – though I kept one hand on his shoulder.

My heart was pounding so hard I could feel it in my throat. I had to sneak a look around the corner again, just to be sure.

There was no mistaking Hap-Canae. I would have known him anywhere, and he'd always looked his best by torchlight. Draped in the gold and amber silks he adored, he still had that unmistakeable swagger. And the charisma, too. No applied magic, this, but a part of what he was. Even from where I stood it tugged at me, trying to curve my mouth into a smile, whispering in my flesh.

Lucky that my first instinct had been to hide. Luckier, perhaps, that the boy Antheranis was with me. Lucky for me, if not for him. I kept my hand tight on his shoulder.

"Oh!" he said, his eyes huge and the same smile I was suppressing bending his mouth.

He was watching Shakanti, of course. She drifted down the steps, her gossamer blue and silver robes billowing around her like smoke, like clouds lit by moonlight. It was hard to tell, but I thought that beneath them she was thinner than ever, scoured to the bone. Her face was veiled. Her charisma felt cold as well-water; the attraction of mystery and the night hunt.

Of course, her charisma had never had the same effect on me as Hap-Canae's, but it was pretty devastating nonetheless. I wondered if being so close to two full moons was increasing her powers. It wasn't a pleasant thought; she was one dangerous bitch without any extra help.

A litter glowed at the foot of the steps, crusted with gold paint, and jewels, and more gold, and a few more jewels, not to mention bronze bells polished to a glare and hanging from every available projection.

That had to be Hap-Canae's choice. Shakanti, at least, had some taste.

Yellow-robed acolytes and general attendants swarmed like ants, bowing their backs to help the Avatars into the glittering monstrosity of a litter. Seeing them supported on those straining shoulders helped dampen the dual effects of fear and charisma and get some good healthy anger burning in my gut.

And guilt, of course. Those people with their narrow-nosed, slim faces and long eyes; I knew them. The deep bronze skin, black hair bound with beads and glowing with the occasional flash of hennaed red. The lithe, graceful bodies, some already twisting under the weight of their work.

My people, once.

The litter finally moved off, with the trumpet-blowers going ahead, blaring the presence of godhead through the streets.

A few of the fame-hungry still clustering around the steps waved and cheered, but (bless the Scalentines for their short attention-span) these demigods were already old news, and there were nothing like the crowds there must have been when they arrived.

Their departure took them past the front of the alley, and I pressed myself and Antheranis back into the shadows, but they never paused.

Dark flowers bloomed in front of my eyes and I gulped air. The boy shifted his shoulder under my hand and I realised I'd been gripping too hard. I managed to let go. "Sorry, my lord."

Antheranis rubbed his shoulder, peering out of the alley in the wake of the procession. "Who are they?"

"Do you have gods?"

"Of course! But... they were *gods?*"

"Demigods. Avatars."

"Our gods do not *walk about,*" he said, sounding offended.

I thought of those sweating backs, bent to the weight of the litter. "Nor do they, it seems. Forgive me, my lord, but I need to get you back to your father."

He scowled. "Madam Steel? Why do you hide from them?"

"That's nothing you need to know."

"Really, they would..." he drew a hand across his throat.

"Yes."

"My father, perhaps, can help," he said, looking up at me.

"I appreciate the thought, but he's best out of it." And besides, though I enjoyed Antheran's company, when all was done he was only a client. He had no reason to get involved.

Besides, I liked the man. I didn't want him drawing their attention.

I looked at the boy. "How about a bargain? I won't tell your father what sort of dive I found you in, and you won't mention what just happened."

He pondered for a moment. "What you will tell him?"

"That you came to visit Essie and I decided to escort you back."

He blushed, all the way to the top of his bald head, bless him. "Madam Steel? If I ask Father, he would pay, would you take me, to see the things that are not pretty? The real?"

Ouch. I hadn't bargained for that. "Just now, my lord..."

"Please to call me Antheranis."

"As you wish. But just now, having me as an escort... well, let's just say it might not make you as safe as your father would wish. Why not ask Essie?"

"I could not take her to such places!"

I grinned. Essie was born in King of Stone, a rat's scuttle from Ropemakers Row. A *brave* rat. She could use her knee like a fist and her fist like a siege-weapon, and if there was anything that could make her blush I'd yet to hear of it. But let him cherish his illusions a bit longer. "Perhaps we can get one of the others to do it. In the meantime, my lor... Antheranis, if you please..." I gestured him towards the Moons in Splendour, where his father was staying.

He pouted, but obeyed.

TIRESANA

I WENT TO the ceremonies, and to Hap-Canae's bed when I couldn't avoid it. When I rose from it I smelled like him, of cardamom and myrrh; I bathed for hours, trying to scrub it from me.

I seduced my way into the locked sections of the libraries, pretending I thought them a good place for assignations. Leaving my conquest exhausted and comatose, I stuffed ancient scrolls up my sleeves, shuffling things about so it wouldn't be noticed that anything was missing.

That didn't last. Neglected as the libraries appeared to me, it was soon apparent that the librarians kept a careful check on the scrolls, even those they weren't allowed to read themselves. They didn't question me, of course; I was an Avatar. But their anxiety was obvious. I dared not take a scroll out for more than a few hours.

I knew there was a danger that the Avatars might notice, but I hoped they would not. After all, I was not looking for the same thing they were. I was looking for a way to become less, not more. The minute Ranay could bear to let go of the scrolls I took them back and thrust them in among the others.

I met Ranay in unused corners, in empty temples thick with incense-scented dust, in windowless rooms buried at the heart of the temple where the faded wall-paintings looked down on us with flat gilded eyes. *The more he found, the more fascinated he became; the more eager for knowledge.*

The legend said that the gods had created the Avatars before they left this plane, to do their will and stand for them before the people. And yet it seemed, from the older texts, that perhaps this was not quite how things had happened. That the gods had gone, and then, some uncertain time later, there were the Avatars.

Ranay said that what he had found suggested that the gods had not wanted or desired such creatures. That perhaps the Avatars had been only High Priests and Priestesses who had, somehow, found a way to gain power that maybe the gods had never meant them to have.

It made sense to me. What sane gods would have given so much power to creatures like them?

Of course, that assumed the gods were sane to start with.

One day he pulled out a scroll and held it up to the window. "There were others before you, you said. Other Avatars of Babaska?"

"Yes," I said.

"Look."

The ink was old and faded, the words almost gone. A lot of stuff about loosening chains, and cutting bonds, 'and the jewel of the gods shall open the gate.' Ranay tapped the scroll. Scratched next to the words were two faint marks. A sort of crossbar, and a thing like a fat bird's claw.

"Turn it the other way up," Ranay said.

And there they were: a lotus, and a sword.

Babaska's mark, made by a human hand. What did it mean?

I ran the tip of my finger over it. I wasn't sure if I could feel the faint roughness, or if it was just my imagination. It woke a memory in me, but I couldn't grasp it. "You think one of them, one of the other Babaskas, did this?"

"Yes. I've seen others, I didn't know what they meant. But look."

He tilted the page, and at the bottom were more marks. Hastily scrawled with the tip of a knife, in a rounded childish hand, barely visible, were words. "Power lies here, the force divine. If Bahaska find this, heed my sign."

"'The jewel of the gods will open the gate'?" I said. "Do you think that means that the jewel, whatever it is, will give them what they want?"

"True godhead. Unlimited power."

"Yes."

We looked at each other, and I could see the horror in his eyes, knew it was reflected in my own.

I banished the fear the only way I knew, and he did no more work that night.

Later, as I lay awake, listening to him breathing – even the sound of his breath was precious to me – I wondered. Why would the last Avatar of Bahaska have left such a message? I understood why she didn't destroy the scroll, it might have been noticed. But surely, marking the passage like that would only draw attention to it? What if it had not been Ranay, but one of the Avatars, who found it?

And what if the Avatars were watching us already, wondering what I was looking for?

I could never sleep for long, those nights. Yet frightened as I was, impatient as I was to be free and human again, seeing Ranay bent over the scrolls by lamplight, working until he was so weary he could barely stay awake for a kiss, I knew a strange, fragile happiness.

"THERE IS TO be a battle," Lohiria said, her long gold hair rippling and whispering like seas of corn; not that we had seen any such harvest, not for a long time.

"A battle?" Fighting, at least, I knew how to do. Life and death was simple in comparison to what was going on in my head. "Are we under attack? Who is it?"

"Mihiria."

"What?"

"We want to have a battle. And since you are in charge of the soldiers, you must be there."

"But I don't understand... you're fighting each other?"

She sighed. "Really, how you ended up as Babaska's Avatar... still, I suppose fighting and fornication don't take that much sense. We pick a place. We each pick one of two villages or two towns or two families. We tell them they must defend our honour, and off they go. As the Avatar of Soldiers, you have to be there. Now do you understand?"

Of course I did. I wondered how I could ever have been so stupid.

There was no enemy. Where would an enemy have come from? Hardly anyone came to Tiresana.

The soldiers were only pieces in a game, not people, not to the Avatars. And I'd been as bad as the rest, failing to see, as they died at my feet, that they were dying for nothing; believing I was doing something that had meaning, defending something, when all I was defending was some other Avatar's pride. They didn't interfere with each other, but they played games.

What would I do, among the soldiers? Urge them on to waste their lives, to show an honour and courage that the Avatars had long forgotten, if ever they knew such things?

Anything I could give them, courage or strength, in such little portions as I could, would mean someone else's death. I was steeped in death, in deception, in ugliness.

I had to do something. I went looking for a place to meet Ranay, desperate to talk to him, frantic to hear that he had found a way to destroy this sick power inside me.

If I'd had any sense I'd have met him openly. To bed priests was part of my role, and would have been perfectly acceptable. As it was, I grew increasingly nervous. I was afraid Lohiria would recognise him and become suspicious; though the woman had the brains of a fish, she had, like all of them, a vicious streak.

I was certain I was watched, and kept seeking out new places to meet him. One night, I discovered a part of the temple that was plain and unpainted: a newer part, but almost as dusty as the corridors around the altar-stone and equally unguarded.

I went looking for a room that would lock (not that it would make the slightest difference, if the Avatars came). I pushed open a door and found I was surrounded by the dead.

The room was full of stone sarcophagi, beached boats on a dry shore. There were no names, no engraved steles, no mention at all of who lay within them.

Lifting the lantern, I saw something lying on one of them. It looked like a rag, as though someone had been dusting the tombs.

I picked it up. It was a piece of silver gossamer; or had been, before it was torn and bloodied and washed and mended and stitched until it was just a web of broken threads held together with tiny, obsessive stitches.

Renavir's scarf.

Still clutching it, I stepped back.

My foot hit something that clinked and rolled away, shining.

A ring. Not left on a tomb, this, but simply discarded, or lost. I knew even before I looked closer that it would be the ring Aka-Tete had given to Jonat. The soft metal was dented. I didn't know if I had done that, or if it had fallen from Jonat's limp hand, when they put her in her coffin. She had got thinner, those last days.

I looked at my own ring, and imagined Hap-Canae placing it on my coffin, with a regretful sigh.

The truth sank into me, colder than well water.

All the girls I had trained with were dead, disposed of like dogs that wouldn't breed true. The bodies had not been dumped in the desert, or the Rohin, but disposed of almost... decently. It was as though the Avatars had wanted to hide, even from themselves, what they had done; to cover murder with a slab of decency.

Why didn't you run, Jonat? You knew something was very wrong. Why didn't you run?

I heard her voice as though she was standing there.

"Because I still loved him. Because I hoped I was wrong. Because I tried to make you understand, and perhaps we could have run together, but you wouldn't see it; you were stupid, and a coward."

I realised that those who had trained us must also be dead; Livaia, with her grace and humour, all those pretty young men and women, and all the fight trainers. Farren, perhaps, might have survived. But apart from that...

They weren't here; had they been given to the sands? Was it only because the girls had been potential Avatars that they had been granted the cold grace of a proper tomb?

There were two or three older sarcophagi, too. There had, of course, been at least one other Avatar of Babaska. She had 'proved unworthy of the role,' Shakanti had said. How many more had there been? Running my hands over the chilly stone, I wondered how they had done it. It's hard to kill an Avatar.

I remembered, finally, that I was supposed to meet Ranay. I had just enough sense to mess the dust about to hide the marks I'd left, and drop Renavir's scarf back on her coffin.

There was a lock of silver-white hair lying there too. It seemed that Shakanti, in her own strange, twisted way, might have mourned her protégé.

It probably meant she'd taken the trouble to kill her herself.

CHAPTER
TWENTY-SIX

I GOT A message to Antheran's suite, and he came down the stairs to the main hall at such a pace that he tripped on his robes and only saved himself a bad fall by clutching the banister. He forced himself to a walk, his face rigid, and advanced on Antheranis, who, having seen his father's face, was now trembling quite badly.

He wasn't the only one, I realised, when Antheran, ignoring him, took my hand in a fervent but distinctly shaky clasp. "Babylon. Antheranis, you will go to our suite and you will await me there." The boy shuffled off, casting a scared look over his shoulder.

"He's quite well, my lord," I said. "Came to visit Essie. I thought you'd prefer I brought him back to you myself."

"I can see he is well. Whether he will be feeling quite so well in another hour is entirely a different matter. And I shall have to dismiss his bodyguard."

I looked over at the boy, who was hovering miserably at the foot of the stairs, scuffing the floor with his foot, and occasionally casting apprehensive glances at us.

"May I make a suggestion, my lord?"

"You think I should just punish the bodyguard?" He looked down at his hand, and I realised the knuckles were split. "I already broke the man's jaw. I was... a little upset."

"Don't dismiss the guard. He's going to be twice as careful now, and if he's any sense, grateful that he hasn't been turned out. Boys your son's age are like cats – they can get through gaps you wouldn't think possible, before you can turn around." I had reason to know; I'd hauled more than a few curious youngsters out of the Lantern over the years. There'd been that boy the other day who'd wriggled in through some hole or other.

"I shall think about it. Thank you, Babylon." He leaned close, and pressed a pouch into my hand. "That is only a token, a nothing," he said. For 'nothing,' it was pretty heavy. "You brought my son back safe to me. If you need *anything*..." His voice shook for a moment.

"Thank you, Antheran." I kept my own voice low – I normally addressed him as 'my lord' in public. "Believe me, he's fine."

"This time." He drew a deep breath and turned towards his son, who put his shoulders back and raised his chin. It was time I left.

I ABANDONED THE idea of a drink and headed back to the Lantern. This wasn't going to be pleasant, but I'd done enough of putting off the unpleasant recently.

Previous was on the door, pulling at her new bracers. I could see the red marks on her wrists, where they'd rubbed.

"We need to chat," I said.

I called Unusual down from where he was still dancing attendance on Cruel. He stationed himself out front, looking so grim that I said, "Unusual."

"Yes."

"We don't know who did it, and we don't need any more trouble. So no haring off after anyone on suspicion, all right?"

"Right."

I was uncomfortably aware that I was echoing what the Chief had said to me. I didn't want to think about the Chief right now. We'd spatted before, but never like that.

"So what's this about?" Previous said.

"Come upstairs, okay?" I took her into my room, shut the door behind us and got the wine out of the cupboard. Then I put it back, and got out my bottle of golden instead. I wondered if perhaps I should go down and find out where Flower kept his extra-special bottle, then realised I was just delaying. I poured us both a good knock of the stuff.

"Babylon?" she said.

"You seen Frithlit today?"

"Not since yesterday. Why?"

"How much do you know about him?"

"*Frithlit?* I thought this was going to be about whatever the hells is going on with you!"

"Huh?"

"Come on, Babylon. You've got a scar on your face that looks at least three years old, but wasn't there last week. You've been twitchy as a cat on a windy day ever since Clariel turned up yesterday..."

"Was it only yesterday?" I was honestly surprised.

"Yes. So what's going on?"

"Later. Previous... look. Those bracers Frithlit gave you... someone cheated Bannerman's out of a pair like that. The matching greaves are in his window."

She looked down at the bracers, with their delicate running deer, and her coppery brows drew together. Then she sighed. "Oh, Thukret's hairy balls." She drank her golden off at a gulp and held out her glass. I hesitated for a moment, then refilled it.

"You think he bought them off some bloke in the Sideways Road, or the Break, maybe? Thought he was getting a bargain?" she said.

"Umm... no, honey. I don't think so."

She sighed again, heavier than before. "No. No, nor do I."

"You don't?"

She turned the glass around in her fingers, staring at it. "You know when we met? He'd just come out of the Sideways Road. I know the sort of games they run, but I thought he was some tourist who'd got caught, you know? But there's been other things."

"Like?"

"I caught him in your office yesterday. He said he was looking for you, but... and the day the Vessels came?"

"Mmm."

"Well, he told me he hadn't been here long, but he knows a lot about the law, doesn't he?"

"Maybe too much for someone on the right side of it, you mean?"

"Yeah." She drank the rest of the golden, sniffed hard, stood up and started to unbuckle the bracers. "And he's been asking questions."

"Like what?" I said, suddenly even more worried. What if Frithlit wasn't just a lowlife fixer, but a lowlife fixer who'd been hired by the Avatars? What if he'd gone off to tell them about the woman who ran a brothel, who had a scar on her jaw...

Previous glanced up at me, and I could see there were tears in her eyes. Previous! I'd seen her take a blade right through the arm without crying. I didn't care if Frithlit was working for the Avatars; if I got my hands on that mouse-eared little creep, he was going to *seriously* regret it, just for hurting her.

"Stuff about what sort of money the place earns, and where we did our banking and... well. So I started asking a few, too. And he just sort of slid out of answering. What should I do with these, take 'em back to Bannerman's? Think he'll have me arrested?"

"Previous..."

"Don't," she said. "I've been an idiot. That's all there is to it."

"But that isn't all there is to it, is it?"

"Oh," she said. And then laughed, a little hard laugh, like a cough. "Funny, I actually forgot for a minute. Yes. I'm pregnant. Dumb, eh?"

"We'll deal with it," I said. "Whatever you want to do, we'll deal with it."

"What I *want* to do is take that little wretch by the scruff and throw him to the Twins, is what I *want*."

"I don't blame you. Give me the bracers, okay? I'll sort that out, at least. And Previous?"

"Yeah."

"If he comes back here, don't kill him, all right? Just tell him to bugger off, punch him if you like, but don't kill him."

She snorted. "I'll just tell him he's about to be a daddy. If that doesn't send him running for the hills, nothing will."

She's not the type for hugs, so I slapped her on the shoulder. She gave about half a grin, which was pretty good, considering, and made for the door. She stopped halfway through, and turned around.

"Babylon?"

"Yes?"

"I'm used to watching your back, but I can't do it if I don't know where the spear's coming from."

"I know," I said.

As I WALKED back into town with Fain's money still in my coat, and the bracers wrapped in a piece of cloth, I realised I was skulking close to walls, like a cat avoiding unpleasant children. I don't *skulk*. It made me even angrier than I was already. I forced myself towards the middle of the pavement and inserted myself into the stream of people going into the main entrance of the Exchange. The low roar of business and the clatter of coin echoed off the soaring ceilings and lethally polished floors. Exchange guards in yellow-and-brown striped jerkins stood at intervals along the walls, or wandered about, eyeing everyone.

People were exchanging samples of goods and currencies, doing deals that filled the holds of ships and emptied the coffers of kings. Many of the traders were casting signals, strings of hand-gestures so rapid their hands looked like flickering wings: the lingua franca of finance. One language I never managed to learn.

Hugging the walls like they were my best client, I tried to work my way around to the cashiers without drawing attention to myself. I had that constant itchy crawl along my spine that didn't mean I was being watched, but meant my spine wished it had eyes.

I'd barely visited the Exchange Hall since I first arrived in Scalentine, weary of running and thinking I'd left my past behind. Damn fool that I was. When I had any money to put in, I tended to dump it and get out of there as soon as possible. The place made me twitchy.

"Madam Steel?"

I was on my feet with my hand on my sword before I thought, *they wouldn't call me that.*

There was a little round man in front of me, with oiled hair and beard, his hands flying up in horror. "Sheath, sheath! Drawing steel in the Exchange hall? What are you thinking?"

"I wasn't." They're excessively touchy about people waving weapons around in there; a guard was already eyeing us, ready to head our way. The little man raised his hand to show he didn't think I was going to cut his throat.

Wonderful. I'd drawn attention to myself for no reason at all. But why shouldn't I? This was my city, I should be able to draw attention if I damned well pleased.

I tried to push my anger down and looked at the man in front of me. I had a feeling this man had been a client, anyways I knew him, but I couldn't dredge up his name for my life.

"How do you know me?" I said.

"We have met before, and of course, I know that ring." He nodded at my hand. "Did you want to talk about the arrangement?"

I gaped like a landed fish, I'm sure. "Arrangement?"

"Yes. Your loan."

"Loan?"

"Are you quite well?" he said.

"I'd feel a damn sight better if I understood anything you just said. What loan?"

"The loan I was arranging for you..." His high colour began to wash out of his face, like linen bleaching in the sun. "Oh. Oh dear, I think you'd better come with me."

"I'm going nowhere until you tell me what you're talking about."

He looked around the hall. "Please, this is best done out of range of curious ears."

"Not moving."

He glared. "Very well. A young man came to me yesterday morning. He had your signature, and your seal..."

"*What?*"

"That ring. The same you showed when you borrowed money from us several years ago, to set up your... ah... place of business."

Ah. So I had been a client of *his*, rather than the other way around.

"Are you telling me someone borrowed against my name?"

"In your name. He said he was your emissary in the matter."

I looked at him. He started to back away, raising his hands protectively. "We haven't given it to him yet! It was a considerable amount, it had to be transferred... but we had no reason not to believe him. The signature, the seal...."

I raised my hand, looked at it. "This ring?"

"Of course."

"It's never been off my hand..." I started to say. But of course, it had. I'd taken it off to bathe, and to sleep.

I had been bathing, and had been interrupted. And who had been waiting outside in the hall? Frithlit. Charming little Frithlit, with his wide eyes and his crinkly ears.

And the ring had been covered in soap, and the soap missing. It was an old trick; you want to make a copy of something, take an impression in a chunk of soap. Use it as a mould.

"Tell me," I said, "what did he look like?"

"Slight. Shorter than me. Blue skin..."

I cut him off. "You, Mister, just arranged to lend money to a fraudster who ripped off Bannerman's two days ago, and who knows how many other people before that. Or since."

He raised his hands and made a series of flickering gestures, without taking his eyes off me. I glanced up and saw one of the cashiers make a short gesture back to him. "What?" I said.

"The loan has been cancelled. I have placed a small sum of fifty silver in your account to compensate you for the inconvenience. I do hope this will not affect our future business relationship."

"I hope not too," I said, handing him the bag of coin I was carrying, and realising I'd left the other bag at home, dammit. "This is to go with that fifty silver. I'd take it... *kindly* if you don't give it to anyone else who happens to turn up carrying my seal."

He bowed low and started to make a lot of protestations about how pleased he was and that if I needed anything...

"Just tell me when he left, and if you know where he went."

"Yesterday." He spread his hands. "Unfortunately, he did not inform me of his plans, and had he done so, one must doubt whether the information would be accurate."

"If he comes back here, I want to know."

The banker smiled, for the first time, stroking his beard. "He will. We were going to give him the money this afternoon. He's due to collect it in less than an hour." He flicked his hands at the cashier again.

I said, "I'll wait for him. Out of sight. That'll help compensate me for the inconvenience."

"Of course," he said, then glanced down at my sword. "But please... we can't have any *unpleasantness*. I have already arranged for a message to be sent to the militia."

"Get a lot into a few flicks of the fingers, don't you?" I said. "You should be in the profession."

"Madam! I'm a happily married man."

"I'm not surprised," I said. "Look, I just want to be personally sure that the greasy little fraud is under lock and key."

So he found me a room to wait in, and I sat there, fretting. And fretting some more. And watching a brass clock under a glass dome tick through the minutes, all its little wheels working.

At least I'd caught up to Frithlit before he cleaned me out, but what else might he have got in my name, and with my ring?

And what about poor old Previous?

And what was I going to do about the thrice-damned bloody Avatars?

There was nothing, absolutely nothing, in that room except me and the clock, and too much time to think, with very little to show for it. I ran through some training moves, just for something to do, and nearly ran through the banker as well, when he opened the door without warning.

He squeaked; fortunately I'd time to pull the blow. "Madam Steel?"

"Is he here?"

"It's the militia, Madam. They want to talk to you."

"What? Where's Frithlit?"

"He... er... hasn't arrived." The banker, looking disconcerted, tugged at his beard.

I wondered for a moment, with a sudden surge of hope, if the Chief was here, but why he'd have come looking for me and how he'd have known I was here I couldn't imagine. "You'd better take me to the millies, then."

It wasn't the Chief. It was Roflet, the blonde young officer with the eyelashes. He was standing very straight, with his hands by his sides, all his flirtatious charm put away. "I understand you were looking for Frithlit Oprentic, Madam Steel."

"If that's his name, I was, yes. Little bastard tried to rob me. Gave one of my crew a pair of bracers he'd conned out of Bannerman's, too." I dropped the package on the table. "These. Seems he didn't give a toss if she was caught wearing them and accused of robbery. He forged a copy of my seal-ring and tried to get money in my name – I suppose the banker told you."

Roflet glanced at the package. "I see. When did you discover the forgery?"

"About an hour ago, when I came here."

"Can you tell me when you saw him last?"

I thought back. He'd been there when we were looking after Cruel. "Yesterday, about mid-afternoon, I think."

"And you haven't seen him since."

"No. Why? Who's he ripped off this time?"

"Possibly someone who took it rather badly. We just found his body."

TIRESANA

I WANDERED TOWARDS *the meeting-place we'd arranged, barely seeing what was around me; seeing only those cold sarcophagi, the pathetic little relics. The torn scarf, the dented ring.*

Ranay came towards me with his hands held out. I don't know what he saw on my face, but he looked stricken. "What is it?"

The worst of it was the sense that I'd known, somewhere, in the back of my mind. I'd suspected things were wrong, that we were being lied to.

I'd done nothing. And now all of them but me were dead.

I shook my head. I felt strange, afloat. He took my hands. "You're cold." Outside the sun was a bronze hammer; the precinct swam with heat. I hadn't even realised my hands were freezing.

"Yes."

He pressed my hands to his chest to warm them, wrapped me close in his arms. I buried my head in his neck, in the clean fresh scent of him.

"Help me," I said.

"Tell me."

So I told him.

He just held me for a long time, stroking my hair.

"I hate them," I said, into his shoulder. "I hate them and I don't know what to do."

"*You don't have to be one of them anymore, Ebi. I found something.*"

"*You did?*"

"*Yes, I think so. If I have read the scrolls correctly, you must shed your blood on the altar, and place your hands where you placed them before, and you'll be free. Not an Avatar any longer.*"

I should have felt relief. I did. And yet, I realised; I was planning to run. I was Babaska's Avatar. Babaska didn't run from anything. Strategic retreat, yes, but never cowardice. I thought of those soldiers, in their stinking barracks; I thought of the dead girls – Velance, Jonat, Renavir. Adissi. How many more?

If I stopped being an Avatar, I'd have nothing to fight them with. Nothing at all.

I put my arms around him. "*So many people are dying, Ranay. For nothing. While I'm still... this, while I still have some power, I think we should tell them.*"

"*Tell them?*"

"*What the Avatars are.*"

He looked at me, silent. I felt a weight on my heart. He'd said he would do anything I asked; he hadn't promised to die for a forlorn hope. Maybe I would have to do this alone.

But that wasn't what troubled him. "*Ebi,*" he said, "*I'm not sure it will work.*"

"*What do you mean?*"

He took my hands. "*I've been a priest longer than you've been an Avatar. I've seen them at the temples. Do you know that the worse things get, the more they come to worship? People are so frightened; they see how things are, the dust where the crops used to be, the eyeless children. But the Avatars are powerful. People believe in their power; they're desperate to believe in something. You're going to be telling them that power's hollow. I don't think they'll want to listen.*"

I thought about it.

"Then maybe we should just start with me. Maybe... maybe we can get them to understand, if we tell them about me, if we can prove it, then maybe they'll believe."

He nodded. *"Perhaps. When a temple starts to fall, it doesn't go all at once. It starts with a little crack, that spreads and widens. Do you have a way to make one?"*

"There are people who knew me. Before. If we can find them..."

Not the master. Certainly not the mistress. But Radan, Sesh, Kyrl, they knew me. They would know me now, however much I'd changed.

"There's something I need you to do," I said. *"Get a message to Babaska's temple at Pryat, to be passed on to the cousin of the Priestess there."*

"What message?"

"'Tell Kyrl...'" I thought for a long time.

"'Tell Kyrl I'm about to risk everything on a bad hand, and does she fancy joining the game?'"

He repeated it, until he had it by heart.

"Ranay, did you find any more of those things about the godhead jewel?"

"Yes. A few."

"Were there more of those marks? Because I think I might have seen them before." The scroll Hap-Canae had found in the library, the one he'd burned; that too had had something about godhead on it. True godhead that came with blade and flower.

"I found two or three more. Always upside-down to the text. Perhaps she hoped that they wouldn't realise it was her mark."

I wondered who she had been. Alone, frightened, trying to leave clues, not knowing if anyone would ever find them, already feeling her death breathing down her neck.

"If we found the jewel, could we destroy it, do you think?" I said. *"Stop them from ever using it?"*

"Maybe. But things like that... even if we could find it, it's not always easy to destroy such a thing. Or safe."

And we didn't even know what it was. All we could do was start to undermine them the best we could. I knew it might be a long time before Kyrl could get to me; if she could. If she was still alive. So, readying the ground, we started to chisel cracks. Whispers among the supplicants at the temples. Rumour, spreading on the hot summer wind.

CHAPTER
TWENTY-SEVEN

FRITHLIT WAS DEAD. Through the shock I felt a sting; not sorrow, exactly, but a kind of regret. He'd been a fraudster and a lowlife, but he wasn't the worst and, hells, when I first met him, I'd actually *liked* him. And so had Previous. Oh, sweet All. Breaking this news to her was going to be even more fun than the last time.

"What happened?"

"No-one knows. The last anyone saw of him alive, he was at a card game in the Moon and Mackerel, down on the docks, this afternoon."

Why in the name of all that was sane Frithlit would choose to get into a dodgy card game when he had a big chunk of someone else's money at the Exchange, just waiting to be walked off with, was beyond me. But maybe he was someone who couldn't resist just one more scam. I've met the type: always overreaching.

"Did he try and pull a con?"

"No-one made a fuss about being cheated. But apparently there was interest in a certain ring he was wearing; a lot of interest. Someone tried to buy it from him, and he said no. They were very insistent, offered a considerable amount of money, and he still said no."

"A ring?"

I stared at the ring on my finger. So did Roflet. "Deep red, with a sword and lotus carved in the stone," he said. "From what our informant said, there has been some interest in a ring like that, the last few days."

"But who'd have wanted it? It isn't even real!" Except, I realised, no-one knew that, apart from me and Frithlit.

"All we were able to find out," Roflet said, "is that money was being offered to find that ring, and take it to a contact at the Blue Sun. And the victim wasn't wearing any jewellery when we found him." His eyes, very blue, were as cold as Clariel's. "So you only just discovered the forgery? And the theft of the bracers?"

"Yes, I told you."

"Because some people might think that was a motive."

"A... wait a minute. You don't think *I* killed him? Last time I saw him I didn't even know he was a thief!"

"You were, however, extremely angry. You're a trained fighter, are you not, Madam Steel?"

I *was* getting angry now, and hauled on my temper hard. "A fighter, yes. I am not a murderer. And if I'd caught Frithlit, I'd certainly have been tempted to slap him bluer than he was already, for trying to steal from me, and even more for being a rotten deceiving little fraud who hurt a good friend of mine, but kill him? There are worse things he could have done, Officer Roflet. Much worse. I don't kill people over trivialities."

At his expression, I realised I could possibly have put that better. "And you don't know anything about why someone – several someones – might have been trying to buy a copy of your ring?" he said.

"No. I mean, unless everyone's suddenly got the same idea as Frithlit and is planning to rip me off, but frankly, anyone who thinks I've got that kind of money..." I shut up as a new idea fought its way to the front of my brain, and my throat closed.

"Madam Steel?"

"The Blue Sun."

"I'm sorry?"

"You said, a contact at the Blue Sun. Was he burned? Frithlit?"

"Burned?" Roflet looked startled. "No, he was drowned. The tide rolled him back in. It was only luck we found him so quickly, otherwise he might have been washed out through Portal Bealach and that would have been it."

Drowned. Shakanti, I had no doubt at all. Even that mad bitch had realised turning him to stone might cause comment.

What if they had come to Scalentine, not for me, but for my ring? But how had they traced it? Followed it from portal to portal?

The seer. I remembered the seer; that eyeless, self-possessed young man. Had they used him to find the ring? *I have a bent for metal*, he'd said. They must have done; him or someone like him. Not that the how of it mattered. They'd found it, or so they thought. But the real question remained.

Why did they want it? Did they actually want it at all, or was it only a way to track me? And why *now*?

Roflet cleared his throat, making me start. I'd almost forgotten he was there.

"Why burned?" he said.

"What? Oh, I don't know... I thought... maybe fire magic..." It was a rubbish explanation and we both knew it.

"If you think you may know something, Madam Steel, the Chief would appreciate it if you let us know."

"Yes. How is he?" I said, before I could stop myself.

"Still working."

"Still? Isn't he getting kind of close to Change now?"

"I'm sure he'll take himself off duty as soon as he feels it necessary," Roflet said.

I stared at the ring, trying to force my brain to work.

What if I told him, right now, that I suspected the Avatars might have something to do with this death? Even if he believed me, it would mean telling him, someone I barely knew, more about the past than I was comfortable with. And what would they do? Arrest the Avatars?

Hardly. The Diplomatic Section would step in before you could say 'Neutral Territory.'

But if I didn't tell them, and it came out anyway? What would the Chief think of me then?

"Officer Roflet? Do you know anything about some demigods who were staying at the Blue Moon?"

"Demigods? Oh, that lot who caused such a fuss a few days ago? They're gone."

"Gone."

Gone.

That meant, if it meant anything, that it had been the ring they wanted, not me. I was, strangely, conscious of a kind of wounded pride. I'd mattered so little, then?

"Yes, they're gone. Why?" Roflet said.

"I... I thought... I don't know. They were staying at the Blue Sun."

"You think *demigods* might have had something to do with this?"

"Well, he's dead, and they're gone..."

"Why, exactly, do you think demigods would go to the trouble of murdering a petty criminal?"

Because murder's what they do, I thought, and only just stopped myself from saying so.

I shrugged. If they were off-plane, they were out of the militia's jurisdiction in any case. Which meant the Chief couldn't do anything. Which meant there was no point troubling him with it. *You're fudging, Babylon. Be honest with yourself, at least. You just don't want to tell him.* "Silly, I suppose," I said. "We've enough murderers right here on Scalentine. Why look elsewhere for 'em?"

"Indeed," he said. "Murderers are usually someone the victim knew, after all. We're going to want to talk to you again, Madam Steel." He picked up his helmet. "Let us know if you're planning to travel off-plane, if you please. And if you think of anything, please contact us."

TIRESANA

THE HOTTEST TIME *of the year. Summer fever raging in the town, the stink of sickness on the air. No ceremonies now to distract me – or to keep me out of Hap-Canae's way. He had tired of his little priestess and was seeking me out again.*

The thought of bedding him made my gorge rise. I couldn't claim illness; Avatars didn't get sick. I kept myself occupied, said it would do the soldiers stationed at the nearby fort good to see their Avatar. I brought Ranay as part of my retinue, I was scared to leave him where the other Avatars might notice him. He was reluctant to leave his studies; he couldn't bring the most important scrolls with him, in case someone noticed they were missing. But he studied as best he could, seeking through obscure and ancient texts for more references to the jewel of godhead, while I spent time with the soldiers.

They seemed happy to be visited, if underfed and anxious, like everyone else. Some already had the fever; I sat and held one boy's hot dry hand, and he looked at me with over-bright wondering eyes. I listened to the sounds of soldiers all around me, telling stories as they mended their kit and grumbled about the food. They offered me the best of it, and I got angry and told them to give it to the sick. Then, when no-one could see, I cried, dry painful sobs without tears.

They left little offerings outside the sickroom: thin beer, terrible wine, a fine sharp dagger. All they had, and more than they could afford.

The boy recovered, got up, still looking top-heavy, his head too big for the rest of him, staggered weak-legged out to his mates who slapped him (carefully) on the back and looked at me as though I deserved their love.

How could I leave them?

I might have thrown a three, but I had to stay in the game until the end.

We went home. Or at least, back to the Temple of All the Gods.

HAP-CANAE MET ME on my return, smiling, and reaching out to cup my chin. "You are taking your duties very seriously." The touch of his fingers on my skin was horrible to me. I knew he was thinking of bed, and I wondered how good a whore I really was, to bed someone I hated, and not let it show.

I tried to smile back. "They seemed to like it."

"I hear you sat at the bed of a sick boy. Do you really think that is appropriate for the Avatar of a goddess of war?"

"Babaska did it," I said.

"Did she? Hmm."

"Yes. I read it. I should do what she did, shouldn't I?"

"I suppose so." But his mouth turned down, and he said, "If I were you, I should bathe. An Avatar shouldn't smell of sickness."

Grateful when I was supposed to be hurt, I sneaked out to find Ranay.

CHAPTER
TWENTY-EIGHT

I WENT HOME, and found Previous, and told her about Frithlit.

She didn't cry, this time. She just sat there, her freckles standing out like bloodspatters on her white face. I told Laney to make her a potion, and to be careful what she put in it. I didn't tell her Previous was pregnant, but she'd guessed, anyway.

You can't keep a secret from my crew; or at least, not that sort of secret.

They were, for the moment, distracted from worrying about me by worrying about Previous instead.

They'd gone. The Avatars had been, and gone. They'd left without tracing me, without showing the slightest desire to look for me.

Perhaps I could forget it. Forget they'd ever turned up, and go back to my life.

Only I couldn't. I spent another mostly sleepless night, and at dawn I got up, and went out, and went to the Lodestone.

TIRESANA

I REMEMBER THE room, empty but for dozens of driftweed seedpods floating on the air and piling in corners like milky ghosts. The first tang of autumn in the air. Me with my stolen light, and Ranay, glowing with nothing but youth and health.

"I had an answer to your message," he said.

I had almost forgotten. "What did it say?"

"That she'll play. And, Ebi, I think I have found the jewel."

"What?"

He held up the scroll he was carrying, and laughed. "You'll never guess!"

I took his other hand. "Oh, Ranay." I felt the first uprush of hope rise in me, green as spring rushes.

We smiled at each other, and over his shoulder I saw the door open.

Hap-Canae walked into the room.

"Oh, you silly child," he said. "You've spoiled everything."

The scent of myrrh and cardamom was in my nostrils as he put his hand on Ranay's shoulder, and then there was the scent of burning meat. Ranay didn't even have time to cry out; his eyes looked puzzled, the pupils widening with shock, as they reflected the flames of his own robes. The scroll in his hand flamed briefly, and was ash. Then his face blackened. The flames were scorching my hands. I let go, and my darling love fell in smoking pieces at my feet.

The Touch of the Sun.

Hap-Canae staggered a little; weak, from using the power. I could have got past him then, but I was staring at what was left of Ranay. By the time I'd gathered my senses and reached for my sword, one of the Messehwhy stalked into the room, with that heavy-bellied, swaying walk, and sniffed at the remains. I ran for the door, past the thing, and straight into Rohikanta, whose hair and beard drenched me with warm, musty-smelling water. Horrified, nauseated, I tried to fight, but Aka-Tete was with him; the skulls at his waist grinned up at me, and his touch on my arm made my eyes go dark, and the sword fall from my hand.

If I'd had longer to grow into my powers, to learn how to use them, I might have escaped, I suppose. But though you can wound them, it's hard to kill an Avatar.

They must have planned what happened next as soon as they realised I wasn't playing their game – or maybe they'd planned it long ago. This was the second time, at least, that they'd tried to depose Babaska's Avatar; there may have been more. Had the others, too, dared to care for those who worshipped them? Had they threatened the careful palace of glitter and falsehood that the Avatars had built around themselves?

In any case, I was to be the last. The gods were gone, and who was left to care what was done in their name?

We had been more successful than we knew, Ranay and I. The rumours of the Avatar of Babaska's humanity were spreading like fire in the dried-out fields.

So they decided to unmake Babaska; not to take her out of the pantheon – that would only arouse further suspicion – but to make her a shadow, a demon. Her positive aspects would be assigned to other gods; she would represent only darkness, blind lust, blood lust. This is what happens, the message would say. This is what happens when you dare suspect a goddess of humanity.

Her name was stricken from the steles, gouged from the monuments, her statues destroyed, her priests and priestesses murdered or driven from their temples. Shakanti took great pleasure in telling me every detail; thinking, I suppose, that I might still care.

And while I could, I felt sorry for the dead, and for those who'd worshipped Babaska, but after a while, I couldn't think about them at all. Because the Avatars decided to show Babaska was either powerless, or cruel, or both; that she would not even protect her own Avatar.

They took over the temple that had been Babaska's. I watched as her statue was smashed. Her head, the hair bound up for fighting, the scar on her cheek like a crack in the stone, rolled past me, ended up on its back, blind eyes staring at the sky. They raised a pillar of stone, and chained me to it with adamant. They made sure the priests witnessed it, so that the story, or at least the version of it that they wanted, would become legend. A tale to terrify children.

If they couldn't be gods, they'd be feared as gods, by any means they could.

IT'S HARD TO kill an Avatar. You can have the flesh gnawed from your bones by wild dogs, and live. You can see someone with your innards in their fist, and live. You can feel beetles scurry in the hollows of your skull, and live. I... lived. I don't know how long for; it could have been days or a century. It was... I was... nothing but pain, and horror. I became familiar with many different textures and colours of pain: purple-black drumbeats, jagged reds, screaming yellows.

I learned the precise prickling vileness of beetles' feet on the inside of my skin. The feeling of a broken bone grinding in the torn flesh, like blinding white fire. A tooth ripped out by the root, a kind of wailing in the skull. The body reduced to meat, wrenched from the bone by dog's teeth, the way the tendons pull and stretch before they tear, the feel of hot breath on raw flesh.

And I healed, of course, because I was an Avatar.

Then it would begin again.

Each time I healed a little more slowly, and a little less completely. Each time I prayed that this was it, that I was finally dying. I longed for death as I had never longed for anything. I screamed death's name, muttered it when I could no longer scream. I saw, or hallucinated, Aka-Tete, the skulls he wore clicking and whispering Babaska, Babaska; I promised him whatever he desired if only, afterwards, he would kill me, but he always turned away.

Still I felt death edging closer, little by little, slow as oil, slower than blood, across the tiled floor.

Sometimes I thought I felt that wordless, assessing gaze inside my head, that might or might not be the goddess. I cried out to it for help, and before long I cursed it, and then I was no longer sure which I was doing or even if it was really there.

Hap-Canae didn't take part in the torture. He didn't stop it, of course; he just... avoided the unpleasantness. I dreamed, sometimes, that he stood in the door and watched, with no expression except faint regret.

I dreamed of Ranay, too. I dreamed that we were on a barge, sailing away. "They told me you were dead," I said, and he told me it had all been a trick to deceive the Avatars, and smiled so sweetly. But before I could take him in my arms I always woke, and grief rolled over me like a night without dawn. And eventually the pain was greater than sorrow, greater than any memory of love or pleasure or sweetness, and eventually, when I remembered him, I only envied the quickness of his death.

CHAPTER
TWENTY-NINE
Day 6
1 day to Twomoon

IT WAS TOO early for sensible people to be about. The Lodestone was full of quiet bustle and the clean smells of fresh produce.

Clariel was in the little yard at the back, frowning over a crate of round, pinkish vegetables the size of hen's eggs, packed in straw. I didn't know why she was frowning – they looked pretty good to me.

"Babylon," she said, without looking up. "I am very busy. This is not the time."

"Sorry, it's important."

She sighed, and shivered her wings. "What is it, Babylon? I can only give you a minute, no more."

"Did those visiting demigods dine here? Hap-Canae, or Shakanti?" It was hard to say those names aloud. They had an ugly flavour even now; blood, drying on hot tiles. Incense, and the ripe stench of open guts.

I was watching Clariel very carefully, or I wouldn't have noticed the slightly increased rigidity of her features. Distaste, or something like it, and I didn't think it was directed at me.

"Surely you do not think *they* have anything to do with your missing girl?"

Of course, she didn't know Enthemmerlee had been found. I was doing more lying and fudging than I found comfortable, at the moment, but... "Maybe," I said.

"The information I gave you before was not sufficiently helpful?"

"Sorry."

Clariel's the only person I know who can sigh with an edge. "Come, then."

The little room at the side of the yard was a cold store. I didn't know you could stack potatoes that neatly; it was almost frightening. It made me think of the room at the temple of the Vessels, for some reason – probably because the smell of harsh soap almost overwhelmed the fresh earthy smell of the vegetables.

"Well?" I said.

"Yes, they dined here."

"And?"

"I am not unhappy that they have left Scalentine." Her wings ruffled.

"So," I said. "Bad customers?"

"I am used to clients who expect the best. But they were... exceptionally demanding." Her eyes burned, but she set her mouth firmly. Though she was obviously longing to vent her fury, the habit of not gossiping about her clients was too deeply ingrained.

I turned away and picked up one of the small crisp carrots, lined up like soldiers on the countertop. "Clariel, I'm not asking for gossip. I just want to know if they said why they were here."

"If I tell you..." she tapped the edge of an immaculate shelf with her forefinger. "Flower comes to work for me."

I felt a jab, as though something inside me was splitting apart. I tried to ignore it. "I can't promise that," I said. "I don't own him. You can certainly ask, make any offer you want." What else could I say?

"This goes no further, Babylon."

"I wasn't planning on it."

"They were looking for something."

The carrot broke in my fingers. "Did they say what, and what for?"

"Please do not make free with the supplies." She bent down and picked up the fallen half of carrot. "I calculate the numbers very carefully.

"It was some*thing*," she said, looking at me far too shrewdly. "Not some*one*. There was one who smelled rather too much of some unsubtle scent. He asked if I was interested in old things, old ornaments. I asked what he meant, and he said they were looking for the things of old times, things of the dead. Possibly he meant antiques. I advised them to try Glimmering Lane."

"How did you... you speak their language?"

"No. They had some Lithan; badly pronounced."

"Thank you," I said. "I have to go."

I walked out, still clutching half a carrot.

Things of the dead. I didn't like that phrase, not one bit.

GLIMMERING LANE IS another place where the rich go to spend their spare money. There isn't a single shop where you could buy anything *useful*. Chairs too fragile to sit on; glass too thin to use, and jewellery so expensive that you wouldn't dare wear it out, for fear every robber in Scalentine would be drawn to it like flies to a corpse.

I edged into the first shop, clutching my scabbard against my leg so it wouldn't sweep something off a shelf and cost me a month's profit.

"Can I help you, Madam?" A young man oiled up to me.

"I'd like to ask you about some people who may have been in here."

By the time I'd been through four or five of them, being treated like a customer when I walked in and a vagrant when they discovered I wanted information rather than insolvency, I was in a rare temper and ready to go home.

I almost passed by the next place: it looked shut. The windows were dim, the few artefacts in them – a battered cauldron, a tray of dusty rings, a dented goblet – didn't look like the sort of thing that would appeal to the Avatars. But I caught a glimpse of a figure moving about in the gloom, and went in.

The place was yellowy dim, and smelled of dry age. The proprietor was a frail, but very upright old woman, with thick gold-rimmed glasses balanced heavily on a fragile nose and grey hair in a bun from which little wisps and trails escaped to float around her head. She was peering at the spine of a book so old the title would have been unreadable even in decent light. "With you in a moment," she said, and a flare of witchlight suddenly bloomed over her left shoulder, sparking twinkles and glows in the depths of the shop. "Hmmph. No, really, I don't think so. A third-generation copy, at best." She put the book down on the counter, and looked at me with eyes bright as swordpoints.

"I'm sorry to bother you. I wanted to know if some people had been here, looking for something, but..."

"You're Babylon Steel."

"Um... yes?"

"A friend of Mokraine's."

"Yes."

"Sad. Very sad," she said. "He was a great man, you know. Not a good one, but a great one. Now..." She shook her head. "Who, and looking for what?"

"Sorry? Oh. Demigods, from Tiresana. Seeking something," I said.

"Oh, yes. They were rude, even for demigods. I gathered they were looking for something they believed to be a deifact. Not unusual. Well, deifacts are, of necessity, unusual, but entities seeking them out are sadly common. You're Tiresan yourself."

"I..."

"You'd rather it wasn't known? Of course."

"Thank you. What's a deifact?"

"Something that turns a being into a god."

There was a soft explosion of light in my head, and I leaned on the counter. The woman asked if I was all right. I shook my

head, and looked at my ring. In the low light, the stone glowed
deep red, like a heart.

*And with her sword she cuts the way to power. True godhead
comes only with blade and flower.*

How many years was it, since I'd read those words? Was this
really it, the thing they had been seeking for so long?

Ranay, holding up the scroll, smiling. *"You'll never guess."*

Was that what he'd meant to tell me? That the jewel of godhead
was my own ring?

Wouldn't that be a fine joke, if this ring, gathering dust in the
temple treasury, tossed to a silly girl like a rag doll to a wailing
child, had been all along the talisman they longed for? Hap-
Canae had had the secret in his hand, not once, but twice. The
ring he had given away, the manuscript he had burned.

I laughed, a strange barking laugh in the dusty shop. The
woman simply folded her hands and stood, waiting.

If I was right, then they thought they had found it. How
delighted they must have been; to have found what they sought
so easily, with so little trouble to themselves. It must have seemed
to them proof that they deserved it. Only one little murder. After
so many, what did it matter?

And how blisteringly furious they would be when they
discovered they had a copy, and not the real thing at all.

"A deifact."

"Yes."

My mind buzzed and whirled.

If it was true, I could try and rid myself of the thing. Have it
melted down, have the stone shattered. Then if they did come
back looking for it, once they discovered they'd been duped, it
would do them no good.

But objects of power are not always easy to dispose of. Or
safe. Ranay had said as much. And it had clung to me all these
years, that ring; I'd never been able to sell it.

It had never turned me into a god, though. I'm fairly sure I'd
have noticed.

"Would you like some water?" the woman said.

I nodded. She poured it into a battered pewter tumbler. It was cool and sweet and I drank gratefully.

"How would you tell if something was a deifact?" I said. "How does such a thing work?"

"Oh, a variety of ways, when and if they exist at all. I don't carry such items. Too much trouble, even if the genuine article can be got, which, mostly, it can't."

"I shouldn't imagine so. We'd be up to our knees in gods."

"Oh, it would be very unlikely to work on Scalentine. There are certain safeguards, you know."

I hadn't been on Scalentine all this time, though. I'd passed through a dozen planes or more.

"I told them," she said, "that anything proclaimed to be a deifact is more likely to be the province of fraudsters. They left. Why people think such a thing is worth having I will never understand," she said.

"Er... no?"

"I seek to understand how the universe works," she said. "Attaining godhead, by comparison, lacks ambition." She smiled, at herself, or at others' folly, I couldn't really tell.

"I wonder," I said. "Would you look at something for me?"

"Certainly."

I took off my ring, and handed it to her. She stared at it, lit up the witchlight again, and stared some more. Then she sighed.

"An object of power, no doubt, but not my field. You might find it worth talking to Mokraine."

I walked out of the shop feeling as though my head were full of wool, and wrapped up in the middle of it were a lot of people, all shouting.

TIRESANA

ONE EVENING, I had had more of a chance to heal than usual, because it was the dark of the moon, and Shakanti's powers were weak. She retired to her rooms, and didn't have the energy for torture. Perhaps, too, she was simply losing interest.

I struggled to the surface of a dream of swimming in river water, cool and sweet; reluctant, as always by then, to wake at all. I saw Kyrl, heavier than I remembered. Sesh. Lanky Sesh, who'd punched any man who looked at me funny.

I thought they were hallucinations – I was having them quite a lot by then. I babbled at them, saying that if they were real, I'd ask them to kill me. Because Shakanti would be back, eventually. "They say you can't kill an Avatar," I said, "but you just need to find out how. It's in the scrolls, somewhere. Ranay could have found it. It was easy to kill Ranay, he wasn't an Avatar. Hap-Canae said he loved me but he burned my love all away."

"Shh, please, hush," Kyrl said. She was red with shock and anger.

Sesh was crying. Somehow the sight of that brought me more to myself. I'd never seen him cry, not ever.

"Sesh."

"It's me, honey cake."

"Sesh, are you really here?"

"Hush, Ebi. It is you? It really is our Ebi?"

"Please kill me."

They looked at each other. Then Sesh got a vial from his pouch, and tilted it to my lips. "Hush, Ebi. Sssh. It's all over now."

Then there was blissful, painless nothing.

I WOKE IN *darkness, and realised that I was cold, but not in pain. I could feel rough cloth against my skin, binding my arms to my sides. I pulled free – my strength had come back – and felt about with my hands, realised I was not chained, but trapped; walls of stone enclosed me, no more than four inches from me in any direction.*

It took me a few minutes to realise I was in a sarcophagus. I pushed against the lid, but I'd used up my strength ripping my way out of the bandages, and couldn't shift it.

And trapped in here, I was only going to get weaker.

Was this the final punishment they had decided to visit on me? To bury me alive? I knew Avatars were hard to kill, but without water, without food, surely even an Avatar would die eventually. Just very, very slowly.

I thought of Sesh and Kyrl, and realised they must have been a dream.

Perhaps I should have been panicking, screaming, clawing at the stone, but I wasn't. Partly it was just being out of pain; the wonderful, blissful blankness of it. What numbing pleasure it was to have only the small discomfort of chilly stone beneath me, instead of unremitting agony that paused only to be renewed.

I stopped pushing at the lid. I realised I didn't even want to escape. I just wanted to be left there, to die in peace.

But it wasn't to be. I heard a scraping noise, and there was a flickering line of yellow light that stung my eyes.

"Ebi. Ebi!"

"Sesh?"

"You're alive... Praise be, you're alive. We weren't sure; we had to believe..."

He and Kyrl helped me out of the sarcophagus. I recognised the room.

"You're real," I said.

"Yes, Ebi." Kyrl said. "We saw... oh, if I ever get the chance! What was done to you, they should die. They should all die for it."

"You're better," Sesh said.

"Yes. Apart from this." I touched the scar on my face. "That never goes. Everything else... heals. What did you do?" I said.

"A potion. It mimics death. We didn't even know if it would work, you being... you know. An Avatar. Before we knew what they'd turned you into, we were going to use it to get you away, if we needed to. The state you were in, we were half afraid it really would kill you, but..."

"Death I'd still have thanked you for," I said.

Sesh was looking at me with a strange, almost greedy wonder, as though I was some rare thing that might disappear any moment. "It's true, then."

"What is?"

"The Avatars are human. All of them, not just you?"

"Yes. And knowing it got Ranay killed. We have to get away."

"I know." He nodded to Kyrl, who heaved into the coffin a cloth-wrapped form.

I stared at it.

"Just in case," Kyrl said. "I don't know why they should ever look, but if they do, they'll find a body here. Summer fever, poor child, and no-one to bury her. Come."

"No," I said. "If I leave and I'm still an Avatar, they'll find me. We need to get to the altar-stone."

I wasn't sure it would work. But I knew that if they found me, we were all dead, or worse.

And almost more than escape, I wanted to rid myself of this sick, stolen power.

We crept through the corridors, keeping to the back ways, but still, we had to pass Hap-Canae's rooms.

As it was night, we were probably safe, but nonetheless I was paralysed for precious moments, unable to go past the door, in case he should realise, somehow, even in his sleep, that I was there.

In the end they lifted me off my feet, and scurried past with me. I wondered if he had someone else in there, some other young girl, wrapped in silk, stunned with love.

She wouldn't end up as Babaska's Avatar, at least.

We made it to the ancient corridor. And here the obsessive secrecy of the Avatars worked for us; there were, still, no guards.

The dust rose up around us like a convocation of ghosts. I thought I could see in it the faces of all the other girls: of Velance and Jonat and Renavir, of Adissi, pleading in stone. All the soldiers who'd died for nothing. And the poor girl in the tent, whose name I couldn't even remember.

But the words, yes, the words I could remember. I whispered them.

Insiteth

Abea

Iatenteth

Hai ena

The floor hummed against my bare feet, but for a long, dreadful moment, nothing happened. It was long enough for me to think it had all been for nothing, to think we would still be standing there when they found us. Then, the doors swung open.

The altar sat within, looking like nothing but an ancient chunk of rock.

"Give me a knife," I said.

They looked at each other. "What do you think I'm going to do?" I said. "I need to spill some blood – my blood – on the altar-stone, to give the power back. Give me a knife, or cut me yourself, I don't care, just hurry!"

Sesh gave me his knife and I cut my left hand, then, holding the knife awkwardly, my right. After everything the pain hardly registered. I was shaking, though, and cut a little deeper than

I meant. Quickly, before the wounds could heal, I slapped my bleeding hands into the cupped dents.

It hurt so much I couldn't even scream. My back bent like a bow, but my hands stayed on the stone as if welded there. The ring I still wore burned against my finger until I thought it would scorch the bone itself. I thought I was, finally, dying.

I felt that gaze inside my head for the last time, assessing. Go away, I thought at it. You didn't help me. You didn't save Ranay. You let all your worshippers suffer and you did nothing, so leave me alone!

Was it even Babaska at all, had it ever been anything but my own bewildered mind? I had no way to know, and hurt too much to care.

There was a horrible, tearing feeling inside me, as though something that had been fastened to me with a thousand threads of my own flesh and soul were being ripped away. My hands slipped from the stone and I collapsed back onto the floor.

I hurt. But I could feel all through me that I was, once again, human.

They hauled me up and we ran, me still in my bloodied burial robe, on my bruised human feet. We made it out of the temple. How many people they'd bribed to look the other way, I dread to think; it must have cost them a year's wages and a lifetime of favours. Luckily the post of temple guard was little more than a sinecure; it meant a great deal of standing about, and polishing one's kit, and a good pension, but no-one had attacked the temples in a hundred years. Who would dare?

We travelled through the night, under the bright, distant stars; Babaska wielding her sword against nothing; the crouched Leopard, the turning Wheel. They told me that they'd had help – from ex-priestesses of Babaska, who'd gone into hiding. From soldiers, and from whores. All of them terrified, all of them worshipping in secret, all of them risking death to save a symbol – who couldn't save a single one of them.

I asked after Radan, and they told me he'd died, in his sleep, one night on the road. "He was worried about you, too," Sesh said. "We told him we'd check up on you, see that all was well, and that seemed to make him happy, and next morning..."

I wanted to cry, but I didn't seem to have any tears left in me.

We stopped at an abandoned inn on the road out of town. Sesh had stored some supplies there: food, clothes, sandmules, and a sword. It felt good to have one again, but it wasn't enough, not nearly enough.

"I'm going to Mantek," I said. "The portal."

They looked at each other.

"If you stay," Sesh said, "we can tell people. Maybe we can change things."

"I can't, Sesh..."

"Sesh, shut up. You saw how it was. How can you ask her?" Kyrl said. "It isn't fair."

"No." Sesh smiled at me, but there was regret in it. "I'm sorry, Ebi. I am."

"You can't fight them, Sesh. They... I tried."

"But what will you do?" Kyrl said. "How will you survive?"

"I'm a good fighter, now. Even without being... what I was, I'm good. I can earn with that. I..." I didn't say I could earn my living whoring, too. Sesh was always oddly prissy about such things, especially where I was concerned. "You'd be safer if you came with me."

"Through the portal." Kyrl frowned and fiddled with her knife. "I'll –" she swallowed. "I'll come with you, if you want."

She'd risked the wrath of the Avatars for me, but the thought of leaving horrified her. A true Tiresan, Kyrl. Tiresans don't leave.

"No," I said. "No. Better this way; then, if they do come after me, they won't find you. I wish I could give you something." All the jewels and weapons and fine robes that had been hung on me, and here I was, with nothing to my name but a second-hand sword and an old ring. I kept thinking I should take the ring off, in case someone recognised it, but somehow I always forgot.

"You did give us something," Sesh said. "We know how the Avatars were made. And we know they can be unmade."

I gripped his hands. "Sesh. You saw what was done to me. You think they'd hesitate a moment to do the same to you if they even suspect that you know? You know what they did to Ranay. I loved him. Do you want to know how many times I cursed his name? How much I envied him his quick death? Let it go. They can't be fought."

Gently, he unclasped my hands. My nails had left red crescents in his flesh. "Anything can be fought."

"You can fight a tidal wave, but it doesn't mean you can win. Kyrl, tell him. Please."

"He knows, lass. So do I. You get yourself away and keep safe. We'll look after ourselves."

We hugged, and then they rode away, and I headed to Mantek alone, feeling as hollow as a dried gourd.

CHAPTER
THIRTY

I FINALLY RAN down Mokraine outside the Blue Griffon theatre, just around the corner from Gallock's, waiting for the actors to come out. There's nothing like a failed audition for generating emotion.

"Mokraine."

"Babylon, my enchantress..." His eyes were veined and wandering, his hands shaking. The familiar leaned against his leg, watching me with its three blood-drop eyes.

"Meet me in Gallock's when you're done here?" I said. "I'll buy you lunch."

He didn't ask why, just nodded, his eyes already back on the doorway, where the sound of voices was growing louder.

I didn't want to watch him feed. I went into Gallock's and sat nursing a cup of thick dark coffee until he showed up, flushed and glassy. Gallock glared at the familiar, but said nothing, just banged crockery about in a pointed way.

Mokraine ate little of a good meal, his mind on other flavours. When I thought he had come down enough to pay attention, I said, "Can you tell me anything about this?" I held out my ring.

"Your ring? What do you plan to give me next? A shoe, perhaps? A feather?"

"Mokraine. It's important. Please. I need to know what it is."

With a shrug, he took it.

"Oh," he said softly. "Now *this*... this is interesting." Without taking his eyes off the ring, he started to poke about in his pockets with his free hand.

"What do you need?" I said.

"I used to have an eyeglass... never mind. May I put it on?"

I hesitated. It had never done anything to me that I knew of, but...

Mokraine saw the look on my face and his own, just for a moment, changed. I caught a glimpse of the man he'd been; not a good one, but a great one, with all the arrogance of someone who was the best at what he did.

He looked away. "No matter. I think the wearing of it is only part of what it is intended for."

"Is it a... deifact?"

He gave a small cough of laughter. "A deifact! No. Almost the reverse."

"What do you mean?"

"I wish I had my books," he said.

"We can go to your place," I said.

"Oh, no. I don't have them anymore."

"What happened to them?"

He stared into the distance. "I sold them, I think. Probably, yes. But even without them, I can tell you, this... is an object of power, but it does not *contain* power; it has no magic within it. It is more like a portal."

"I've been wearing a *portal*?"

"Not precisely," he said. "But it links to something. And whatever it links to is stronger now, or I might have noticed it before. The alignment."

"The what?"

"The alignment. The syzygy. Here, it manifests as Twomoon. On other planes, in different ways. It is a time when things move into place, when places and powers not otherwise conjoined link like a necklace on the breast of the All. But this one, this is a Greater Syzygy. More aligns, now. More doorways open. This happens once in seven years, Babylon. It was a Greater Syzygy when I made my experiment."

"Oh."

"Where did it come from, this ring?" Mokraine said.

I told him what I thought he needed to know, as briefly and sharply as I could. He nodded, now and then, his gaze wandering from the ring, to my face, to somewhere far. "I don't know why I kept it," I said. "I didn't wear it for a long time. I thought about selling it, sometimes, but somehow I always managed to get some food, or money, or a job, and I'd forget."

And then, when I settled in Scalentine, I actually started using it as my seal. I suppose it had been a kind of defiance. A statement, that I was safe, and wasn't going to run anymore.

Hah.

"Perhaps it did not want to be sold," Mokraine said.

"How can it *want* anything?"

"It was created to do a certain job. It is trying to make sure that job is done."

I was somewhat disturbed by the idea that this thing, this lump of metal and stone, had been having a hand in its own destiny. And mine, come to that.

"What is its job?"

"I believe that as a glass focuses sunlight, turning it intense and powerful, to blacken and burn, so this diffuses, radiates."

"Diffuses *what?*"

"Whatever power is passed through it, of course. It is meant to take a concentrated power, and flow it out, into..." he stared at the wall. "Earth. Earth and sky."

"Not people?"

"I don't think so, no."

"But you're not sure?"

"Not entirely."

I tried to think, sipping the cooling coffee.

The ring diffused power. The power stored in the altar? Diffused it to where, and to what purpose?

But the scrolls said that the jewel created godhead. And yet, at least one of those paragraphs had been written in a different hand. And marked. The marks left behind, the marks left by, perhaps, previous Avatars of Babaska. Warning marks.

Upside down.

I looked at Mokraine. He was awake, this time, at least. In the Break of Dawn he'd been comatose. I remembered the cloaked figures at the next table, long, pale fingers tapping a card.

The High King, reversed.

The tarot. The tarot turns up everywhere.

"If you find this, heed my *sign!*" I said. "That's what it said. Not my words, my *sign*. And the symbols were reversed!"

Mokraine looked bemused, but I felt suddenly clear. The sword and lotus, upside down. *This means the reverse of what it says.*

The scrolls indicated that the jewel would bring the Avatars power. The last Avatar of Babaska had meant for the Avatars to find those messages in the scrolls, to use the ring, to rob themselves of power. But she hadn't been certain it would happen; perhaps the ring was already lost, by then. So she'd left a message, for the next Avatar of Babaska. *Find the ring. Use it. End this. End them.*

Perhaps she had already known that she didn't have long.

"Mokraine? Who do you think made the ring?"

He shrugged. Of course, he could hardly be expected to know. Who *had* made it? Someone who thought it might be needed. A priest, a priestess, an Avatar... maybe even a goddess.

"You said it's stronger now? What does that mean?"

"It means that it is ready to do its job; the alignment is probably a necessary part of the ceremony."

Which meant I had to do this while the planes were still in alignment, *and* assuming the Avatars didn't complete the ceremony and discover they'd been sold a dud before I could get there.

"How long does alignment last? I mean, is it anything like a normal full moon?"

"That is a matter for some discussion. Alignment is generally considered to last four days. Its apex will be in two days time, *here*. At about three o'clock. On other planes, of course, they measure time differently. In some, time *is* different."

Two days.

"Is there anything else I need to know?"

"You are planning to use it?" He looked at me with a surprising level of interest. "Well, the rite it is most likely to succeed if performed at the height of the alignment."

"I'm not an astronomer, Mokraine. How do I tell?"

"This ring is made to be used like a seal, to be placed somewhere to close the connection. There should be a specific home for it." A specific home... I pushed my mind back. The altar. I remembered the last time I'd had my hands on it. As well as the handholds, there was a circular depression in the centre of the altar, about the size of a copper coin.

Or the size of my seal.

"If I am right," Mokraine said, "that place is likely to change its appearance as the correct time approaches."

"Yeah, that's... not exactly specific, is it? How do you tell? Can you just put the ring there, and wait?"

"Oh, no!" He looked at me, shocked. "This is, almost certainly, a transference operation of one of the Late Entheranic systems."

"You what?"

"There are a number of systems of magical operation, Babylon. The Late Entheranic required, as a rule, very precise timing; they used a high degree of ceremony, too, but the ceremony was generally mere embellishment. In most of the Falnaway systems, on the other hand, the ceremony is the very bones of the thing. Without it..."

"Mokraine? Matter in hand?"

"My apologies. But I believe the ring must be placed within a few very specific moments. Too early, or too late, and the consequences could be unfortunate."

I wasn't fooled by the casual way he said 'unfortunate' – this was a man who had messed around with viciously dangerous magicks on a daily basis for years. And ended up addicted and ruined, of course.

"Right. Thanks."

"And, of course, it will have to be worn, to operate. That's why it's made in the shape of a ring. The Entheranic systems always leave such clues."

"Worn."

"Yes. May I?"

I gave it back to him.

He looked at it for a long time, running his thumb over the carving. "There may be more," he said. "But I would need to do further research."

"I don't think there's time." I realised he looked exhausted. He handed me the ring. I put it on. "Thanks, Mokraine. And I'm sorry."

"For what?"

"For troubling you."

"Hmm." He was staring over my shoulder again, and I thought he was already drifting off, his mind turning towards his next feed. "No, I think perhaps... Babylon?"

"Yes?"

He touched my hand, and I tried not to flinch; I owed him that much. "Thank you," he said.

"What for?"

He gave an odd, twisted smile, raised my hand to his lips, and kissed it. He didn't feed, just kissed it. His lips were dry. "Try to stay alive," he said.

TIRESANA

MANTEK SEEMED BUSY to me, with goods coming and going – later I would realise that healthy trade looked a damn sight busier, but then I was still an ignorant girl who thought all the worlds could not be bigger than the deserts of Tiresana.

Mantek is a dry-land portal. Never having seen one before, I stood amazed at the glowing arc that hummed and shimmered, that seemed to twine with voices just below hearing. The brilliant haze that filled it parted around mundane carts, hauled by beasts with their eyes and ears wrapped in cloth.

There were guards, but they were, like the temple guards, mainly ceremonial: fine uniforms, flashy weapons more polished than used. They paid me no mind at all. But I was still Tiresan enough to stand shaking and choking at the threshold; my feet seeming welded to the sand-gritted tiles, until I heard a shout behind me, and both the guards looked that way.

They've found me, I thought, as I ran through in the wake of a departing trade-caravan, feeling for the first time that strange internal shudder, of both body and mind.

I had no idea what was on the other side. It turned out to be a much colder world than Tiresana. My main impression of it was that everything was grey. The buildings, the people. I didn't stay – I ran for the next portal and the plane beyond, which was even colder. I spent my first few weeks freezing and half starved, grateful to get what clients I could, if only for the *body heat, until I got work with a warlord's personal guard, some good, if flashy, gear, and my first experience of fighting in snow and the way a corpse left overnight creaks in the frost as though protesting the cold.*

I kept moving, selling my sword-arm or my body, whichever would get me fed and far away. I got sharp and silent and hard. Someone called me Steel, and it stuck.

I took a job as guard, with a caravan trading silks and pack beasts. Off duty, I'd fallen asleep. I slept a lot, those days, dull heavy sleeps like being buried in dust, ugly dreams jerking me awake. Mostly dreams of being back in the temple, in chains.

One night I woke terrified, smelling sand and heat and river mud, and grabbed one of the on-duty guards. "Where are we?"

He shrugged. "They call it Babylon."

I looked out. There were a thousand stars blazing above me, but I didn't know them. Babaska and her sword were gone.

Why I took the name, I don't know. A memory, a whim.

But the place was too much like Tiresana. I stayed only long enough to collect my wages before I ran for the next portal.

I don't know how many times I did that. If I'd known more about portals I might have been more cautious. Travellers who do a lot of portal-running, long-distance traders and the guards they employ, are tough, careful, and take a lot of precautions.

As it was, I was luckier than that level of carelessness deserved. I could have ended up dead, stranded, Faded. But I just kept running. For years.

I kept my head down and stayed out of trouble and was as lonely as a tomb in the deep desert. The lovers I took, whether it was a paid transaction or not, took the edge off the loneliness, and reminded me that I could feel something good.

But I was always looking over my shoulder, and I always moved on.

Eventually, having gone for four or five years without a sign of pursuit, I stopped jumping at every shadow. I began to weary of never having a place of my own, of the brief and broken friendships. I met up with Previous, and started to feel more connected, more human with every day in her company. Yet still, I kept moving. I would wake one morning and find some excuse to get going again, though in fact it was mostly just a feeling in my blood that it was time to move on. And she came with me, willingly.

We were staying in Larians, a pleasant enough city, when the feeling came again. My excuse was a merchant who I in no way took to, who was convinced that enough money would change my mind. I could have dissuaded him, but instead, Previous and I took a ship up the Druthain river, and through what turned out to be Portal Bealach.

We landed at Scalentine docks, where those of us without specific business on Scalentine were sent to the Reception Hall.

The Chief was there briefing the guards to keep an eye out for some troublemaker or other. He cast an eye over the new arrivals and saw me and Previous, leaning against the wall, both a little grey with portal sickness. He came over. "You speak Lithan?"

"Some," I said.

"Good. Welcome to Scalentine. I'm head of the militia. We're here to deal with trouble, so please don't make any. There are clean, cheap places to stay in Harvest Street and the Barrel Downs. Stay out of an area called King of Stone, don't get into any card games in the Sideways Road. If anyone causes you problems, find someone wearing this uniform," he gestured at his own; brilliant red, with brass buttons.

"That shouldn't be difficult," I said, and saw that melancholy grin for the first time.

"You'd be surprised," he said, "how hard it is for some people. You'd think they were avoiding us on purpose. You two are soldiers, yes?

"Mostly."

"Killing people is frowned on. But we can always use trained fighters in the militia."

He nodded, and moved away.
I looked at Previous. "What do you think?"
"Let's try it out, eh? Stay here a while, see how it goes."
We both found the place suited our minds.

CHAPTER
THIRTY-ONE

"BABYLON," PRINCE ANTHERAN bowed over my hand. "This is a charming surprise. Please to come in, sit."

His suite at the Moons in Splendour was perfectly chosen: tasteful enough to make his rich visitors feel at home, without being so extravagant that they would be certain he was overcharging them. His servants were so smoothly unobtrusive, they might have been Fades, like Bliss.

"How is your son?" I said, settling myself into a chair which embraced me like a lover. I hadn't been in surroundings this luxurious since I left the temple.

"Well, thanks to you. Though I have no doubt that even now, he is writing a poem about the cruelty and lack of understanding of fathers, which will be poorly hidden, so that I may find it and feel suitably chastened."

Despite myself, I laughed. "I think he is fortunate in his father, my lord."

"I hope so." He shook his head. "I wish his mother were alive; I think perhaps she would deal with him better. She was a woman of most superior understanding. I am tempted to stop bringing him on these trips, yet he must learn the business, and left at home... ah, well."

After we had been supplied with spice tea and a number of dishes of little salty delicacies, I said, "I hate to do this to you, my lord, but I wondered if I might call in that favour."

He gave a brilliant smile. "How can you even ask? I feared, being the woman of fierce honour that you are" – I hoped he didn't notice me wince – "that you would never do so, and the weight of it would hang over me until my dying day. Anything that is within my power, I will do."

"That's an extravagant promise, my lord, I hope you don't have cause to regret it."

"Babylon. You brought my son safely back to me. *Anything* I can do, I will."

I'd been thinking about my next words very carefully indeed. I didn't want to do anything to remind him that he'd made a potentially careless remark during one of our moments of intimacy: he would still, being the man he was, follow through on his promise, but he'd never forgive me for using such information against him, and it would *ruin* the Lantern's reputation.

I took a deep breath. "I once heard, I can't remember where, that it might be possible to travel with great speed, between the planes, without being held up by unnecessary paperwork."

His hand paused in the act of reaching for a salted vine flower, then moved on.

"And if I should happen to have heard something similar, how would that be of help to you?" he said.

"I need to travel to Tiresana, extremely fast. Before the end of the" – what had Mokraine called it? – "the syzygy. I thought perhaps you could, possibly, assist me to do that."

"Hmm." He looked at me over the rim of his cup for a long moment, then put it down with a decisive snap. "Of course."

I must have looked surprised. He spread his hands. "Babylon, I told you. Anything. And I will of course provide you with assistance. I would ask only that my name is not, now or in the future, connected with this in any way."

"I understand."

"However, I do not know Tiresana, I don't believe I have ever traded there."

My stomach went hollow. "Oh."

"If you can tell me which planes it links to, however, perhaps I can help you."

I forced my mind back. I'd been in such a panic... the guards at the portal had been skinny creatures with naked ratlike tails... I'd leapt at the first chance to leave, but I'd been on that plane for a few days at least... what the hells was it called? Kai or Nai or Flamp or some damn thing.

"No... it's..." Something buzzed against the window. "Flai!" I almost shouted. Antheran looked startled. I lowered my voice. "It links to Flai."

"Flai." Antheran frowned at the air, then snapped his fingers. "Ah. Yes. We are in Twomoon. You are fortunate. At alignment, there is a way to get there quite quickly, if you are willing to risk discomfort. You may even be able to avoid having to do too much negotiating; there are many who wish to take these fast routes while they are open. Simply being open-handed and persuasive can speed things considerably."

"I'll remember."

"Remember also that you will need to return before alignment is over, otherwise you will have to wait a year, or go the long way around. That could take several years in itself."

"I'll remember." Though it crossed my mind that I might not have to worry about coming back.

"Only with knowledge can one be properly prepared," Antheran said.

I could only shake my head in admiration. "You know, I'm not at all surprised you've managed to restore your family's fortunes, my lord. If I wasn't asking you a big enough favour already, I'd ask you to look at my accounts as well. You could probably turn us enough profit for Flower to sprinkle gold-leaf on the breakfast sausages."

"Certainly, if you wish."

"I wasn't serious," I said.

"I was. Accounts are of the greatest importance."

"Not compared to this. I *have* to get there before the end of the Alignment."

"Yes? Then we must deal with this immediately. And later, I will have someone look at your accounts. Though I do not recommend gold-leaf on sausage. It would be vulgar, and you are not vulgar."

Leaving me open-mouthed at *that* fairly astonishing assessment, Antheran clapped his hands, and his servants were sent scurrying.

It was a bit like watching a storm wind fling bits of leaf and random debris past your window as you sit in comfort with a glass in your hand. I ended up with a set of directions, a bundle of currencies, and a sheaf of papers.

I MOVED AROUND my room, running my hands over the curtains, and the bedspread, half-consciously saying farewell to it. I would have to talk to the others. I didn't know what I was going to tell them, though. The fattening moons rose in the sky. Twomoon began tomorrow, and in two days, according to Mokraine, the syzygy would reach its apex on Tiresana.

I could just leave it. They've gone.

But I couldn't. For one thing, though they might have gone, they could come back, threaten me, threaten my crew.

And for another...

Bent figures, struggling under the weight of a litter. A dead boy, his cheek on his hand, on a blood-muddied field. Jonat's eyes, wide and knowing and frightened.

Through the window I saw a figure approach the Red Lantern. And stop, and turn, and turn back. Even in my current state, I felt faintly amused. Plenty of people act that way, on their first visit. A few steps forward, a hesitation, a turn.

I realised it was a woman, stocky, wearing a short practical cape and breeches in dun-coloured leather. She got nearly to the steps, where Cruel, the bandage around her head giving her a piratical look, was lounging on guard. Then the woman looked up, and saw me.

I knew her, but it was a moment before I placed her. Mirril, the butcher. Somehow I didn't think she was here as a client.

"Missus Steel?"

"That's me."

"I..." She glanced at Cruel, who gave her a smile like a polished blade.

"Look, it's cold," I said. "If you've something to say, you can say it as well inside as out in the street."

She didn't move.

A long wavering howl rose from somewhere over towards the Druthain, and Mirril jumped, her hands clutching at the edges of her cape.

I said, "I'm busy. If you're too worried about being polluted by what goes on here to come in and talk in the warm, say what you've got to say and let's get it over with, all right?"

"It isn't that," she said in a rush. "It's just, I don't know, if I'm seen here, you see, it's..."

"You think actually walking through the door is more compromising to your virtue than standing talking to me on the step for all to see? I'm shutting the window now. You can come in, or not, as you please."

She scurried up the steps. Cruel bowed her through the door extravagantly, and I took her into the Little Parlour. She looked around, her gaze going from the cushions, to a half-finished sketch of Essie Jivrais had left on the table, to the curtains.

"Not what you expected?" I said.

She shook her head. "This isn't... I just wanted to say, I'm sorry. I'm sorry I cut you off, you've been good customers. But I've my daughter, you see."

"If you think that I would ever, under any circumstances, allow a child to take part in this business, you can leave now."

"I never thought that. It's not that sort of place, everyone knows that."

"So why? First off, why'd you cut us off, and second, why are you here?"

She blushed the dark, angry blush of a middle-aged woman not used to being caught out. "I got a chance at a good client. A big 'un. And I got a daughter to raise on my own, I can't afford to turn down work."

"I don't see what this has to do with me. So you dumped us for a better client. Fine. Well, we've found ourselves another butcher, we'll manage."

"Thing is, I didn't think there was anything to it, when she said yon man was a priest. Plenty of them around, I thought."

"I'm not following you, lady, and I've got things to do. If this is a roundabout way of saying you'd like us back on your lists, I'll fetch Flower and you can talk to him. Now if you don't mind..."

"Listen!" she said. "That order I got? It was for the Vessels of Purity."

The bloody and thrice-damned Vessels. Again. "And what's that got to do with me?" I said.

"The man who came along, he said mine looked like a good place. Clean, he said. Cleanest he'd seen. He liked that. He asked me about my other clients, and I told him, the Lodestone, and how they were known for their food; and Pippit, she's my daughter, she goes and pipes up with the name of the Lantern, not knowing any better, because of you having a reputation for good food, too." She glanced up at me, half embarrassed, half angry.

I didn't say anything.

"So he says..." – she took a breath, folding her arms under her bosom – "he says that that was a pity. He made it obvious, see, that if I dealt with you..."

"He'd whisk that big fat order out from under your nose," I said. "Wait a minute, did your daughter tell him what sort of place this was?"

"'Course she didn't! I didn't bring her up to mention such things!"

"Which means he knew already," I said. "That's odd, don't you think? That a priest of the Vessels should know about a brothel? Or maybe not, since they made a point of coming here, causing ructions and distress all around. Maybe that's what they do, go searching around for places of sin. Wonder what they do if they can't find any? *Why* are you here?"

"They came here?"

"They stood outside, two of them, scaring off clients until they realised they were breaking the law. So?"

The woman was twisting her hands in a fold of her cloak, wrenching the material into a rope like she was trying to wring out the long-dried dye. "I should have come before," she said. "When she came back, and told me, but I had so much on, I just told her to take a different route and stay out of his way. What was I to do?"

"What are you talking about?"

"The priest," she said. "Pippit was doing an order for the Hen and Chickens, just riverwards of you, and she came past here, and she stopped, because, she said, she always liked to look and see what the girls were wearing, especially the Fey, and I know Flower, sometimes he'd give Pippit a little treat, a cake or something, guess she was hoping he'd be about, and he came out of the alley and he started talking to her."

"Who did? You mean Flower?"

"No! This priest. He said things to her. Things about sin, and how she'd get tainted, and how she should stay away or be scoured in the cleansing fires. Well, the first time it happened, I didn't think much to it, she knows not to let anyone mess with her. But he was there again, next time, and somehow he had her scared. She started going the long way round, and she had to tell me 'cause it took longer and she knows I worry if she's late. She's a good girl that way."

"I'm sure she is. You tell the militia?"

"The militia? Well, no. I mean, he hadn't done anything but talk, and she recognised him from when he came to the shop.

Just a bit too much god in him, that's what I thought. Only she's been fretting, worried, and to be straight, so have I. Because you've got young girls here – I know, I don't mean children – but still, I thought he might be trouble for you. I thought maybe I should come."

"Bloody right, you should. I'd have appreciated knowing some ranting hate-monger was hanging around my jalla." Then something in my brain went *click*. "Which alley?"

"What?"

I kept my voice under control with an effort. "Which... alley... did this *priest* come out of?"

"Just down there... Dice something?"

"Twodice Row," I said. "You should have come earlier."

"What..." The colour dropped out of her face, leaving it yellowy, like an old candle. "Was someone hurt? Did he do something?"

"You saw that bandage Cruel was wearing? The girl on the door? He damn near stove her skull in."

"Oh, sweet All protect us." Her knees went, and she collapsed on the nearest sofa. "Pippit... he was talking to Pippit..."

"Hey, now." I poured a measure of golden from the decanter on the table and gave it to her. She drank it down without a blink, and the colour rushed back into her face.

"So this priest. A Vessel?"

"Pippit said so. He had the mask."

I remembered the birdlike flicker of grey I'd seen, when I was looking out of my window. "All right. We're going to the militia, right now."

"But Pippit's on her own, in the shop; I can't leave her, I have to go..."

"We'll take her with us. They'll want to talk to her anyway."

I told Cruel what was up as I was leaving. "Tell the others. Let in no-one, *no-one*, we don't recognise. Understand? We got any clients in?"

She shook her head. "Not that I know of. Too close to Twomoon."

"Good. In that case, no clients either. Right?"

"If he comes, we'll be ready," she said.

I wasn't going to let one more girl die at his hands, not if there was a chance I could stop it. As soon as the twisted little creep was in the hands of the militia, I'd be gone.

Back to Tiresana. I felt my stomach curdle at the thought.

ANY OTHER CITY, any other time, we'd have made a strange threesome, me and Mirril the butcher and neat little Pippit. Her mother clutched the girl's hand as though afraid she'd float away, glaring around at anyone who came too close.

But this was Scalentine, and close on Twomoon. The streets rang with the boom and crackle and sulphurous tang of fire-magic; the portals hummed and burned. The sky danced with light. Closer to hand, brass blared, drums throbbed, and a procession spilled down the street.

They were little blue people from some plane I didn't know; dancers in costumes of multicoloured rags, their tall hats glittering with sequins; musicians playing great curved brass horns, so long the bowls were supported on little wheels; riders on fat beasts like grey sheep, slung about with drums the riders played with their heels.

Mirril clutched Pippit close to her, and the girl squirmed. The grinning dancers tossed paper-wrapped sweetmeats at passers-by. I caught one on a reflex, but for once I had no appetite. I managed to wave and give something like a smile, and gave the sweet to Pippit. The procession trailed noisily away.

As we moved into King of Stone, towards the barracks, the streets were packed with moon-dancers, driven to a spinning frenzy by Twomoon, their wide silvery skirts and long white hair flying out as they whirled themselves to exhaustion. There were wailing luck-singers and people hawking cures for weredom (*they'd* be away on their toes if they saw a militia uniform). There were junny-men with their steaming jugs of happy juice; banta-cake sellers, for those with stone mouths and steel digestive tracts; the green-robed, slate-skinned priesthood of the Church of the Glorification wandering through the crowd, handing out little wooden mice.

No Vessels. Not one.

The barracks was packed to the walls. People pushed past, shouting; the only space was around a dozen weres on the turn who didn't have a safe room of their own and were queuing for the ones provided by the city. They were already jumpy and hairing up. Pippit stared around, wide-eyed. She didn't seem scared, just interested.

A middle-aged woman, with a tall, sullen, wild-haired boy in tow, was pleading with Roflet.

"Madam," he said, "we can't just lock him up."

"But you can see it! Look at him! He's changed, he's not like my good boy anymore, he doesn't do his chores, he argues, he won't bathe! He's a were! I know weres have to be locked up during Twomoon, I'm doing my duty, that's all!"

The boy glanced at us, Pippit giggled and he flushed.

"Ma'am, he's not a were," Roflet said. "He's just fourteen. We don't lock people up for that."

Eventually she went away, still towing the poor lad by the wrist, claiming that it was all wrong and if her son ran amuck it wouldn't be her fault.

Mirril and I made it to the front of the queue, finally, and when they asked us what we wanted, I said, "We've got information that might help with finding out who killed the girl down in King of Stone."

Mirril made a choking sound. She hadn't, of course, known about the dead girl, and I hadn't thought to tell her. One of these days I'm going to have to learn when to apply tact *outside* the bedroom.

"Chief's office," Roflet said.

Mirril started to jabber as soon as the door shut behind us, telling the whole story, and the Chief held up his hand. Paw.

She shut up.

I'd never seen him on duty so late in his Change – they must have been really pushed. His shoulders were massive, and smooth silver and black hair was growing up his neck and cheeks to meet the mane that tumbled down his shoulders. His jaw was longer, his nails had become claws; he was starting to look a lot like a lion.

He looked at Pippit. "You remember what this man said?" His teeth were changing, too, making his speech slightly mushy.

She chewed her thumb. "I don't know," she said. "I mean, some things, but not, you know, what he actually said in his actual sort of words. What sort of were are you?"

"Well, no-one's quite sure. No-one knows where I come from, see." He winked at the girl. "Now, anything you can remember? What he said, way he looked, anything."

She stared at the table with those big solemn eyes, looking exactly as she had working at her slate. "Well, he said stuff about how the god didn't like the Lantern. That it was full of bad people, people who did lots of sin, and I shouldn't go there. That I'd be... rotten."

"Rotten?"

"A word like rotten."

The Chief looked at me. He loses some words, closer he gets to Change.

"Maybe... corrupt?" I said.

"Yes!" She looked delighted. "Corrupt. He said there was corrupting and iniquity. And stuff. And he was creepy."

"Creepy how?" the Chief said.

"Well he was talking at me and at me, it was like it didn't matter if I listened or not, and he didn't even *know* me."

I glanced at the Chief. A Vessel, talking to a woman? Even one as young as this?

"And I tried to get on and do my rounds, and he just kept

talking. And when I was there again and he was there *again*, he saw me, and he sort of *shook,* and his voice was all funny. He said things about me being still an innocent, and that I could yet be saved, but I had to stay away from the... corrupting.

"Then he held his hands up like this." She held hers up, the fingers hooked, the thumbs spread. A strangler's grip. "And said something about the Purest protect her innocence, for otherwise His Servant must do cleaning, or something."

There was a hitching sound. Mirril had one red, work-roughened hand to her mouth, and you could barely see anything of her face except her eyes, fixed on her daughter, as though afraid she might disappear.

"It wasn't like he was talking to me at all," Pippit said. "Maybe his god. I don't know. Anyway I said I was sure he was right and I wouldn't go there again and I went home." She dropped her hands and gave the Chief a bright-eyed look, like the good student I'm sure she was.

"Very good," he said, after a moment. "Thank you, Pippit." He was working hard to keep it out, but I could hear the undertone in his voice, that growl waiting to burst out of his throat.

I sympathised. It was lucky, very lucky for the Vessels, that I wasn't an Avatar any longer. Right then I'd have given a great deal to have the power to go through whoever was responsible like... well, like Babaska would have done.

Roflet gave both Pippit and her shaking mother some water, and turned to the Chief. "What now?"

The Chief frowned, his eyes almost disappearing in hair. "Don't know for certain it was a priest, just the mask. Anyway, a hundred priests in the city. More. Can't bring 'em all in on suss." He looked at Pippit. "Anything else? He ever take his mask off?"

She shook her head.

He held his hands up. "Any rings?"

"No. He didn't have any rings. His hands were very clean.

They looked all scrubbed, like Mum's do when she's getting ready to cut the meat?"

"Clean hands."

"Yes. Very clean. He smelled of soap. Not just clean-clean, but really strong soap. Like Mum uses in the shop."

I saw Mirril frown, as if something was twitching at her memory. Something was twitching at mine, too. Something to do with the Vessels, again, but I couldn't quite grasp it.

"Why the *mask?*" the Chief said. "He can't be a Vessel. No sense to it. A mask is meant to say, here's a Vessel. Look. But..."

"Wearing a mask *implicates* the Vessels, doesn't it?" Roflet said.

"Yes."

"Well, yes," I said, "but..." But I shut up, because I could see the point. The mask of the Vessels was a statement. To wear the mask meant you were acting as a Vessel. And the Vessels knew that they couldn't commit murder, as Vessels, and get away with it...

My head hurt.

"So, we need to talk to them again," the Chief said. "They're not going to like it. Diplomatic section won't, either. After all, Vessels have been being co-operative, right? Good upstanding citizens..."

"Yeah," I said. "Funny, that, isn't it?"

The Chief gave me a look. His eyes had changed, but they were as sharp as ever. "What?"

"Well, that changed kind of sudden, didn't it? One minute, they're all *we demand this, we demand that, no whore has a right to question anything we do*, and the next they're all apologies. And money. And they've been hanging around my jalla, too; not just the day they were obvious about it. We've caught glimpses of them. Now, I thought it was because they were hoping to catch us out on something, breaking the law, maybe. But what if that wasn't it?"

"You think maybe they..." he glanced at Mirril and Pippit

and broke off. "Ma'am, you go home. May need to talk to you again. You get your customers to pick up their own orders, for now; or hire someone to do your running. Someone not to be messed with, okay?"

Mirril said something but I didn't hear it, because another of those soft explosions had just gone off behind my eyes. "*Soap*," I said. "And clean hands. Really, really clean. I was thinking of asking him to do our floors, looked like he'd had practice. And he's allowed to talk to women. They're not."

"What?" the Chief said, but Mirril was looking at me with a sort of dawning horror.

"It's not a priest. It's the administrator. That smooth-oiling little shit Denarven."

Mirril stood up, convulsively, knocking her chair over, and clutched a bemused Pippit to her.

"Mum, what?"

"He knows where she lives." She was staring through the Chief at some horrible imagining. "He came to the shop. I should have remembered. The *soap*. He's the man who does business for them. Sweet All protect and preserve us, it's *him*. The man who came with the order... he knows where we *live*..."

"Hold it, hold it," the Chief said. "Tell. Slow."

We did. Well, I told him why the soap had struck a chord. And Mirril babbled, poor woman. I couldn't blame her. Any anger I'd felt towards her had long drained away.

When she wound down, or just exhausted herself, the Chief said, "Roflet. Want Bothley, and probably Jennan. Couple more."

"Jennan's off duty, Chief."

"You pick, then. Want polite, but tough. They're coming to temple with me. You, take Mirril and her daughter home and stay with 'em."

Roflet opened his mouth, and the Chief held up that big paw again. "We're short staffed, it's Twomoon, whole city's going mad, don't want to hear it. Want someone who can deal if this twistfart shows up. You got the duty. Babylon, know you want to get back to your crew, right now want you with me. You warned them, yes?"

"Yes. Place is locked up like a chastity belt. But why do you want me with you?"

"Want the Vessels thrown. You throw 'em."

"Chief?" Roflet said. "Are you sure?"

"About what?" he growled.

And it really was a growl. Roflet put himself between the Chief and the doorway, which was actually fairly brave.

"One, you're taking a civilian. Two, you're *very* close to Change and very angry, Chief."

Bitternut reached out, lifted all six-foot-something of Roflet in his two hands, and moved him to one side. Then he left.

I followed. When Roflet grabbed my arm I was so tight-wound I was within an ace of hitting him.

"*Don't let him kill anyone*," he said. "He kills, when he's in Change, he's finished. You understand me? He's the best we've got. You'd better look to him."

"I understand," I said, shaking him off.

"And try not to get yourself killed, either. That'd look bad for him."

THE CARRIAGE DREW up at the temple precinct in a scatter of gravel. The guards at the top of the steps lowered their spears, saw the uniforms, raised their spears again, and looked confused. The older one nodded to the younger, who went inside.

"Babylon. Keep shut."

"Yes, Chief." He was getting more monosyllabic by the minute, and I began to wonder if Roflet had been right. I might want to tear out throats myself, but I didn't want the Chief to. It would end him. And not just his career.

"The Purest sees all," said the guard, fixing his gaze firmly on the middle distance so as not to meet any of the eyes in front of him. "Abase yourself before the gaze of the Purest."

"Abase... no," the Chief said. He had straightened up, and it was only the flicker of a muscle in his jaw that told me how hard he was working to keep himself under control. "Chief of the City Militia, see. Abasing's not what I do. Only to laws of this city. Temple being in the city. How about you send out someone to talk to me? *Could* come in, but it'd be rude. Prefer to treat our citizens with respect."

There was a flicker of movement at the arrow-slit window in the wall above us, where someone was listening.

The younger guard returned, and took up his post. From within the temple the prow of one of those vile masks emerged, like the ghost of a bird.

The priest was young, by his bearing. There were eyeholes in his mask, through which he glared as though we were rubbish that had blown into their nice clean precinct.

"Follow me," he said. He tried to inject chilly disdain into his voice, but something, maybe the mask, gave it a hollow ring.

We were led to the same little room where I had first seen Denarven; which ended up pretty crowded what with me, the Chief and the three other militia boys, all of them large. Denarven wasn't there. Instead, there were another two masked priests, one with the bowed neck and bent shoulders of an old man.

His mask had no eyeholes.

His left hand rested on the younger priest's right shoulder like an ancient root. The tips of his skinny fingers were faintly purple, the rest of his skin had a yellowish tint, except where veins ridged it like seams of porphyry. His fingers moved in a rapid drumming. His right hand was held out, palm up, at waist level, trembling like a leaf in some faint constant breeze.

"This is the Father of the Inner Temple. He asks why you have come to disturb our meditations," the young priest said.

"He speak for himself?" the Chief said.

I realised that the young priest was drumming with his fingers on the palm of the old man's right hand as the Chief spoke.

"The Father of the Inner Temple has not spoken aloud to

anyone other than the Purest in many years, and in return the Purest has blessed him with deafness. He is no longer distracted from the Glory by the chatterings of a crude and corrupt world. We believe that before long he will also be blessed with blindness, as the Purest's highest favour. This one" – the young priest gestured at himself – "is the Father's chosen mouthpiece."

"Hmm. But he's dealing with us."

"He believes that the Purest wishes it."

"Wonder why the Vessels have decided to be so very cooperative just recently. Twomoons, is it?"

Drumming.

"The Father says we take no note of how many stones are in the sky. All celestial objects are under the gaze of the Purest. The Purest does not wish his followers to be distracted from their duties towards Him. He wishes us to co-operate in order that all may return to contemplation of His greatness."

"Good. Cooperation I like. Your man at the gate, very cooperative. Didn't ask why we were here, didn't fob us off with some low-grade acolyte. Brought us straight to the Father here. Even though" – he gestured at me – "talking to women, not done, is it? Send 'em to the administrator. So why not this time?"

"We wish to act as good citizens."

"Chief?" I said.

"What?"

"They won't talk to me, but could you ask them something for me?"

"Ask."

"When they came and stood outside the Lantern, to put customers off, I understood. Didn't like it, but understood the motive. But then they stopped. And paid us money for the inconvenience. And they didn't try the same trick anywhere else. So why not? What happened?"

There was no response. Of course. They didn't speak to women. Chief Bitternut growled the question again, his shortening patience in every roughened syllable.

"We were advised that it would not be in our best interest to act in this way," the Mouthpiece said.

"Who advised you?" Bitternut said.

The old priest's head trembled, the mask like a bird's skull strung up and shivering in the breeze; his fingers drummed.

The Mouthpiece said, "Administrator Denarven."

The Chief and I looked at each other.

"He warned them off," I said. "He didn't want them hanging about. He was afraid they'd spot him. He'd already targeted the place." And more pieces began to fall together. *When a great temple falls, it starts with a crack.* "You can pretend not to hear me," I said. "But I know you do. I saw two of your priests in Buckler Row, just after a girl was found, murdered. They said they were out 'spreading the light of the Purest.' Me, I call it hunting. *You already knew.* You might not have known who, not yet, but you *knew* one of your own was involved. But you wouldn't go to the militia. You had to stay *pure.*"

Even with faces hidden, you can tell a lot from bodies. I saw the old man's shoulders hunch a fraction. I'd been right.

The Chief got it, too. Perhaps, at that stage, he could actually smell it. He leaned forward, and the Mouthpiece winced back, almost dislodging the old priest's hand from his shoulder.

"Tell me. How long you known you hiding a murderer?" the Chief said, his voice very soft.

"That is a terrible accusation, to make in our own precinct!"

"Precinct stands inside Scalentine. People of Scalentine my..." – his lip curved up from his teeth – "my pack. Maybe it happened before. Before you came to Scalentine. Did you run, thinking you'd leave the stink behind? Can smell it. Smell it through all that scouring."

"If murder has been committed, do you think that knowing, we would do nothing?"

The Chief gave a hard, bitter smile that showed more teeth than maybe it should. "Maybe. Nature of the crime. A purification? Is that what you think? Not supposed to go near women, are you? Not supposed to look at them, think of them, certainly not touch them. But he touched her. Hands on her neck, crushed. There was more. You want to know? Or you know already? No purity in it, Father. What was done to her? Corrupt to the bone. Now *where is he?*"

The Father raised his masked, trembling head; seeking, maybe, to hear the voice of his god. Whether he did or not, I don't know. But his fingers drummed on the young man's shoulder, and the Mouthpiece spoke.

"We still do not know for certain that he has done this thing. This city is alive with sin; we are here to do the work of the Purest, to bring light into the darkness. There were many more likely possibilities than that one so closely connected to us was involved."

"Closely connected?" The Chief said. "He's one of you."

"*He* is not a priest. He was a child of corruption, you understand?"

Child of corruption? So his mother, perhaps, had been a whore – or just unlucky.

"He could never be a priest," the Mouthpiece said. "He asked. He asked, often. He believed a life of contemplation might help him with certain... troubles of the mind, that he had. But it was not possible. I meditated long upon it and the Purest showed me the way. We permitted him to enter the temple as an administrator. He is efficient. Adept. Careful. He does for us what we cannot do without risk to our souls; he deals with the corrupting world."

The Chief said, "Where is he?"

"We are responsible for him."

The Chief's voice was thickening by the minute, but his next words carried an edge like a Gillalune blade. "Maybe you are."

There was a silence.

"We cannot tell you where he is. We do not know."

The Chief's shoulders were hunching in a disturbing way. "All right," he said. "Search temple. Babylon, you're first."

"No!" The mouthpiece yelped. The Father's fingers blurred with speed. "He is not there. He was out, ordering bread, fruit, something."

I wondered for a moment if Denarven was aware how little they knew or cared what he did for them every day, in their unworldliness, too busy contemplating glory to notice where supper came from. Out ordering bread... how many bakers were there, in Scalentine?

Then I remembered something else and an awful weakening feeling shot up through me. "Cruel... she was wearing my cloak, with the hood up; in those heels, she's nearly as tall as me. Chief, he thought it was *me*. It was because of me. I came to the temple. You were right. I blundered in... I drew his attention... he'll go there. He'll go to the Lantern."

"Then so will we," Bitternut growled. "As for you..." he looked at the priests. "Ask forgiveness of your god, if you dare."

OF COURSE, THERE was Previous, and Flower, and the Twins... I kept telling myself this as the coach belted along rocking madly from side to side. I was squashed between one of the officers and Bitternut. I could feel the muscles of the Chief's arm twitch and shudder. Some of it was the Change.

I glanced upwards. The sky was a deepening blue, and the moons were showing above the rooftops, fat and glowing frosty. Time had become an enemy, creeping into camp while the guard's attention was elsewhere. But I had to deal with Denarven first. This was here. This was now. This was my *crew*.

"Chief?"

He didn't answer. I wasn't sure he still could. We pulled into a side street near the Lantern, jumped down, and tethered the horses – they were of that stolid militia breed that can cope with weres and almost anything else, mainly due to having dough for brains.

"I see Previous," I said, looking out of the side street. "Looks all right so far. Chief? Why don't you leave these three with me, and head back?"

He glared at me. His eyes were bright green now, with long pupils. He didn't move.

Roflet had been right, damn him.

I thought as fast as I could. "Why don't I go in?" I said. "If he's watching, he'll be expecting me, not you. Yes?" I was beginning to hope for more than one reason that Denarven was a long way away.

One of the millies said, "Is there a back entrance? He might be sneaking around out there."

"Yes. Down that alley there, right and right, a blue-painted gate. Why don't you and the Chief go have a look? That still leaves these two big lads to keep an eye on the front, right?"

"Chief?" the officer said. "This way?"

Bitternut made a sound I had to take for assent, having no choice, but at least he started to follow the man.

"All right," I said to the other two. "I'm going inside. We're going to make some noise inside in a bit, see if we can draw him out. Or in. You just watch out for anyone making for the door, all right?"

"Yes, ma'am," they said, and saluted.

It must have been something in my voice. Sometimes these things come back to you.

I went up to the door. "Hey, Previous."

"Babylon."

"Everything smooth?"

"So far. What's going on?"

"Act like I'm telling you a rude joke, or something, okay? There may be eyes on us and we need to look normal."

Her eyebrows flicked briefly upwards and then she gave a staccato, not very convincing laugh.

I told her about Denarven, and she swore, then laughed again, worse than before, to cover it.

"Seen someone hanging about, the last few days. Might have been him," I said.

"Purity mask?" she said, not taking her eyes off the street.

"Yeah."

"Me too. Thought they were just keeping an eye on the place in case any of their worshippers went off the straight and narrow. So it's that slinking administrator," Previous said. I could see her grip tighten on her spear.

"That's the one."

"Cold bastard."

"Yep. Is Flower out back?" I said.

"The Twins."

"That should put him off. On the other hand, it might encourage him. Those two are walking sin if I've ever seen it. Right, this is the plan. We make it sound like a ruckus upstairs, you run in, the Twins do the same, take up stations just inside, out of sight of the doors and windows. Make a lot of noise upstairs so it looks like you've all been pulled in to cope with that. If he's watching for an opportunity, he'll slip in then. All right?"

"'Plan'?"

"I had to think of this on the run, all right?"

"You're the boss."

"That's me." I went inside and told the others, stationed myself at the shadowed end of the upstairs corridor. A scent of bittersweet smoke in the corridor; Laney, preparing some potion or other. Whatever it was, it would be nasty. Good.

A few minutes later, there was a yell from upstairs, running feet, and Previous and the Twins came charging in.

I watched while Previous slipped to one side and stood out of sight of the still-open front door. The Twins based themselves by the kitchen and the foot of the stairs. Flower was in Laney's room; everyone else was scattered hither and yon, eyes open and at the ready. Luckily we'd no clients to deal with, not on Twomoon.

I wasn't expecting Denarven to be armed, but if he was, and things got nasty, I thought I could deal. He was an administrator, not a soldier.

The minutes shuffled by. I couldn't see out the back – where were the millies, and the Chief? Was the Chief all right? I'd never seen him all the way into his Change. How much control did he have?

And was Denarven really crazy enough, or desperate enough, to try and sneak in? Was he even here? Or was he at Mirril's place? Or had he got wind of the chase, and tried to get passage on a boat out of the docks, through the portal, to spread his poison on another plane?

The sky outside the windows began to darken. Flower and Laney were still yelling and making slamming-the-furniture-around noises, but in a pause I heard the Twins whispering to each other. Previous, who'd had plenty of experience of guard duty, was standing immovable as a stone and still had her eyes fixed on the door. Ireq was watching the back. I shifted my feet.

He wasn't coming. I began to worry about Mirril and her daughter. And the other houses, and the freelancers... it had been stupid to assume he would come. He was probably in some dingy little room now, with his hands on the neck of some fragile girl. I'd wasted everyone's time. I sheathed my sword. Better make sure the Chief was all right.

I heard a noise and started to turn; the mask came straight at me, like some grim revenant, out of the dark corridor. His grey robes flickered around him like smoke.

I didn't have time to wonder how the hells he'd got in before he slammed right into me and almost had me off my feet. I went down on one knee, got an elbow in his ribs. I heard a crack, didn't slow him at all. Pushed myself up, grabbed his arm, tried to spin him round, get him down on the floor. He twisted out of my grasp.

I'm a foot taller and a sight stronger, but he's burning with some kind of dreadful energy, baking off him like a fever. I can hear him, a chopped up hiss, fragments of words; sin and darkness and whores and hate. Mask against my face, cold, the beak of it digging into me. I get him down on his knees, but he's eeled out from under me again, hands around my neck. Black flowers blooming – *no*. After what I've lived through, I'm damned if I'll die here, at his hands. Get his wrist, haul back; feel/hear something break in his wrist, slam his arm against the floor. He's *still* trying. Get a knee under him. Thundering sound, screams.

Weight's gone off me, all at once. What?

The mask flying backwards along the corridor; hard to work out what was happening, but something had Denarven by the back of his robes.

I could hear him beginning to choke, the mask hanging askew, making him look as though his neck were broken.

I could hear something else, too: a low, raw growl.

I saw the eyes over Denarven's shoulder: luminescent green. Claws sunk in Denarven's arm and thigh.

"Chief! Hold up!" Damn, that hurt, that little bastard had really dug his fingers into my throat. "Chief?"

He'd backed into a corner. Denarven was clawing at the neck of his robes; the mask cracked, then broke open down the middle, showing his face.

I'm not sure he even knew the Chief was there. His gaze was rigidly fixed on mine. The neck of his robe tore, and he reached out his hands, those hands he'd tried to scrub clean.

There was blood trickling from his arm and leg, soaking his robes. Even I could smell it, and it would be going straight to the Chief's gut.

I could hear the others behind me. Previous had shot up the stairs after the Chief, and was hovering at the top of them. Someone – Flower and Laney? – at my back. I could hear tight, frightened breathing; lots of them, maybe the whole crew. I didn't dare look to see where everyone was, didn't dare take my eyes off the Chief.

"All of you, back off."

"Babylon..."

"Do it. I'm all right. Chief, come on. We've got him. There's enough of us to hold him."

Laney said, "That's right. We're all fine, Chief. Why don't you let us take him, now?"

There might have been words in what the Chief said next, but I couldn't get them. It was mostly growling.

"Chief, you can't kill him. He has to go to trial. Him and the Vessels both. Come on, now." I moved forward, slow. "Chief, you can't kill him. You're still on duty. This is my fault, I should have made you go home. But you and me, we take responsibility for our actions, don't we? And I don't want to see you on trial when it should be him and those who could have stopped him. You kill him and they'll weasel out of it somehow, you know that."

Of course I'd wanted Denarven dead, the second I knew he was the one who'd killed that girl, but he wasn't worth the Chief's career. He wasn't worth the dust on the Chief's feet.

"Come on, Chief. Let him be. We can take care of him. We'll see him dealt with. We can even give him to the Twins, how about that?"

I heard a kerfuffle downstairs and doors slamming, more footsteps and someone yelling, "Chief! Oh, *shit...*"

The Chief's head turned, just for a second. I dived forward, grabbed Denarven under the arms and rolled backward, hearing a ripping sound, slinging him past me, putting myself between him and the Chief.

The Chief's head snapped round, and he roared.

Somewhere a million miles away I heard a high sweet note, like the trill of a bird, and a muffled groan. Laney said, "There."

I didn't dare move my eyes.

I was on my back, looking up at the Chief. His eyes glowed, and his claws, still bloody from Denarven, flexed. His shoulders were hunched like a mountain range. Ragged bits of cloth still clung to him. He'd a tail, now, and it was flicking back and forward; it brushed the floor. I could hear it, because everyone else had gone intensely quiet.

Then he dropped his head, and nudged me in the shoulder. Hard. He lowered himself until he was lying in the hallway like a sphinx, and gave a sort of groan.

I sat up, slowly, and patted him on one huge shoulder. "C'mon, Chief. We'll make you comfortable. Come with me."

He was still tensed like a bowstring, I'd felt it when I patted his shoulder. We passed the collapsed shape of Denarven, his split mask lying either side of his head like an open oyster shell, his slack face its poisoned pearl.

The Chief's upper lip rippled over his teeth, but I managed to persuade him down the stairs with one hand in his mane.

We'd got to the bottom when I realised we'd been joined by Roflet, who was glaring at me like I'd murdered his favourite grandmother. "Chief?" he said. "You. Steel. What happened?"

The Chief snarled.

"Let me just get him safe, Officer," I said. I led him down to the Basement. He looked at the great thick door with its barred window, and looked at me. Then he nudged me again, and went inside.

I closed the door, and stood blinking at it for a moment.

Cruel and Unusual came up, and locked the door with an iron key the length of my forearm.

"Babylon," Cruel said. "Hey, Babylon."

"Hmm. What?"

"Here."

She put a glass in my hand. It was golden. I took a gulp; it burned like several hells going down, but after that, it helped.

"Right," I said, sounding as though I'd been yelling orders in the field all day. "Make sure he has food and water."

"Yes."

"Bedding. Blankets."

"Yes."

"Steel."

I was aware of Roflet standing behind Cruel, with his arms folded. I said, "We can look after him here until Twomoon's over, unless you've got secure transport and somewhere for him?"

"I'll send someone to fetch him." He obviously didn't trust me. I was vaguely sorry for it, but great leaden waves of weariness were beginning to come over me and I was in no state to do any bridge-mending.

"Right. Laney? What's happening with the arsehole?"

"Wandering the shadow," she said, from the top of the stairs. "He'll stay that way a while, I think, but can we please get him out of here? He makes me feel ill."

Ireq, stolid as ever, began to sweep up where the millies had tracked mud in. Previous came in from the back, white as Flower's apron. "I found where he got in. Out back, where the pipes run from the scullery. So small. I meant to look, when you told me about that boy, but I never did... Gods, Babylon. I'm so *sorry.*"

"What?"

"Remember the boys who got in? There was one not long ago, I said I'd find the place. Denarven must have been watching even then. Maybe he saw one of them get in."

"Don't take it on, Previous," I said. "It's my fault, I should have checked. I've been unbelievably stupid." In more ways than one, I thought, resting my hand on the door of the room where the Chief was pacing up and down.

Flower, with the look of someone handling a full bucket of puke, scooped up Denarven and trudged down the stairs with him slung over one arm. He dumped him at Roflet's feet.

"That him?" Roflet said.

"That's him," I said. "He doesn't look like much, but watch him if he wakes. Make sure he's secured. He's..." I blinked, shook my head. "Crazed. Berserker type, you know?"

"Right."

Roflet started snapping out orders. I realised he had half a dozen other militia with him. They bundled Denarven away, like rubbish. I slid down the wall, because somehow it seemed easier to do that. In fact, the floor felt really comfortable. I'd just stay there a while, keep an eye on the Chief, until my head cleared.

I could still hear him pacing the floor behind me. I laid my hand back on the door as though it might be some comfort to him.

"Babylon. Babylon!"

"What?"

"You can't sleep here."

"I can't sleep at all. I have to go..." I had to go somewhere. I had something that needed doing. But I couldn't remember what it was.

I was vaguely aware of someone – Flower, probably – getting a hand under my arm and half-carrying me to my room, and then I wasn't aware of much else for a while.

CHAPTER
THIRTY-TWO

Day 7
First Day of Twomoon

WHEN I WOKE up it was late morning, bright pale sun falling through the gap in the curtains. I was still in my bloodstained clothes.

Things started dropping into my head like big jagged stones. Denarven, *in my jalla,* among my friends. The Chief.

I raised a hand to brush blood-bristled hair out of my face, and my ring caught the light.

Oh, sweet All. The ring. Tiresana.

I got up, feeling every bruise, and pulled back the curtains. The moons were both visible high in the blue: Inshallee like the ghost of a rose, Beriand like the memory of a spring leaf. I wondered how Enthemmerlee was doing this morning; her change must be well on its way by now.

The Chief had no choice about his, but she'd chosen hers. She'd taken it on, because she thought it needed doing.

I washed hastily, pulled on a robe and went downstairs.

Unusual was just on his way up from the cellar. "Morning," he said. "How are you?"

"Bruises. Sore throat. How's the Chief?"

"Millies came for him this morning."

"Oh. How was he?"

"Touchy."

"Ah."

"S'all right. No one was hurt, they just had a bit of a struggle getting him into the coach. You seen the coach they use for that sort of thing? It's something. Like a strongbox on wheels, built of iron thick as a door. Takes six horses to pull it." His eyes were gleaming.

"Unusual... what would *we* use it for?"

"I'm sure I could think of something. Anyway, they got him in. He kept trying to get upstairs, for some reason, but they made it eventually."

"Right." I yawned so wide my jaw creaked. "So long as he's okay. I need some breakfast."

Flower was waiting in the hall, with his arms folded, his apron as clean as virtue, his tusks gleaming. Laney and Previous were ranged to either side, Laney quivering with indignation so that the feathers on the neck of her gown fluffed up like a hen's, Previous turning her dented helmet over in her hands and scowling fiercely.

"What's going on?" I said.

"Isn't it time you told us that?" Flower said.

"Look, I'm horrified that Denarven got in here, I take total responsibility for that. No, shut up, Previous, it was up to me and I didn't do it."

"It's not that little squit we're talking about," Flower said, "Though why the hells you didn't let me tackle him..." he went off into his own language, which I don't speak, but it didn't sound complimentary. Then he switched back to Lithan.

"For an intelligent woman, Babylon, you can be pretty stupid."

That was no news to me.

"Which doesn't mean *we* are," Flower went on. "You've been going around looking like you just got volunteered for a suicide mission the last few days. Clariel's turned up, *here*."

"So much for that deglamour she was wearing," I muttered.

Flower waved a hand. "Please. You think I can't smell the Lodestone kitchens? Then Darask Fain, of all people. You haul Previous down the sewers, come back drenched in blood..."

"It wasn't ours."

"Not the point. You haven't been telling us what's going on."

"Look, it's sorted," I said. "Denarven's in custody, Enthemmerlee's safe."

"Enthemmerlee!" Laney actually stamped her foot, and her eyes were shading to red. This is never a good sign in a Fey. "It's *you* we're worried about. There are things going on you're not telling us, Babylon."

"Laney, I know, and I'm sorry. I never meant for things to get this crazed." I looked at them all. There was no way of avoiding this – or at least, not unless I was prepared to sneak out of my own place, out of my own life, like a thief. And I wasn't going to, not this time. "Look, you'd better all come into the kitchen."

We sat around the big scrubbed table, except for Flower, who started cutting meat. I rested my hands on the clean, dented wood, for the comfort of it.

"Listen," I said. "I have something I have to do, and I have to go, now. Today. And, well, there's a fair chance I won't make it back. So... I just needed to tell you. I haven't... there's money. Damn. I can't leave you my seal. You'll have to... I need paper. I'll give you my signature, for the banker at the Exchange. Sorry. I should have gone there earlier, I didn't think..."

"Wait," Previous said. "Hold up. What?"

I sighed. "I can't tell you the whole story, I haven't time, but there are people I need to deal with. I have to make things right."

"But who are they?" Laney said.

"Avatars. Demigods, if you like. On my home plane. They, well, let's just say I think they stole the power they have and it's up to me to take it away. And I can only do it during Twomoon. I may be too late already, I'd have gone yesterday if... anyway. I have to go."

There was a silence while everyone looked at each other, then they were all talking at once. I held up my hand, and for once, they shut up. "I'm sorry, I really am. I hate to leave you like this, but judging by yesterday, you'll all be safer if I'm out of the way."

"We'll come with you!" Laney said. "We can help."

"No, Laney. I've put you all in enough danger recently, I'm damned if I'm dragging you to Tiresana with me. It's not Scalentine, you know. The Avatars have powers, there. I've seen them use them. They can kill, and they'll do it. Because you're in the way, or just because they feel like it. And killing's not even the worst of it... no. No-one's coming with me."

"So you're just going to leave?" Flower said. His apron was smeared with blood.

"I don't have a choice."

They looked at each other. Then Flower brought the cleaver down on the chopping board, where it stuck, the blade gleaming in the mellow autumn sun. "At least let me make you up some food. The All knows what sort of rubbish you'll get travelling."

"Thank you, Flower. Laney, if you can, I need something that will work against charisma. Can you..."

She sniffed. "I suppose so."

NO-ONE BUT Flower was about when I left. I could hear movement in the rooms, but not one of them came out.

I knew they were angry, but I hadn't realised *how* angry. I'd have welcomed even an argument, though it would have delayed me more, which I couldn't afford. Silently, Flower handed me the package of food, and a battered hipflask.

"I put some golden in there."

"Thanks. Flower..."

"You'll miss the tide," he said; he put a heavy hand on my shoulder and turned away. When I got outside I realised there wasn't even anyone guarding the front. I wondered whether I should say something, but Flower had pulled the door shut.

I walked towards the docks feeling like her again, that silent, hard-bitten woman with an empty heart and little else but scars. I managed to get passage on the *Misty Morning,* heading for Galent.

My one advantage was that I was fairly certain the Avatars would travel in comfort, in luxury as far as they could manage it. If I sacrificed everything to speed, I could get there, if not ahead of them, then at least hard at their backs.

I stood on the deck, listening to the roar and chatter of the docks, the creak of ropes and snap of sails. The light of the portal arc flared off the water like another kind of liquid, rich and thick. I could see the tower in the town square; I realised I was peering to see if I could make out the Red Lantern. As the anchor chain rattled up, I turned away. I gripped the rail, and shut my eyes as we passed through the portal.

I'd almost forgotten that bone deep inward shudder – the sense that all your insides have shifted slightly to the left of your outsides – that comes with passing a portal. In all my years of travelling I'd never got used to it.

The *Misty Morning* was a stripped-down merchant vessel, made to outrun her competitors. She had few comforts. We didn't stop at Larians, the city that mirrors Scalentine on the far side of Bealach portal, but bucked our way through the storm-passes of Flogen and the Lower Reaches and rode the alignment tides to Galent. Three hours. Empty in the stomach and shaking in the legs, I disembarked, handed out bribes and smiles at high speed, and went through the portal to Loth, where in a thick heat buzzing with insects the size of my hand I hired a vehicle of light strong wood, drawn by three pairs of leggy, nervous beasts with four legs, huge eyes, long necks and soft grey feathers. Their driver looked like a fat green dog. The thing was fast, but damned uncomfortable; I was thrown around like a dried pea in a child's rattle. Three more hours, or thereabouts.

I tumbled out, bruised, at Ithackt and headed straight for the portal. I had a nasty hour or so there, trying to be smiling and persuasive with my stomach doing somersaults, handing out Antheran's bits of paper and more bribes than an aunt with her favourite nephews. Finally I was allowed through.

From there another overland; I hired... something. It was biddable, steerable, fast, and knew the road. It seemed to be some sort of mobile shrub with a kind of wooden scoop in which one sat, while brushlike legs whisked along the dusty purple track. Around me, spires of gleaming black rock jabbed at the greenish sky. Another portal. Busy; lots of people, all in a hurry. No need for bribes, I was waved through impatiently. By now I was so tired and sick I could hardly stand, or see. Time, sliding past me like the road. A ship of sorts; driven by teams of rowers, across a lake of thick pink fluid that smelled of dying flowers, where half-seen creatures like huge, slate-coloured ghosts swam alongside, the slow balletic sweep of their great fanlike fins sending out ripples of roseate light.

Another portal city. Slow conversations with greedy officials, fumbling among the currencies I still had, all made worse by my inability to string together more than half a sentence by then. Finally, with a lurch, I fell through the threshold into Flai, barely conscious.

Someone hauled me up and dumped me on a hard bench. Once things stopped swaying like a topmast in a storm, I opened my eyes.

The architecture was familiar; the residents of Flai seem to have a liking for everything square, grey and cold. I started to shiver, and dug in my pack for something to throw over me, then remembered I'd only packed a spare shirt.

I put it on. I was surrounded by Flaians: green-marbled skin, skeletal features, ratty naked tails, no hair.

One of them bent over me, and said, in bad Lithan, "You can't stay here. Transit here only. Where you going?"

"Tiresana."

"Next transport for Tiresana portal, over there, you go wait."

Once I could stand, I went to where they had pointed: a boxy shelter that didn't do much to hold off a chilly penetrating drizzle.

I remembered this. The shuttered, unfriendly look of the streets, the grim slab-like building they'd created around the portal, the smoky metallic smell that was the result of something they mined in the hills above the town.

When I'd come through I'd stayed barely a day, so eager to be as far away as I could, that I'd taken up with the first group leaving within hours who'd wanted a guard. Flai has two portals that I know of; I'd left through the other one.

If I'd known all this time how close to Tiresana I was during alignment, I'd probably have reached Scalentine and just kept running.

The transport arrived, grey. A wheeled cart, drawn by miserable looking droop-necked beasts. Also grey. We plodded through the rain.

Once I'd put one of Flower's honey-cakes in my clangingly hollow stomach and recovered a little, I stared out at veils of rain sweeping the grey hills. I was gripping the side of the cart as though the pressure of my hands could speed it. The beasts moved in a slow, muddy trudge towards the Tiresana portal; I knew we were going faster than I could have on foot, but I felt time hissing at my back.

The more I tried not to think about the Lantern, the more images crowded me: Flower putting food on the table, roaring for people to eat while it was hot; Essie and Jivrais thundering up and down the stairs, giggling; Laney putting on the Fey Princess for all she was worth with a new client, and the expression on her face when she got an extremely expensive and extraordinarily ugly necklace for her pains. Previous red-faced with laughter as she hauled in someone who'd tried to run without paying... and been tripped by his own unlaced trousers, ending up face-down and bare-arsed at the bottom of the steps. Ireq, watching it all, barely speaking, often smiling. And the Chief, seated over the chess-board, his long finger tapping the corner of his mouth as he considered his next move. The melancholy lines of his face lifting into a smile. My last sight of him, changed, pacing, still marked with the blood of the madman he'd hauled off me.

By the time we reached Ithakt, the portal town to Tiresana, I was beyond weeping; cold and grey and empty as the Flai landscape.

Ithakt was yet another lump of blocky buildings, almost identical to the one we'd left. The familiar and by now, to me, fairly loathsome hum of a portal was audible before the cart pulled to a halt; the beasts simply stopping, as though they saw no point in walking further, ever again.

There was a certain tension in the air. Flaians are hard to read, at least for me. But in most races a tendency to shift about, look over one's shoulder, and keep half-consciously checking for your weapons is definitely a sign of nerves.

I wondered what they knew, or guessed.

And for the first time there were Tiresans: thin, weary, scared, decked with packs and rolled sleeping mats and squalling babies. Tiresans, leaving. How bad had things got? Tiresans don't leave. Except for me.

I knew there was hardly any chance I'd be recognised, not after all this time. But still I stooped, ducked my head, turned my face away. No-one was looking anyway; they were more concerned with keeping track of children and goods and dealing with their own terrors than eyeing another rain-drenched refugee.

The guards were herding them onto transports, heading them out. I wondered where they were all going.

The guards were the only ones who looked at me. They made no attempt to stop me, although they cast glances at each other as I stood looking at the portal. It was smaller than I remembered, its arc an uneasy shifting mix of grey and orange, casting queasy lights on the rough stone floor.

For a moment I wasn't sure if I could do it.

I could still turn back. I could go home, and be safe – for as long as it took the Avatars to realise their mistake and come looking for me. Or as long as it took for me to sicken of my own cowardice.

I took a deep breath, squared my shoulders, and with one hand on my sword, I stepped through.

I felt that subterranean shudder and then the smell of ghost-lilies and desert and sandmules, the smell of my past, closed over me like a hungry mouth.

MY KNEES BUCKLED, but at least this time I didn't fall.

The portal town of Mantek had grown a little since I'd left, but not much, in more than ten years, and the newer buildings looked shoddy and dull. It was disturbingly quiet; even those waiting to leave (all Tiresans, every one of them, nor a foreign trader to be seen) stood meekly, waiting. When I'd left it had been a bustling, comfortingly crowded place.

Perhaps because I'd been the only one entering, rather than leaving, a few people glanced at me. Some of the glances seemed to linger a little too long. I told myself I was being foolish.

As I came out into the open, the sun had just dropped below the horizon. I remembered it all. The particular pale blue of the sky, the dusty purple outline of the mountains in the distance, the fleshy curves of the dunes rolling towards the horizon.

I could hear something else that was all too familiar: the hissing, fussing and bellowing of sandmules from a nearby livery stable. Sandmules. That was one thing I'd been happy to leave behind.

This lot looked worse than I remembered: scraggy, ribby, harsh-coated, wall-eyed and vicious. I took my time over it, trying to choose the one that looked healthiest and least psychotic.

I was putting off the moment of actually heading for the Temple, I knew. I had finally picked one and was getting ready to bargain with the owner when a voice behind me said, "Thukret's hairy balls, those are ugly beasts."

"*Previous?*"

I turned around.

Previous, Laney, Flower and the Twins were standing there. Previous was flushed and sweating; Laney, wearing strangely practical garments of plain linen, her green eyes rimmed red, looked so sick she was almost the same colour as Flower, who was holding her up and scowling at me. The Twins were, as always, as neat and self-contained as cats. Even Cruel's bandage looked as jaunty as a pirate's bandanna.

"You honestly thought we'd just let you *go?*" Flower said.

I clutched at the neck of the nearest sandmule to steady myself, and it bawled a protest. "No, no. I can't believe you did this. How? How did you... never mind. You have to go home, all of you."

"Why?" Previous said. "And frankly, after what we went through catching up with you, I'd rather fight Nederans. *Drunk* Nederans."

I took a breath, looked around; the ostler had drifted outside to gossip with a friend, and was out of earshot. I grasped Previous by the shoulders. "The Avatars. If they think for a moment that you might be a threat, they will have you killed, or tear your guts out and keep you alive just to make an example of you. Do you understand me? I'm not taking you lot anywhere near them. Please. Go home."

"Who said anything about 'taking'?" Cruel said, stretching elegantly. "We're not servants, as you've often pointed out. We want to take a little trip, well, who's to stop us?"

"Cruel, you don't even know what you'd be facing!"

She shrugged. "Then you'd better tell us, hadn't you?"

"No! Please." I was so caught between fury, tears, gratitude and terror I could barely get the words out. "Hap-Canae burned my lover to death in front of my eyes, just by touching him. You think I want to see that happen to you?"

"Babylon." Flower loomed over me. He wasn't wearing his apron; he looked odd without it, somehow much bigger, and more muscular, and more dangerous. A great long scar, paler green than the rest of his skin, ran from his left shoulder to the right of his waist.

He shook his head. "Look at you. If I ever thought a little thing like you was going to be trying to keep *me* safe... what sort of life do you think I had before I arrived in Scalentine? Or any of us? You think we were all wrapped in silk and petals? You have any idea how many times I've fought for my life? Never mind, I'll tell you later. Just accept that I do know how to look after myself."

"And Laney?" I said, "you can't even *walk*."

"Oh, Babylon, darling, really," Laney rasped. "It's just portal sickness, I'll be over it in an hour or so. And we're not on Scalentine, are we? I mean, I won't have the same powers I would in my own plane, but still." Laney managed a small, but thoroughly disconcerting smile. "Let's just say, you've never met the Lady Lanetherai, and neither have they. I mean, how do you think we *got* here?"

"We can all manage," Cruel said. "Trust me." Unusual nodded.

"So what's the plan?" Previous said.

"Plan? The *plan* was for me to leave you lot safe behind me, that was the *plan*."

"We'll have to make a new one, then, won't we?" Previous said.

UNABLE TO STOP them hiring their own sandmules (they just threw Empire coinage at the man until he collapsed in a heap of gibbering gratitude) I realised that the only thing I could do, that might stop them, was tell them everything.

There was no time. I would have to talk as we rode.

There was a house beside the livery stable. Outside was a small, headless statue; heavy-breasted, a sword at its side.

Babaska. All of her statues had been broken, of course. But I could see the stains where someone had poured wine at her feet, and a few crumbs of bread.

A couple of women were leaning in the doorway, looking weary and underfed. "A little company?" one called out, in broken Lithan. "We'll make you welcome."

"Sorry, ladies," Cruel said. "Here on business."

The whores glanced at me too, and glanced again. I supposed it was the crew. It could hardly be me. When I'd been Babaska's Avatar, I'd been a sixteen year old girl with an Avatar's charisma and glow. Now, I was a slightly-used woman a good few years older, and the description 'handsome' was as close as I was going to get. But there were other considerations...

"There is one thing you can do for us," I said. "Scarves. Head wraps, for the dust. We'll pay well."

One of the women scurried inside and came out with armfuls of cloth: turquoise and emerald, rose and scarlet, threaded with gold. Hoarded treasure.

As I took the scarves one of the women smiled at me, and drew her finger along her jaw, in exactly the place I bore my scar. Where Babaska bore hers. I could see a faint line, like a smudge of kohl, along her jaw.

Before I could puzzle it out, she bowed, and hurried back inside.

"Here," I said to the others. "Put these on. Wrap it over your head and around your face." I demonstrated; my hands remembered, moving as though I'd done it only yesterday.

"Must we?" Unusual scowled at his scarf, which was a vivid yellow.

"Yes, unless you want a mouth full of grit and a face like a stonemason's before we've been on the road an hour. Besides, in case you hadn't noticed, there wasn't any other foreign trade coming through the portal. There were never many people on this plane who weren't Tiresan, and I'd rather not have everyone noticing us, if you don't mind."

"And that's supposed to work on me how?" Flower said.

"Dammit, Flower... yes, all right, but at least cover your head. They might not notice the rest of you once it's dark."

The evening shadows were stretching long and blue across the desert, and the wild dogs began to howl. We saw a few of them: pathetic and mange-ridden for the most part, slinking among the thin clumps of whistle-grass and biteweed, their shadows far more threatening than themselves.

As I SETTLED back into the sandmule's stride, once as familiar to me as my own, I kept drawing breath to speak. The sandmules' feet with their great soft pads went *thup, thup* on the cracked hardpan. The stars burned hard and far. I could hear the crew's soft comments, but they were mostly quiet, and I knew they were waiting.

In the end, I stared at the sandmule's great veined ears as they twitched and furled, and said, "I was an orphan lucky to get taken in as a servant. I was Chosen, I thought, to be trained as a priestess..."

I told them about the Avatars, and how I had become one; about the girls, about what I had done and failed to do. My voice sounded strange to me – young, distant, like the memory of Ebi.

I told them about the way I'd been punished, and how I had run, abandoning my friends, the soldiers and whores I was supposed to protect. I told them about the ring. Both rings.

By the time I trailed into silence, I felt numb, and a long way from everything.

No-one said anything for a while. Then Previous pulled up alongside me, and patted me on the arm. "Sounds to me like these bastards are well overdue for a kicking," she said.

"Kicking's the least of it," Flower growled. "When I get hold of them..." his mule made a hoarse whine of protest as his hands tightened hard on the reins.

I turned my mule to face them.

Laney's eyes were glowing brilliant scarlet, and she was crying. It made her look as though she were weeping blood, and I shuddered to my bones.

"Now you've heard," I said. "You know what you're facing. So. One last time. Will you go home?"

They just looked at me, stubborn as a wall.

"Oh, arse on the lot of you," I said. I wrenched the sandmule around so my back was to them, because seeing your battle-leader in tears isn't generally good for morale, and we set off again.

Previous coughed, and said, "So. You're sort of an ex-goddess of war, then."

"Not quite. Avatar. And ex, yes. Definitely *ex*."

"No wonder you're so bloody good at fighting."

"Hah. Not that good, I've still got the bruises from our last training bout, remember?"

"Hey, yeah. So, I beat you, eh?"

"To a pulp, thank you very much. Don't sound so damn pleased with yourself, Previous. I'm no Avatar any longer."

"Don't ruin her moment of glory," Laney said. "If she wants to have beaten up a goddess, let her."

"Fine, fine. I'll keep it in mind next time she wants to lame me for life."

"And you were a goddess of sex, as well?" Laney said. "You could really make men swoon just by looking at them?"

"And? You can do that anyway," I said.

"Not *all* of them." She pouted.

"Even you couldn't handle *every* man in the planes."

"I wouldn't mind the chance to try."

I felt hollowed out with exhaustion, but oddly light, as though there were space in my head for the first time in a very long time. "I suppose I'd better try and come up with a plan, then," I said.

"Well, yes, that *might* be useful," said Laney.

"How does the ring actually work?" Cruel said. "We need to know that before we can plan anything, don't we?"

"From what Mokraine said, it has to be placed into some kind of hollow. There's a place in the altar that looks the right shape."

"So if we can get in there," Previous said, "you can just pop it in there and we run and it goes boom?"

"Not quite. For one thing it has to be placed when something happens – Mokraine said the appearance of the altar will change. It has to be put there at the right time. Also, someone has to be wearing it."

"Ah. Did he say anything about what *happens* to the person who's wearing it?"

"No. But the power is supposed to sort of dissipate out. That doesn't sound so bad," I said, as cheerfully as I could manage.

"So," Laney said. "Why don't you just swap the one you've got for the one *they've* got, and they'll use it, and they'll go foof? Or the power will go foof, which is just as good."

I stared at her. "Just swap them."

"Well, yes, if you can find where they're keeping the fake one, why not?"

I didn't answer for a moment, thinking. Could it *really* work like that? I felt a rising hope. Maybe I could just swap the real ring for the fake, get my crew the hells out of there, and let the Avatars do the job for me. Bring about their own destruction.

"Where would they keep the ring?" Flower said.

"They trust each other about as much as hyenas around a corpse. They'd keep it somewhere they could all keep an eye on it, until it was time for the ceremony. Somewhere safe, but neutral; nowhere anyone else might happen on it. There's only one place I can think of... the altar-room."

"They'd keep it in the room where the ceremony's supposed to happen?" Laney said. "Really? What if something went wrong? What if someone got in? Will there be guards?"

"There never used to be, because they didn't want anyone

knowing it was there. And because of the opening spell. But it would be sensible to assume they'd have taken *some* precautions. And so should we. They have charisma, all of them. Very strong."

"Well you did ask for an anti-charisma potion," Laney said. "So I assumed we might need it. I dosed everyone before we left. Honestly, Babylon."

"So all the time I thought I was leaving you behind... how the hells *did* you follow me, anyway?"

"You mentioned Tiresana," Unusual said. "After that, all we had to do was keep after you. The trouble wasn't that, it was keeping out of sight until it was too late for you to give us the slip."

"But I had papers..."

"We had me," Laney said. "Oh, and some money."

"Whose money?"

"The money you forgot to take to the Exchange. The rest of Fain's and the money from the Vessels and Lord Antheran."

"Oh, great. So are we broke again?"

"Well, not *entirely.*"

We raced the night across the desert, stopping only to water the beasts and ourselves at a well in a patch of scrub, dying trees, and the remains of a few scattered walls.

The well had Rohikanta's head carved on it, with fish frolicking in his beard. I realised I knew the place. But when I'd last seen it there had been a small but vigorous market here, people selling dried fruit and water-bottles and fortunes. Now, nothing but a smear of silty water, and the well.

Previous doused her face, and looked up, dripping. "Wouldn't hurt to have a diversion on hand," she said. "Something to get any guards looking the other way."

"I can do that," Laney said. "I think..." she shook out her sleeves, gave the nearest palm tree a calculating look, raised her hand, and flicked her fingers.

A fat spark the size of an orange shot out of her hand, danced around the tree, giggling, zoomed out over the pool, dipped to meet its own reflection with a hiss, bounced up, and shot up into the night, still giggling.

"Well..." Previous said, doubt in her voice.

Laney was scowling at her hand, and looked pale. "Drat."

"What?" I said.

"There's something wrong here. That was *hard*. Much harder than it should have been. *And* it didn't work."

"Like on Scalentine?" I said.

"Oh no. On Scalentine it's like, you can only, I don't know, you can only shout so loudly. After that you can't shout any louder however hard you try; something damps the noise down as it leaves. Here... it's more like something's stopping your voice working properly in the first place. And it feels *wrong*."

"Well, I suppose Scalentine isn't the only plane where magic works differently."

"I may have to stick with illusions, then," Laney said. "Botheration. Do they *have* Fey here?"

"I'd never seen any until I left. Tiresana didn't interact much with other planes; I suppose the Avatars preferred it that way. They always acted as though the portal didn't exist."

"Who'd they have their wars with, then?" said Previous.

"Each other. They sent their soldiers out to fight as though they were chess-pieces. It was a game to them."

I heard Previous swear under her breath.

"Laney," I said. "Can you do a deglamour?"

"No. But I can *dim* you, I can do that even on Scalentine."

"What does that do?"

"I'll show you."

"No! Don't. If things aren't working right you might not be able to do it when you need to. What is it?"

"It blurs your edges. Makes you sort of shadowy. Remember when that client came calling and he had such terrible breath, and he was asking for me? That's how I got past him. It only really works if it's dark, though."

"Laney... why didn't you just *say?*" I said.

"Because it was funnier watching you try and find a tactful way to tell him."

"Yes, well, never mind that. Do you know how long you can do it for?"

She shrugged.

"All right, we'll see how we go. As to the Avatars... I doubt they'd leave one alone to guard it. They don't trust each other that much. So it'll be two or three if they're there."

"How do we deal with them?" Flower said.

"You don't. If there *are* Avatars there, we have to get them away from the room for long enough, without confronting them. They've different powers, all nasty if not deadly. Shakanti can control any water in the vicinity; that shouldn't be a problem at the heart of the temple, even *she's* probably not mad enough to flood the whole place to get rid of us, but she can also turn you to stone, or drive you mad. Some of the others I never saw use their powers, so I don't know what they can do, but I'd not risk a stand-up fight with any of them."

"So we just need to draw them away? Well, I can do *that*," Laney said.

"You have to give me long enough to get in, get past whatever they *have* got set up, and swap the rings. *If* I'm right and the damn thing's actually there. If not, I'll have to rethink."

"What are they likely to have?" said Cruel. "Wards?"

"No. There's almost no magic here but for the Avatars' own powers. Traps or deadfalls, maybe. I don't know."

Cruel and Unusual looked at each other. "You brought the ropes?" Cruel said.

Unusual just smiled and patted the bag he was carrying.

"What else have you got in there?" I said. "No, don't tell me, I'm not sure I want to know. Laney, can you create an illusion of one of the Avatars?"

"Not without knowing what they look like. And not at the same time as dimming."

"Damn."

"*You* know what they look like, though."

"Yes, but I can't draw for donkeyshit." I thought. "Right. Once we get there, the dawn worship will be starting. We should have a chance to see at least some of them, *if* they bother to attend to their worshippers when they've godhead on their minds."

THE STATUES OF the gods rose out of the desert. Arrogance in stone; so vauntingly huge it seemed as though even the vast temple they guarded hadn't been enough to contain them. One was broken off at the waist, a gap like a lost tooth; Babaska's.

So old, those statues. As old, perhaps, as the altar-stone itself. But the altar was solid, and these were hollow. I looked at them, thinking hard.

There were others ahead of us, travelling in the cool of the night; people driving thin, bawling herd animals, carts of dusty vegetables. All those priests take a lot of feeding. People with offerings of gold and perfume, meat and roots. I thought of Adissi, with her handful of pebbles. Did the statue that had been a living girl still stand in the temple at Pella?

Shakanti was insane, but Hap-Canae wasn't. He'd always known exactly what he was doing, and had no excuse but a selfishness so bone-deep you couldn't dig it out with a three foot blade. Though admittedly, the thought of trying didn't exactly displease me.

Maybe I'd get the chance before he burned me to charcoal.

CHAPTER
THIRTY-THREE

Day 10
Second Day of Twomoon

A THIN LINE of light was showing on the horizon when we entered Akran. The great torches at the gate, clasped in the hands of statues fifty feet high, hissed and sent flickering yellow light across the sand and over the people, catching on patched armour and gimcrack jewellery and sunken eyes.

There were a few non-Tiresans present; what little external trade there was, of course, was almost certain to end up here. I'd the scarf on still, pulled up over my nose. But still, people looked. I hoped it was just my height; I was taller by a head than most Tiresans. Flower, of course, was even taller. If I'd known they were going to be such damn fools and come with me, I'd have made some attempt to make us look more like traders.

Trudging through the gate, we limped and drooped and kept our faces covered. There were hundreds of people in the precinct: cartloads of vegetables and bawling beasts going towards the kitchens, priests and priestesses from other temples with messages and requests, guards and porters and acolytes.

And of course, worshippers: pregnant and would-be pregnant women heading to the temple of Meisheté with its blood red tiles; young girls, their hair dressed with flowers if they could get them, to Shakanti's silvery-walled temple. Others prostrated themselves in the middle of the precinct, hoping for the notice of any god or Avatar who deigned to look their way.

Here and there, even in the half-light, I spotted that dark streak along the jaw-line. On men and women, young and old. Some looked like soldiers; some like whores. Some like neither. On one or two the scar was a real one – self-inflicted, by the look.

"What does it mean?" Laney asked me. "That mark?"

"I think perhaps Babaska still has her worshippers. One of the whores back at Mantek had the same mark. They're taking a hell of a risk, though."

I looked around the precinct, a little puzzled. It was the same, and yet, not quite. There seemed to be more space somehow. Then I realised it was not that the precinct was bigger, but that worshippers were fewer. Perhaps, for many, the faint hope of a favour was no longer sufficient to drag them here.

No-one paid us any attention as we worked our way around the edge of the precinct to Babaska's temple.

"We'll have to be careful. Her worship was discouraged, vigorously. We shouldn't be seen going in if we can help it," I said.

We edged and shuffled, climbing, one by one, up the part of the steps that was still in deepest shadow, freezing if anyone seemed to be looking our way.

Bits of Babaska's statue lay about, like a giant child's toy, flung down in a temper. Curses had been carved around the entrance, promises of doom and misery on those who dared worship Babaska of the Bloody Hand, the Traitress.

The pillar still stood, grey stone stabbing up, the blackened chains hanging silent against it. Dark stains scored its sides. I could hear the sound of beetles skittering in my skull.

Behind that pillar was the door that would take us inside the maze of tunnels that led to the altar-room. Babaska's face smiled blindly at me from the floor. I had to go in, before someone noticed us, but I couldn't.

"Oh," Unusual said softly behind me. "You were right. Look."

Just inside the threshold, a flicker of colour. A handful of wilted flowers, tucked beneath the statue's shattered hand. A bracelet of blue beads. The gleam of a copper coin; a small well-sharpened dagger.

Offerings. Who were these people, still hoping for help from she who could no longer grant it?

But maybe I could. I gripped the lintel and forced myself to step through, my heart cold in my throat. Shadows scuttered away from my feet. Beetles; it was as much as I could do not to cry out.

I brushed one of the chains as I moved past the pillar, and it chinked faintly. I put my hand on the wall to steady myself.

"Babylon?" Laney said.

"I'm all right."

The altar had been hacked to pieces, but the screen was still there, its hundreds of little figures still frozen in love and war.

The door behind it was locked, of course.

"We may need to break it," I said. "But I don't want to draw attention." I looked over my shoulder. The precinct was brightening rapidly, light beginning to spill into the temple. "Previous, go to the door, but stay out of sight. You should see a temple over to the left, lots of gold about it, priests in yellow robes outside. Are they there?"

Previous picked her way through the debris, and peered out. "Yes, I see it. Bunch of priests and worshippers."

"There's someone up on the temple roof, see them?"

"Yes."

"They'll drop their hand when they see the sun, and all the priests will sing out. Previous, drop your hand when they do. When she does, Flower, hit the door."

We stood in the cool whispering shadows for what seemed like endless minutes, until, finally, Previous dropped her hand. To a clash of brass and a shout of chanting, Flower dropped his shoulder and barged the door.

It cracked right across, the gilded wood shuddering and splitting. Flower began to tear it away, then we all put our hands to it.

I made them wait while I went through.

The stairs behind it were silent, deserted. Light was beginning to paint the walls pale. Dust lay thick on the steps.

Feeling like a ghost of myself, I led the others up the stairs, paused for a moment, and turned left. Past the room where the sarcophagus was; where I had lain. Past the room where our trainers had instructed us in seduction. Silent, these rooms, now. Left to the beetles and the dust.

We passed a window that looked down into the inner precinct. I risked a glance and saw Meisheté, in her aspect as a heavily pregnant woman, heading no doubt for the back entrance to her temple. Even in the low dawn light I could see she had that blooming glow, the essence of a healthy, welcome pregnancy, her eyes shining in their shadowed surrounds. I thought of the women I'd seen outside, swollen bellies on skeletal frames; the skinny huge-eyed children. *Go,* I thought. *Eat up the praise you don't deserve.*

Even now, when they were about to gorge on power, they had to wrench out the last drop of worship.

Previous peered out beside me. "Is she..."

"No. It's an illusion, one of her Aspects. They're all barren. Sssh." I beckoned Laney up behind me. "Look, there's Meisheté. And..." Behind her, strolling along, Hap-Canae. He'd always loved the worship, bathed in it like sunlight.

"That's him, isn't it?" Laney whispered. "Well, I understand why you fell for him – that... *yrrkennish paiketh.*"

"The what?" I said.

Laney – *Laney* – actually blushed. "It's... never mind. Just don't ever say it if you're around Fey. Seriously. Ever. Who's that?"

"Shakanti," I said, grabbing Laney's arm and pulling her back as Shakanti's head tilted like a hawk's, her hair drifting about in the morning breeze, strands of silver shining like spider web.

"She's the one who... *oh.*" Laney's hands, fine and fragile as china, curled into claws, and her eyes glimmered scarlet. "Oh, Babylon, let me..."

"Sshh. Listen."

Below us Shakanti approached Hap-Canae, and their voices came clearly up to us. I gestured the others to silence.

"...those women will be of no use at all," Shakanti said. "We should go back." I remembered that voice. I still heard it, on bad nights.

"No," Hap-Canae said. "We must go on." His voice was exactly the same, every rich syllable as rounded and full of caressing warmth as I remembered. "Nothing must seem different today. We discussed this. Emptying the precinct for the creation of an Avatar may have been one of the things that started these rumours."

"Once it is done, these whores and brawling peasants will pay for their heresy." Her voice was the same, too: glass and silver, gleaming ice over death-cold depths.

"Yes. *Once it is done*. After the morning worship."

He drew her away, and with a suspicious glance backwards – the woman had the paranoid instincts of a sheep-killing dog – she went.

"What did they say?" Laney said.

"It doesn't matter," I whispered, though I wondered. Heresy. The whispers that Ranay and I had started. Sesh had wanted to fight the Avatars, and perhaps in his own way he had; more whispers, about the true nature of the Avatars. He'd have been good at it. He was always a storyteller, Sesh. "Keep away from the windows, and keep quiet."

As we approached the corridor where the altar-room was, I waved the others back behind me and held up a hand to keep them still. A breeze skittered past us, sending the dust swirling.

I peeked around the corner. Two tall, hawk-faced women in their robes of grey and blue, their long pale hair in constant motion. Lohiria and Mihiria; Avatars of the goddesses of the east and west winds.

It made sense. They'd always fought like bantams, for all they were twins. If any of the Avatars could be trusted not to band together, it would be those two. They were staring in opposite directions, the set of their shoulders making it plain they'd been arguing. I drew the crew back.

"Now listen," I said. "You need to stay here, out of sight. There are two Avatars guarding the door, and I have to get them away. Laney, can you make me an illusion of Shakanti? The woman with the silver hair? Voice as well?"

"Yes. But... you really want to be *her*?"

"I have to," I said. "They're scared of her, and she's known for telling the truth, even if she always did it to hurt. She's the only choice."

"Well, if you're sure..."

"I am. The rest of you, wait for my signal. Laney? Glam me up."

Laney hunched her shoulders and narrowed her eyes, and colour streamed from her fingers. The illusion poured over me like cold water. For a moment I couldn't see anything except a swirl of blue and silver, then it settled.

My real eyes were slightly below where Shakanti's were, my body bulkier than hers; it felt rather like wearing a badly fitting helmet.

Laney was looking relieved, but anxious. "I don't know how long it will hold, Babylon," she whispered.

"I'll do this as fast as I can." I would have to. Morning worship would take no more than an hour, and Shakanti was already suspicious.

I walked around the corner. Even Laney couldn't make me walk with Shakanti's drifting, arrogant elegance. I hoped they wouldn't notice.

"Shakanti? What are you doing here?" Lohiria said. "I thought the *greater* Avatars were to receive worship as usual this morning."

"The others may be as foolish as they wish," I said. I could hear Shakanti's voice over my own, slightly out of time. It almost threw me.

"Is something wrong?" Lohiria said. "We have waited hours. I still don't see why we couldn't have one of the priests guard it; we could always have killed them after."

"It was necessary," I said.

They looked at each other, and I wondered if they could sense something wrong. I was sweating cold.

"Have they *still* not decided?" Mihiria said. "I thought it was all done. We know that only an Avatar can use the ring, we must all be present, and then the power will flow into all of us," Mihiria snapped, twitching at her robes. "I can't see why there is all this waiting about. Wait, wait, wait. We've waited centuries." She glanced at me, warily, as though she might have gone too far.

"You'll wait longer," I said. "Tell me, who ordered the statue of Babaska broken?" If it had been Shakanti herself I would have to fudge somehow.

"What? Why?" Lohiria said.

I said, hoping I sounded like Shakanti in a mood of thinning patience, "Well, who was it?"

"You *know* it was Hap-Canae," said Mihiria.

"And why do you think he ordered it?" I said.

"He said it was part of the destruction of her worship; really, I don't know what this has to do with anything," Mihiria whined.

"He has tricked us all," I said.

"What?" Lohiria glared at Mihiria. "I *told* you!"

Mihiria said, "What do you mean? What is he doing?"

"The statues. The power will go through the statues. That's why he had Babaska's broken. Her no longer having an Avatar, he didn't know what would happen if power went there. Hap-Canae meant not to be at the ceremony; to make some excuse. If he is inside the statue of himself when the ring is placed, then he will take all the power to himself. He will leave us with nothing."

"The statues?" Mihiria said.

"Where is Hap-Canae?" Lohiria said. "Why didn't you stop him?"

"It is dawn," I said. "My powers are weakening as his grow. I only just discovered this; how could *I* stop him?"

"But if we need to be inside the statues," said Mihiria, "who will place the ring?"

"We don't *need* to be," I said. "It is only if one wishes to divert power from others, to keep it all for oneself. If we are all present for the ceremony, then things will go as planned, an equal share for all."

I saw Mihiria's face change as she realised that she, too, had a statue.

So did Lohiria.

"We'll stop him," they said.

"There are two of us, our powers don't fade with the hours," Lohiria said. "The room is still guarded *inside*."

"We'll come straight back," Mihiria said. "But if something happens to keep us away, if Hap-Canae defeats us, don't let them stop the ceremony!"

"Yes," said Lohiria. "Better that we should sacrifice ourselves, and the rest of you take up your rightful places!"

Before I could even answer, they picked up their skirts and ran, trying to outpace each other. Sacrifice themselves, my backside; they just wanted to get to their own statues.

The door stood before me, as it had all that time ago. A good chunk of my life, it had been, since then. To the altar-stone I suppose it was nothing; a bare blink of time.

I could hear something moving in the room beyond; a dull scraping, like the body of an armoured man dragged across stone. Lohiria had said the room was guarded inside.

I beckoned the others.

Laney had gone so white she was almost transparent, and was shuddering all over.

"Laney. Laney! You can take it off now!"

She let out an explosive breath that ended in a harsh cough, and staggered. I felt Shakanti's likeness run off me, and shuddered with relief.

We took turns listening at the door, but none of us could work out what the noise was.

"Never mind; whatever it is, I have to go in," I said. "And one last time; if the Avatars turn up, just *run*. Get the hells out of here, make for the portal, and get off Tiresana. No arguments. There'll be nothing you can do, and I don't want the last thing I hear to be my friends dying. Understood?"

They looked at each other.

"Understood," Previous said. "Do what you need to do."

The words were in my head, as though I'd heard them the day before. That memory of mine. It wasn't always a blessing, especially here.

I took a breath, and said:

"*Insiteth*

"*Abea*

"*Iatenteth*

"*Hai ena.*"

The dust spiralled around us. Nothing. Then, as I felt failure take me like a sickness, the floor hummed beneath my feet and the doors swung open.

There were no windows in the room; the only light came from the torch on the wall behind us, sputtering near its end. At first I couldn't make out what I was seeing. I could hear that slow, dragging sound, and the floor seemed to be *moving*. About three feet off the ground floated four red glowing lights, each the size of my palm.

Someone moved, letting in more light, and it fell on great scaled backs. Rohikanta's pets, the Messewhy.

They belted forward with that swaying ungainly run, which would look a lot more absurd if it weren't so terrifyingly fast. I leapt back, almost knocking Previous off her feet. Someone shrieked, and the things reared up with a jolt, towering over us, yawing and hissing.

There were thick collars of black metal about their necks, and a chain of the same stuff ran from each to the wall. Adamant. They'd used it to hold me, too; the only material that could hold an Avatar. Or, it seemed, an Avatar's uncanny pet.

They realised they couldn't reach us, and dropped back onto all fours with resounding *thuds*. "Someone bring that torch here," I said.

In the flickering light, I could see a small box on the altar, heavily decorated with lapis and shell. I could only hope I was right, and the fake ring was in there; if not, we were done for.

It was roughly thirty feet from the door to the altar, most of it covered with toothy reptile. The chains were taut at the door, and I realised, as one of the beasts moved to the far end of its length, that they couldn't reach the altar either. That made sense, I supposed; it would be irritating if one of your guards, in a moment of boredom, decided to swallow the thing it was supposed to be guarding. Unfortunately they could cover most of the space between door and altar with no trouble at all.

"Unusual, is there rope in that bag?" I said.

"Of course."

"How are you at throwing it?"

"Straight, weighted or looped?" he said.

"I guess that answers my question. Looped. Can you get loops round those beasties' muzzles, and pull them tight?"

"If they need those chains, Babylon," Unusual said, "I'm thinking even our best rope, which we don't have, wouldn't hold them."

"It doesn't need to hold the whole animal – just its jaw. Their strength is all in their downbite. You can hold their jaws shut with your hands, and they can't open them. Normal ones, anyway."

"There's a normal version?" Previous said.

"Yes. Don't go paddling in the river."

Unusual was coiling the rope over his arm, and squinting into the room. "More light," he said.

A couple of the crew grabbed torches from the wall-brackets. We wouldn't need them for long. The day outside was rising much too fast.

Unusual flicked the rope out, the loop spun lazily through the air, over a beast's snout, and he snugged it tight. The Messeh flung its head about, hissing furiously; Unusual shoved his end of the rope at Flower, who grabbed it and braced.

The other one reared, disturbed, just as Unusual threw again, and the coil caught briefly across its eyes and slid away. It put its great clawed foot down on the rope before Unusual could yank it clear.

He started immediately to make another coil, his eyes never leaving the beast, his hands working by themselves. Behind us in the precinct I could hear the morning worship of Aka-Tete, a deep whispering chant followed by a wailing cry.

We didn't have long.

Unusual raised the coil of rope to his mouth, and blew on it, a gesture I'd seen Kyrl make a hundred times before a tricky throw.

He swung. The rope seemed to hang in the air for an age, like a dream or a vision, then it fell. The Messeh moved its head; Unusual flicked his wrist and the coil slid over its muzzle neat as you please. He yanked. The beast froze, then dropped back to the floor.

"That's not going to hold," Cruel said.

"It'll have to. We can't wait. Stand over there and try and distract them."

The crew moved to one side of the doorway, and began to wave their arms, and whisper invitingly. The beasts turned their heads that way, but as soon as I moved, one turned to watch me.

"Wait..." Laney said. "I can..."

"Laney, no. You're wiped."

"What do they eat?"

"Anything that gets close. Laney..."

She shushed me with a gesture so utterly imperious I couldn't help but admire it, and there, suddenly, was a fat, slow, ripe-smelling hog, on the far side of the room. Both the beasts scrabbled across the floor towards it. I took a breath, and ran for the altar.

The scaly side of the nearest beast was as high as my waist. I ran as I'd not run since I was sixteen, my feet barely seeming to touch the floor, but still, that room was horribly long. Surely it hadn't been so long, all those years ago?

I heard a shout of warning, put on a spurt of speed I didn't have, and felt hot breath on my neck. I dived for the altar, slapped my hands on the surface, and whipped my legs up under me.

I looked down and realised that my hands were half an inch from the handholds. The ones I'd put them in before, when I became an Avatar – and when I stopped being one. I shuddered so hard I almost fell off the altar.

I could hear the beasts hissing and scrabbling behind me, but I was still alive. I grabbed the box, opened it.

Yes. The false ring sat gleaming in the torchlight, with its slight roughness, its artificial shine. I thought briefly of Frithlit; chancer that he was, I doubt he'd ever imagined where his little replica would end up.

No time for triumph. I whipped out the false ring.

I heard a sigh, and a thud. Through the doorway I could just see Laney, crumpled on the floor. The image of the hog disappeared.

"Is she all right?" I called.

"Breathing. She's just drained herself," Flower said, scooping her up into his arms. "Come on, get out of there."

The second Messeh shook its head, clawed at itself, and the single loop of rope dropped to the floor. It opened its jaw – big enough to swallow a cart whole and stuck with ivory daggers – and hissed.

It was still chained, but if I got five feet from the altar, it would have me.

It was suddenly very quiet. And I realised the chanting had stopped.

"Flower, take this! And get them out of here!"

I flung the false ring at him, and he snatched it out of the air.

"Go!" I yelled.

"We're not leaving you!"

And then it was too late. The smell washed over me: myrrh and metal, rotting meat and cardamom and blood, and there they were – Hap-Canae. Aka-Tete. Shakanti. Meisheté.

The crew glanced from them, back to me, and stayed still.

I was cold all through.

"Thieves!" Meisheté said. She raised her hand towards me, her fingers glittering with blood, and Previous stabbed her in the side.

Meisheté hissed with fury, her eyes flaring in their dark surrounds, and flung the curse at Previous instead.

A red shadow seemed to coalesce around her, as she stood staring at the place where her dagger had barely dented Meisheté's skin. Then she dropped to the floor.

"Previous!" I yelled.

"Stupid!" Aka-Tete said to Meisheté. "You might have hit the altar, or the ring! Who knows what that would have done!"

Rohikanta, his hair and beard tumbling white and green like a river over rocks, appeared in the doorway. The Messehwhy reared up at the sight of him. Rohikanta snapped his fingers and the beasts quieted.

Previous was bleeding; a shadow spreading beneath her thighs.

"Previous!"

Her eyelids fluttered. "What..."

"Help her," I said, in Lithan. "Please."

"Who are these people?" Meisheté said, ignoring me.

"Previous," Unusual said. He and his sister knelt, either side of her. "What's happening?" The Avatars ignored them, too.

"Meisheté governs childbirth," I said, still in Lithan, realising what the vicious barren monster had done.

"Oh, no," Cruel said. "Oh, that bitch. Previous... stay with me, sweetheart, please..."

The blood spread dark on the floor, like spilled wine.

Hap-Canae strode towards me, past the Messehwhy – of course, they wouldn't touch an Avatar – and swung his arm.

I ducked, not fast enough, and hit the floor, with the breath knocked out of me. I heard a *crack*. Hap-Canae stood over me, seeming more curious than anything. That scent, that smell of myrrh and cardamom.

"The *ring*, get the *ring!*"

Shakanti.

I tried to get to my feet. Hap-Canae grabbed me by the wrist and hauled me up, yanking the ring off my hand. Pain pulsed out of my wrist in hot waves. Broken. Shit.

"A most audacious thief," he said.

Aka-Tete, in his warrior aspect, blood running from his armour and spilling over the skulls at his waist so they seemed freshly killed, raised his sword. The blood dripped from his hands, disappearing before it hit the floor. I watched it fall.

Hap-Canae held up a hand. "Wait. We have a little time. How did you get in?" he asked me. He hadn't recognised me, but he looked as though some memory was tugging at him.

"Obviously, she fooled those idiot women," Shakanti said. "They will be punished. So will she. Don't kill her yet."

I was panting, now; the pain was getting unpleasant, but it would be worse if Shakanti had her way. Much worse. *Don't think about that. Don't think about it.*

"She got past the Messehwhy, too," Hap-Canae said. He shook me, which hurt. "How did you know about the ring? Who are you?"

"Does it matter?" Aka-Tete said. "Kill her or hold her. Once the ceremony is done, Shakanti can do as she pleases with her, and we'll soon know whatever she has to tell."

I told myself it didn't matter, it didn't matter – Shakanti wouldn't get to me. All I had to do was stay quiet, and wait. I could see little sparks of light in the altar-stone, beginning to whirl and congregate.

"Perhaps you're right." Hap-Canae said, and let me drop.

Shakanti looked at the crew, and actually clapped her hands, like a delighted child. "Why, what sort of creature is that?" she drifted up to Flower, and stroked his arm. "I shall think of something quite special, just for you."

He couldn't understand the words, but he knew who she was. He tried to stare straight ahead, but his lip lifted a fraction, and Shakanti laughed. "What an angry beast. And *what* is it carrying?" She stared at Laney.

Then I saw what was on Laney's hand; not one of her own jewels, too big and clumsy. I realised Flower had put the false ring on Laney's finger, presumably for safekeeping, his own hands being too big.

What if Shakanti noticed it?

She ran one of Laney's tumbling curls through her fingers. Blonde hair is rare on Tiresana; Shakanti's own bone-white veil of it was the closest most people ever saw. Her mouth tightened with distaste, and she dropped the silky strand as though it were filthy. "It has pointed ears," she said. "How... animal."

Laney's limp hand, with the false ring, was almost brushing Shakanti's thigh.

I had to distract her. If it was to work, if we were to have any chance, I had to distract her.

Previous, bleeding. *Don't think of that.*

"Hap-Canae," I said. "Don't you know me?"

"What?"

"It's me, Hap-Canae. I was an Avatar, once." I clutched at his robe with the hand that still worked. He backed away, startled, and I crumpled at his feet. "Hap-Canae, please! I only wanted to be with you again, to have you love me as you once did! Don't you recognise me? I know, I've got old, and ugly, but I thought if I came to the altar, I could be an Avatar again, you could love me again."

"You... oh. You were one of Babaska's Avatars!" he said. "The last one, weren't you? So it wasn't a tomb-robbery, at all. You actually escaped. And then, you realised what you'd thrown away, and came back. *Silly* child."

"Why, I remember *her,*" Shakanti said, turning – thank the All – towards me. "She was Chosen instead of my poor little Renavir, who would have been *so* much better. But *you* chose to run away, didn't you?" She was looking at me, now, far too closely. "You chose the peasants instead of us. And now you have chosen these." She waved a hand at my crew. Previous was white as bone, dying. "You know," she said, "I don't think I believe you."

"What do you mean?" Hap-Canae said.

"She said she wanted to be an Avatar again. But she *never* wanted to be an Avatar, not really." She walked across the room to me, and bent down, and cupped her cold hand under my chin, forcing me to look at her.

I stared into her eyes, trying to lie with my whole face, trying to convince her that I wanted, I *longed* to be an Avatar, to be like her.

I think my hatred must have shown. She shoved me away. "She's lying."

"It doesn't matter," Hap-Canae said. "Kill her later." He put the ring on his finger.

I could hear a humming, now, coming from the altar. It was low, just on the edge of hearing, but with a suggestion of melody, a sense of complexity; as though a long way away, thousands, millions, of voices and instruments were all harmonising together.

"It is time!" Greedy as a child reaching for the honey-jar, Hap-Canae moved forward. *Do it,* I thought. *Do it now, damn you, and maybe we can still save Previous.*

Then I heard, "Flower? What happened?" I looked to the doorway, and there was Laney, opening her eyes, raising her hand to brush the hair out of her face, and Shakanti saw the ring.

"Hap-Canae! Stop!" Shakanti shrieked. "It's a trick, some kind of trick!"

"But..." Hap-Canae said, and stopped, looking at the ring on Laney's hand, looking at me.

"But it was all understood," Aka-Tete said, in his voice of metal and dust. "We will not have such a chance again for many years; it must be done now."

"But *what* must be done?" Shakanti hissed. "Why is she really here? You know how much damage she did!"

"Well, ask her!"

"She will lie!"

They began to argue, as the altar heated and hummed. The two wind-goddesses, obviously having come to what few senses they had, reappeared, looking flustered, and joined in.

Ignored, crouched against the foot of the altar, I heard a voice, in my head. A husky voice, used to yelling across a battlefield, to whispering in a lover's ear. A voice of immense depth and power, attenuated by distance. *Listen to me now, Babylon. Listen to your Goddess.*

Babaska? Now you decide to talk to me? Now? All the times I cried out to you and you didn't answer?

I couldn't. Only at the syzygy. Didn't you wonder, when my mark appeared on you?

I had a few other things on my mind.

Yes. You do what you do because of who you are; but, because of who you are, you are my representative. You bear my scar. You are still mine, Babylon Steel, Ebi that was. And only an Avatar can use the ring.

But if they realise, they won't do it!

They won't. You can. Only an Avatar can use the ring.

You mean I have to...

Yes.

What will happen? When it works?

The power will go where it was meant to.

Babaska?

But there was silence. The voice was gone. No-one was looking at me. If I was going to do it...

I looked down at my hands, human hands, callused here and there from using a sword. I thought of Enthemmerlee, her little cold fingers in mine. Of the Chief, Hargur Bitternut, who'd risked everything to save this life of mine. For what?

The Avatars argued, oblivious to everything around them. Just as usual. I thought of the girls whose bones lay in the room not far from me. Of Previous, bleeding on the cold stone.

No more dead, I thought. *No more girls, no more soldiers, no more dead for you. Except maybe me.*

And I can live with that.

I jumped up, and slapped my hands into the dents in the altar. Hot pain shrieked up my arm from my wrist.

Hap-Canae turned, and howled with fury. He grabbed me, trying to pull me away, but the hold of the altar was too strong.

The power blasted into me, with a roar of light and voices. It split me into a million sparkling golden pieces, spinning through space and time, and rammed me back together.

I was...

The Avatar of Babaska. Flesh and fire. The taste of power in my mouth like metal and blood...

I heard screaming around me.

The desire for battle, to slaughter the enemy, to protect those I fought alongside...

Hands on my waist. Desire rising, ranting: *I could make him mine, any of them mine, with a word, with a thought, with a look. I could seduce the universe...*

I am not a goddess. I am Babylon Steel, and I run the best whorehouse in Scalentine.

You are Babylon Steel, and you are my Avatar.

I am Babylon Steel. I am neither Goddess nor Avatar, I am myself.

The coin-sized dent in the altar was blazing with spinning light, a window into some unknowable plane. I took hold of

Hap-Canae's where it clasped my waist, and ran my fingers along his. I felt him shudder and gasp, and his grip slackened.

Before he could realise what I was doing, I slid the ring from his finger, and onto mine, and slammed the seal down where it belonged.

The humming stopped. The silence was huge.

Suddenly I was terrified, that I'd got it wrong, that Mokraine had got it wrong, that I'd made a total, blind, idiot miscalculation.

Purple-white light exploded out of the altar. I was flung backwards, knocking Hap-Canae over. The floor bucked. I could hear shrieks and groaning stone and the Messehwhy hissing and yawping and somebody wailing and a roaring like the sea.

My hands, ringless now, glowed with light, surrounded by dancing motes of dust. The light of an Avatar. *No, please... I don't want it!*

And then it hit me, the tearing, the feeling of something withdrawing, that had been knit tight to human soul and human flesh, ripping away.

The break in my wrist reappeared with a snap and a hot jab.

Gasping with pain and relief, I scrambled up, looking for my crew. They were huddled against the wall of the corridor, Cruel crouching over Previous to protect her. The air was full of dust, tasting of stone and metal.

Then there was nothing but a room full of people, ageing, groaning, human.

The altar was a silent lump of rock. A great drift of silver hair lay scattered about it; Shakanti's.

"No!" Hap-Canae looked at his hands, veined and big-knuckled. "No..." he pushed himself to his feet.

I ran to Previous. Cruel, rigid-faced, was holding her hand. "It's all right," she said. "All right." Previous was so pale, so dreadfully pale.

"Flower," I said. "Keep them here. If anyone moves, crock them. Cruel, Unusual, you too."

"Right," he said. They ranged themselves across the doorway, blocking it.

I took Previous's hand. "Hey," I said.

Laney dropped beside her, put her hands on Previous's stomach, and said tearfully, "Please. A little. Please. I have some left. I must have some left." But there was no light, no glow and crackle of magic.

"Previous?" I said.

"Hey, Babylon." So quiet I could hardly hear. Her breath smelled like yeast and blood.

"How'd you get your name?" I said.

"Not... drunk enough."

I dug the hip-flask out of my pocket, and tilted it to her mouth; she sipped a little, most of it running down her cheek.

"How about now?" I said.

She managed something that was almost a smile. "Thought you'da guessed. Too eager. Ran in, ahead of the line. Got me in trouble."

"I'll send you to the Chief for training with the militia, how's that?" I said. Her hand was going cold, and I was crying.

"Wouldn't... wouldn't..."

"Hey, sshh, it's all right."

But it wasn't.

MEISHETÉ WAS SITTING with her veiny legs splayed in front of her, staring at nothing. She looked like any middle-aged woman, except for her richly embroidered gown. The butterfly mask colouration around her eyes had gone. I took her by her greying hair and yanked her up, dragged her on her knees to where Previous lay.

Someone was saying my name. Someone was putting their hand on my arm. I shook it off.

"Look at this," I said. "You murdered my friend. A better woman than you will ever be, you evil, useless, vain, cruel *bitch*." I threw her down, and she crouched, shaking, her hair in her face, her hands in Previous's blood. "Stay there."

I saw Cruel start towards me, and Unusual grab her arm and hold her back.

One by one I took them, and dragged them out. Aka-Tete, hollow-cheeked, liver-spotted. The skulls at his waist had gone brown and lost half their teeth. Rohikanta, wispy greying beard still smelling of river mud. Lohiria and Mihiria, skinny middle aged women with lank locks and protuberant eyes. Shakanti, utterly silent, thin as a bone, her long silver hair all gone, bald as rock. Now, *I* was stronger, and anger was raging in me like sickness. I cast them around the body of my friend like offerings.

Hap-Canae was the last. He was clutching the altar, digging his hands into the hollows until they bled. "Where is it?" He whimpered. "Where is it?"

I wasn't sure if he meant the ring, or the power. Both were gone, the ring evaporated as though it had never been.

He had gone pouched and doughy. When I took him by the collar and hauled him to his feet, he clutched at my shirt, leaving wet red marks. "Help me. Bring it back. You and I, we can be gods, Babaska, gods. We *deserve* it." Yellowy rheum clouded those leopard eyes.

"Deserve it? After what you've done? I know what you deserve," I said. I flung him against the others.

They stood or knelt, hardly looking at me and the crew, staring instead at each other, at their own too-human hands.

Aka-Tete managed to drag his chin up, and stare at me. "What right have you?" He said. "Let us go. We are the Avatars of the gods, and we rule this land."

"And a great job you made of it," I said.

"This is nonsense. Get out of the way."

He tried to push past me and I shoved him back, hard. "Don't try that again, or I'll kill you."

"We can get past them," Shakanti said. "Come." She raised her chin ridiculously high, and started to walk towards me.

Flower stepped in front of her, and showed his teeth.

Laney said, "Don't even try it, bitch." Shakanti couldn't have understood her, but the meaning was clear enough. Laney was crackling with anger. Sparks were jumping from her fingers and snapping off the ends of her hair.

"Cruel, Unusual. Rope them together, so they can walk. Laney? You all right?"

"Yes. It's come back. Strong. Too late, Babylon. It's come back too late." She was weeping scarlet, started to say something in the Fey tongue, the air around her shimmering.

"Laney. *Laney.*"

She looked at me, through burning tears.

"No curses. I know. I know you want to, and I want to let you, but it isn't ours to punish them, and not here, where no-one can see. They've got away with too much in secret. It's time to take it out into the sun."

We roped the ex-Avatars together.

Flower carried Previous.

THE PRECINCT WAS ankle-deep in stinking water; the Rohin had flooded. Priests and civilians, their worship disturbed, were huddled on the steps of the temples. Wreaths and bedraggled dead chickens floated in the muddy mess. We were surrounded by muttering and stares as we herded the ex-Avatars out through Babaska's temple into the sun.

"Look," Unusual said. "What is that?"

Something in the skyline above the precinct walls had changed; the statues had a strange, furred look, dotted with flecks of colour.

I realised something was growing on them. Some kind of creeping vine.

People were looking, gathering around us as though drawn by some instinct. I stood on the steps, blinking in the sunlight, wondering what to do now.

One of Hap-Canae's sun-priests splashed towards us, holding his robes above his knees. "That temple is forbidden," he said, obviously grasping for something he could control, unlike the river. "Worship of the Traitress is... who *are* you?"

"We are your Avatars!" Aka-Tete roared, or tried to; his voice was cracked and thin. "Kill this woman! Release us!"

The sun-priest blinked. "Avatars? You're not Avatars! You speak heresy!"

I could feel the crew looking at each other. "Get ready to run for it," I muttered in Lithan. "This could get nasty." I turned to the sun-priest. "No, they're not Avatars anymore, but they were," I said. "And me... I was once the Avatar of Babaska."

"What? No." The sun-priest looked from me, to my crew, to the roped Avatars, and obviously wasn't sure who to accuse of what. "Heresy!" he said, to the general air.

There was silence, the lap of water; a baby wailed suddenly and was hushed.

"Speak," someone called.

"Yes, let's hear it."

"Let her speak!" I could see those who called out; they all bore the jawline mark. How many of them were there?

"Silence!" The sun-priest roared. "They are heretics! Guards!" He motioned to the temple guards who were scattered about. They moved towards us as fast as the water would allow, raising their spears.

There was a swirl of movement in the crowd, and suddenly, somehow, there were people standing between us and the guards.

Many bore the jawline mark. Some of them were obviously courtesans, and a good few were, even more obviously, soldiers, with battered weapons in their hands. They looked at those shiny, unused spears, and grinned.

Temple guard wasn't a post for those with brains, but it wasn't a post for the suicidal, either. The guards halted.

"Listen to her!" A young man with henna in his hair and a smudged kohl-mark on his jaw raised his hands towards me.

"It's the truth of Babaska! The Human Goddess, she speaks! Listen to her!"

"Wait!" I yelled. "I'm no goddess, I never was! None of them are, that's the *point!*"

A tall woman in worn blue robes looked up at me, and smiled. "We know," she said. "We believe the Truth of Babaska, that the Avatars are human."

"Heresy!" came the roar, from priests and priestesses.

"No, it isn't," I roared back. "*This* is what you've worshipped. Recognise them? They've gorged on stolen power while the land crumbled and people died. You know what they did with that power. You *saw.* Now their power's gone, and this is what you're left with."

"Gone where?" The sun-priest scoffed.

"Here! Look!" A man stumbled towards us, his arms full of bright objects. It took me a moment to realise they were gourds, fat and ripe, yellow and green and orange. "The statues are covered with them! There's food, food everywhere!"

Some of the crowd broke and ran, then, to grab what they could. I didn't blame them.

"This is the bounty of the gods!" the sun-priest shouted. I almost had to admire his quick-footedness. "See how they favour us! Worship the gods who give you bounty, bow before their Avatars... these are not Avatars! These are some poor slaves this woman has captured to tempt you into heresy!"

"Silence!" Shakanti surged forward, stopped only by the rope at her waist, glaring. "I am Shakanti! Look on me! Am I not beautiful? Do you not fear me and adore me?"

The priest looked at her, her bald wrinkled head, the shrivelled breasts and sunken ribcage clearly visible through the silvery gauze of her gown, then looked away in obvious embarrassment. "Oh, let the poor creature go," he said. "It's obvious she's mad. You should be ashamed."

Shakanti shrieked with rage, and tried to claw for his face, but couldn't reach.

The other Avatars began to find their voices, then.

"I am Aka-Tete! I am terror, and night!"

"I am Meisheté! I hold your children in my hand!"

They cawed like ragged crows at autumn's end, condemning themselves.

"I am Hap-Canae!" How could that harsh rasp be the voice that had once wrapped me like silk? "The power was given to us by the gods! We had more in our grasp – we could have made this a land of glories!"

"We don't want glories!" A man with battered armour and one arm yelled back. "We want enough to eat, and a decent life! That's what we want!"

The crowd roared agreement; I felt it bearing me up, like the sea.

"Kill 'em! Kill the Avatars!"

"Kill them! Kill them, kill their priests!"

It would be so easy to let that sea wash over me. I wanted them dead, with a bitter fury, and if a few priests died, too, well, hadn't they had a hand in it? Hadn't they lived fat in the Avatars' shadow?

Tiresana's own moon was hanging in the air, full; a pale ghost, just above the horizon.

You and me, Chief, we take responsibility for our actions, don't we?

"Wait!" I held up my hand. Thank the All, they quieted. "I know what they've done," I said. "I was part of it, for a while. For my stupidity, and my cowardice, I am profoundly sorry. Now, you have the right to decide what's done with them" – I took a breath – "and with me, if you so wish." Keeping my eyes on the crowd, I gestured to the crew, "Not these, though. They're friends, who came to help me end it. And they've paid. Paid more than these monsters were ever worth." I swallowed down grief. Later, if I lived, I'd grieve.

The crowd shifted and muttered. The priests were looking nervous, seeing the reins of power jerked out of their hands and the beasts ready to bolt. The Avatars were beginning, at last, to look frightened. I took a hard breath. "Listen," I said to the crowd. "If you decide they should die, that's your privilege. I couldn't blame you. But a very wise and brave young woman recently said to me: 'I must believe that people can choose to do what is right.' So can you? Will you be like the Avatars, or can you be better?"

The silence stretched out deep and long; I could hear my ears humming. I began to realise I was so bone-tired that I was in danger of collapsing and rolling down the steps into the mud.

The floodwater was draining away.

The one-armed soldier spat. "Better than that lot? S'hardly a challenge, is it?"

There were some mutterings of disappointment, but more cheers.

"And me?" I said.

The blue-robed woman looked at me with tears in her eyes. "*You?* We'd never hurt you. You're our hope."

A shudder twisted right up my spine. "No!" I said. "I'm not. Nobody should be. You've got to be your own."

The sun-priest said, "What... but what will we do? We have to keep things in order, we have to..."

"Who gave you that right?"

The sun-priest looked at the Avatars. Then he closed his mouth.

"The gods are gone," I said. "The Avatars are gone. The people are right here."

THEY TRIED TO get me to stay, both the heretics (Babaskans, they called themselves) and the priests. They seemed to think I still had a job to do, but I wasn't having it. I just wanted to get my crew, what was left of them, home. But there were a couple of things that needed doing.

I went to the room of sarcophagi, alone, and said goodbye. I arranged for a stele to be set up, out in the sun, with the girls' names on it. No-one knew the names of the other Avatars of Babaska, so I told them to carve a sword and lotus on it.

Reversed.

Then I asked after Sesh and Kyrl. None of the priests would meet my eye. "Sesh of the house of Lothi and Kyrl Danashta?" The blue-robed woman looked at me, and her face told me everything, even before she spoke. "They spoke of Babaska's Truth," she said, gently. "They were the first. The Avatars... I'm sorry. I'm so sorry."

I hadn't really expected that they'd still be alive, but still, it hurt. And yet they'd been at my side in the shape of those Babaskans, standing in the muddy precinct, demanding to hear the truth.

And before Sesh and Kyrl, of course, *we* had begun it. More than twenty years ago.

Oh, Ranay. It did work, in the end. I wish...

I looked at the priests.

"Make another stele. Put their names on it. Sesh of the house of Lothi; Kyrl Danashta;Ranay, Priest of the Temple of Babaska. Good people have died," I said. "They'd better have died for something worthwhile. Screw this up, and I *will* come back, and I will personally take each one of you to hell. Believe me, I know the way."

They were leading the ex-Avatars away, as we left.

"Wait!" Hap-Canae called to me. "How can you leave me? I was your god!"

"That was then."

"Babaska," he said.

"*Don't call me that.*" Before I thought, my hand shot out. The crack of it meeting his face seemed incredibly loud. "It's not my name. No more than Hap-Canae is yours. Do you remember who you really are? I do. I'm Babylon. Babylon Steel, Ebi that was. And you – you're no-one."

I turned my back on him, and gestured to my crew, and we gathered up our dead and walked away.

*   *   *

As the temple precinct fell behind us, with the sound of laughter and chatter and shrieking children, and the smell of cook fires and sweet squash roasting, I seemed to move in a bubble of silence, in which names buzzed and fluttered against my memory like moths around a lamp. Sesh, Kyrl. Ranay. Previous. Jonat and Renavir. So many deaths. Even Hap-Canae, who might as well be dead; I'd loved him, once, more than my own soul, and if I hadn't been such a fool, how many of those deaths could I have prevented?

It wasn't until I heard someone gasp, and had to look up, that I realised my vision was thick with tears.

"What is it?" I said, hastily rubbing my eyes clear.

"Look," Flower said. "Don't cry, Babylon. Just look."

I looked, blinked, and looked again, and realised that creeping across the baked curves of the desert was a faint, tender flush of green.

We got back slightly more slowly, and easily enough; the syzygy was still in effect. I was leaning on the rail of the boat, on the river between Loth and Galent, when Laney came up beside me. "How's the wrist?" She'd bandaged it before we left.

"All right."

"You're brooding," she said.

I shrugged.

"Previous was a soldier, Babylon. Fighting's what she did. She died with friends, you know. Lots of people don't get that much."

"Yeah." We'd brought her back with us. She had no family I knew of. We'd bury her in the garden. It seemed fitting.

"Babylon, can I ask you something?"

"Sure."

"Well, two things. You became one of them, didn't you? At the end. You changed."

"Yes. I had to. I... only an Avatar could use the ring."

Laney nodded. "I thought so." I waited for her to ask more questions, which I wasn't sure I wanted to answer, but she seemed satisfied.

"I'm still not sure," she said, "why you didn't kill the Avatars. Just *some* of them. Not just because of Previous. Because of what they'd done to *you*." She glanced at me, and sighed. "But then vengeance isn't as important to you as it is to Fey, is it?"

"They're mortal," I said. "They're going to be ordinary, and sick, and old. They're going to spend years knowing they're just those things, and that death is coming for them. They'll never be able to be normal, to just appreciate a warm bed or a good meal. Not after what they've had, and what they were. Seems like vengeance to me."

She looked thoughtful, and then smiled; a cool, Fey smile. "Here," she said.

In her hand was the false ring. Sword and lotus, carved in a red stone. "I didn't know if you'd want it, but I didn't like to just throw it overboard."

I took it from her and held it up. It wasn't an object of power; it wasn't even gold. But it was still a perfectly good ring, and my finger had felt naked without its original.

I slipped it on. Laney, watching, sniffed a little. "Poor old Frithlit."

"He was false, too."

She looked at the ring. "That looks better on you than on me, doesn't it?"

"Big, loud, cheap – yeah, it's definitely more me."

She poked me in the side. "But not false, Babylon. Never false."

THIRTY-FOUR
Day 13
Twomoon Ending

THERE WAS A lot waiting for us when we got back. Twomoon was fading, and the client list was backed up halfway to next week. It didn't help that my wrist was still bound up, but I didn't let Laney do much to it. It felt right to let it heal naturally.

We held the burial first. We patted the cold earth over her; there'd be a headstone, later. In the meantime each of us said what words we felt were best, the things we remembered about her, the things we wished we'd known. It was another bright, frosty day, but somehow it felt as though it should have been raining.

After that I was glad to be busy. I spent a day apologising and rearranging, and had a potentially embarrassing encounter with a quiet young woman I thought was a new client, who actually turned out to be an accountant that Lord Antheran had sent over to help us out. When I showed her the account book and accompanying wodge of paper that acted as my filing system, she looked positively cheerful. Guess some people like a challenge.

I had just seen her settled in with ink, tea and a glint in her eye, when the bell rang.

It was young Roflet, looking fairly grim.

"Madam Steel? I've been asked to fetch you."

There was a cold hollow in my chest. "Is it the Chief? Is he all right?"

"The Chief?" Roflet blinked. "No, ma'am. He's fine."

"Am I under arrest?"

"Not at the moment," he said. "You've been requested to accompany the Chief on a visit to the Temple of the Vessels."

"You... huh? They've *asked* for me? What for?"

"It's to do with Denarven. We had to hand him over to them."

"*What?*" I said.

"Diplomatic Section. They insisted."

"Oh, for... so what did they do? Slap his wrist and send him off-plane to start killing women somewhere else?"

"Apparently not. He's still there. They want you to see him."

I didn't want to see him. But I did want to see the Chief; I'd wanted to see him ever since I got back.

I wasn't ready for it. As soon as I walked into that courtyard with its heavily draped statues I remembered Previous. I saw her leaning against the balustrade in the sun, grinning, her helmet at an angle. I felt such a rush of grief into my throat I had to stop for a moment.

"You all right, Ma'am?" Roflet said.

"Yeah. I'll do. Give me a minute, all right?"

He did. Then an administrator, maskless and grey-gowned as Denarven had been, appeared and gestured for us to follow.

He led us into a chilly little room and left. There, back to his human state, but looking so grim he might as well have been one of the courtyard statues, was Chief Bitternut. In the wall next to his head was a grille, shut. Roflet nodded to the Chief and left.

"So," Bitternut said. "Glad to see you're back in one piece."

"Pretty much," I said.

"Know why we're here?"

"Only what Officer Roflet told me. They've got Denarven here."

"Yes. They seem to think this is going to be some sort of recompense for not having to hand him over to us." He sighed. "Hope they hurry up. It was considered good politics to come, but frankly I'd be happy never to see that crazed little twistfart again."

"Yeah, Chief, about that..."

He gave me a glare. "Don't," he said, and then, the door opened.

It was the Mouthpiece, and the High Priest.

The Chief and I looked at each other.

The High Priest drummed his fingers on the Mouthpiece's hand.

"The High Priest thanks you for attending," the Mouthpiece said. "It is hoped that once you have seen what we have to show you, you will be assured that the unfortunate one has been placed in the best circumstances for true communion with the Purest, to cleanse his soul and lead him to righteousness."

"True communion with the Purest?" the Chief said. You could have etched steel with the acid in his voice.

"Now he will have a life with no distractions from contemplation of the glory," the Mouthpiece said.

He reached out, and opened the grille.

The room beyond was brightly lit, but that would make no difference to the mewling, naked thing that was in it.

It had no eyes. Its wailing, open mouth was tongueless. It had no ears; the place where they had been was sealed over. It had neither hands nor feet nor genitals.

The wounds were cleanly healed, surgically neat.

I've seen war. I've seen terrible things, and done more than a few. I've seen guts spill over my boots.

I've never done what I did then, which was stumble out past the Mouthpiece, pushing him out of the way, lean one hand on the wall, and throw up into the clean-swept courtyard.

I wiped my mouth, and felt a hand on my shoulder.

The Chief.

He said, "They tell me..." He coughed, hard. "They tell me he'll be fed, and kept clean."

The Priest and his Mouthpiece had emerged behind us. "He

will live a life of perfect contemplation, and die the purer," the Mouthpiece said. "Many might envy him."

"Right," I said.

"Do you feel he has been adequately dealt with?" the Mouthpiece said.

"He's been dealt with," I said.

"You feel justice has been served?"

"Something has," the Chief said.

"But you are satisfied."

The Chief looked at me.

"*This* has been dealt with," I said. "Chief?"

"Yeah. *This* is over. You're still citizens of Scalentine. That comes with responsibilities. Don't forget 'em again."

And he took my arm and we walked out of the precinct.

I could feel the tension in him, as he told Roflet, who was waiting at the gate, to go back to the precinct. "Walk you home," he said.

"Thanks."

We walked in silence for some time. Then Bitternut said, "I wanted him dead. I remember... I don't always remember things so well, from Change. But I really wanted him dead."

"So did I," I said. "I think... it would have been cleaner. Dear holy hells. Isn't it *illegal,* what they did to him?"

"Tricky. According to their religion, they're doing this to help him. To improve his chances of redemption. I'll ask, but I think may fall under the Cultural Practice exceptions. Which I'd see burned, if I could, but I don't make the laws."

Something had made Denarven into a killer. *Could* the Vessels have saved him? Could anything? He'd have nothing, now, except the darkness of his own mind. I didn't know what to feel, except a kind of exhausted sickness.

When we got to the Lantern, the Chief walked past me into the blue room. I found him staring down at the chess board, which hadn't been touched since halfway through our last game.

"You're going to lose," he said. A stray lock of hair fell over his eyes, and my fingers twitched to brush it back.

"Probably. So, you want to sit down?" I said.

"Right." He moved away from the board, sank his long limbs into the sofa, and tugged at his fingers, making the joints pop.

"Been a long day," I said. "Beer?"

"Ah, you're a goddess, Babylon," he said, attempting a smile.

"Not anymore," I muttered. "Thank the All."

"What?" he said.

"Nothing." I poured beer, and wine for myself, and sat down next to him. "I'll tell you, one day. When you've got time, and I can face it. I lost a friend. Previous. She got... she died."

"I'm sorry. She was a good sort."

"She was."

He nodded, looking into his beer, which gave me a chance to get control of myself.

Then he said, "You saved me, you know. If I'd killed him..."

"Oh, balls, Chief. You saved *me*, remember?"

"I mean it, Babylon. If I'd killed him, it would have been over for me. And you stopped it, so I just needed to say, thank you."

"There's no need. But you're welcome. Does that mean I'm forgiven?"

"Forgiven?"

"You were angry with me. You had every right."

"Oh! Well. Yes, I was." He stretched his legs out, not looking at me. "Worry about you."

"Oh, is *that* why you... right. Yeah, I do sometimes too. But, you know. You have to do the best you can."

"I'd prefer you didn't get killed," he said.

"Well I'd prefer you didn't, too."

"Glinchen turned up," he said. "Told me about finding the girl."

"Really?"

"Yeah. A bit after the fact, but, you know. So, thanks."

"Stop thanking me, it's making me nervous."

He half-smiled. "What happened to your arm?" he said.

"Broken wrist."

"Ouch. Hurt much?"

"A bit. Laney says it'll take another moon at least to heal."

"No fighting for a while, then."

"Nope."

"So... You heard anything that's going to make my life more difficult?" he said.

"Hardly, I've barely got back."

"Oh, of course. Right."

"Right. Chief?"

"Hmm."

"Hey. Hargur." I don't use his first name much. He looked at me, surprised. "Doesn't have to be a business transaction," I said. "In fact, I'd rather it wasn't one."

"What?"

I leaned over and kissed him, just lightly, in case I was wrong. Turned out I wasn't.

I led him upstairs, trying to ignore Laney's grin and Essie making a thumbs-up gesture. Bitternut caught it, though, and snorted. It was good to hear him laugh. Good to get him into my room, good to finally get him out of his battered clothes and start to get properly acquainted with the long, lean body under them. There was a little musk of the Change still on him, and a little wild still in him. Nothing wrong with that. In fact, part of the fun.

I kissed him, lightly at first, though it took effort, then he pulled me tight against him. Skin to skin, and lips to lips. I felt greedy, starved, wanting all of him at once. Wanting something good and clean and right. No art to it, just desire.

We tumbled backwards onto the bed, still kissing. I tangled my fingers in his long hair, so he couldn't escape. He lifted my breasts, licking and kissing until I was half crazed, and I slid my hand down, feeling him already up and eager. Hands everywhere, clumsy, but good. Hurt my wrist, didn't care.

He had enough sense left to pause, breathing hard, and say, "I need... do you have..." I grinned at him and reached into the cupboard beside the bed.

He had a lovely cock, smooth and clean and silky-skinned. Next time, I would take my time dressing it; this time, we were both too greedy, too hasty. On with the preventative, and in. When he slid inside me, he fitted me as though we'd been designed for each other, and neither of us could wait. We ran for the finish together, arrived panting and growling.

"Well," he said, when he got his breath back.

"*Very* well," I said.

He laughed. Then he leaned up on one elbow and looked at me, and began to run his fingers over my scars, gently, as though he could soothe the wounds that had made them. "Lot of fights."

"You too," I said, tracing one of his in turn, a long pale line that twisted up under his arm.

"You going to tell me about them?" he said.

"Only the good ones," I said. "You know. Where I swung off chandeliers and stuff. And won, obviously."

"All right, then." He kissed me again, and this time, we took our time.

THERE WAS A discreet knock on the door, and I pulled on a robe and got up, leaving Hargur fast asleep.

"What is it?"

"Message for you," Jivrais said. "The boy's waiting for an answer."

I went downstairs, to find a messenger boy, neat and courteous, with a sealed paper. I opened it. *Darask Fain requests the pleasure of your company at lunch, tomorrow, at one o'clock, at the Bronze Bell.*

"Tell him 'yes,'" I said. I wanted a word with Fain. Then I went back upstairs. I was taking the rest of the night for myself. Boss's privilege.

THIRTY-FIVE
Day 14
First Day after Twomoon

THE BRONZE BELL turned out to be one of those exquisitely discreet little places; not a place to be seen, like the Lodestone, but somewhere to be invisible.

Fain was already there when I arrived, a courtesy I appreciated. If I'm kept waiting too long, I tend to get annoyed, and flirt with waiters. "Madam Steel," he said.

"Mr Fain." He looked as good as ever, though his trait seemed to be in abeyance. Of course, Twomoon was over. Still, I'd something with me, in case he tried it on; a little portable dose of an anti-lust potion Laney had given me, but I didn't appear to need it. At least, not yet.

He poured me a glass of wine. "I hear you've been travelling."

"Yes."

"Your business was concluded successfully?"

"I hope so. We'll have to wait and see." I paused. "I lost a friend."

"I'm sorry."

"Me too."

After we ordered our food, I said, "Tell me about Enthemmerlee."

"The last I heard, she was well. Her transformation was successful. Whether it will have the effect she hoped for..." he shrugged.

"So how did her family take it?"

"Shock, fury, accusations of treachery; half the ruling class want her banished to Scalentine, most of the rest want her executed. Half the Ikinchli now think she's a goddess, and the other half think she's a fraud. Her family are about to enter a vicious and probably generations-long feud with the one she was planned to marry into. As I said, volatile."

"The All protect her, then. Poor child."

"Someone needs to. It would help to have someone she trusts there, but they would also need to be someone who can move easily between the different communities, who is without known ties to any one faction, who makes friends easily and can deal with those who are less than friendly."

"That's a lot to ask of a bodyguard."

"Oh, they'd need to be more than that. It's not just her who needs protection, but the entire population of Incandress." He looked, suddenly, very tired. "Incandress could be a great country, a civilisation for all its people, but it's in danger of degenerating into pointless bloodshed."

"People often don't see what's under their noses," I said. There was a pause, while he looked at me until I began to wonder whether I had a smudge on my face or something. "At the risk of sounding brusque, Mr Fain, why *did* you invite me to lunch?"

"You don't think I might do so just for the pleasure of your company?"

"Let's say it would surprise me if that were your only reason."

He gave that slantwise smile and put his knife and fork neatly together. "Your encounter with Enthemmerlee has left her, and the revolutionary faction that supports her, with a great deal of respect for you. The Gudain seem to consider you tried to 'rescue' her from her transformation, and are inclined to regard you in a very positive light."

"How nice of them," I said.

"You are known and liked among the Ikinchli community." Damn, did that mean he knew about Kittack? Probably.

"And you obviously have an ability to handle yourself in difficult circumstances."

I shrugged. "I have a habit of getting into them. I'm trying to break it."

"On Tiresana, I understand, you managed an extremely volatile situation quite remarkably."

"How the hells do you know what happened on Tiresana?" I realised my hand had gone to my jaw. The scar was still there. I kept hoping it would fade, but it didn't.

I was trying not to think about what that might mean.

Fain smiled. "Obviously I would like to hear your own version, if you feel inclined. But didn't you wonder why the militia never questioned you further about the death of one Frithlit Oprentic?"

I stared. With everything that had happened since, I'd almost forgotten that little mouse-eared fraud existed. *Had* existed.

"You arranged that, did you?"

"Let us say I... smoothed things over. After all, his murderers are outside our jurisdiction, are they not?"

"And why would you do that, Mr Fain?"

"Because I want to ask you a favour, which you would find difficult to perform if you were incarcerated."

"A favour."

"How would you feel about acting as an unofficial Scalentine envoy? Firstly to Incandress, later, possibly, elsewhere?"

I almost choked on my wine. *"What?* You're joking. Aren't you?"

"Not at all."

"Well, you should be," I said. "I have a job, and a life, here."

"You wouldn't have to leave them. It would require occasional visits, only."

"Doing what?"

"Observing the situation. Assessing. Creating contacts. Reporting back."

"I believe the word is 'spying,'" I said. "And, no offence intended, but were you drinking before I got here? Because, me? I'm not the discreet type. Nor am I particularly inclined to go about things in the approved fashion. I can hardly imagine anyone less suited."

"Aside from all the reasons I have just given, that is why I am inclined to think you might be precisely suited."

"You... what?"

"Madam Steel..."

"Oh, hells, you might as well go back to Babylon."

He raised his glass. "Let me put it this way. The Diplomatic Section, or some version of it, is as old as Scalentine. And that has its advantages, in terms of experience, and knowledge. But it also has massive disadvantages."

"'The right orders, correctly signed'?" I said.

"Indeed. That sort of attitude can be a dangerous drag on getting things done. You do not seem to suffer from that kind of... over-caution."

That time, I did laugh.

I said, after another glass, that I'd think about it.

And I will.

But I'm going home to the Lantern, first, and I'll invite the Chief to eat supper with me and the crew. He's one of us, now.

It's the best life can offer. Better than godhead any day. Good food, good drink and good companions, safe under a friendly roof.

THE END

ABOUT THE AUTHOR

GAIE SEBOLD WAS born in the US to an American father and English mother, and has lived in the UK most of her life. She now resides in that bit of South East London known as 'not as bad as New Cross.'

She began writing shortly after learning to read, and has produced a large number of words, many of them different.

She has worked as a cleaner (don't laugh, Mum), secretary, till-monkey, stage-tour-manager, editor, and now works for a charity and runs occasional writing workshops. She is an obsessive reader, enthusiastically inefficient gardener and occasional poet.

She has a wonderful boyfriend, a paranoid cat and too much stuff.

Find out more at
www.gaiesebold.com

ACKNOWLEDGEMENTS

A LIST LIKE this is always incomplete and will no doubt riddle me with guilt when I realise who else I haven't mentioned, when it's too late. However.

My parents, for bringing me up in a house full of books and trying to encourage me even when they didn't know why I wanted to write this weird stuff. My sisters, for their constant support. Michelle Crawford, for being a wonderful teacher. The Noises Off bunch – you know who you are. The extraordinary T Party Writers (*http://t-party.org.uk/*) – I really couldn't have done it without you.

Martin Owton for constant nudging. Sarah Ellender, superlative friend, muse, and ever-absorbent shoulder; and Luke, who lets me appropriate her a lot. My lovely agent, John Jarrold. The fabulous people at Solaris.

Dave, for more than I can possibly say. Thanks, sweetie.

And you, dear reader, for being interested enough to read at least this far.

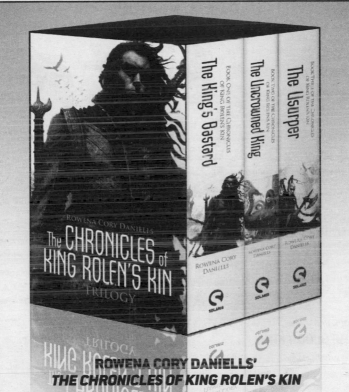

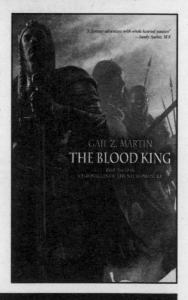

GAIL Z. MARTIN'S
THE CHRONICLES OF THE NECROMANCER

BOOK THREE
DARK HAVEN

ISBN: (UK) 978 1 84416 708 1 • £7.99
ISBN: (US) 978 1 84416 598 8 • $7.99

The kingdom of Margolan lies in ruin. Martris Drayke, the new king, must rebuild his country in the aftermath of battle, while a new war looms on the horizon. Meanwhile Jonmarc Vahanian is now the Lord of Dark Haven, and there is defiance from the vampires of the *Vayash Moru* at the prospect of a mortal leader.

But can he earn their trust, and at what cost?

"A fast-paced tale laced with plenty of action."

– SF Site

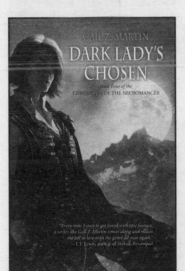

BOOK FOUR
DARK LADY'S CHOSEN

ISBN: (UK) 978 1 84416 830 9 • £7.99
ISBN: (US) 978 1 84416 831 6 • $7.99

Treachery and blood magic threaten King Martris Drayke's hold on the throne he risked everything to win. As the battle against a traitor lord comes to its final days, war, plague and betrayal bring Margolan to the brink of destruction. Civil war looms in Isencroft. And in Dark Haven, Lord Jonmarc Vahanian has bargained his soul for vengeance as he leads the *vayash moru* against a dangerous rogue who would usher in a future drenched in blood.

"Just when you think you know where things are heading, Martin pulls another ace from her sleeve."

– A. J. Hartley, author of The Mask of Atraeus

JULIET E. McKENNA'S
CHRONICLES OF THE LESCARI REVOLUTION

BOOK ONE

IRONS IN THE FIRE

ISBN: (UK) 978 1 906735 82 1 • £7.99
ISBN: (US) 978 1 84416 601 5 • US $8.99/CAN $10.99

The country of Lescar was born out of civil war. Carved out of the collapse of the Old Tormalin Empire, the land has long been laid waste by its rival dukes, while bordering nations look on with indifference or exploit its misery. But a mismatched band of exiles and rebels is agreed that the time has come for change, and they begin to put a scheme together for revolution. Full of rich characters and high adventure, this novel marks the beginning of a thrilling new series.

"Magically convincing and convincingly magical."
– Dan Abnett

BOOK TWO

BLOOD IN THE WATER

ISBN: (UK) 978 1 84416 840 8 • £12.99 (Large Format)
ISBN: (US) 978 1 84416 841 5 • US $7.99/CAN $9.99

Those exiles and rebels determined to bring peace to Lescar discover the true cost of war. Courage and friendships are tested to breaking point. Who will pay such heartbreaking penalties for their boldness? Who will pay the ultimate price?

The dukes of Lescar aren't about to give up their wealth and power without a fight. Nor will they pass up some chance to advance their own interests, if one of their rivals suffers in all this upheaval. The duchesses have their own part to play, more subtle but no less deadly.

"If you're not reading Juliet McKenna, you should be."
– Kate Elliott

BOOK THREE

BANNERS IN THE WIND

ISBN: (UK) 978 1 906735 74 6 • £12.99 (Large Format)
ISBN: (US) 978 1 906735 75 3 • US $7.99/CAN $9.99

A few stones falling in the right place can set a landslide in motion. That's what Lescari exiles told themselves in Vanam as they plotted to overthrow the warring dukes. But who can predict the chaos that follows such a cataclysm? Some will survive against all the odds; friends and foes alike. Hope and alliances will be shattered beyond repair. Unforeseen consequences bring undeserved grief as well as unexpected rewards. Necessity forces uneasy compromise as well as perilous defiance. Wreaking havoc is swift and easy. Building a lasting peace may yet prove an insuperable challenge!

"Shows McKenna at her best."
– Paul Cornell

UK ISBN: 978 1 907519 97 0 • US ISBN: 978 1 907519 96 3 • £7.99/$7.99

The Archmage rules the island of wizards and has banned the use of magecraft in warfare, but there are corsairs raiding the Caladhrian Coast, enslaving villagers and devastating trade. Barons and merchants beg for magical aid, but all help has been refused so far.

Lady Zurenne's husband has been murdered by the corsairs. Now a man she doesn't even know stands as guardian over her and her daughters. Corrain, former captain and now slave, knows that the man is a rogue wizard, illegally selling his skills to the corsairs. If Corrain can escape, he'll see justice done. Unless the Archmage's magewoman, Jilseth, can catch the renegade first, before his disobedience is revealed and the scandal shatters the ruler's hold on power...

The first book in a thrilling new series.

> **"Fantasy in the epic tradition, with compelling narratives,**
> **authentic combat and characters you care about."**
> — Stan Nicholls, author of *Orcs*

BOOK ONE OF THE CURSED KINGDOMS TRILOGY

THE SENTINEL MAGE
EMILY GEE

"An addictive story."
SFX Magazine on Thief With No Shadow

UK ISBN: 978 1 907519 49 9 • US ISBN: 978 1 907519 50 5 • £7.99/$7.99

In a distant corner of the Seven Kingdoms, an ancient curse festers and grows, consuming everything in its path. Only one man can break it: Harkeld of Osgaard, a prince with mage's blood in his veins. But Prince Harkeld has a bounty on his head - and assassins at his heels.

Innis is a gifted shapeshifter. Now she must do the forbidden: become a man. She must stand at Prince Harkeld's side as his armsman, protecting and deceiving him. But the deserts of Masse are more dangerous than the assassins hunting the prince. The curse has woken deadly creatures, and the magic Prince Harkeld loathes may be the only thing standing between him and death.

**"Dark and compelling...
Emily Gee is a storyteller to watch!"**
— *New York Times* Best-Selling Author Nalini Singh

 WWW.SOLARISBOOKS.COM

Follow us on Twitter! www.twitter.com/solarisbooks

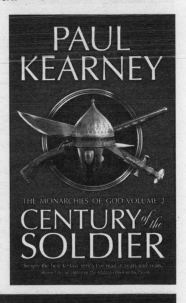

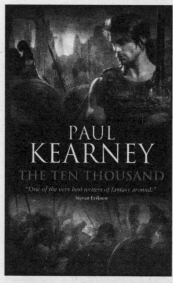
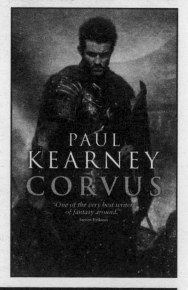

PAUL
KEARNEY
KINGS OF MORNING

"One of the very best writers of fantasy around."
Steven Erikson

UK ISBN: 978 1 907519 38 3 • US ISBN: 978 1 907519 39 0 • £7.99/$7.99

For the first time in recorded history, the ferocious city-states of the Macht now acknowledge a single man as their overlord. Corvus, the strange, brilliant boy-general, is now High King, having united his people in a fearsome, bloody campaign. He is not yet thirty years old.

A generation ago, ten thousand of the Macht marched into the heart of the ancient Asurian Empire, and fought their way back out again, passing into legend. Corvus's father was one of those who undertook that march, and his most trusted general, Rictus, was leader of those ten thousand. But he intends to do more. The preparations will take years, but when they are complete, Corvus will lead an invasion the like of which the world of Kuf has never seen. Under him, the Macht will undertake nothing less than the overthrow of the Asurian Empire.

"Very rarely does an author manage to leave you heartbroken while still allowing you to have enjoyed the book you've read... Kearney captures all the best parts of fantasy and combines them together with grit and realism and enough blood to drown a horse."

— *Fantasy Book Review's* Book the Month